Songs
FROM THIS AND THAT
Country

BY GAIL SIDONIE ŠOBAT

Copyright © 2025 Gail Sidonie Šobat
Enfield & Wizenty (an imprint of Great Plains Publications)
320 Rosedale Ave
Winnipeg, MB R3L 1L8
www.greatplains.mb.ca

All rights reserved. No part of this publication may be reproduced or transmitted in any form or in any means, or stored in a database and retrieval system, without the prior written permission of Great Plains Publications, or, in the case of photocopying or other reprographic copying, a license from Access Copyright (Canadian Copyright Licensing Agency), 1 Yonge Street, Suite 1900, Toronto, Ontario, Canada, M5E 1E5.

No part of this book may be used or reproduced in any manner for the purpose of training artificial intelligence technologies or systems. In accordance with Article 4(3) of the Digital Single Market Directive 2019/790, Great Plains Publications expressly reserves this work from the text and data mining exception.

Great Plains Publications gratefully acknowledges the financial support provided for its publishing program by the Government of Canada through the Canada Book Fund; the Canada Council for the Arts; the Province of Manitoba through the Book Publishing Tax Credit and the Book Publisher Marketing Assistance Program; and the Manitoba Arts Council.

The author gratefully acknowledges the support of the Edmonton Arts Council and the Alberta Foundation for the Arts

Design & Typography by Beth Gillespie

Printed in Canada by Friesens

Library and Archives Canada Cataloguing in Publication

Title: Songs from this and that country / Gail Sidonie Šobat.
Names: Šobat, Gail Sidonie, author.
Identifiers: Canadiana (print) 20250211637 | Canadiana (ebook) 20250214997 | ISBN 9781773371412
  (softcover) | ISBN 9781773371429 (EPUB)
Subjects: LCGFT: Novels.
Classification: LCC PS8587.O23 S66 2025 | DDC C813/.6—dc23

ENVIRONMENTAL BENEFITS STATEMENT

Great Plains Press saved the following resources by printing the pages of this book on chlorine free paper made with 100% post-consumer waste.

TREES	WATER	ENERGY	SOLID WASTE	GREENHOUSE GASES
13 FULLY GROWN	1,100 GALLONS	6 MILLION BTUs	46 POUNDS	5,760 POUNDS

Environmental impact estimates were made using the Environmental Paper Network Paper Calculator 4.0. For more information visit www.papercalculator.org

CERTIFIED CANADIAN PUBLISHER

MIX
Paper | Supporting responsible forestry
FSC® C016845

For the grandparents I didn't know:
Angela and Petar Maniljo Šobat - Serbia
Minodora and Wasyl Bodnaruk - Ukraine

and the ones I did:
Honore and Magdalena Van De Kinder(en) - Belgium
who always loved to hear me sing

Part 1

1

There are many ways to kill your father.

You can perform the ritual dance and then slit his throat, exposed and fresh as in a goat slaying. Go for the jugular. Then sing loudly the victory songs.

You can roast him in the oven, heated to five hundred degrees, as any self-respecting witch would do.

You can chop up, pickle, and preserve him, place him in a jar with the row of jars on the shelf, alongside the canned peaches and pickled carrots.

You can cudgel his brains out. Disembowel. Impale. Behead. Lacerate his femoral artery and watch him bleed out.

You can feed him his own venom or a noxious poison made by your own clever hand. Then see him rot from within and die, writhing, mere hours later.

You can sing a siren song and watch him thrash on the waves and careen into the rocks.

You can raise a boy by hand, then offer the man a gun and see what he does.

You can watch him wasting from some cancerous disease, do nothing but keep vigil and will his fading heartbeat to slow, to slow, to cease.

Or you can put a pillow over him as he sleeps. Lullaby and goodnight.

You can cast him from your life and break his heart.

Or let him cast you from his and watch grief grind him to dust. You can let his own devouring demons consume him from within.

Or so the fairy tale goes: one they never tell; one never writen down the one about how a daughter kills a father, lest she herself self be killed.

2

Once long ago she was born at dawn to the cacophonous chorus of a murder of crows. It was the kind of hot day where rivulets of sweat stream down the back and pool at the base of the spine. The kind of sweltering day where tempers flare and leap to flames incendiary. One of those white-anger days where the light from the harsh sun wavers a warning on the horizon. On such a day was she pushed from the crevasse between her mother's legs into an angry world.

Squalling and fiery red, she burst through membrane onto the scene, eager to join in the fray. A caul-baby, she might have been called Sudbina, Destiny. Except that she was called Mirjam, after her paternal great-grandmother. After the biblical prophet, a daughter of rebellion who sang a song of the Exodus. And with her first appearance began the song that was a scream.

For something was amiss with her digestive system. So several doctors opined. Some pre-ulcerous condition. Or perhaps she was simply a spoiled baby. One medical expert suggested leaving her in a room to cry it out. The harried mother tried this.

But the baby's bawling was incessant, and the mother acquiesced to take her in arms and rock until dawn. Mrs. Capone's neighbourly, old-wife wisdom was to give the infant a drop or two of grappa. The mother had none but did try the cooking sherry. No relief. But quite a good deal of spit up. She'd heard somewhere that a burst of gas from the stove—just a quick whiff, mind you—would do the trick. But she was a smoker and did not trust the gas method. And so she resorted to the only trick in her small-town book: she rock-a-byed the child, walked her around the tiny, rented house until her arms ached, and her feet complained, and her back cricked, and her own eyes drooped with fatigue. Night after night the same ritual. And finally, each time, after perhaps an hour or two or three of wailing, the child would surrender to the soft strokes of her mother's hand upon her swaddled back. And, oh, peace.

The father slept in the basement all the while. He, too, was prone to ulcers. The bleeding kind. From the war. And, of course, as the breadwinner, he needed his sleep.

Sometimes the mother, Luba, would simply drop to exhausted slumber in the bed beside the crib. Other times she would stare at the baby, wondering how she had arrived at this place in her young life. She had not really wanted motherhood, though such were not the thoughts of a nice girl from Rosedale, Alberta, a mere eight miles from the booming city of Drumheller, better known to locals as Drum. As a working girl she had at first transcended her bohunk roots—Rosedale's Ukrainian girls were supposed to marry young and make babies.

And of course, there were the unfortunate circumstances of the conception. None of this felt as though it was meant to be.

An immigrant raised since a toddler in this dry valley, Luba had had bigger dreams. Of working in a bigger shop in Calgary, maybe. Being discovered for the beauty she was, looking a little like Rita Hayworth, in some storefront window. Only prettier, if the boys at the Elks were to be believed. Back then, dancing at the Elks to the swing of big bands, Luba felt as though she could go anywhere, be anything.

But then she'd met Dan, and that had all changed. In a few months they were married. And then followed fifteen years of childlessness, and blame, and more.

Until finally this child. Who was by all reports—relatives', neighbours', babysitters'—a strange child, though Luba had not felt any prescient maternal stirrings, even while she carried the baby. Mirjam, born in a caul. Luba's mother, dead already twenty-five years, would have clucked her tongue at that. And there was no denying the baby was unusual. She stared at the mother with big, wise eyes. Watching, always watching.

Eager to move, she walked at nine and a half months. Running, pushing at life. Quick to temper over lost toys, food she did not relish, and any perception of imprisonment, whether diapers, the playpen, the child harness, the baby gate, the front fence. Once she tore out of the screen door and escaped the yard in a mad rush towards the Red Deer River, lucky to be caught by a neighbour and brought, in a fit of tantrum, home to safety.

She wasn't exactly a happy or content baby, Mirjam. There were those tummy issues. But she was lively. Restless, even. Fiery. Demanding. She wore her mother out.

Luba wondered often in her postpartum days if her daughter Mirjam had a secret. The first time Luba witnessed it, she did not want to believe. The child was only three. Luba did and did not believe in magic.

In the grey-faded shed out back lived a stray tabby. Meowing, she'd meandered into their lives during Mirjam's third summer. Together mother and child had made her a bed, for Luba could see that the cat was engorged and pregnant. One sunny, dry day, less than a week later, Luba and Mirjam sat watching through motes of dust in the arid air of the shed as the mother cat gave birth to four kittens. Mirjam, gape-mouthed and fascinated, observed the she-tabby lick the babies clean. She sighed when the mewing, squirming kittens nuzzled in to take the teats. And it was love—sure, and fierce, and possessive.

Days later, Walter, the neighbour boy, years older and cruel as boys can be, came over and suggested that they let the kittens swim in Mirjam's pool.

Her three-year-old logic saw this as a lovely idea in the heat of the sun, and she helped Walter drop the kittens, one by one, into the inflatable plastic pool, site of so much of her own delight these long summer days.

Only by chance did Luba glance up in time from her dishes and streak outside to the pool to scoop out the miserable tiny felines. Walter darted away before she could catch him by the ear. But Mirjam listened quietly and attentively as her mother cautioned her about the near-fatal results of her actions, spurred on by the neighbour boy. Luba towel-dried the cats and returned them to their anxious mother. Then she watched as Mirjam haunted the short fence that divided the two yards. Eventually, Walter ventured outside again. At the kitchen window, Luba shuddered to see the look Mirjam gave the boy. Heedless, he raced off on his small bike onto the street.

A screech of brakes propelled her outside, potato peeler still in hand. An old Ford pickup had struck the boy's bike, sending him flying many feet through the air. Now she could spy his distraught mother weeping over his form. The ambulance screeched into the street. And Luba held Mirjam tightly in her arms, against her knees. Mirjam watching, watching.

Sirens blaring, the boy was rushed to the hospital.

"I did it."

"What did you say, Mirjam?"

"It was me."

"Don't be silly," Luba said. She felt a kind of terror take root in her heart.

"For hurting the kitty cats."

Luba merely shook her head, tried to dislodge the unsettled thoughts of possibilities whirling in her mind. Tried to dismiss the old wives' tales about caul-born babies.

The boy lived but was simple. He grew into one of those men whose sentences are garbled and nonsensical. Walter went to the special school in town. Wore adult diapers. Drooled. Outlived his parents but spent a dullard's life in an institution.

And Mirjam never again in her life spoke to him.

3

I came home from the war and my hair had turned white. I was almost twenty-four years old.

Go on, the psychologist said.

It was an honourable discharge.

The man in the chair opposite nodded.

Eventually, it grew back black. But with streaks of grey, even so.

Even so.

I had nightmares. For years. And when a car would backfire I'd duck for cover. Under a table, a desk, whatever was nearest. It was completely involuntary.

Tell me about before the war.

Like my childhood?

We could start there.

I was a Depression baby. Born thirteen pounds.

Really? That big?

My mother was a big woman. We weren't starving. In fact, we'd been quite affluent before the crash. My dad ran a little store in Drumheller. Sold the baked goods that my mother and sister handmade each morning. The Anglos, despite turning their noses up at our immigrant ways, were glad enough to eat the pastries our women made. Thin as paper, my mother's pastry. It would melt in your mouth. Butter and egg and sugar and flour and then more butter. Pita, it's called, though nothing like what you'd call pita bread. No, it's a dessert. Filled with sweet apples and cinnamon. Or cheese curds and sugar. They used the kitchen table to spread out the dough. My sister learned from my mother. She never used a measuring cup. Went by the feel of the dough. She had a gift. They both did. My mother was ... an amazing woman.

When they lost the store, she kept the family together, kept the garden, the chickens, a cow, while my dad moped around, getting laid off from the mine, looking for jobs he never kept or got. He was not a labourer, my dad. And those were the only jobs in the valley. He spoke four languages. What good are four languages in the coalmines?

My mother hated what she saw as his laziness. So, after he was laid off a last time, he packed up off to Edmonton where he got a clerk's job for measly pay.

He died there of mouth cancer. It ate away half his face. In St. Joe's Hospital. It's a condominium complex now, can you believe? They buried him with some other guy in a pauper's grave.

Good riddance, my mother said. And it was.

Dan paused. Glanced around the room, its walls a soft hue of washed sky. His left leg was paining him. The damn sofa was too low. Christ. This new-age furniture. Who was it made for? Just like everything else in the damn world. The young. Who gave a fuck about the elders anymore? Even the soft lamp next to him was too damn dim to give any meaningful light. What was the point if you couldn't see the page before you? How could the psychologist, this man to whom he was assigned, possibly see enough to be scribbling so intently? Possibly have enough illumination to read all the books that lined the shelves? Probably didn't. They were there just for show. Just like all show-offy guys with degrees. He squinted to read the titles. *Narrative Therapy. The DSM-III-R. On Narcissism.*

Jesus H. Christ, that he, Danilo, had to be here at all. Here in this claustrophobic closet with this prying asshole. Then he swallowed. Something had to be done. If there were to be any reconciliation with Lu. Dan reached for the glass of water on the coffee table before him. Even that was too damn low.

Your mother?

Like I said. An amazing woman. She didn't spare the rod, mind you. But I deserved every lick I got. Today you'd say I was an abused child. But back then, it was just discipline. I don't resent her for it. She was a singer, my mom. Used to sing all day, songs from the old country.

Where were you in the birth order?

Youngest. There were seven of us. Anka, Maria, Jovanka, Jovan, Bosilka, Dušan, who died at birth, and me. Joe was already grown up and married to Evica—Eva—in Chicago. He died young. Of blood poisoning from a razor cut. Can you believe it? Those days there was no penicillin. Poison travelled to his brain. His whole face and head swelled up. When my mother got the telegram, she dropped to her knees in grief. I can still see the moment. The telegram fluttering to the ground as if in slow motion, like in a movie.

Their little daughter died of black measles a year or so later.

And soon after that, Eva was decapitated in a commuter train accident.

Gruesome.

Yes. She never sang again.

I should say not.

No, not Eva. My mother. After Joe's death. And I became her favourite, I suppose. My sisters say so anyway. In Serbian culture, the boy is the darling. Bosilka called me Majka's pasha.

Do you regret not having a son?

I regret having a daughter.

He felt the flicker of ire beginning in his stomach. She. She was the reason for this interrogation. But it wouldn't do to lose his cool here. Not now. Not under court orders. Luba's directive. So Dan took another sip of water. Tried to douse the smoulder.

There was anger and resentment in your childhood home.

No. Not really. My mom was not so fond of my dad, after the business faltered. After Joe's death. She felt he coerced my brother to leave Canada. But then dad left for Edmonton. It was a happy home. Mainly.

Your mother used physical force as a disciplinary tactic.

You make it sound like she was the military police. She wasn't like that! She was a warm woman, impossibly kind!

Alright.

She had a temper, but then so do my sisters. So do I.

Yes.

Dan watched the doctor's pen scribble across the open page of his black notebook. Somewhere out in the city streets a police siren whined. His stomach grumbled uncomfortably. He hoped he wasn't going to have a session with his ulcers.

I shouldn't have hit her.

No.

I'm sorry.

I'm sure you are.

It won't happen again.

That's why we're here, Dan. To try to make sure that it doesn't.

Is there a pill you can prescribe for me?

I'm not that kind of doctor. And no, there is no pill.

Are you sure?

Pretty sure, yes.

I just wondered. Because that would be a simple solution, wouldn't it? If I just took a pill and it calmed me down, so I didn't—

There are pills to calm you down, but I don't think that's what you need in this instance.

What? What do I need, doctor?

More time. More talk.

He thought about the weeks of therapy ahead of him. Then the course on anger management. Would any of this matter? Could it ever work again between him and Luba? Damn that shrew of a daughter! What passes between a man and wife should stay between them! Why did she interfere? He would never speak to her again. Never.

That's about it for our time together this week. The doctor came back into Dan's focus.

Oh. Okay. Thanks.

I'll see you again, next session.

He rose stiffly and took his hat in hand. No one wore a hat these days, except on the golf course maybe. Dan had turned a fine figure in a hat, once. Long ago now. But old habits die hard. He turned to the door.

Do you think I'm getting better?

It's early days, Dan. And it's not about you getting better.

I'd like to be.

4

Once there was a great and powerful despot whose now-dead wife had born him no sons, but instead three daughters. The eldest was named Milosti (Grace); the middle daughter, Vera (Faith); and the youngest, Sudbina (Destiny). Sudbina was the despot's darling favourite and a gifted and musical child. They lived in a castle near the Velika Morava and the daughters could watch the river flowing as they looked up from their needlework or their books, out through the windows of the keep.

The three girls stayed much of the year in the tower keep, attended solely by their lady servants, because of the threat of Turkish skirmishes or those who would come to pillage the castle and destroy the peace of the land so fairly ruled by their father the despot. During fine weather, they visited the gardens, and otherwise the girls were permitted access only to the inner courtyards and private chambers. On festivals and on their saints' days the sisters were allowed into the other castle apartments where dwelled the despot and his liveried officials. Such occasions were joyous, marked with music and feasting and dance, often led by the court harpist, a masterful player who bore a curious birthmark in the shape of a harp on his left forearm. It was always difficult afterwards to return to the boredom and confinement of the tower. Milosti and Vera bore this graciously enough, Sudbina less and less so with each passing year.

Finally, in the spring of a time when the marauders were busy elsewhere, the despot determined it was seemly for his eldest to marry. Milosti, who had clever sewing fingers and a sweet smile, was known to many young men throughout the land. Had she been asked, she might have chosen her fourteenth cousin once removed—a strapping lad she had met on a saint's festival date the year prior—and he her. But her father chose otherwise: a feudal lord with whom he sought a deeper alliance.

Though the man was past his prime and reputedly too often into his cups, Milosti acquiesced, as befitting her name. The sisters fashioned her wedding garments and linens, and the day of the nuptials rose fair and clear. Man and woman became husband and wife; the despot solidified an alliance and a new fealty. Many toasts were drunk that eve to the couple, wishing them health and strong sons. Several guests gambled that from the look in the new groom's eye, there would be a child born within the year.

Milosti rode away to her new lord's castle, while Vera and Sudbina returned to their quarters. And so, three became two. Days turned to weeks turned to months.

"Do you not feel"—Sudbina spoke as much to the leaden windowpane before her as to her sister behind her, posed at the mirror and brushing her hair—"there is somehow something we are missing?"

"I, too, miss our Milosti. But she is with child and unable to visit."

"I don't mean Milosti, though certainly I miss her. But the very idea that we might venture out to visit her. Why is that denied us?"

"Because dearest Sudbina, as well you know, there are dangers and perils. Our father knows how best to keep his despotate and his daughters safe."

"Imprisoned, rather." But this the girl said under her breath, for she knew where Vera's loyalties ultimately lay. Best to keep a silent tongue and one's thoughts in one's own head.

In due course, the despot, in a fey mood after a summer with a grand harvest and an autumn of good hunting, felt it only fitting that his second daughter should wed. He chose for her another lord, prosperous and plump, who offered a bride price the despot could not refuse. Vera had only met the man once, at a feast where he had marvelled at her nimble-footed dancing, but she fully trusted her father's choice.

The wedding feast was a sumptuous and grand affair attended by many of the despot's dignitaries and subjects. Milosti, with an infant mewling in her arms and another on the way, was allowed to attend and so briefly reunite with her dear sisters. At the great table, the merry new husband feasted and then hand-fed his new wife sweetmeats, one after another, and refilled her wine cup with cheerful admonishment that she must be sure to drain it, so that they were both quite red-faced with excess.

That evening, when Vera was carried away by her lord and Milosti by hers, Sudbina climbed with heavy feet and heart back to the keep. As the sole remaining daughter, she had much time on her hands and naught much to occupy her lonely days. She was the least accomplished sister at needlework. So more and more often that task now fell to the lady servants. She was, however, a superb singer, ofttimes singing at the court harpist's side for her father's pleasure. But these days her songs turned to laments. Sudbina took up her perch at the window and spent her hours sighing and singing sad little tunes.

Days turned to weeks turned to months.

5

Revenge: an intergenerational game for the whole family.

The Ottoman Turks defeated the Serbs on the Field of Kosovo in 1389. Mirjam heard from infancy about this bloody battle and medieval grudges held and nurtured since then. About the wall of skulls the Turks spitefully assembled. The cutting off of noses, ears, hands, penises, women's breasts: atrocities were the Turkish article. It was clear from the outset that she was meant to hate Turks.

But she didn't. She loved Turkish singer Leyla Gencer, introduced to her by a singing teacher, and the soprano's gorgeous rendering of "Bell'alme generose" from Rossini's *Elisabetta, Regina d'Inghilterra*.

Then there were the Croats. Particularly the rapacious Ustaše, those traitors in bed with Hitler and his Axis. Those same slaughterers who disemboweled and impaled and humiliated so many Serbs in World War II. Catholic bastards, all Croats. Pope ass-kissers. She was to hate Croatians, too.

But she had acted out before her mirror, "Tatiana's Letter Scene," singing tearfully along with Croatian diva Sena Jurinac.

Above all, she was urged to hate the Muslims. Jihadists. Infidels. Assassins. Terrorists. Turks-in-disguise. Mohammed-loving Arabs. Mirjam was instructed to hate Bosnian Muslims and Albanians, and by extension all Muslims.

But she had sung with her choir Kara Karayev's beautiful "Autumn," revelling in its Eastern intonation.

So in the heat of hatred, well instructed as she was, instead Mirjam hated Serbs.

And yet she, herself, was one. Or partly so. Because her father was a Serb (although her mother's roots were Ukrainian). Because she was born in Canada. But her father insisted, telling her again and again with growing warmth: she would ever be a Serb so long as she had a drop of Serbian blood. This fact—despite the accident of her birth in a social-democratic country made up of First Nations, Metis, Inuit and French-Canadians and Anglo-Canadians and many, many immigrants of many, many different ethnicities, hues, and religions who did not disintegrate into ethnic violence—Mirjam could never escape: there was an element of Serbianism dwelling in her person like a parasite, try though she might to shake off the yoke of the old country and assume fully the mantle of Canadian.

Being Serbian made shame rise to the back of her mouth.

Perhaps it was the flame of madness that touched her father's eyes when he spoke of a land, Serbia, that he did not know, had never known, having arrived via steamship in Montreal as a mere infant. Perhaps it was Mirjam's learning in high school social studies that it was a Serb who assassinated Archduke Ferdinand II and his wife, setting the match to the fuse of

World War 1. Perhaps it was the ugly talk of her uncles around the kitchen table after too much homemade plum brandy. Talk of ethnic divisions and superiorities and others' inferiorities and the myth of a greater heavenly Serbia at any and all cost. For the first eight years of her life, she thought "Pgh-Tito!" to be the communist dictator's full name, so many times had she heard him thus reviled.

The one-sidedness of her family's discussions made her simmer with anger and sting with impotence. But a child, moreover a daughter, was meant to be still and keep her tongue. Questions, debate, challenges were not tolerated or were met with a swift slap, a sharp, venomous retaliation. Harsh, stinging words.

Her Serbian father had the drama and arrogance of his people, but also the charisma and generosity, she recognized. When he was jovial or playful, which happened less and less as the daughter grew, Dan was the father of her daydreams, like the TV dads of her favourite sitcoms. At his best he was demonstrative, playful, even kind. She could understand why her mother had fallen in love with such a man, why friends and family found him warm and delightful. But when he turned, it could be sudden as a summer storm. Just when Mirjam might let herself again trust him, he would betray that trust with a cruel word, a cuff to the cheek. So following Luba's example, Mirjam learned to tread softly about the house as if afraid to make the floorboards creak, never certain which of the patriarch's serpent heads would appear: the charmer or the spitting cobra. The rooms of the various houses they lived in were suffocating with the strain of saying the right words in the right tone of voice at the right time. And timing was everything with a Serbian father who could stroke the kitten in one instant, and in another throttle the cat.

Later, when she was deep in her professional life as a singer, Mirjam's humiliation at her own Serbianism grew from associations of Serbs with the word genocide and the names Milošević, Karadžić, Mladić. From the grainy footage of the Siege of Sarajevo, the horrific photos of mass graves of Srebrenica, pictures of smug Batko, the Monster of Grbavica. From images of endless piles of skulls and bones.

From talk-radio eyewitness accounts of Serbian cruelties inflicted incessantly and without regard to age or gender or culpability of victims. From rape after rape after rape. These made her search her own face in the mirror, looking for the murderous Serb lurking beneath her skin. These made her wish to take a knife to herself and cut out the pound or more of flesh that linked her with Serbia.

Though she knew, frustratingly, that the media was not reporting the entire story, neither did her family tell all. The whole truth. Perplexed by the various versions of the history of the old country and its new incarnations, as she grew from child to teen to woman, so too, increasingly unabated, did her confusion and disgust about and at all things Serbian.

It was not surprising that her hatred of Serbia began to conflate with despising her Serbian father.

In fact, this loathing was well established at the age of ten. On a camping trip to the Rocky Mountains.

The day had been spent in the confines of an overly hot Buick Skylark, her father at the wheel and irritated by the holiday traffic on the Trans-Canada Highway. Jerks who weaved across the centre line. Asshole campers who blocked the view to pass or slowed to snail's pace the trail of travellers behind them. Crappy campsites that were already full by 4 p.m. Her father's resentment about the entry fee to Banff National Park.

Finally, they pulled into the Johnston Canyon campsite. They might have been awed by the beauty, their own insignificance at the foot of the mountains. Instead, they were distracted. A sullen silence had descended between Mirjam's parents because her mother's advice that they should phone ahead from home to reserve a spot had gone unheeded. They'd been lucky to get a substandard place in the campsite. It was late and everyone was past hungry. Lu set about making supper while Dan fought with the pump to the Coleman gas stove. Cautioned not to dawdle, Mirjam was sent for water from the taps near the washrooms. At last the propane flame was lit and the potatoes were boiling.

Her father turned his attention to setting up the tent trailer. Mother and daughter held their breath. While this should have been an easy assembly, for some reason Dan was always daunted by the task. He worked himself into a sweaty crossness that persisted even after the frame was raised, the canvas snapped into place, and throughout their supper of cold ham and potatoes. Tonight, there would be no campfire with marshmallows, Mirjam realized as her chin sank further into the palm of her cupped hand.

"Sit up and eat!" Dan's bark roused his brooding daughter.

"I'm finished."

"Then help your mother clear up instead of sitting on your

prat like a sulky baby!"

Mirjam rose and cleared the Melmac plates, then dried the sudsy dishes her mother washed in the water she'd heated on the Coleman. Clearly, it would be an early bedtime tonight. Mirjam would have to read by flashlight under the sleeping bag.

Sure enough, her mother went off to the washroom soon after the dishes were finished and the food stored away from the bears. Mirjam donned her pink flannel pajamas and began to crawl into one of the beds of the tent trailer. Her legs, long and brown and not entirely under her pre-teen control, knocked the small travel clock from the makeshift bedside table. Her father, outside finishing his before-bed cigarette, threw open the canvas flap.

"What the hell was that?"

"I dropped it." Mirjam was turning the clock over in her hands, willing it to still work. The clear plastic face was cracked. But the second hand was still operating. She sighed in relief.

"You little idiot!" Dan crunched out his cigarette and stormed into the trailer.

"Give me that!" He tore it from her hands. "It's broken."

"It's not bro—"

"What do you call this?" He held up the cracked face to her own. "You little bitch!"

Mirjam could feel blood rushing to her face and down her neck. The campground was full. Everyone could hear this altercation through the thin canvas. Everyone. Everyone would know that she was a little bitch.

"All you do is break things!"

This was clearly not true, but there was no arguing with her father when he was like this. Mirjam felt the familiar sickness fill her stomach. "It was an accident."

Dan struck her. "Shut up!" He was fuming now. "Shut up and get into bed, bitch!"

She crawled meekly into her sleeping bag and turned her back to her father as the trailer continued to shake with his rage. Hot tears streamed down her cheeks, and she forced back sniffles. If he knew she was crying there'd be more to come and maybe worse. He has a Serb's temper, all her aunts liked to warn her.

After a seeming eternity, her mother returned to the trailer. Lu knew nothing of what had just happened. Mirjam was used to her father picking his moments of fury carefully, often in her mother's absence, when the girl was most vulnerable. The unfairness of the attack stung her. Such a small thing. A replaceable cheap clock. Such a cruel overreaction. Such public humiliation. How could she face the other campers tomorrow? She'd have to hide out in the tent trailer and there was no way her parents would allow that, not since they'd saved and planned for this camping trip on her behalf. It was all ruined now. The bitch would be turned out for all the world to see.

Tomorrow he would come to her, repentant. "Daddy's sorry. Daddy loves you. Do you still love Daddy?"

And she would be expected to say, yes. All is forgiven. But it wasn't and it wouldn't be. Too many times this scene had been repeated in her ten short years. Her irrational irate parent. Followed by contrition and simpering affection. It made her weep all the harder. And she couldn't even blow her nose. The sick feeling in her stomach hardened into a little knot of hate.

Mirjam waited for her parents to fall asleep in the chilly darkness and plotted against her father: *I will find a way to make the tent trailer fall on your head so that your brains are dashed out and they spill all over your stupid puke-green golf shirt and then I'll laugh and Mommy and me will go on like you never existed.*

The next day, the frame of the tent trailer did collapse on them as they sat inside eating breakfast, away from the morning drizzle. But no one was hurt.

Her father simply cursed and leapt in time to catch and secure the frame. He reset and then locked the mechanism.

Lu paled as she observed her daughter's smirking face when Dan returned to the little table.

Mirjam said nothing, only munched her cereal and glanced at the cracked face of the little clock. It ticked away, oblivious to her family, marking their secrets.

6

1946. The war was over. Some visibly maimed and scarred, some invisibly but inalterably damaged, the boys returned to Drumheller and the valley. Lu had earlier lost two former beaus in the Battle of Britain. Casual boyfriends. Casualties. She and most of Rosedale had turned out for their humble memorial services. There wasn't much to be shipped home; no remains remained, except the memories of two homegrown boys downed in their prime. Memorial plaques and plinths were set for the valley's thousand soldiers and airmen killed. Monuments to the dead were erected; wreaths were laid. The whole valley mourned for lost youth, for loss and waste.

To assuage the collective grief, the town went dancing. Live, hot swing bands from Calgary or farther away played at the Elks. Lu wore high heels, a plum skirt with a peplum jacket, her hat at a jaunty angle. She sashayed into the cigarette-smoke filled hall her shapely legs in those nylons repaired again and again through the war years. Friday and Saturday dances at the Elks, the live bands whipped up the boys—Bob, Tat, Doug and half a dozen other former servicemen—smitten and sniffing. Marking territory.

Lu was a looker and she knew it, too. Hadn't everyone said so? Her jealous sisters? Her boss's wife? Her boss who snuck a pinch whenever his better half wasn't looking? She cut a figure. Popped the eyes. Lu could have her pick. Of even the Anglo fellas.

And then Danilo Popović who'd become just-Dan Pope overseas. With his movie star looks and crooner's voice, all spit and polish and sophistication. No trace of Slavic accent now. Something she, a bohunk from the Rosedale sticks, could surely appreciate. He'd seen the world. Even his aftershave spoke of worldliness. His pants were ironed razor sharp. His shirts starched crisp. His suits smartly tailored. His hair and nails, fastidious. And Jesus, could he dance. Enough to sweep a small-town girl off her pumps. Somewhere between "Mood Indigo" and "In the Mood," she was swept.

Married in a civil ceremony, just her cousin and his best friend as witnesses, Dan and Lu couldn't wait to tear their clothes off and dive into each other. They honeymooned for a halcyon week in Edmonton at the Hotel MacDonald. Paid for with the cash Lu had saved up from her job, the one she'd left to get married. After she'd paid the balance Dan owed the Drumheller jeweller for both her engagement and wedding rings, her purse was empty, but what did it matter when her heart was so full? The newlyweds moved right into their little rented apartment upon returning to town. And three days later, over the matter of her burning his breakfast toast, Dan hit her for the first time.

Lu considered her options. She was decidedly Catholic, if a somewhat lapsed one, so there was no possibility of annulment. Her mother had dropped dead of a heart attack when Luba was ten, so she couldn't turn to her. Lu's sisters were much older harpies, none of them given to giving much more than criticism. Besides, she well knew the old axiom her sister Bella would offer about made beds to lie in. Lu's father had kicked her unceremoniously out of the Rosedale shack at fifteen, claiming it was time she got to work. Too many mouths to feed, although she was the last. Having immediately taken up with the town whore, and soon afterwards siring three more half-siblings, her father had had little or nothing more to do with his youngest daughter from his first marriage. They'd barely exchanged a sentence between them in three years. Luba had only finished grade eleven, had used up every cent she had saved for secretarial college for marriage and the trappings.

In 1947 in the Badlands, there were no shelters. There was no Oprah to help a lost woman find her spirit and her strength. There was but the realization that a woman with nothing, from nothing, could do nothing except to accept her lot.

Especially since this was the second week of her marriage, and Dan's explosion was likely her fault anyway because he had to head off to work and needed everything to be just so for the start of his workday.

Burnt toast. Spilt milk.

Lu put some ice from the icebox on her cheek, later applied some paint and powder. Set her jaw. Ignored her wounded heart. The make-up sex that evening was spectacular.

And Dan didn't smack her again until her declaration that she would return to work.

"No wife of mine!"

"But Dan, the store wants me back. Think of how the money could help us. We could save up for our own business."

"Did you hear me the first time? Jesus, are you deaf or just stupid or both?"

His hand was vicious and sure. Dan stormed out of the apartment.

She nursed her cheek and wept.

Her husband, stinking of cigarettes and gin, crept back to their bed after midnight, repentant and newly resolved. "Awright, Shweetheart. Jus' til we get ahead." He groped.

She acquiesced.

And so, Lu learned to tiptoe through her marriage and her life.

It will take Luba more than forty-five years to work up the courage to leave Dan. Who returns to Dane and Dano and Danilo with growing Serbian fervour and nationalist sentiment in his senior years. Whose violence and anger correspondingly grow. As her heart grows correspondingly cold and finally frozen towards him.

In the meantime, she will miscarry twice and bear him a stillborn son. A willful daughter. Bitter resentment that will turn to bad dream.

In his haunting of her dreams, she will be the girl of her youth with that crown of thick hair coiled and coifed about her head like some luxurious towel. He will take hold of her locks to uncoil and pull them straight. His fierce stare will meet her eyes, and then he will begin to wrap her own hair about her neck, once, twice. The noose will tighten. Constrict. Lu will find that she cannot breathe or break free of his entrapment. And when Luba starts awake, her own bedsheet will be wound about her neck and she will be mortified to learn that she has wet herself.

7

Mirjam is a singer. It is what she was set upon this earth to do, she believes. To be precise, she is both an adept actress and a coloratura mezzo-soprano. She has been singing since she could talk, studying music seriously since she was fourteen, performing with increasing frequency on professional stages since twenty-two. She has a Bachelor of Music and a Master of Music in Opera and Voice. Now again at university, she is taking post-graduate Master classes, on full scholarship, studying with the famous Professor Weinstein from Germany. Famous for his profound understanding of German lieder and for the number of women's underpants he has assailed.

Mirjam is currently hunting for hers. In the utter darkness of Professor Weinstein's windowless and cluttered office and rehearsal room. He has spent the past two hours first hammering away with her on a difficult Schubert lied, and then hammering her on the closed lid of the upright Steinway piano. She trips over a stack of music books.

"Dammit. Helmut. Some light, please."

A match strikes and for a few fluttering seconds she can see his face but little else beyond the meagre flame's radius. She knows he is reclining on the mat where the two of them collapsed après their sexual rondo.

"But Liebchen. If I find the lights, we must return to Herr Professor and Fräulein Pope."

Mirjam lurches towards some article of her clothing and the light extinguishes. "Really, Helmut?" Her voice is hushed as she tries to distinguish leg from arm and type of garment. The university rehearsal walls are stupidly thin. Voices and a violin playing and replaying a passage are easily audible. The soundproofing is for shit.

"After this?"

"But of course, Liebchen." His tone is matter of fact, patient. "I am your teacher. We must be prudent. But really ..." he lights another match, "must you go so soon? I haven't another appointment until 4 p.m."

"Yes, Helmut. I have to go. I'm picking up my mother. We're looking for apartments. She hates when I'm late." Mirjam manages to find her flip phone in the pocket of her pants. "Christ, it's 2:45. I'm already late." She hits auto dial, but there is no answer. "She's left without me, I guess." Mirjam shuts the phone. Pulls on her jeans. Sans the panties she cannot find.

"Then I guess there is time for at least a kiss?" Helmut's tone has thickened. He strikes another match. Holds it nearer his stomach that is only slightly paunched. For an older man he looks very good. Delicious. The flicker is enough to show Mirjam that his ample cock has thickened, too. Immediately, she feels a responsive flutter. The crotch of her jeans is instantly saturated.

The room goes black again. "Come." Helmut's whisper is

still that of a master in command. In the darkness, she heads towards his voice. Stubs her toe on something and falls to her knees. But she can feel his heat nearby. Reaches out a hand and touches his thigh.

"Clumsy girl," Helmut chuckles and lights another match. "Here you go. Let's try again with the major scales in glissando, shall we?" He puts his left hand on the back of her head, lowering it towards him. Blows out the match. "On the downbeat. Begin. Ah."

Just before he reaches the climax of the piece, he pulls her head away.

"These wretched tight-trussed trousers restrict your breathing." His hands guide her to standing over him. Helmut unzips with precision. Slides a finger in. She shudders, panting. "You see? I know of what I speak." Then he pulls her jeans to her knees and buries his face. She is awash in his vocalise murmuring. Her diaphragm lifts with desire.

He frees first one leg and then another from her jeans and lowers Mirjam down onto himself, erect and sure as his conducting baton. "First largo." He whispers in her ear. "You know this movement." And then she is fucking him. And he lets her. And she has moved to andante. Allegro. Presto. He finds her mouth and kisses her deeply so that she will not soprano-shriek like the last time. Crescendo.

Their coda is at the door of his rehearsal room. He straightens her hair, which can only be called just-fucked, regardless of his spurious efforts.

A colleague is coming down the hall. Helmut straightens to professorial. "Until next week, then."

"Er—yes, Herr Weinstein."

Helmut closes the door and Mirjam walks away sore and bewildered. In her heart and elsewhere.

Inside his office, awash now with overhead light and the smell of lieder-lust, the professor surveys the room, turns to the music stand, takes up a piece of sheet music with his right hand, pockets her thong with his left.

※

"You're late. And your hair."

"Ma. Don't start. I'm juggling grad school, teaching classes, and finding time to practice. Today's rehearsal. Um. Things went later than expected. I can't dictate what my profs will do or ask of me. I'm here now. Look, the agent hasn't even arrived yet."

Luba, in attempting to tame her daughter's mad hair, gives her a sniff. She knows that smell. But says nothing. The agent pulls up in a silver Honda Civic. Howie, in his dated suit, bald dome glistening in the heat of being late, apologizes three times. There are greetings with the building manager as mother and daughter are granted entrance to the modest flat.

This is their eighth apartment viewing. The others have all been too pricey. Wrong neighbourhood. Too small. Not near enough to the mall. No elevator. No air conditioning. Luba is driving her daughter crazy, and vice versa. Mirjam is seldom on time and always preoccupied.

"Well, what do you think, Mrs. Pope?"

Luba is running the taps, checking out the linen closet space. "It's Bodnaruk. I'm going back to my maiden name."

Mirjam starts. This is news to her. But she doesn't disapprove.

"I'll take it, if you'll have the building manager clean the place again. This time with a professional carpet cleaner."

Her mother is thorough. There is no doubt. Mirjam grins in relief. She likes the place, too. Brightly lit from southeast windows, a tasteful Berber carpet, sizable rooms and a neat little kitchen. There is even a little fireplace off the living and dining room.

Luba signs the lease, fills out the post-dated cheques, shakes hands with the agent. Mirjam calls the moving company to arrange to transport her mother's furniture out of storage where it has been sitting for several weeks. Move-in day will be Saturday and this is Wednesday.

In celebration, mother and daughter go for lunch, for shawarma and falafel, food outside of their respective ethnic culinary upbringing, yet not so far from Mirjam's Serbian side, whether speaking of geography or cuisine.

"I'll help you hang the pictures. Maybe we can get you a whole new bath set, Ma."

"That'd be nice." Lu adds a little more humus to her pita. "The extra room. That could be for you, you know."

Mirjam sighs. She knew this had been coming. "Sure. On special occasions. Christmas."

"I was thinking more permanently."

"I know. But it wouldn't be good for either of us. You know it, Ma. We'd be at each other like cats."

"I don't know..."

"Yeah. You do." Mirjam thinks of her own small apartment, imagines further naked duets with Helmut. "I have to have my own place. I'm thirty, Ma. And I have the piano. I have to rehearse. I have my own students. Then there are my classes to prep: the ones I'm taking, the ones I teach in the music department."

"You could do that at my place. You could save up some money. We could find room for the piano—"

"Isn't going to happen, Ma. Wouldn't work. I'd like us to stay friends, because we are friends, Ma. And that's kind of ... you know ... what I want for us." Mirjam puts another forkful of tabbouleh salad into her mouth.

"Guess you should know something ..."

"What?" Mirjam knows well the various melodies of her mother's voice and doesn't particularly like the sound of this one.

"Your father," Luba takes a sip of her iced tea. "He's been released from jail."

※

Daddy said a not-nice word; he had nicked himself shaving. Mirjam, crying in her bedroom, heard this and her heart looked up from its sorrow and was glad.

Earlier in the day, she'd set the quilt on fire. It was an accident. She had been making a tent. And tents are dark, so she needed a lantern. Down to the basement. So many cobwebs.

Spiders. But Mirjam was fearless. After all, being five had some advantages. In the light of the single overhead bulb, she first found the flashlight. But the batteries were dead. Hanging just out of reach was the trouble light. There was Daddy's toolbox. Stepping up onto it, suddenly Mirjam was just tall enough. She carried the light in its cage and the long snaky cord back to her room.

She read *One Fish, Two Fish* in the glow under her tent. Then *If I Had Duck Feet*. These were her mother's gifts to her. Every outing to big-city Calgary meant a book.

And there were two purchased for every dentist visit. Mirjam loved books. She had taught herself to read. She especially liked *The Illustrated Grimm's Fairy Tales* and stories about witches. There were only two things that Mirjam loved more than books. Music and ice cream. So when the calliope notes of the ice cream truck sounded along her street, she was drawn like a child enchanted to the piper. Mirjam aborted her book reading and scrammed down the stairs, out the doors with her piggybank in hand.

A scorching smell drew her father into her bedroom. The ancient quilt had begun to smoke, and a hole was burning where the trouble light touched the grey satin. He erupted as Cronus out the back door. Strode over to the swing set where, oblivious, Mirjam was eating her Creamsicle. In one stroke, he knocked the ice cream splat onto the paving blocks underfoot. In another, he nearly knocked his daughter's head from her shoulders into next Tuesday. Or so it felt.

Then he was pulling her off the swing. Carting her up the

stairs. ChiChi the Chihuahua scampered in terror, seeking safety from the eruption. The furious god threw the daughter into her bedroom. Shook the charred evidence of her misdeeds before the shaking child. Slammed the bedroom door almost to splintering. And Mirjam was alone.

She could hear the voices down below. Lu had returned from grocery shopping. Daddy's words were virulent and vicious. Mommy's were placating.

Mirjam was alone for a very long time in her room. She cried for a very long time.

Then she heard Daddy climb the stairs and enter the bathroom. Run the water. He swore and Mirjam's tears abated. He stormed out of the house for his tee time.

He did not yet know how rotten his swing would be that afternoon. Splice after splice. Dan did not make par on any of the nine holes.

Soon after his departure, when Lu came into Mirjam's bedroom with a cheese sandwich and milk, the girl was playing with Velveteen Bunny and Toad. Bunny was the misunderstood, much maligned and long suffering. Toad, returning from a sub-par golf game, had a flat tire on his roadster. Mirjam was singing softly to herself,

"Husha, husha, we all fall down."

❧

"What will you do?"
"I'll move into my new apartment. Move on with my life."

"Does he know you're here, Ma?"

"Of course, he does. We sold the house when—when all this happened. He knows I choose to be near you."

"Will you get another restraining order?"

"Do I need to? Across provinces or something?"

"Likely."

"Maybe he'll stay in Mission."

"Daddy? Not bloody likely. There's no one there to beat up anymore. He'll come sniffing around for you eventually."

"Probably. Eventually." Lu pats her daughter's hand. "I'll be fine, Mirjam. I've got my pension. My little job at Woolco."

Mirjam sighs. Her mother has turned into a senior stereotype. Was there anything more depressing than becoming a salesclerk at a transnational corporate greedbox store? No benefits. Pissy hours.

"I know you don't approve. But it's something. To keep me busy. My mind occupied. And besides," Lu smiles wryly, "those tickets to your concerts aren't getting cheaper as you rise to fame."

"Ma. I can always get you comps."

"I like to pay my own way."

"Comps are legit, Ma. They're for family and friends."

"Then save them for your friends."

Mirjam shakes her head.

"Your boyfriends."

"I don't have a boyfriend. No one permanent, anyway."

"Don't you think I'm well aware of that?"

"Please, Ma! Don't start." She still feels the present of Helmut's recent presence in her. Time to change the subject.

"So I will likely know by Christmas if I'm going to be chosen to sing the lead soprano part in Dr. Weinstein's new concert opera."

"What will that mean?"

"A—it will be an honour. B—I will know what to sing for my graduate performance. C—it will likely lead to other jobs and critical notice. If I sing well enough."

"Of course, you will. You're always brilliant."

Mirjam smiles across the table at her stage mother and best cheerleader. Lu would not know whether or not Mirjam had hit the high C purely in "Adele's Laughing Song," but would be stunned and delighted at her daughter's performance regardless.

As Luba pays the bill, Mirjam considers what Dan's coming to Calgary will mean. Does he know yet who had called the police? Will his fingers next find her throat? Or will he try again to assault Luba?

Or might he manage to have an accident on the Trans-Canada Highway as he zooms feverishly towards them?

She wonders if any cellmate had raped Dan during his week-long incarceration in the Mission jail.

Mirjam hopes so.

8

I am a boy watching...
Go on.

 My mother is in the hot kitchen fussing over the coal oven and stove. There is the smell of bread baking. And she is making soup. Tongue soup. It is a family favourite. Delicious. A Serbian recipe. Tongue is such a cheap cut at the butcher's. And we have fallen on hard times again. My father cannot hold a job in the valley. For the life of him.

 How old are you at this point, Dan?

 Maybe ten. He, Tata, has come home. His shoulders are stooped. I think he has been crying. His hat is in his hand as he speaks to Majka. But I can't hear his words. I can only guess that he tells her he has been laid off from the Atlas Mine again. Her voice whips him like the wind through the eaves of our house on a stormy winter night. I wish Tata would stand up to her. But even I can see that he is puny before her. He is already sick with cancer, and she knows it. But Majka is right. Tata has failed us. Again. He is broken.

 So she takes the cast iron frying pan to him.

 Tata does not come to the supper table that evening to eat

the tongue soup. When I ask about him, Mama bats me across the head. Usually, I am her favourite. The baby. The last son. I should know better. When her mood is dark as the coal in the hills.

I see Tata later, maybe the next day? He sits on the greying front stoop. I see how shrunken he is and that he has a blackened eye. I watch his shaky hand put a plug of chewing tobacco in his cheek. He pulls me to him. Danilo, my son. My son. He buries his face in my shoulder, and when he pulls away, my shirt is wet.

Soon after that—days or weeks later—my father stands at our door next to a worn-out leather suitcase wrapped around with a leather belt. He is dressed in his suit, shiny from too much pressing, atop a threadbare white shirt with a striped, black tie. His hair and moustache are very neat. I can smell the pomade. Under his arm Tata carries a package of his best-loved books. His fingers clutch a paper bag, a lunch my sister Maria has packed him. His fingernails are trim and clean. I look down, trying to hide how I am feeling, especially from my mother ....

And how are you feeling at this pivotal moment in your young life?

How do you think? I am losing my father, damn it! And I am my mother's pet. I am supposed to be her ally in all things!

You are in a very difficult position, especially for a young boy. You've been asked to choose, perhaps not directly, but the implication is very clear.

If I don't choose Majka, she will not love me.

I see. And that is unthinkable.

Yes.

Especially for a ten-year-old.

Yes.

Can you remember anything more about that day?

I remember, looking down, that Tata's shoes, though very old, have been polished. They are almost shining. I remember that he embraces us all. Except Majka, who stands straight as a poker before him. So he touches her face. Tentatively. Tenderly. But she says nothing, not even goodbye. Then he bends down to me and says, Be a good boy, a good little man for Majka, won't you? in Serbian. I'll never forget his words. They are the last I ever hear him speak.

And then?

He walks away in the dust.

Where does he go?

To Edmonton on the train. To a clerk's job for shitty pay that he sends back to Majka, or almost all of it, after he pays for his room and board at the Allen Block. That lasts a few months. Maybe half a year. Until the cancer begins to eat him alive.

Majka never goes to visit him. She tells us there is no money. My grown-up married sisters make the trip, one by one. As each returns, she recounts the progress of the disease. First, his cheek. Then, the rest of his tongue. His lips. His throat. Finally, his brain.

He sends letters and then they stop. And then my cousin who lives in Edmonton writes to us. Tata is dead. Majka says, drop him in a hole. We can't afford to have him sent home. I have to write the letter because she is illiterate. And in the note, she curses Tata. An ancient Serbian women's curse on him and all his ancestors.

That's very harsh.

In all other regards, as I told you, she was a warm and loving woman. But I know she was glad to be rid of him, once and for all.

You shouldn't have been the one to write such words.

I guess not.

You needed to grieve, to mark his death.

I never did.

You were a child. That letter was not a child's burden. That was not your hate, but hers.

No.

It wasn't your fault, Dan, the leaving. The abandonment. You didn't do these things to your father.

But I stood by my mother. All of her life.

You were a good son. To both your parents.

Not to Tata.

What could you have done?

Never written Majka's hateful words. Her curse. I could have written to him in Edmonton. Told him I loved him. Run after him that day.

Run away to Edmonton?

Yes, I could have done that.

At ten? In the Depression? With an overbearing mother? No money, no means?

I might have.

You were a child. You are not to blame. Not for the deterioration of their marriage. Not for the violence in that home. Not for his leaving. Not for his death. Especially not that.

I am ... as weak as he—

Why? Because you weep for this profound loss in your life?

Yes. I blubber like he did. And he was powerless.

We all are, Dan. Sometimes. It's not a crime.

Men are—are supposed to be the backbone.

So I've heard. So we're told. But I wonder. And precisely how was your father not the backbone? He loved you, your mother, your siblings? He worked when he could?

But he didn't provide. Enough.

It was the Depression.

Others worked.

Many didn't. Look. There are billions of men on this earth who, because of circumstances, cannot provide enough for their families. Are they all weak, Dan?

Yes!

That is what you really believe?

Yes. No. I don't know. What do you want me to answer?

What you believe. What you think.

Then yes. I think men who don't provide for their families have no backbone.

Alright, I'll take you at your word. Let's go on. Your daughter located the grave? She wrote to the Edmonton Cemetery to inquire about it, I believe you said.

She did. Luba and I were visiting her on my sixty-fifth birthday. She gave me a card and the letter from the cemetery. Petar Maniljo Popović. 1882-1933. There was a plot number and an invitation to contact their offices for further details.

So in some ways, the abandonment was abated. Your mother's curse unhexed by your daughter's words.

I hate her.
And that is why we are here.
Hate her.
Whom exactly do you hate?
Her.

9

"What do you know of the Turk?" She had paused in her singing during an afternoon spent in the company of the court harpist.

"Why, Despoina, I—I know as much as you."

She dropped her voice to a hush so that the lady-in-waiting nodding off near the great fireplace could not hear. "Is it true, think you, that the infidel spears babies, ravishes women, eviscerates old babas and saws off the heads of our men?"

"So the tales tell. But such are also the ugly rumours about the warriors of this, your land."

"I've heard these whispers but never believed."

"You have been reading the books in your father's great library."

"I have. In secret. I am not permitted."

"That is between you and your conscience, not for me to tattle or judge. What do the pages tell you?"

"That the infidel is never to be trusted, that the sultan would have us all impaled, drawn and quartered, would he could."

"And the lore of other times and other places?"

"True, those books tell a similar tale: that in war there is always savagery, measure for measure. One loses an eye, so half-blind, will likewise poke out the eye of his foe, if he meets with opportunity."

"Thirst for revenge seems unquenchable." The harpist softly plucked a melody in a minor key.

"My father can never forget Kosovo."

"No, though many generations have passed."

"Lazar will be avenged, so my father promises."

The harpist retuned. "The Ottomans are many things, I suspect, my lady. Cruel masters, yes. But also poets and artists, weavers and mystics, dancers and musicians. Turks are the architects of great buildings. Astronomers and physicians, farmers, peasants. Warriors, yes. But no people—not yours, not mine, not the Ottomans—are so easily summed up by their worst actions."

They sang a song then. And another.

Somewhere leagues away, her father's men had madly set to fire a peasant village where the people, hoping to fill their bellies, were withholding taxes.

Somewhere further leagues away, boys were summarily rounded up from a village and taken to the great city as slaves to convert and become Janissaries. In another, a baby was roasted on a spit over a cooking fire before a small crowd of laughing soldiers. In another, a collection of heads was placed in a sack to be delivered to the leader. In another, a collection of eyeballs. In another, a man was impaled mouth to anus on a sharpened wooden stake embedded in the ground. In another, a man was forced to have sex with his son and the son afterwards to castrate the father. In another, a young girlchild was raped before her mother and grandmother who had already been ravaged and lay bleeding and pleading before the attackers. In another, a small boy was sawed in half by his family's captors—his horrified watching parents' heads rolled within the hour. In another, Catholic, Orthodox, Muslim, gypsy, and Jew were flayed alive, corpses left to rot in the sun. In another a pregnant woman was skewered on a meat hook, her fetus kicking its last, while soldiers drained her lifeless breasts of milk. All in the name of might.

Safe in his military tent, the despot took to bed a woman captive. He did not ask nor care which god she worshipped. He gulped *rakija* and feasted on roasted lamb while his drunken men danced the Hora outside before the great fire.

Safe in his palace, the sultan stepped in his silver-soled slippers towards the harem. The young women presented themselves for his pleasure and he selected his favourite whom he would take to his luxurious bed. They would drink wine and eat meze, delighting in the roast lamb. The court musicians would play their tamburs while the sultan and his concubine rutted away the night.

Safe in her father's castle keep, Sudbina, like the rest of the despot's family, could not hear the sighs of grief and mourning, the wails of victory and defeat, the grunts of mounting and ravishing. She would eat and drink and sleep without nightmare. She would return to her books but would find no answers.

10

It is a beautiful eighteen-karat gold pocket watch on a finely wrought, thirty-inch gold chain. Two initials are engraved on the front in a beautiful Edwardian script: *AP.* The clockwork and movement are impeccably precision timed. If the back casing is pried open with a fingernail, one can watch the world of miniature cogs and wheels beat as though attuned to the human heart. A pleasant ticking is audible. The face of the watch and its delicate Roman numerals are protected by a crystal. A second hand pulses along steadily, in a smaller circle directly at the bottom where the number six would be. The effect of sound and movement is mesmerizing, almost trancelike. To peer at its face is to forget that one is marking the passing of one's hours. One's life.

It was a wedding gift from her husband. The dust cover of the movement is engraved in Cyrillic with their wedding date, November 3, 1910. "From Petar." The man who whisked her off to a new world. From her beloved home. Her Serbia. Far from her childhood home in Bunić, Lika. From whence Petar, visiting his relatives, stole her away with dreams of grandeur in Belgrade, where he worked briefly as a translator. Only to promise her even greater things after the Great War with a life in Canada.

Canada: a cold country with a frigid welcome to foreigners who spoke a strange language, cooked strange stinking meals, worshipped in a strange church. Serbs were nobodies in this land. Fit only to work the coalmines in the Badlands, alongside the Croats, curse them and their mothers, every last one. And segregated from the main town, where the Anglos lived and flourished and went about their perfect lives, Serbs were treated like so much rubbish. Thick-tongued, thick-pawed, thick-headed, the English thought them. Well, she thought little enough of the Anglo *kopilad*. Little enough to learn very little of their ugly language her entire life.

She'd had her girls, of course. And her Jovan. Until he died. And her mother's heart broke and never recovered. One by one the girls grew up and married and moved away. Everyone in this country moved. Such migrations baffled her. What of family? Tradition? What of home? But they left her. To Edmonton. To Victoria. To Miami, Florida. Two of them married Anglos, God above, help them. Changed their names. Newly baptized, they resettled elsewhere and far away. She seldom saw them or her grandchildren. At least Maria married a Serb. So what if he sometimes hit her? Sometimes she deserved it, too. He was a good man, a hard worker otherwise. Maria need only duck the blows when he drank and keep her thoughts to herself. There was a roof over her head, food on her table. And they were in town, near her mother. Angela would have very much liked to be near her own mother, now long dead and buried. Petar took her from Serbia and she never saw her *majka* again. Maria was lucky to have a man and a mother close by.

And then her Dane was born. Beloved gift of Angela's menopausal years. She would teach him what she knew of the old country. He wouldn't forsake her. Danilo was destined for the priesthood; she could feel it. And then he would never stray far from her. He would tend to her in her old age. What need then would she have of a man who was useless as was her husband? The one getting ready in his one good suit for this photo on this hot dry day for the photographer. As if they could afford such a luxury. But Petar insisted. A photo of their boy Dane; a photo of Maria's family, her husband Eli, their tossing sons Branko and Milan; a photo of everyone together. Another with just the two of them.

She fixes her steel wool hair, once so black. She fixes the watch on its chain upon her breast. She fixes her eyes—the same that had once looked so warmly on the young suitor who'd courted her many years ago—fiercely at the camera lens. She fixes her chin against this photograph effrontery. Petar puts his hand on her shoulder. The photographer's bulb pops loudly.

As Maria and she lay the table for the family picnic, Angela hums a little tune, one from the old country about Serbian battles and victories. The lamb is turning on its spit and Eli is salting it. Then he and Petar pass a bottle between them. Her old eyes miss nothing.

Dane comes crying with a cut knee. Milan and Branko have pushed him down the silt hill and he has scraped himself and landed on a cactus. She tends to her wounded child, kissing him and lulling his sobs as she washes and dresses the scrape. He takes hold of her watch on its chain still around her neck.

One day it will be yours to mark the time, she tells him. It is gold for a golden boy. A treasure for my treasure.

Later, she boxes the older boys about their ears. They love and fear her. It is the way with the whole family. Dane looks on, smugly. It is always good to be the family victor. It will become his addiction.

Love and fear, emblematic of the woman and the land from which she sprang, are writ on her face in the photographs taken that hot summer day. Her body is rigid with will and defiance. And in her eyes that lock on the viewer is the curse of her people: a consuming, dangerous love to fuel the fire of nationalistic fervour, setting ablaze deadly and murderous skirmishes. Fear of loss and of difference further fans the flame of hatred, a loathing that dwells deeply and permanently in the depths, in the belly of the beast, eventually, to swell and become an inferno. A chaotic, possessive wildfire. A devouring devil that will swallow whole families and villages and cities. It cannot and will not be sated. Such is the way of the beast that glares through the woman's eyes.

From mother to son this legacy passes, as if via glance, imperceptibly between them. Stories. Songs. Silences. Poison soaked up and stored away for later use when it can be decanted, concentrated then heated. Boiling oil to be poured down the towers. Catapults of sharpened stone and flaming hurdle, flung to flatten or inflame the adversary in the wars between countries or between lovers or children.

The lamb whose throat was slit that morning is served up for the feast. The men dance the Hora and drink too much homemade chokecherry wine. They weep for Serbia, telling tales of Croatian betrayal.

Across town the Croats dance the same dance, tell the same stories, but reverse the villains, at their own feast on this day of feasts.

Angela looks up from the basin of soapy water where she is washing dishes as Maria dries. Surrounding her in the violet gloaming are the hills, their ridges like wrinkled, aging flesh, not unlike her own. She feels the valley will swallow her and her family and her history up. Angela looks up as though to appeal to the first stars, but the hoodoos along the eastern ridge are like teeth laughing at her, poised to devour. She is caught, a worm on the hook, in the great mouth of this foreign, incomprehensible land with its fossil history of ferocious creatures she did not know existed until she came here, until she saw their bulk, their bleached articulated bones on artful display, and finally recognized extinction.

The watch and the photo, faded by time and lies, all shrouded in flimsy, yellowed tissue, sit abandoned in a wooden cigar box. The textured indigo stamp with 'Habana, Cuba' is torn apart on the lid's edge. There is a picture of a pretty, dark-haired girl whose lips are parted to reveal perfect teeth, whose hair is adorned with a hibiscus blossom, and who offers up an open cigar case. She, more than the contents of the box, interests the teenager, who wonders where she might find such a flower for her own hair. Finally, she fingers the contents of the box, long emptied of cigars. Mirjam cannot name the faces in the photograph except for her father, aunt, and uncle. She cannot remember the name of her grandmother. A vague recollection of 'Peter' for her grandfather bubbles to the surface. Everyone looks old and outdated.

The watch no longer works, and its crystal is shattered. All the mechanical bits stopped years ago, and no one took the time or cared to repair them. Uninterested in the workings, Mirjam turns her attention to the face. She prefers digital to the Roman numerals she has always had such trouble deciphering, so snaps the lid shut. Mirjam barely makes out the initials on the watch case, so overwrought with flourish is the engraved script. No family member she knows has a name that begins with A.

Perhaps her grandmother's name was Anna? The woman is long dead, died decades before her granddaughter's conception and birth. Mirjam knows nothing of her grandmother's life, cares and wonders less. There is a knitted afghan heirloom that is rather pretty, mouldering in a hope chest that the girl seldom opens.

Because there are other hopes awaiting. She is sixteen, and a musical life, a siren singing on the waves, already beckons to her. Hastily, the tissue is replaced; the box is closed. A girl gazes back at a girl. Mirjam adjusts her own auburn hair, tries shaping it along her face as in the photo, wondering how many months it will take to reach her mid-back. She longs for the glamour of the habanera, hopes she will be as seductive as the girl on the cigar box cover, dreams of playing the role of Carmen.

Her Serbian grandparents and their troubled family and national histories barely flicker in her consciousness. Mirjam is a thoroughly modern Canadian girl. Serbia reminds her of acerbic, something you spit up.

11

Her father is back in the city. He has purchased a very expensive car and rented a downtown apartment in a brand-new building. Tonight they are having dinner together, father and daughter, so that Dan, as he told her tersely on the answering machine, can explain his side of the story. He has made *punjena paprika*, stuffed peppers, a recipe passed down from his mother.

Mirjam has bitten her nails nearly to the quick. She is wearing a black pencil skirt and a white blouse and carries a bottle of Malbec in her leather shoulder bag. She presses the building buzzer and her father permits her entrance. He lives on the eleventh floor. Her bladder painfully resists the ascent in the elevator.

Danilo meets her at the door and embraces her warmly. As always, Mirjam is repulsed at his touch, but does not push him away, at least initially. Finally, she tells him that she must pee and he steps back to usher her into his apartment and to the bathroom. In the privacy of the small room, she can smell his aftershave. She recognizes pictures on the wall that were in her childhood home, sees that he has purchased a new towel set and shower curtain in a deep forest green.

When she emerges from the bathroom, Dane gives her a tour. The view of Calgary and the mountains to the west is spectacular. Expensive camel-coloured leather sofas face a gas fireplace. Her father has a new Sony TV. A glass dining table, ringed with plush wine-red chairs, is set for two. Near the imitation Christmas tree, too-early purchased and loaded with matching silver decorations and lights from Sears, Kenwood stereo speakers whisper a Serbian folk melody. Inexplicably, a king-sized bed and matching dark wood bureau are crammed into a modest-sized bedroom. There are prints of exotic elsewheres, vague and interchangeable on the eggshell walls of the bedroom, down the halls, and back in the living and dining room. There are no photographs. Nothing to speak of a home or a family or a life before the schism.

Mirjam opens the wine and pours it into wine glasses as Dan puts the white casserole dish, its colourful contents bubbling and aromatic, upon potholders on the table. He ladles out a pepper and thick tomato sauce onto her plate, then serves himself. She raises her forkful to blow on the pepper.

"So you're settled in. It all looks very ... nice, Daddy."

"I still know some people in retail in this town. I got some deals."

"Ma's working at Woolco, did you know?"

"Woolco is an American bastard. It's eating up this country like a cancer."

Mirjam shrugs and swallows her first mouthful. The green pepper is sharp and soft. Its flavour has permeated the rice and hamburger, augmented by the onion and garlic she knows her father has used liberally in the dish. "Just as good as always."

She smiles at him, nodding approval for his culinary skills, and takes a sip of wine. The Malbec has yet to fully open, but it is bright and hopeful for this tentative meal.

Her father works his knife into the steaming pepper on his plate. "I could get you something, too, if you need for your apartment."

"Thanks. I could use a vacuum cleaner. Mine died last week."

"Good, a vacuum. What else? Anything you'd like. Bora, who works at Eaton's, is my friend and can get me merchandise wholesale. A TV?"

"Thanks, no. I don't watch much, and my little set is just fine."

"A new table? This one was a steal."

"No Daddy. I have your and Ma's old one. The red and chrome."

"That old set? You should get a new table and chairs."

"Really I don't. I don't want anything."

He looks hurt.

"For now, I'm fine. Just the vacuum. Would be great."

She searches for something else to say. Fills her glass with wine and tops his up. "What will you do now that you're back in Calgary?"

"Oh, I'll keep busy. I can help Bora out. And I bought a membership at the golf club. It has a golfing dome, so I'm practising my drive and my swing—two, three times a week."

"Good. That's good."

They eat in silence. The CD has finished, so Dan rises to change it. He puts on Sinatra. At one time all he listened to were the crooners, the Rat Pack, the Big Bands, Rosemary Clooney—and he, himself, possessed a rich, caressing voice. He was Mirjam's first musical teacher; they would sing together in the house, in the car, with Luba's applause encouraging their shared vocal talents. Mirjam had learned many of the tunes of the era before she turned to classical studies with a professional vocal coach. So she has a particular fondness for Old Blue Eyes. It's only in the last ten years that Dan has turned to old-country music. Ancient folksongs. Battle epics. Mirjam prefers to fly with Frank to the moon rather than hear of heavenly Serbia. Swing music reminds her of the tales her mother told her, how her father, a great dancer, had loved to jitterbug and foxtrot. It was how they met. At a dance in Drumheller. The beginning of a flawed love affair, just before the fall.

"Have some more." Dan begins ladling another helping of steaming pepper onto her plate.

"Not too much, Daddy."

"Have to watch that *velika guzica*." He chuckles.

"Don't remind me."

"We come from the same stock."

It's true. Her father's rear end, like her aunts', like her own, is ample. Mirjam has always called it the Serbian curse. She is an hourglass fifty years too late. So she pours more wine.

"Ma's got a nice place, too. It's northwest. No view. But quite comfortable."

"How is your singing?"

Mirjam pauses. "It's fine. Going well, actually. I'll be singing a new concert opera."

"Oh, before I forget. Bora is roasting a lamb on Sunday,

January 14. There is a feast day for Saint Sava at the Orthodox Church. I want you to come. Maybe you could sing."

"I'll see."

"It's weeks away. You love lamb."

"It depends on my rehearsal schedule. Rehearsals are very intense. This new piece is difficult."

"You don't want to come."

"It's not that, Daddy."

"You're too busy to spend time with your father."

"I don't spend much time with Ma, either."

"I didn't ask. What's a concert opera?"

"Usually a composition with a sacred text. You know, like Handel's *Messiah*. But this is a modern concert opera with a secular text, the Greek myth of Myrrha."

"Who is he?"

"Myrrha is a she, the daughter of her father Cinyras, whom she seduces."

"Who would write such a story, make it into a song?"

"A concert opera. Ovid wrote the story, actually, or his version is best known. But the concert opera is a composition, a new work by my professor, Helmut Weinstein."

Dan abruptly rises to clear the plates.

"It's an honour to sing it, really. I'm honoured," she tells his back.

She can feel his temper rippling through the galley kitchen and around the walls to where she still sits at the table. Scraping plates and clanging cutlery telegraph his displeasure. Mirjam removes her napkin and puts it on the table, resolving not to invite him to her Master's concert.

Dan returns with two demitasses fragrant with espresso. He sets these down, leaves, then returns with a plate of bakeshop sweets. All this while Sinatra's got her under his skin. Dan sits in his chair and clears his throat. He will not look at Mirjam. Father and daughter add sugar cubes to their cups. She tries again, willing her voice to gentle.

"Were you ... you know ... okay? In Mission?"

Dan shrugs. "I was in a jail cell. The one she sent me to. What do you think?"

"I think. I think—Don't blame Ma. You can't blame her."

Mirjam cannot reveal more, cannot bring herself to tell her father that it was she, in Calgary, who had, in fact, called the Mission RCMP about his violent attack on her mother. The night Luba, in abject terror, called her landline. On that very particular Sunday night when Mirjam, having just felated the visiting German singing professor for the first time, had, of happenstance, come home soon afterwards, rather than spend the night, despite his insistence. Luba's desperate voice cried out from the Fraser Valley across the interior and over the Rockies, "He's pummeling me!" and then the line went dead.

The receiver remained in the daughter's frozen hand, until she heaved a great sigh and the inertia passed. Shakily, she dialed 911 and was forwarded to the RCMP in Mission, BC who dispatched a car immediately. For the better part of an hour, Mirjam kept dialing her parents' phone number. Eventually, her mother called from a neighbour's next-door condo. She was safe. She didn't want Mirjam to fly out. Dan was in lock-up.

On the following day, a Monday, Mirjam's university class was interrupted by a secretary bringing news of an emergency phone call. Mirjam left her curious students to take the call from RCMP Sergeant Bromley of Mission, BC, asking for details of the assault. There was little to relate except for Dan's history of violence. Mirjam hung up the phone and immediately tried her mother. There was no answer. Vibrating, the singer returned to her vocal production class.

She had put her father behind bars. And now she must sing.

"I shouldn't have hit her."

"No. That's very true."

"But you don't know how that woman pushes and goads! You don't know the hell I've lived through. Especially after we lost the business. She blamed me. I know it! I could see it in her eyes, hear it in her voice. So many years ... I could do nothing to please her. Even once we got back on our feet and the new business took off."

Mirjam swallows a mouthful of the sweet, strong coffee. She blinks, once, twice. Nelson Riddle's orchestra plays an interlude. "Maybe an upright. A Hoover. Instead of a cylinder like my old Electrolux."

Dane nods, puts down his small cup. "I don't think you should sing about such things. The money we spent on your singing lessons, accompanists, festivals, the piano, your fancy degrees. And this is how you repay us by singing dirt and filth."

"It's not—dirt. It's myth. A powerful story. Ma doesn't mind."

He snorted. "No, of course, *she* wouldn't."

"What does that mean?"

"It means you should have a little respect."

"Respect? For Ma? I do—"

"For your father. How I'd feel about such things. My reputation."

"Pardon?"

"Singing that song by that German."

"You don't even know him, Daddy."

"I know Germans."

"You can't know all Germans, just because you fought in the war."

"Don't tell me what I don't know!" The heat of his sudden flash makes her start.

Mirjam shakes her head. How did they get to this place? How is it possible to conflate Greek mythology and modern classical composition with Nazi Germany and the Second World War? How did her singing a concert opera turn into some kind of a pejorative reflection upon her father? She wants to be gone now. At home in front of the piano. Or curled up with a book. Any place but here with this madman who is her father. She rises from the table.

"I'd better go. I have an early class that I still have to finish planning."

"Of course you do."

He withdraws now into a pout familiar as a tired old refrain. He does not walk her to the door. Her hand is on the doorknob when the knife of his voice reaches her back.

"Tell her I'm done. My lawyer will be in touch very soon. Tell her."

"Tell her yourself."

Alone in the elevator, she leans her forehead against the cool metal of the sliding door. Why had she come? Why make amends, or pretend to, with this man she will never again love? Why waste her time and energy when she could have been home rehearsing or out with friends or tangled in the bedsheets with Helmut?

Mirjam steps from the elevator and into the dusk. The birds are singing their goodnight songs to each other. A lone crow caws. There is a chill promise in the late autumn air, and she makes another to herself.

12

Repeatedly, Sudbina sought an audience with her father the despot. As she was his favourite and he was loath to yet marry her off, he denied her requests, thinking marriage was on the girl's mind, now that her sisters were wed. Instead, he busied himself with military exercises and war and fighting.

Sudbina was not easily put off. Each time he returned to the castle, she repeated her request to see her father. Each time she was denied. But finally, after a particularly fatiguing three-day skirmish with the insurgents, the despot relented and allowed his daughter into his antechamber.

"Father, I am come to ask if I might be permitted to visit your library. The days are long in the castle keep now that I alone remain of your daughters. I am tired of the books there, having read them all many times over."

The despot felt instantly relieved, certain that this small bequest would in no way endanger the girl or take her and her lovely singing from him prematurely. He smiled indulgently, well knowing she had been availing herself secretly of his tomes for some time. "Yes, daughter Sudbina. This I grant you."

In gratitude for this freedom to learn and know, Sudbina,

accompanied by the court harpist, sang her father his favourite songs, easing his burdens and lulling him to sleep.

On the morn, she fairly flew to the library where, according to her will and whimsy, she busied herself in the books of her father's rich collection. In this way, she joined soldiers on the battlefield, lords and their retinue, heroes on their quests. She saw faraway lands, mythical beasts, magical portents. In the evenings she would return to the keep and dazzle the lady servants with stories and songs she composed about the adventures she'd read. Days turned to weeks turned to months.

"Father, I have another request to make of you." Sudbina had scarce finished her lay, and the court harpist's strings had yet to grow still in the great firelit hall of her sire. The despot was home from yet another military foray. His bones were weary and his wits dulled by wine.

"Yes, my fair child of the golden voice?"

"That is it precisely, dear father. I wish to visit my sister, Milosti. To bring her the tales and tunes of her former home. She is yet again with child, and it has been many months since St. Stefan's feast when last I saw her or her babes."

The despot sat upright on his throne. "No!"

"Father, I am wasting away with idleness here in your castle."

"The Turk will murder you within an hour."

"Father, to stay within these fortress walls is to be imprisoned."

"Perhaps it is time you were married."

"What? And exchange one gaol for another? Besides"—she softened her voice to a soothing alto—"it is not time for me to leave my father permanently. Who else would sing to you and ease your troubles?" Sudbina touched his hand gently. "I ask only to visit my dear sister, to travel with your guards to her castle and stay but a fortnight. I will be with your armed and able men. Indeed, even the harpist could come along as extra companion."

"A harpist for protection?" the father grumbled, though he trusted this one almost as he would a son. So, too, he'd heard the lore about such musicians and their propensity for making magic with their instruments. But that was the stuff of women's gossip. He shook his head.

The man with the harp spoke melodically. "It would be an honour to accompany the despoina."

Sudbina beamed at him and turned pleading eyes upon her father, who finally sighed, resigned. "I have many misgivings. You must travel through the woods and there lives Baba Roga, that wretched hag."

"Old wives' tales, Father!"

"There are highway robbers and forest brigands."

"Your men are skilled combatants for such rogues."

"So many perils ..."

"Yes, there are Turks and witches and thieves, but we will evade them all safely there and back, Father; you will see. Your men are so well trained under your command. We'll not stray by the wayside or take foolhardy risks. Trust them. And trust your daughter, Sudbina."

At last, the despot grudgingly acquiesced and plans were made for the journey.

On the momentous morning, discordant notes from the crows at the window casement roused her. Sudbina rose and eschewed her waiting women, choosing instead to dress herself in a riding vest, breeches and cape. She'd had them purposefully, if reluctantly, make for her travels. The girl did not yet know how to ride a horse, but she intended to learn, unbeknownst to her father.

A company of nine—the harpist; a bevy of six guards; one trembling waiting woman, Elenya; and Sudbina—set off that fine March day, with birdsong as a farewell chorus and the despot, heart in throat, watching his dearest possession depart.

13

Luba carefully reconciles every penny in her account, every cheque she has written in the past month, with her bank statement. Though her daughter has recommended that she pay her bills at the debit machine, Lu resists. She likes the surety of her own calculations, the meticulous checking off of cheques cleared through the bank, the paper record of transactions and expenditures of a life. At least she knows she has lived through yet another month and made it to the end without bankruptcy. She can balance that much. Luba fears financial ruin as much as she does another Depression, especially now that she is on her own. Especially now that she must live off her small pension and her minimum wage from two part-time jobs.

That is, until the court orders Dan to pay her some form of support. If the court so rules.

Lu's meeting with a divorce lawyer was a disheartening and expensive proposition. At the conclusion of a one-hundred-and-fifty-dollar hour, she felt her life a failure, her marriage a forty-five-year mistake. Leaving the plush office of the woman attorney a third her age, Luba struggled to swallow a sense of humiliation.

How had her story become a battered book, cover torn asunder, for the remainder bin? Had it really been fifty-some years since she danced at the Elks and worked in Claire's selling dresses and dreams to other hometown girls and women? What of her own dreams? She cannot remember them now. How did she become a senior citizen in a city she no longer recognizes and where she has only a daughter for a friend? Who is the woman Luba, now that the best years of her life have flown and she has little else but a puny pension and a beaten sense of self?

But these are momentary self-indulgent thoughts. The bankbook balances. Lu has a new part-time job at Safeway as a sampler hostess, another as a Woolco salesclerk, and a good pair of shoes that so far have eased the impact of the concrete floors on her knees and back and corns. She glances down at her hands, their crepe-y skin and a small bump of cartilage that she never before noticed. Her wedding and engagement rings, those same she herself paid for years ago, are tucked away in her jewellery box. Lu has no heart for them. Unadorned and still sturdy, her fingers unbent by arthritis, Luba wills her hands to put away the tools of her banking machinations and put some coffee on for her daughter, who has promised to visit this afternoon.

The phone rings.

"Hello Lu?"

"Dan." She panics. How did he get her number? Does he know where she lives? Then she remembers that she chose not to unlist her telephone number because of the extra cost and regrets her parsimony. Still, he can't know her address, at least not yet.

"I'm in Calgary."

"I know. Mirjam told me."

"I was wondering ... would you like to go for coffee?"

"Coffee."

"Yes, we could—could talk."

"I don't. Dan, I don't really want to talk to you right now."

"Maybe in a week then?"

"I don't know."

"Okay, I'll call you back in a week."

Lu still clutches the receiver to her breast when Mirjam lets herself in the apartment with her key. She is instantly at her mother's side. "Ma? Have you had bad news? What's happened?"

"Your father."

"Is he—is he dead? Did he kill himself?"

"No. He wants to have coffee."

"What? I hope you told him to go fuck himself."

"No, not that."

"Well, what did he say?"

"He's going to call me back."

"Jesus." Mirjam pours them each a mug of black coffee and takes the phone from her mother's hands, replacing it on the charger. They sit together on the rose-coloured sofa.

"What are you going to do? Change your number?"

"No."

"I'll call him. Tell him to leave you alone."

"No, you won't. I'm quite capable of handling this myself."

"Meaning?"

"I'll go for coffee. What can it hurt? I need to be civil to him."

"Why? After what he did—"

"Because, Mirjam, of you. We're in this together, he and I, for the rest of our lives."

"Don't put this on me, Ma."

"I'm not. I'm just thinking about the future. Yours. Mine." Lu takes a sip from her mug. "Let's be honest. Our money, your inheritance, is tied up in all of this."

"I don't care about that, Ma."

"I do. I happen to care very much."

Lu paints her face. First the eyebrows, two surprising bows. Then powder and blush to disguise the enlarged pores. She outlines her mouth resolutely in a deep cinnabar and fills in her lips with Carnadine Caper. Last night she re-touched her roots with Nice and Easy Hazelnut Glow. Though Luba knows she no longer turns young men's brains to paste, she acknowledges that she still turns out well. Flipping the new scarf from Mirjam about her neck, she exits and locks her apartment door, then walks down to the parking lot.

Easing out of the alley, Lu works at orienting herself and navigating the Tercel through rush-hour traffic. Why did they choose this ridiculous time to meet? So many one-way streets downtown. Which direction is the river again? Why didn't she just take the CTrain? Because, she tells herself, her own car means a quick escape, if necessary. Luba makes a decision and turns north. She hopes it is the right way.

City workers along 17th Avenue are putting up Christmas lights, winking promises as the afternoon light fades. Billboards insist with ridiculous prematurity that Christmas begins at Eaton's, and Lu makes a mental note to buy a gift of lingerie for Mirjam, having already cut the coupon out of *The Calgary Herald* and tucked it in her purse. Will she buy Dan a gift? It's only October. Still time to consider.

※

The Tim Hortons parking lot is not too busy despite the time of day. Lunch is well over and the evening crowd has yet to appear. Schools have emptied of gum-smacking, idiot teenagers who descend like vultures at 3:30 p.m. to loiter, unscrew saltshakers, and make stupid googly eyes at each other, punctuated by intrusive bleatings. Dan detests their daily coup d'etats.

He has arrived forty-five minutes early. He sits in his Lincoln Town Car, idling the engine for the heater and listening to the right-wing talk show radio host he admires. Finally, at a quarter to the hour, Dan switches off the engine, pockets his keys and enters Tim Hortons. Gloria, the little Oriental girl he quite likes, is not working today. He orders a double-double and a French cruller from a tarty-looking tattooed twenty-something, then picks a seat by the window, quite away from other patrons. Tinny music comes over the coffee shop speakers. Dan finds it invasive and annoying.

Like his daughter's music. Not the songs that she sang, but the music that blared regularly out from behind her closed bedroom door. Dan lost count of the times he flung open that door to tell her to turn the damn music down. How she managed to get through high school and her undergrad degree while listening to that crap was beyond him. He is sure she has a hearing problem by now. After all the money they'd spent on her singing lessons and her education, she'd find a way to undo it all and go deaf, he is certain. Then that would be the end of her career, wouldn't it? Serve her right. Chasing after dreams of stardom. Where did that ever get anybody? Sure, there were the Bings and the Dinos and the Sammy Davis Jrs. But what kind of life was being a classical singer? Who could survive on that unless you were a Pavarotti? And Mirjam is certainly no tenor.

No, this music business is going to be another of her stupid pipe dreams, Dan can tell. Then she'll come crawling back to him, looking for money to fund her next fly-by-night scheme. Well, not this time. Danilo has bigger things on his mind. Like the reconciliation of his marriage, for one thing.

He wonders if Luba has got lost. The woman has no sense of direction. Like the time he took her to Yugoslavia, years ago before all this business erupted in the old country. She couldn't find her way back from the market to the hotel, silly thing. Dan smiles at the memory. He'd had to go on a search to find her, several blocks from the hotel, map billowing in her hand, agitated and headed the wrong way. Leading her by the elbow, he'd guided her safely into the hotel lobby lounge where she'd collapsed in a chair and ordered a drink. They'd laughed together then. He wonders if he will ever again hear Lu's laugh and feels himself tearing up at the notion.

But there she is now, pulling slowly into a space, her usual timid approach to parking. Dan watches as she leaves the car and finds her way across the asphalt to the entrance. He feels blood rushing to his face and ears as he rises to greet her. She sees him and waves him back, motioning for him to stay seated while she purchases her own cup of coffee.

So this is the way it is going to be, is it? Luba paying her own way.

She maneuvers past the tables over to where he sits. Luba puts her steaming mug down. "Hello Dan."

"Hi Luba. You look good. Very good. A nice scarf."

Lu takes the seat across from him. Dan finds her too bright in this beige plastic place, though they have had coffee together at Tim Hortons for many years, before all this.

"Mirjam gave it to me as a gift."

Dane does not want to discuss their daughter with his estranged wife. Mirjam is a tinderbox between them.

He looks older, Lu thinks. A little puffy around the eyes. As usual, Dan is impeccably groomed, his silver hair trim, his face clean-shaven, his clothes tidy and his shoes polished. But she can see that he has suffered. Dan has trouble meeting her eyes.

She knows, as usual, she must begin. "I went to a lawyer." Dan's hand shakes as he raises his coffee cup.

"And I know what I'm entitled to, Dan. I also know what our finances are, better than you do."

His look is nitroglycerin. The usual sickness rises in Lu's throat, but she will not be thwarted. "I know what will happen to our money if we live apart. And how that will affect Mirjam in the end."

Dan does not trust himself to speak, but merely grunts.

"So I have a proposal."

This surprises him.

"We buy a place together and move in."

Dan cannot believe that her mouth is making these sounds. He thought that Lu would never forgive him. Would insist on a divorce. Would cut him from her life.

"We reconcile the marriage, with conditions."

"Yes?" He is eager to hear everything she has to say.

"Separate bedrooms. The sex is over."

He looks down into his coffee. He is impotent. Years of smoking. There have been times when he coerced Lu into oral sex. She complied, but never willingly. And the results had been less than hoped for.

"You turn the accounts back over to me. We visit a lawyer and draw up a new will."

Dan nods. Soon after he was released from jail, he changed his will to remove both his wife and daughter as heirs. It was stupid, he knows now. But he was so angry and hurt. Now, for Lu ... he can agree to this remedy.

"And finally, if you ever hit me again, it will be over between us forever."

"I'll never do it again."

Lu says nothing, but takes a sip of her coffee.

"I'm—I'm sorry, Lu. I'm sorry I—I hit you." Dan is nearly crying. He feels a fool in Tim Hortons. But he is so relieved at this unexpected offer from Luba. A warmth rushes over him, and he reaches for her hand.

Luba, however, pulls it away. "I also want you to go for counselling. Get some help."

"I'm taking an anger management course. It's a condition of

my sentence."

"A course is not enough, Dan, for what ails you. You need ... you've always needed therapy." Lu knows that she has crossed a threshold. She can't quite believe her boldness. Wonders if it's the caffeine. Her heart is a trapped animal in her ribcage, even though she knows she is in a coffee shop and Dan would not dare raise his hand to her in public.

"O—okay."

"I mean it, Dan. You hit me for the final time in Mission. I want us to be very clear on that and on this: nothing about this proposal is subject to negotiation, Dan. Do you understand?"

"Yes, Luba. I understand." Dan deeply resents her tone, but he suppresses his feelings, the ugly ire that threatens to command him as it has always done, as she rises to go. "When can we start ... to look for a place?" Dan follows her to the door and out into the bright afternoon.

"Next week, I think. Give me the weekend to break the news to Mirjam."

She leaves him and dashes over to her car. He waves at her and Luba drives away. Dan realizes that she has not smiled once during their past half hour together.

A clot of teenagers tumbles over to where he is standing at the door. They are dressed in those stupid flannel pants, plaid jackets and combat boots. He finds them and their piercings abhorrent and longs to take a fist to cuff them out of their self-absorption. He raises his arm but is overcome by a cramp and must instantly lower it, rubbing gingerly the muscle in his tricep. And the youth pass him by.

14

Aphrodite, goddess of love and desire
What cruel trick have you played
On Myrrha your sister
How have I come to this state?
Why are you so resolute
Your back to me defiant
You say that I have crawled into my father's lap
To take up that power which belongs to him
I have but this to say: why did you, goddess,
Turn my desire to my father
Away from other suitors
What cruel caprice
To play with Myrrha's heart!

It is a difficult, dramatic piece with a vocally challenging recitative. Rehearsals are demanding, made even more so by the demanding genius who commandeers the singing and then her body. Sometimes after he has groped and felt her, moistened her to climax or taken her from behind at a moment of vigour and heightened passion that interrupts their rehearsal, Helmut will demand that she sing again. Sometimes full afternoons are spent in this manner of repetitive singing and fucking. Mirjam is both exhausted and exhilarated. She both fears and is attracted to the idea that she may be falling in love with her master, and she is not unaware of the Svengalian implications and complications of such feelings. She begins the recit again, hoping to err only on the side of lust.

"Again. You must not breathe here. But here. Come, I will show you." Helmut steps behind his student and places his hands on her ribcage. She sings and can feel his warm breath on her neck. His hands will her to breathe at the appropriate place in the text and the music. She feels profoundly his intent.

And then Helmut's hands slip under her blouse to cup her breasts. In but a measure, he is pinching her nipples and they grow instantly erect at his insistence.

"That is what I wanted." Mirjam's breathing is ragged, and Helmut lowers her to the floor. "Now, the introduction and *sforzando!*"

There is no doubt that they are also making progress musically. Helmut is very pleased with her interpretation of the text and music. Much rides on her performance—for them both. Herr Professor Helmut Weinstein has not had a musical success for some years; his last musical setting of *Richard III* received only tepid reviews in Frankfurt. That lacklustre reception is in large part why he accepted the invitation to this university as a visiting scholar. Feeling both diminished and claustrophobic in his home country, Helmut considers the Prairie and a small university to be a fitting departure from the past few years of his lagging career. He has been working on his concert opera for seven of those years and is determined to finish it in Calgary, where it will be debuted with the impressive string section of the city's very fine philharmonic orchestra. Expecting a provincial, uninspiring institution, Herr Weinstein feels instead that he was suitably courted and admired by the fawning administration. His stipend is generous, and he has been wined and dined appropriately. Most interestingly, Helmut was pleasantly surprised to find a mezzo of Mirjam's calibre, youth, and vaguely European beauty. She thought him a genius from the start. He thought she was Jewish when first they met but was not startled to learn that she was Slavic to the bones. And they are good bones, indeed.

Mirjam is most amenable to work with, besides her obvious charms. She gets on well with the tenor who is singing the part of the father, Cinyras, as well as the soprano who sings the part of Aphrodite. Helmut wondered why his lead had not already fostered a career. She told him that she did have an emerging singing career, but that opportunities weren't as many for singers of her ilk in this cold country. He has promised to take her with him back to Germany and to introduce her to audiences there, if the concert opera does as well as they all hope here.

What he likes best about Mirjam is her discretion. He has not told her about Hannelore or the children back home, and she has not asked. They focus exclusively on their passions: music and lovemaking. All in all, Canada is turning out to be a most hospitable and accommodating country.

Beautiful maiden
Who are you
That have so lithely
Slipped into my life
My dreams
My bed?
You with your linen thigh
Your rose-scented hair
You seem almost as young and coltish as
My daughter
Surely, this gift
In my later life is a mercy bestowed
By great Aphrodite herself.

Every afternoon the late-season crows communally roost on the roof of the Department of Music building. They eye her when she hurries down the steps, and one or another follow her as though familiar with her route, her routine. A pair might wait outside the Second Cup while she gets her morning coffee and muffin.

As she waits for a fresh brew, Mirjam glances at the complimentary newspaper's headlines, then flips through the pages to the buried news story: *Serbs massacre 62 Bosniak children in Srebrenica, 100 more wounded.* She wonders at this man, Ratko Mladić and his brothers in arms, including the ever-smirking Slobodon Milošević. Who raised such boys, such sociopaths?

Her father's aunts doted on their own sons, hated Tito, and sometimes still shake the tired rug of fervent nationalism. But how does that mutate to mass violence or lead to massacres? To ethnic cleansing? Does Mirjam, herself, carry a related gene? She shakes her head as if to dislodge the vile thought.

Cup in hand, Mirjam exits the shop, and the crows flap after her as she muses down the street and to the market. Dark thoughts of pillaged villages and systematic rape gradually pivot to tonight when she will cook Helmut dinner. It is the first time he will come to her apartment, the first time they will make love in her bed. The first time they will be between new cotton sheets as opposed to strewn sheets of music as they have yet to make it from his studio to his bedroom. Mirjam anticipates the meal and the newness of this experience as she chooses with particular passion the aubergines.

Still the crows hover under the clouds as she takes the CTrain back to her place not far from the university, Helmut a refrain running through her thoughts while the black birds wing after her, settling occasionally on the power lines, like quarter notes on a staff. What piece do they represent? Beethoven's opening to the *Fifth*? Ravel's *Bolero*? She cannot tell what crow symphony is playing out.

Mirjam spills out of the train with her packages and most of her wits. Now that she is nearly home, she finds she is nervous about tonight with Helmut. There is that butterfly feeling of stage fright as always before a performance. Overhead, the birds caw without melody as she traipses the sidewalk to her walk-up.

In her small kitchen, in between sips of chilled Pinot Grigio, she salts the eggplant slices and sets the sauce to bubbling. Outside the unwashed window, on a dead elder branch that needs culling, one lone crow eyes her doings.

As she sautés the onions, Mirjam thinks about a difficult passage in the concert opera. There is a rather abrupt time signature change in the final movement, and she has yet to master the transition and the feel of the new tempo. Helmut has been working her diligently on the time. It also marks the most emotionally fraught interval of the entire piece, the moment when the daughter recognizes her great sin, and yet determines to carry on her licentious affair with her father. It is a horrendous reckoning with self.

She adds the ground beef to the skillet, skillfully sprinkling in the mint and cinnamon, stirring and adjusting the heat. Mirjam knows that when she finally commands the passage in question, she will have the secret of the character, Myrrha. She puzzles over her stumbling as she adds a little flour for thickening. There have been other, equally challenging pieces of music and movements within them that she has learned to perfect with practice and repetition and good coaching. Now she works with one of the best, and still this part of the concert opera eludes her.

On the next burner the béchamel sauce is beginning to bubble, so she reduces the heat and takes the whisk to the mixture. This part is taking such time to hone, to settle in her voice, to embody the character and the intent, the text and the breathing. The debut is but a month away. Mirjam is concerned about timing. She glances at the clock and refills her glass.

Helmut will help her, she is certain, as he has been doing so patiently these months. He will not relent and leave her stranded before she absorbs the character and the music. And she will command the time change, the passage, the role. Though she may slip in rehearsal, she will not fall at the concert hall. Not at the performance. Not with this man who is growing ever more central in her life and her work. She finds her breath quickening. It has little to do with the pastry she is spreading with the rolling pin on the counter and everything to do with what is happening between her thighs.

Berlin. What will they do together in that city? Take up an apartment together on the Rosenstrasse? Will they meander the unified streets and haunt old world cafés? How will she fit into his world there? Will she find work? Singing roles? Join a company? Helmut has hinted that she will have the career she has dreamed of most of her life. Will she augment her singing time with teaching private lessons or as a sessional instructor at a conservatory? Will he introduce her to the right people—influential directors and conductors? She wonders if her voice will continue to thrill him, and if that is enough, fears there will come other sopranos to usurp her in his attentions, as there one day must. Mirjam wonders most if they will be a couple outside the walls of Helmut's office, a question she has not dared utter to his face. She worries that his desire for her will wane to familiarity and boredom with proximity and the passage of time.

She drops an egg on the floor and cracks her head on the open cupboard as she rises from cleaning up the mess. The pain is sharp and familiar.

When Helmut arrives at 6 p.m., the table is set, dinner is ready, and the bottle is empty.

They drink another. And another. Consuming. The meal. Each other. A consummate performance.

Locked in his arms après sex, pillow talk is brief and perfunctory. Helmut details for her the coming concert opera performance and the ensuing trip to Berlin for the forthcoming German debut.

In a month, she will be in the spotlight, as will he and his great masterwork. She must understand what is riding on this. Mirjam assures the maestro with her mouth and her lips and her tongue.

He does not stay the night but leaves before dawn. Why, she cannot fathom.

Something about timing. Time.

Time. We fracture it. We pull patterns out of its magic hat. We mark it, make it, try to manipulate and crack it. But it remains unassailable.

Time. We break it into measures. 3/4. 12/8. Double time. Half time. Common time. Beat me daddy, eight to the bar. We syncopate. Skip a beat. Ritard and accelerando. Sometimes get ahead of the beat or lag behind. Cheat time. Or have no sense of it. We sustain in legato. Approach with rubato. Or break with staccato. We rest. Sometimes for whole or many measures. Breathe and sing. Sing the time.

Count the time. Time and numbers and breaths that make a song, and a song strung with another to make a suite or concert opera or operetta or musical or grand opera. To make a life of singing, a singing life, one needs time.

We measure a song by its measures, by the time it takes to learn and memorize and master. The number of times we sing it so that it becomes locked in the mind and in muscle memory. The time it takes to call oneself a singer. Ten thousand hours, they say. So little time, really, in the measure of an immeasurable universe. And how many songs does one really get to sing in a finite life? The songs are limited to time. Music. Singing. Living. All about time. Timing.

She wonders at the timing of this relationship between her and Helmut. One never knows why or when such passion pitches between a first and third movement. She tries not to overthink, a habit of hers in singing and lovemaking that Helmut has tried to break. She must not spend too much time in thinking, he has repeatedly told his lead soprano, only in the execution and the surrender.

Mirjam sets the alarm clock and turns on her side.

Oh, Aphrodite
Cruel mistress
I would smite thee
Were I not bound as I am
With these feet of clay
To this temporal realm

It is three o'clock in the afternoon a mere three days later when, alone in Helmut's studio, Mirjam discovers the Eudora e-mail from Hannelore open on the maestro's computer screen. He has absented himself to visit the dean and does not know much about computers or personal web security. From his carelessness, Mirjam has quickly ascertained that in addition to a wife there are several children, the youngest boy a fifteen-year-old. As well, there seems to be at least one other mistress in Munich with whom Helmut communicates intimately and regularly. Mirjam carefully forwards to herself the offending e-mails for safekeeping.

In shock, the singer wanders aimlessly about the university campus for two hours under the watchful eyes of her totem black birds. When she pauses to buy a Frappuccino, shock has expanded to cool plotting.

She considers tearing his heart out, a fitting response apropos of the concert opera and Greek goddesses seething with rage. She considers e-mailing Helmut's wife, the children, or at very least, the mistress. They are not at fault, she realizes, though the latter would be the most satisfying to enlighten and disavow of any illusions she might harbour. She considers something more sinister and directly related to this master who has deceived her, or at the very least dissembled by omission.

There is little she can do, however, prior to the debut, as she does not want to unseat Helmut and thwart her own potential career. She needs the concert opera and an international performance and exposure as much as Helmut does. No, instead Mirjam will bide her time.

When she fucks him later that night, he is certainly responsive, but curious about the intensity of her ardour and her new proclivity for binding.

"Too much thinking," she trills into his ear as she rises in time again.

15

They were not long past the castle when Sudbina ordered the lead guard to quit his rowan mare and give her leave to ride. The young woman stood stubbornly in front of the carriage and horse in which she, the waiting woman, and the harpist travelled, and refused to give way. As the massive guard and the stubborn despoina argued for a quarter of an hour, Elenya fretted and the harpist looked on, amused. Finally, the guard agreed with the proviso that he hold the reins and lead the horse. And so the first afternoon passed slowly with Sudbina becoming used to the shift and pitch of a horse's back between her legs. When at last they stopped, and while the fire and evening meal were being prepared and the tents hoisted, she insisted the guard teach her to mount and dismount, and afterwards to groom and feed the mare. In the morning, she was adamant that she ride again, and the guard taught her to saddle, and the beginning lessons of trotting and cantering. The travelling of the retinue was unhurried, but Sudbina had no wish to hasten the passage of her time of freedom from her father's keep.

By week's end, her thighs had toughened their muscles,

and she was adept at the basics, as well as turning and stopping her mount. Sudbina grew fond of the guard, whose name was Dragan, and his lovely mare, Lika. She further convinced him to let her try her hand at archery, and he found her an able student.

Each night passed thus. Members of the company set camp and prepared the evening meal. The despoina practised the arts of horsemanship and grooming, fitting arrow to bow while the harpist looked on and began to compose a lay about the despoina's journey.

On the twelfth day, they came to a deep wood, though they had skirted others or ridden through thin copses at other places along the trip. This forest there was no escaping: it was thick and far-ranging, the stuff of fairy tales and highwayman lore.

But at the other end, after but a week-long journey more, lay the castle of her sister, so pass through they must. If they stayed on the track, Dragan predicted, they would meet no danger.

But if such were the case, there would be no story. As misfortune would have it, on the evening of the first night under the dark canopy of trees, the company was attacked. Seven bandits who'd sniffed out a royal party had rightly guessed that there were riches to be pilfered. Silent rogues, they slashed the throat of the two night-guards and leapt upon the five who sat about the fire. At the sound of struggle, the despoina sprung from her sleep and picked up her bow. Her waiting woman was beside her in a heartbeat. Sudbina fitted her arrow and shot true. A first rodent fell dead at the fireside. She loaded again and a second toppled. Her father's men managed to stave off three who were upon them, Dragan unsheathing his sword to smite another. But the last large brute crept up behind her waiting woman and put knifepoint to Elenya's throat.

"I'll kill her if you don't call off your men and surrender your silver and—" His harsh command was cut short by the garrote of a harp string strung surely and suddenly about the knave's throat. The harpist drew the string taut and tauter.

Sudbina felt a spurt of blood and spittle against her own throat as the man succumbed and slipped to the ground.

Breathless, the travellers regrouped about the fire. Sudbina consoled the wailing waiting woman, and the men tended to wounds—some minor, some worse.

"You were very quick and brave, my lady," a musical voice spoke at her ear.

Sudbina turned to the minstrel. "As were you." The harpist bowed. Their eyes met over the sobbing head of Elenya pulled close to Sudbina's breast.

Dragan argued for returning to the castle, but Sudbina insisted that they were closer to her sister's safekeeping than her father's. "Surely, for our return, my sister and her husband will lend us men for the journey home." The guard bowed to her bidding, but not without reservation.

And so nine were now seven. The remaining guards made their comrades graves, and the harpist played a lament over the bodies. Those of the robbers were left in the open, their gaping eyes certain to be plucked out by eager crows, their bodies carrion for the beasts of the forest.

Sleep was shallow and broken for the remainder of the

night. As she finally succumbed to exhaustion, Sudbina thought she heard the forest laughing.

A sober group began the next morning's travel. Few words passed between them, except for muttered misgivings about continuing this journey. At midday, they found a huge tree had fallen across the path, and so the carriage that carried Elenya, the harpist, and certain of the supplies had to be abandoned. The maidservant and the harpist, who himself was a fine horseman, rode one of the horses now bereft of its original rider, and Dragan rode the other, now freed of the carriage. And so the party travelled through that downcast day into afternoon shadows.

16

She nearly burned the damn house down. Set the quilt on fire because she'd left the trouble light on underneath it. She was making a goddamn tent to read under. And then got disinterested or sidetracked. Like she always does.

Teenagers take impulsive risks, sometimes.

She wasn't a teenager.

How old was she?

Four, maybe five.

I see. And you hold a four- or five-year-old accountable for a juvenile act of carelessness? All these years later. Many would see this as a humorous anecdote, a tale to be told at family gatherings. Surely, dangerous at the time. But almost thirty years later?

She disobeyed me. And put us all in peril.

Did the fire spread from the quilt?

No, I came in time and managed to douse it with water. The quilt was ruined.

A family heirloom?

No, just an old quilt.

And then what happened?

I spanked her silly to Sunday.

Was this a frequent occurrence?

Spanking? I don't believe in negotiating with a five-year-old, if that's what you mean. I'm a firm supporter of 'Spare the rod; spoil the child,' just like my mother before me. She used a thick wooden spoon, a belt, a willow switch. I used my hand. Kids need disciplining.

You mean corporal punishment.

Call it any fancy name you want, Doc. But I'm not into these new-age parenting techniques. I don't see anything good that's come of letting kids run amok. Nothing except laziness and entitlement, bad manners and piercings.

What happened next?

After the spanking? I forgave her. We carried on. She got over it.

You're sure.

Yes.

Did you?

Yes.

Then why does this incident still make you angry?

Because she defied me.

Like your mother defied your father. And left him feeling impotent.

Sure, drag my mother into it. It's what you headshrinkers do, isn't it? Everything's got to do with my mother for you guys, doesn't it?

Dane wished this session was over. He glanced at the clock. Thirty-eight minutes to go. His left butt cheek was already numb from the damn couch designed by some faggot who didn't give a shit about what it was like to be a senior citizen. Resentment at Lu and at this sentence to life therapy roiled in his stomach. He pulled a roll of Rolaids out of his pocket and popped two into his mouth.

Feeling okay, Dan?

Ulcers. From the war. Part of the reason for my honourable discharge, like I told you before.

And the other reason?

An injury. The butt of my machine gun recoiled into my jaw and broke most of my teeth. Not long after Ortona as we were heading for Rimini. I landed in the medical hospital and then was shipped home. Guess they figured after the injury and almost six years of active duty, I'd done my time, so I deserved the false teeth and a discharge.

Dane grimaced and burped softly. His stomach felt like a swirling toilet. He did not tell the shrink that he'd been cleaning his gun. Had known of its recoil problem and deliberately set the gun too near his jaw, hoping for a minor injury and an escape from Armageddon. He did not tell the man sitting across from him that two days earlier, Chester Smith, a red-headed son from the valley, a good Anglo boy who'd befriended Dane in high school and who'd miraculously ended up in the same battalion with Dan as his sergeant, had had his head blown clear off his young body in the heat of battle to smash the Gothic Line. That Dan, in shock and grief, had soiled his pants for a second time that day. That he had not known whether to attend to the twitching torso and legs of his comrade or to the head and had instinctively chosen the latter. That crawling on his knees and elbows, flat on his gut through the mud over to the head of his best friend, he had held it in his hands. Had witnessed Chester's blinking eyes in a blood-smeared face, his mouth opening and shutting as though hoping to share an ultimate secret with Dan. Chester's brain signal tapping out its final synapses while the rest of his body shat and spat out blood until his heart stopped a few beats later and ten yards over. That Danilo had gazed into Chester's eyes and seen. Terror certainly. But also accusation. Why Chester? Why not Dan? And that within two nightmarish days and sleepless nights Dan Pope had half-consciously found a way home and out of the horror of Italy and the end of the war.

And now this idiot with his several degrees and his comfortable life, bought by the deaths of thousands of young boys like Chester, sat smug and oblivious to the kinds of things Dane had seen and done overseas and thought he could analyze him. Figure it all out with book smarts. As if anyone could rake through the muck and blood that he'd clawed and marched through across Europe and North Africa. As if anyone could take back the fact that he'd killed men his own age and younger. As if anyone should try.

He'd gotten out alive. And that was that. What did any of it have to do with his daughter or his wife or the reconciliation of his broken marriage? Dane didn't realize that he'd spoken this last aloud.

Well, maybe, Dan, something in you is broken.

And you think you can fix me? Set me right like a broken arm? Repair the damage?

That's not really how I work. But maybe you can do those things or begin to.

Dane leaned forward. How long will it take?

It's not like physiotherapy, Dan. You're not "healed" after so many sessions.

I'm not sick.

Just a choice of word relating to the work of physio. Think instead of us getting at the clockworks. Looking closely at the cogs and wheels. Fine watches need tinkering and resetting, maintenance throughout the life of the timepiece. I think that's a better analogy, after what you've experienced in your lifetime.

Danilo sighed. He could really see no point to this exercise. He wanted ten or twelve steps to controlling his anger and one piece of paper declaring him fit and fine. But there was the agreement with Luba. He circled back in his mind to the earlier thread of questioning.

She deserved every spanking she ever got from me, just like I did from my mom. Once I got it so hard from her for telling a lie that I couldn't sit down for a week.

And you think that is normal parental discipline?

Sure as hell do.

Well, nowadays, common wisdom is that such physical punishment is not normal. Nor healthy. It's called abuse, Dan.

Not where I come from.

The law would not agree with you on that, Dan. Your mother could be charged with child abuse today. I know it was different in the thirties, but the current laws are in place for a reason. We've learned that such treatment seriously harms kids. *You were harmed by that harsh treatment.*

I came out okay.

Is that why we're here, Dan? Because you're okay?

Dan looked at his hands. The dark skin was showing its age around the knuckles and the backs were more sinewy than he remembered.

Look, I'm not saying this is the whole answer or that it gets you off the hook for your own actions and behaviour. But it's a recognized fact that the way your mother treated you likely injured your young psyche. You were a child, terrified by this woman. You saw her bully your own father into submission, then, in essence, banish him. Could it be that you feared all of your young life similarly being turned out of the house and rejected? You loved her deeply, by your own admission, but lived in peril of losing that love? In that house, you cottoned to the fact that it was only a matter of time before she erupted again and threatened you either with physical violence or emotional abuse or the withdrawal of her love or all of the above?

Still looking into his hands, Dan nodded.

I always begged afterwards for her forgiveness, her love.

A young child should not have to beg for either, Dan.

I—I did the same for Luba. Afterwards.

That fits a well-known pattern, Dan.

And Mirjam. But she didn't forgive.

※

In fact, Mirjam's eyes, once dried of their tears would turn to agates. He did not remember when he'd first taken note of this change. Certainly not in her toddler years when she had adored him and ridden his shoulders nightly up the stairs to her little attic bedroom. Nor when he played with her on the swing set, or when they sang simple songs together that he taught her. No, the hardness had come later and with it the rebellion. But even at four or five, he had glimpsed it in her expression after he'd pleaded for her forgiveness and reassurance of love: her little rigid body did not acquiesce. As he stood up from the bed where he'd tried to hug Mirjam, he smacked and cut open the side of his head near the hairline, on the sharp edge of the sloping roof. A smile stole across his daughter's small face.

Luba had bandaged the wound, but it left a small scar he could still see today, a little crescent just like the cut of a daughter's smile.

※

She didn't?
She was always a willful child. Untamable.
And you feel we should tame children?
It's called growing up.
But don't they do that on their own?
If they're allowed to run wild, they turn into animals. Or whores.
Is your daughter an animal?
No.
A whore?
Dan shrugged.
You think your daughter is a prostitute?
He waved his hand. No, not like that.
You mean that she is sexually promiscuous.

She's had a lot of boyfriends. But has never settled down. I doubt if she'll ever get married.

And that's what you wish for her?

Doesn't every father?

I'm not sure about every father. I'm asking about you.

Yes, I think she should find a man and build a home and have children.

And live happily ever after?

You're mocking me.

I'm not intending to. I'm just filling in the familiar fairy tale.

Does it have to end that way?

Well, we all die.

Yes, but I'm meaning your daughter's destiny. Does it have to follow that narrative?

How else should it be?

I'm not sure there's necessarily a *should*. Might it be possible for her to live another story? One of her own design.

So now life is a story.

In a way, yes, it is.

Well then, it's a story that doesn't get any easier. She needs to have money and security. She has neither right now.

And marriage and family will assure her of these things?

She'll have a better chance at them.

What if she doesn't want a husband or children?

She doesn't. So she says.

You don't believe her.

I think she's kidding herself.

What does she say she wants?

A singing career.

And you're against this idea.

I think it's crazy.

Why?

Because it's hard to make a living being a singer. It's shaky ground. There's no stability. It's feast or famine in that crazy world.

And you're afraid for her.

I'm afraid she'll end up ...

On the streets.

Without anything. Losing everything.

Did something similar happen to you, Dan?

I'm a kid from the Depression. The wolf was always at the door.

But you said your family was alright. You always had enough to eat. Your mother made sure of that.

Still, we were always aware of the dust and the poverty just outside. We didn't have much but an old house peeling paint and the clothes on our backs. Money was a constant worry. And then, later, after the war, I built a business—retail—and ... I lost it all.

You filed for bankruptcy.

Yes. But I climbed back up from the pit and rebuilt it all and more again. I didn't waste my life chasing dreams, did I?

Did you have a dream, Dan, say ... after the war when you first got home?

Dane gestured towards the certificates on the soft-hued wall. I wanted that. I wanted to go to university. To be a lawyer.

But?

But there wasn't enough money. What I had, I gave to my

mom. She was elderly. Dying of heart disease and diabetes. I just couldn't ... leave her in the valley and come to the city.

Drumheller to Calgary, that's not very far, is it Dan?

It's a lifetime ago. You can't know how it was. There was no way. I had to—to be the man of the house once I returned from overseas. I was afraid of—

Of your mother dying?

Yes.

Of your failing?

Go to hell.

I think we'll stop there for today. I can see you're angry.

I don't know what I pay you for! This all seems like smoke and mirrors to me.

You think I'm a charlatan. A fraud.

I think I'm wasting my money.

Let's try again next week, shall we?

Kiss my ass.

17

Luba tapes shut the box she's finished packing. This is the last of the china. She feels as though she's been packing and unpacking her entire life.

"I hate this, Ma." Mirjam is helping out with the remaining kitchen items.

"I know you do."

"I can't believe you trust him enough to move back in with him."

"I don't entirely trust him. But I am. And really, Mirjam, it's my decision to make. And I wanted ... I want to be settled in before Christmas, so we can all be together again."

"Great." Mirjam moves away.

She hears her daughter sigh audibly in the next room. Luba moves to the crystal and begins taking water goblets out of the china cabinet to wrap. Rolling them meticulously into brown packing paper along the table, she puts each gently into a nest of paper shavings in the bought boxes. Her hands know exactly what to do. They are old and practiced.

She'd trailed Dan from Drumheller to Calgary shortly after their marriage that followed quickly upon his mother's death. He'd found an ideal site in a happening fashion district. Couldn't Lu just taste the potential? This was the right move.

So Luba gave up her job at the Drumheller dress shop. Left her friends and her family in the valley to begin her and Dan's own business in the city, another ladies' dress shop, with the money she and Dan had saved.

And then the first miscarriage. After his initial resistance to Lu's working, Dan breathed a sigh of relief when she resumed work after a week's respite from her loss of the baby. His former nonsense about a working wife was over. Especially when they opened the doors to their store in Calgary and they had to work ridiculous hours. She did the books, cleaned the shop floors, the windows, the bathroom. Greeted and courted the customers, ordered the fashions, merchandised the shop, though Dan made displays, too. And the women swooned over his dark good looks, often buying more clothing than they'd intended because of his flattering attentions—after all, the war was over and they could afford the extra pennies, a few new indulgences. Times were good. The store prospered for several years.

Until she and Dan lost the lease. Even after they'd sold Dan's beautiful Studebaker, they soon couldn't afford to buy new stock or the newest fashions. Then creditors began calling. Stock dwindled pathetically on the racks. And the worries welled up in Lu even as she swelled with another child. The boy she lost seven months in. After which Dan stepped out most nights, sometimes not returning until dawn. She knew better than to challenge him, and besides she was caught up in her own suffering for the stillborn son they'd buried hastily and cheaply.

And then one evening, Dan returned home near midnight with a can of gas and a burning desire for insurance money.

Lu begged him to stop. He struck her across the face, then proceeded to douse gas about the apartment.

"Dan, don't be a fool," she shrieked through tears and snot and a bloody nose, "the insurance company will never buy this. The agents will see right through you, through this—this crazy ruse!"

And finally, Dan saw reason. Just in time. She stripped away the matchbox in his hand and began carefully mopping up the kerosene, while he slumped at the red and chrome kitchen table, the one he'd bought her in more prosperous times, on an April day she'd remembered as very happy.

Finished her task, with the smell of kerosene still hovering in the air despite the open windows, she gingerly placed her hand on his slumped shoulder. He'd turned then and burrowed his face into her breast, sobbing and seeking absolution. He took her to bed and they'd conceived another child. And the next morning Lu found the piece of paper in his suit jacket pocket—a receipt from a motel on the north side of the city. Luba could sense her life turning into a bad popular song.

Its refrain ran through her mind as they packed up the store for receivership. As she began filling out the forms for bankruptcy. As Luba wrapped their belongings for the trip back to Drumheller, where they would live in a cheap clapboard one-room apartment infested with mice, Dan repeatedly assured her that it would only be until the baby came, until the couple could get back on their feet.

Luba will one day learn the name of the woman who shared that motel room with Dan. Forty-seven years later, Delores McKenzie, a former regular customer at the old store location, will somehow find the address and write to her, begging pardon for sleeping with her husband. Lu will toss this letter in the trash, along with her coffee grounds and regret. Regret that she hadn't tossed Dan to Delores when she'd had the chance.

But then there would have been no Mirjam.

"Ma! I said, do you want this old suitcase full of old shoes?"

"No," Luba finishes wrapping up the last of the red wine glasses. "That's your father's and those are his shoes. He'll never miss them."

Luba can picture the ratty thing, probably smelling of mildew and age.

It is the same suitcase Dan packed when he took the job selling pots and pans door to door throughout the valley's small centres and farms—Drumheller, East Coulee, Cambria, Wayne, Rosedale, Midland—and beyond—Delia, Hannah, Munsen, Rumsey, Bisecker, Bassano, Three Hills, Big Valley, Stettler—an occupation Luba could see was doomed from the start. How could they prosper from such an enterprise?

Which housewife or farmwife needed pots and pans that she couldn't buy at Stedmans? Of course, Dan had to borrow money from his Serbian relatives to buy the second-hand Chevrolet Styleline he'd needed for this latest scheme. Lu took a job at the five-and-dime store in town during the day and enrolled at the secretarial evening school while her husband hit the road and made but five sales over the course of his fourteen-month tinker's career. In the meantime, she kept the one-room apartment they could scarcely afford, trapping more mice than she could count, and where, alone, she miscarried again while Dan was out of town. He'd sent her a dozen roses that were still on the red kitchen table, seared and withered, when he returned some weeks later, having suddenly resigned from the business of selling pots and pans.

Dan began to mutter about Calgary again. Another move. More possibilities back in the big city. He paced the apartment, trying to convince her until Lu wanted to scream. He did not touch her during this time, either in anger or in their shallow pull-out bed. Neither did he say a further word about the miscarriage, not even when she finally tossed out the flowers, dried reminders of a loss only she seemed to remember.

Keeping her grief in check, Lu rolled her pennies and managed to enroll in additional courses. Then Dan caught wind of an opportunity with White Rose, an oil company, and took to the road again, making sales on its behalf. At least there was a base salary along with commissions. At least he was home some weekends. At least she was getting along in her classes, acing the basic accounting, bookkeeping, stenography and Dictaphone courses, learning to type in triplicate, finally receiving her certificate and a letter of reference from her instructor, Miss Margaret Benson, extolling Mrs. Luba Pope's virtues as a nice young woman, a hard worker who could accurately type one hundred words a minute.

When he told her that White Rose was offering him a promotion requiring that they move to Calgary, Lu immediately put her resume in order, gave her notice at the store, and quietly began packing. Once again, she kissed her family and familiarity goodbye and drove away with Dan and his dreams. She landed a stenographer and receptionist job only days after they'd returned to Calgary. Dan's new position at White Rose meant that he spent a week in the city and three weeks on the road for the company.

It all seemed from the Christmas cards home and the infrequent family visits to and from Drum that things were progressing as everyone had hoped.

But Dan didn't feel he was progressing. He felt overlooked by his superiors, passed by for promotions that his lessers were awarded. Some prick with a kiss-ass attitude. Another bastard who was the nephew of the president. A brown-noser who bought the boss's good opinion with a bottle of Crown Royal at Christmas. Dan did well in sales; his numbers were good, couldn't they see? Lu listened, but if she said the wrong thing, even in consolation, at the wrong time to Dan, the flint was lit and the powder exploded.

"Are you made of stupid? Shut up when I'm talking to you. Your father threw you out for the bitch you are!" The assaults weren't nightly. They weren't even that frequent, largely because Lu recognized when and how to keep her tone civil, learning some of the warning signs that preceded Dan's eruptions. But they were still frightening and irrational and not wholly predictable. Sometimes, Luba would wake in the night in fear that a blow was coming, sit upright in terror, only to recall mid-palpitation that Dan was away on a sales trip.

He, for his part, seemed to know which words would most wound her heart and how best to strike so the bruises wouldn't show. To Lu, his fits of rage seemed to her so calculated when she lay sleepless or rose before dawn to smoke cigarettes and wonder at her life, in retrospect. How could his words shear away her confidence so certainly, otherwise? Three weeks of peace and she would mend the tapestry of her self and resolve variously to patch up the marriage, be a better wife, or leave him. One week at home and he would once again rip her resolve asunder.

Keeping Lu shut up and away from making meaningful friendships was part of the unspoken strategy. Dan would hang up on anyone who called for her, assuring Lu that her colleagues at work were a bunch of chippies and broads she shouldn't be associating with, lest they lead her astray so she would become like them—alone and discarded. So she eschewed deeper friendships with the girls at work out of shame and fear of repercussions. And Dan was always careful and canny whenever the relatives visited; he valued their good opinion. Never did they suspect a brute lurked behind his easy and friendly smile, his open hospitality.

So only once in those early Calgary years did Lu have to

apply pancake makeup to a blackened eye. If anyone in the steno pool noticed, they never said.

And why through the bludgeoning words and fists and the aftermath sex that felt like whoredom did she not leave him? She thought she could. She thought she would. Luba even packed and hid a bag, but he roughed her up good the night he found it; for days her ribs and back ached when she moved, even merely to type. She secreted a little money here and there, but then there was always some emergency or unforeseen expense. The car needed new tires. They owed some tax money. A bad tooth needed fixing. And maybe once a Catholic, always a Catholic—Luba just couldn't find a way to walk out the door.

And sometimes Dan's scythe words rang with a bitter truth. She was less than a woman. She couldn't conceive and carry a healthy baby to term. What good was she, really? Maybe if she really wanted a baby, a healthy child would be granted her. It was her fault for not longing to be a mother, especially after two miscarriages. This she must change. Dan so wanted a son. And Lu could learn to be more supportive. She would have to. Or Dan would leave her. And for some reason that terrified her most of all.

Even before there was Mirjam.

"Ma, look at this!" Mirjam enters the dining room, passes her a photo of mother and daughter toasting the camera with their pina coladas at a nightclub in Waikiki. Still an undergraduate student, Mirjam had used a portion of her scholarship money to purchase two budget flights to Hawaii and a week's accommodation in a condo. Luba had first demurred but finally accepted her sixtieth birthday present. She'd dipped into her savings for some spending money and bought the dress Mirjam had worn for the photo earlier that same day.

"That's such a nice picture of you in that gorgeous jade jersey."

"Of you, too. I still wear that dress. Why did you bury the picture away?"

"Well, that moment was lovely, but—"

"Jesus, Ma. Are you still on that after all this time?"

"I was terrified."

"I was safe."

"You didn't come home that night after you went away with that ... Hawaiian."

"It was nothing. He was a nice guy."

"A one-night stand while I worried all night and almost took up smoking again."

"Oh yeah. Lay that on me. It was what it was. Did you never in your youth?" Mirjam snorts at her mother's shock. "No, what am I saying? Though it would have done you good to get away from Daddy."

"You couldn't do that in my day."

"I guess not. But times change. And I wasn't a kid. I knew what I was doing. And he was so good looking." She sighs.

"It was the fight afterwards, between us."

"I was hungover and tired. I apologized."

"I know."

"You didn't talk to me for twenty-four hours."

"I hate fighting."

"I know you do." She watches her mother's expression. Luba is elsewhere, likely back in some dark time with Dan. "I could kill him."

"Don't, Mirjam. Leave it be." She passes the photo back to her daughter. "It was still a nice time, in the end."

"In the end, yes." Mirjam smiles down at the image. "I'd like a copy."

"I'll get one made at London Drugs. And I'll get a frame for this one and yours, too, if you like."

❦

On October 31st, a crisp fall day, as she carefully ironed his suit jacket, Luba found another phone number scrawled on a matchbook in Dan's pocket. She dialed the number, and a woman's voice told her all that she needed to know. Lu lit the matches one by one, finally burning the booklet in the ashtray. That evening, she made her plan while doling out candy to the neighbourhood goblins.

Dan came home late, tired from his time on the road, dejected at his sales results. Luba lay naked on the new brown nylon couch they'd bought on credit. She knew she still had a great body. And she performed all his favourite tricks, made all the right noises. With a little chicanery and fakery, Dan's deflation rose.

A few weeks later her dresses were already tight around the midriff.

On Friday, June 13th, a summer day swollen with humidity, Dan hung his White Rose boss upside down outside of a three-storey building. For calling him a liar, for daring to suggest that Dan had fudged his sales numbers—and he had—Dan, in fury, had grabbed his superior by the throat, grappled him into a headlock, and shoved him outside the window, madly lowering the manager down so that he held him only by his ankles, threatening to drop him if he didn't recant. Officemates came running in at the screams. Several men pulled Dan off while others pulled the boss back to safety.

With menace, Dan shook off his colleagues and walked out of the White Rose offices before the shrieking manager could string together a coherent, "you're fired!" In a move he fancied was a nod to Gary Cooper, Dan never looked back.

Luba was eight months pregnant. White-faced and wondering how she would buy milk for the baby, she sat huge and still at the red and chrome kitchen table, listening to Dan's delusional version of events and trying to breathe. Then she rose calmly and walked to the phone to call her boss to ask for the job she'd just left, after the little shower the office girls had given her. She could start back on Monday. Lu worked four more weeks until she was nearly bursting. Evenings, she somehow wrapped up their belongings and cleaned the house, despite her fatigue, her weeping, and her swollen feet. She ignored the doctor's orders to take it easy, to ease up on the smoking, although she cut down to six or seven cigarettes a day.

Dan had taken a job back at Stedmans department store in Drumheller, and so they were going home, again, after the birth of the child who fretted and kicked as though sensing the marital and financial tension from the womb.

And in July, three days after Lu had quit work a second time, Mirjam, screeching ferociously, was born at the Foothills Hospital. A very healthy nine pounds. All the fingers and toes. And furious.

"Caul babies have magic," the maternity nurse who looked like an old crow told her.

Luba slipped to sleep at her words, exhausted and unable to produce enough milk for the infant.

Dan held the child and tried to soothe her. An adept nurse took her from him and offered the baby a bottle, and Mirjam drank greedily. When she finally lay asleep in the bassinet, he admitted later to Lu, she was beautiful—a full head of dark reddish curls and his mother's expression.

※

"Ma, l have to go now. l have a lesson at five."

"l know."

"Are you okay with the rest?"

"l think we're pretty much done. The movers will finish the rest tomorrow."

Mirjam wraps her Angora scarf about the collar of her cashmere coat, both gifts from Luba, who follows her to the door. "Thanks for everything."

Mother and daughter hug. "l wish ... W—would you have gone back to him if I'd agreed to move in with you when you asked me, Ma?"

Luba shrugs. "Who knows what would have been, Mirjam? I only know this. Today. Don't worry, Sweetheart. I'll be fine."

She closes the door on her grown child. How did she get to be such an age, thirty-one, and so accomplished?

※

From babyhood onwards, if she wasn't running away, she was singing. There were piano lessons from a young age. Lu insisted and Dan could recognize his daughter's early talent. Mirjam sang in the school choir and as soloist in little festivals in Drumheller. She was competitive and loved the stage. So Luba always found the money for Mirjam's clothes, her books, her records, her music, her lessons, even if it meant she, herself, wore the same sad winter coat for seven years. She and Dan attended every concert and music recital faithfully.

Meanwhile, he continued at Stedmans and became manager. Lu worked at the post office as a typist. They got on. And gradually crawled out of debt, finally repaying the uncle in Serbia in full. They were denied business loans again and again, but Lu tucked money away, if only in small incremental savings.

Lu and Mirjam would walk along the dry hills after the heat of the summer day or when the air turned to crackling fall or in the frost of winter or the chill of spring. They would hold hands only briefly, as Mirjam forged ahead up a slope, heedless of cactus or heights, laughing when she reached the top, capturing the castle before her puffing mother. Once there they would watch the shimmering heat in the arid moonscape around them or gaze at the moon hovering over the ancient creviced face of the Badlands. Mirjam might spill out her dreams while Lu quietly smoked and silently resolved to see her realize them, even though she had long forgotten her own. Sometimes when Mirjam spoke or Mirjam sang, her heart full of all of life and time and potential, Luba thought she might break apart with love.

Her daughter had few friends, because she loved fiercely and such ferocity is seldom matched or reciprocated. Sometimes Luba feared what Mirjam might do to those who did not requite her affections or who did her some small injury. The sprained ankles of her daughter's peers at hopscotch after some squabble always gave Lu pause. Once she puzzled over a storm that hailed only over Midland where she knew lived a friend who'd fallen out with Mirjam. She spoke to her then about forgiveness, about the imperfections of human beings, about patience. She hoped this was enough and feared it was not.

Particularly when Dan announced at dinner that the family was moving yet again. This time to Edmonton, where he had a chance to buy in to an appliance business, an already successful venture that a Serbian friend of a Serbian friend had begun. Luba held her breath in dread that Mirjam would deliver her fork across the red and chrome table and straight into Dan's heart.

Instead, the girl ran to her bedroom and began a wild trashing of her things. Dan leapt up from the table after her, but Lu was quicker and barred the way and his fist from touching the girl.

"She's just upset, Dan," Lu panted. "Let me deal with her."

"The little bitch ..."

"What did you expect? Time, Dan, she just needs a little time."

She stared him down. They'd had fights over Mirjam many times, more and more frequently as the girl entered adolescence. Lu intervened whenever she was home and Dan's ire and his hand rose up against their daughter, so that his wrath was redirected to his wife. But she did not know of the times when Dan, enraged at Mirjam's lip or insolence, had hit her in her mother's absence. The old house would tremble, as if shaking to tell these secrets, for Mirjam never did. But in this instance, Dan slammed the wall in heat and frustration, then returned to the kitchen to finish his meal and simmer down.

Luba entered her daughter's upturned bedroom and worked for the better part of an hour to calm her. Only at the promise of singing lessons with a reputable teacher in the capital city did Mirjam's tears and fury finally abate.

So once more, Luba put their lives into boxes, swept up the debris of years, bade farewell to the valley and the people she loved, and moved with her daughter and husband to another beginning.

Mirjam was fourteen. Luba was fifty.

She put a down payment on the very first house they'd ever purchased, after years of renting. It was a modest, three-bedroom bungalow on the western fringe of the city, but Luba felt a stability she'd not had before in her life. Dan started up at the appliance store and she managed a transfer to the main branch of the post office. And Mirjam sang, eventually winning a scholarship to attend Opera McGill.

After dropping their daughter off in Montreal, they returned to Edmonton—parents who were suddenly empty-nesters—and Lu packed up their lives again in preparation for the move to Mission. There they would begin the penultimate chapter of their lives, largely as strangers to each other, even though they'd occupied the same bed for most of their respective lives. How odd it felt to be suddenly thrust back into coupledom.

What did she do with those years apart from her daughter? Visited Mirjam when she could afford it. Avoided the massing of torrential clouds in her home. Tried to keep a civil tongue in her head when Dan was impatient or unreasonable. Felt his full-fisted fury when she couldn't.

And then came the confrontation about moving back to Calgary to be nearer to Mirjam. Like a jealous god, Dan had denied her this one request, after all she had done for him, for this sham of a marriage. So Luba had spoken out and dared to confront the tyrant. And he had raised his hand, again and again. Raining down blows without mercy, he sought to cement his reign of terror or to kill her trying. Through blood and tears, she could see the whites of his eyes rolled up and back.

Lu managed to pull away, managed to grab the portable phone and hit speed dial.

And Mirjam, her angel of a daughter, made the call that delivered a mother.

After charging Dan with assault, Lu sought and received a restraining order. He stayed in jail while she spent seventy-two hours non-stop in a daze, willing her hands to do what they knew best how to do, wrap and pack and tape. A gypsy called to the road again, Lu then flew to Calgary and to Mirjam, a mother and child reunion.

In the darkness, on the bed that she will strip in the morning before the movers arrive, the bed that she will never again share with Dan, Luba wonders. She wonders about moving back to live with her husband. She wonders about time, used and spent. How can she be sixty-seven? What has she done with all the hours? Time that seemed so infinite when she was a girl, frivolous and wasteful, and finally there is so little left. She wonders at the notion of happiness. Is Mirjam happy? Is she? And Luba is once again moving.

18

Shadows deepened into slate-black night. Without stars or moon as guide, the travellers knew it would be best to halt their progress, to make camp and try to keep warm by the fire from the forest's wet chill. The harpist snared a rabbit in one of his wires set as trap. Dragan gutted and cleaned the hare to make a stew for which all were grateful. One of the guards tossed in fever from a deep wound, now infected and festering.

Elenya tended to him as best she could. The others took shifts of three hours in pairs to keep watch through the long night. Sudbina insisted that she and the harpist take their turn—everyone needed sleep—and the guards could not argue this. An exhausted pall had fallen across the entire company.

She and the harpist took up their respective posts to the east and west of the camp: the despoina stood, bow in hand, upon a fallen tree, and the harpist melted into the darkness of a huge oak. Sudbina tried to tune her ears to the sounds of the great wood, to distinguish between ordinary night sounds and others more sinister. It seemed that though the company slept, the forest was fully awake with rustling leaves and snapping twigs, the hoot of an owl, the swoop of bats.

Sometime around midnight, the harpist gave a low whistle, a soft trill of melody. Sudbina looked towards the sound and saw a single tiny flickering light appear, followed by another and another. Soon there were many dancing diminutive lights westward where she knew the harpist to be. Sudbina marvelled at the sight against the velvet blackness. She leapt from her place and walked towards the spectacle.

The lights seemed as beacons. Sensing her approach, the harpist held out his arm to meet her.

"Shall we follow?" she whispered.

"I think not. These may be a decoy to trick us from our watch. Or perhaps marsh lights that pull us towards quicksand and death."

They stared in wonder as the lights gavotted to and fro above their heads and then away, as though willing them to follow. But the two watch-keeps stayed, and gradually the lights dimmed and dissipated. A grey dawn rose shortly thereafter, but no one came to relieve them, so Sudbina returned to her former post and waited.

When still no relief arrived by full sun, she and the harpist padded back into camp to find the one injured guard raving, while all the other members of the party seemed succumbed to a curious ague. The harpist built up the fire and tended to the horses. Sudbina tried to attend the sick but knew nothing of the healing arts. Instead, she gathered water from a nearby spring to add to the dwindling stew.

At noon the harpist left camp, returning within several hours with more hares he had snared. He taught the despoina how to gut and clean and how to cook the meat on a spit. It was the first meal she had ever prepared in her life. She asked him to teach her to set snare and hunt.

"How did you, a musician, learn these skills?"

"I was not born in your father's royal court. Those of us who are not must ... learn to feed and fare for ourselves."

"So when did you take up the harp? Whenever did you have the time?"

"From my grandmother, who taught me many hours by firelight in the evenings. She had a gift." He shrugged. "And this gift she passed to me. From my father, I learned to hunt and ride, and from a luthier uncle to work wood and craft instruments. Eventually, I built my own harp."

"Why did you leave your people?"

He winced and she thought he wished not to speak of some painful memory.

Finally, he cleared his throat. "My family ... was lost to me. I found myself alone."

"You needn't tell—"

"I found solace in my harp. I guess this"—the harpist indicated his harp-shaped birthmark—"was my destiny. Music called. I would be a minstrel. For several years I was itinerant. I earned my bread in village squares and at festivals. In time, your father, the despot, came to hear of me. And so I came into his employ."

"I was then a small girl."

"I recall. Though I was not many years your elder."

Their eyes met over the flames. Something of a flame leapt unexpectedly in the despoina's chest. She rose abruptly.

"Play a tune, then, harpist. A healing melody while I try to feed our ailing companions."

This he did as Sudbina spooned broth into mouths and wiped brows damp with fever. Neither Dragan nor the other three guards roused for more than to swallow a few mouthfuls. But the music seemed to still the rants of the injured guard, who finally dropped to sleep. Elenya tried to rise and help the despoina, but Sudbina gently pushed her back down, the waiting woman having no strength to resist.

At gloaming, the pair finished their own meal and considered what best to do the coming day. Perhaps their comrades would be well enough to travel onwards.

Perhaps they might themselves forge ahead to her sister's land and bring back medicines and help. Tonight, they agreed, both needed rest. They would alternate watch shifts, and the harpist took the first.

Again at midnight, while on her watch, Sudbina spied the play of lights and thought to follow them, but she recalled the minstrel's warning. Though he had discovered neither dangerous shifting sands nor vile marsh in the immediate forest, the lights could well be decoys. She thought of her father and how grieved he would be to know of this setback, how worried he would be for her safety. So instead of following her curiosity, she chose instead caution.

At dawn, she came back to camp to find that the injured guard had died in the night. The musician stood over his body, harping a soft dirge.

And so seven were now six.

19

Many are the songs of the Serbs. They are a singing people, a singing nation. Long ballads about defeating the Ottoman Turks, about Serbian courage and perseverance through all suffering and even in defeat. Great rousing epic poem-songs about Dušan the Mighty, his fiery and violent deeds in service of his god, his Orthodox Church and his country. Sad elegiac laments about King Petar and his losses. More recent sentimental songs emerging from the terrors and sorrows of the Second World War and its aftermath. Serbs have sung out their embellished history and glory in so many songs.

Angela Sekul grew up singing some of these melodies, memorizing the words taught to her by her brothers, as she could not read, and many such tunes were not written down but passed along orally from generation to generation, some over many hundreds of years. When she became Angela Popović she then passed this musical oral history on to her children: Anka, Maria, Jovanka, Jovan, Bosilka, Dušan and finally, Danilo, who was most musical of all. No one under her roof would forget the haunting beauty of the songs and the tales of great Serbs and their deeds.

Sometimes Angela would set fairy tales and folktales to music for her children. And so they came to admire the water-nymph Vilas, fear the terrible dragon Aždaja and the horned witch Baba Roga, who liked best to feast upon fat, lazy or indulged children. But eventually Angela's theme would always return to the land of her girlhood, the old country, and she would croon a final goodnight lullaby of remembrance over the cradle of her baby sons or the dark curly heads of her sleeping daughters.

These same tunes her brothers sang their children, who became men who dreamed of a return to Serbia's greatness, even as they emigrated to Canada and the United States. Eyes alight with the flame of nationhood, they would sing drunkenly together at any family gathering, the bottle of *šljivovica* passed eagerly and generously between them until they danced the Hora madly or fell down drunk, whichever came first, and often both.

And such were the songs so often on the lips of cousin Stefan who came to visit for a month from Miami, Florida, bringing with him money for Danilo to purchase outright the appliance business in Edmonton, the great booming capital city of Alberta, Canada, or so Dan had written of it to his elderly Uncle Velimir, who was once again loaning him the money. Like Dan, Stefan was fifty-seven, but he prided himself on his thick head of still-black hair, his muscled body—that of a much younger man—the product of a personal trainer and hard sweat, his fluency in Serbo-Croatian, and his trim moustache. He had the air of a man who considered himself descended from kings, an arrogance that came of being born into wealth and privilege.

He commanded any room he entered, and he infiltrated all of the rooms of their lives.

Stefan tried vainly to teach his comely sixteen-year-old cousin the great songs of the old country, but Mirjam would have none of it. She had the voice of an *anđeo* and yet was studying the music of the Germans and the Italians, the French, instead of her own people. Stefan's eyes followed Mirjam relentlessly whenever the girl entered the room and hungered after her when she left.

"Pagh! That one," Dan emptied his shot glass and poured his cousin and himself another hit of Canadian whiskey, "she wants to be a Barbra Streisand, or something."

"A Jew?"

"Better than a Croat or a Kosovar!"

And the two laughed and sang, arms slung about each other's shoulders, well into the night.

On three subsequent Sundays, Stefan tried to convince Luba and Mirjam to join him and Dane at the city's Serbian Orthodox Church. Neither would go, and Luba raised an eyebrow at Dan, who had never been a religious man or even a believer, despite his mother's best attempts. He'd seen too much in the war, he claimed, to make that leap of faith. And yet, he followed Stefan as though one of the faithful. At least it gave Lu the morning off from cooking and serving so that she could focus on the books for the business, and the accounts for the expansion of the appliance store in the west end, which for two years now had been turning a profit.

On the final day of his visit, Cousin Stefan spoke with tears in his eyes about his own youngest son, born to his second wife, Milena, whom he'd married in Belgrade and brought back to Florida. Though only ten years old, Yvan, born and raised in the United States of America, longed to go back to the old country, if only Tito, blast him, would at last die and free Serbia from his tyranny.

"Sit up and listen for once in your life," her father barked. Mirjam did as she was told, correcting her posture at the table, silently seething at this old bore and his stupid son.

"Do you know what the Ustaše did to us in the war?"

"Yes."

"They betrayed us to the Nazis. They set fire to our villages. They ripped open our women's breasts with knives!"

This appalling detail would haunt her for several nights, as her father intended.

"Tito has forced us to live with our enemies, side by side. But we will never forget our Mother Serbia." Stefan wiped away more tears.

"I thought you lived in Fort Lauderdale."

"I do now. But! My parents ensured that I never forget where we come from!"

Dan piped up, "And neither should you, Mirjam."

Luba, serving a traditional lamb stew, winked at her daughter, and Mirjam unclenched her fists under the table.

She ran away after supper, heading for the bleachers of the nearby soccer field where she was to meet Emile, a mixed-race boy she was seeing on the quiet because she knew her father would never approve. He was tall and limber, a soccer athlete originally from Senegal who was in her social studies class. His lips pushed against hers in heat until his tongue thrilled a way into her mouth. He was a secret song she shared with no one. That night he walked her home through the dark suburban streets, as far as she would allow him, and left her with a kiss that would follow her to her bed. Mirjam did not notice that Cousin Stefan saw all from behind the spare-room curtain.

When he came to her later in the night, she was deeply asleep. He crouched next to her bed, touched her hair with one hand and opened his pants with the other.

He saw her eyes flicker awake by the light of the Disney nightlight, a childhood remnant that she refused to relinquish.

"Ssh," Stefan told her as he stroked himself.

"I'm going to call my father ..."

"I don't think so. That is, not if you don't want a beating."

Her eyebrows were question marks.

"I saw you with that Black boy—that *crnčuga*. I know what your father would do to you ... and especially to him, Mirjam."

This sent a jolt of paralyzing panic down her spine. Stefan felt her fear and his lust grew.

"You can touch it if you want." And finally she saw his engorged intent. "Or I can touch you." He slid his hand under the covers to her breast. Then down further to between her legs where she was still wet from earlier thoughts of Emile.

"I see that you want it, too," he spoke softly to her ear as he fingered her. "Does your Black boyfriend touch you like this?"

Mirjam clenched her eyes and tried to will this monster away. Tried not to feel anything at his touch. But his hand was urgent, persistent. And she hated her body silently as it betrayed her and succumbed to a shuddering desire she did not want to feel. When she opened her lids again, she could see his ugliness in the semi-darkness.

"You can put your mouth on me if you want to." He moved himself closer to her face.

A cold low sound came out of Mirjam's mouth. "I'll do it, but you'll regret it."

He grabbed her hair and she cried out.

"Shut up!" Stefan's grip loosened only slightly. "Don't wake your parents, Mirjam, or there'll be so much trouble, I promise you!" he hissed. "Just be a good girl and suck."

When he had finished, she spat him out in revulsion as he zipped up. "I leave tomorrow, and this will be our little secret, won't it, Mirjam? And so will your *crno* boyfriend. But if you breathe a word, you know I can convince your father that this was all your idea and that you fucked that *crnčuga*." He shut the door on her and her deed.

Mirjam considered his parting words for half an hour, then, hoping fervently he was asleep, rose quietly and tiptoed down the hallway to the washroom, locking the door securely behind her. She stared at her pale reflection. What was she now? The thought made her sick. Inside the medicine cabinet she found the Scope and gulped up the cold-hot blue liquid, swirling and spitting her self-disgust repeatedly, until she'd emptied the bottle.

Creeping back to bed, she avoided her cousin's spare bedroom door and wedged a chair under the doorknob inside her own room. Then the shivering began and did not abate even after she'd drawn more covers over her shoulders and head, trying to hide her shame. Hot tears wet her pillow. Something hard knocked at her heart. Finally, at the sound of the first birds, she let it in.

Claiming an early morning choir practice, Mirjam left early for school and so avoided saying goodbye to her cousin Stefan, who left at noon back to Florida.

His was an effortless journey home, a pleasant and uneventful flight, and he was greeted warmly at the airport by his wife, his son, and his father. Stefan had only good things to say about Canada, the Canadian relatives and their generous hospitality.

But that night and on many others, when Stefan approached his wife or she him, he could not will himself to rise.

Seventeen years later and thousands of miles away, while Mirjam is singing on a concert stage, a young man will raise his gun, aim it at a certain Sniper Alley and take a certain shot. A young woman will fall dead in that deadly street of Sarajevo. But a city rebel will correctly estimate the exact origin of the sniper on the hill and retaliate with a barrage of land-air missiles that will, for once, strike directly on target, ripping human bodies on the hill to fragments. One of those bodies will be that of a young man named Yvan, who will not have the chance to die with a fervent national song on his lips.

20

Calgary's Jack Singer Concert Hall is a stage Mirjam has dreamed of performing on for most of her adult life. She has sung on smaller, excellent stages at universities and in cities throughout Canada and various states. But Jack Singer, almost acoustically perfect, is considered one of the best performance venues in North America, and it is in her hometown. Preparations in the rehearsal hall have been lovely and productive, but the moments on the stage with the Calgary Philharmonic are most sublime. To sing in such a space, to sing such a fine concert opera, with world-class musicians and orchestra under the brilliant direction of the maestro, her lover, is near divine. It is all the stuff of a singer's dreams.

Her struggles with the difficult timing over, Mirjam is now more confident that she will breeze through the challenging passage and indeed, the entire concert opera. She and the other principal singers feel they are prepared and have discussed with much excitement the momentous debut. The well-practiced chamber choir sounds gorgeous. Mirjam herself is in excellent voice and she and Helmut agree that she will peak in performance just at the right time—this very night.

On this Saturday prior to call, Mirjam is resting her voice throughout the day.

She swallows her opening-night jitters with herbal tea and lemon. Her beautiful gown—Luba's gift to her—hangs glittering on the back of her bedroom door. Soon she will shower and allow the steam to infiltrate her sinuses and her throat. For now, she sits in her thick terry bathrobe at the chrome and red table by the window, watching crows come and go in the mountain ash tree across the street.

The doorbell rings and Mirjam is surprised and rather touched to find Helmut at the threshold with flowers and a small black case. She lets him enter and moves to speak, but he puts a finger to her lips.

"Don't speak. These are for you, Liebchen," he whispers, handing her the bouquet and staying very near her as she places the flowers—a huge bunch of wax white calla lilies—in water. "As is this, in a manner of speaking," he adds, placing the slim case on the table beside the vase.

Helmut thumbs open the catch. On a bed of green velvet, an exquisite conducting baton lies within. Its handle and tapered tip are antique ivory with tortoiseshell inlay and a shaft of solid ebony. The maestro picks it up and strokes it lovingly, "It belonged to Mahler. I bid many, many Deutsche Marks for this antiquity, this auspicious baton, for this important evening. I feared it would not arrive in time from Germany, but here it is at last. See the engraving? 'To his beloved composer Gustav Mahler.'"

Helmut places the baton in her hands and Mirjam wonders at its beauty and craftsmanship.

"A birthday gift to the composer from the Austrian Kronprinz in 1901."

Mirjam puzzles over the history, and then remembers just as Helmut confirms, "The Archduke Ferdinand of Austria." She shudders and hands the baton back to the conductor.

"Why do you shiver?" Helmut draws her near. "This talisman will mark a new beginning—for you and for me, Liebchen," he tells her ear, then very deliberately and slowly inserts the tip of his tongue. And suddenly she is weak-kneed and pushing against him while his mouth works down her neck. Helmut unfastens her bathrobe with a deft hand. His lips reach her breast, and he touches the baton to her thighs which she opens for him. She gasps when he places the tip against her. But then he stops and pulls himself up and away from her. The nakedness of the moment is jarring.

"No, no, my Liebchen, not now. We must not climax too early," he takes a moment to wave the tip of the baton beneath his nose. "But later, I can promise you, we will revisit this delicious motif." Carefully, Helmut places the baton back in its case and snaps it shut. He turns to Mirjam, who has quickly closed her robe, pulls close to her and kisses her deeply.

"I know you will soar tonight, Mirjam ... my Myrrha. You never disappoint."

And while she is still blinking to regain her equilibrium, Helmut departs.

She wonders how this man can have such a somatic effect on her, why she cannot resist his seduction. Clearly, there is an imbalance in this coupling that is and isn't a relationship, especially now that she knows of Helmut's other life in Germany.

On this demanding day, he has left her limp with desire when she should be centred and focused on the rigours of the coming evening. And he's treated her little better than an organ grinder promising a banana for the performing monkey if she gets it just right. A bitter taste fills her mouth. She would like nothing better than to turn Helmut away when he comes, expectant and pressing, to her door post-show. To forbid him entrance. But her body knows she will not.

Mirjam turns the shower taps on full heat. She stands naked before the mirror as the steam rises. The glass fogs, and she watches her nipples fade, her shoulders cloud, her face disappear. Finally, she turns away from the mirror to adjust the water temperature and steps into the shower stall. The heat at first touch is a shock.

Gradually, as her skin accepts the water, she immerses herself beneath the showerhead. Rivulets form on her shoulders and trail down her olive skin, between her breasts and across her stomach. Mirjam sighs and breathes, breathes and sighs. Hot, moist air fills her lungs, and she begins to hum.

Eventually the humming evolves to scales and runs, rising and descending. Sound fills her head and the small shower cubicle and trails around her naked body. Notes ripple across the back of her small palate, across her tongue. Diaphragm lifted, she feels alight with resonance and breath. A baptism of music and water.

Mirjam towels off and wraps another about her thick hair. Continuing to breathe deeply, she applies her makeup, dries and tames her auburn curls, replaying the concert opera in her head. As she silently rehearses her lyrics, she eats a light salad and drinks another cup of herbal tea.

Tonight, she will forget Mirjam to assume the character of Myrrha, the challenging role she has painstakingly rehearsed and prepared for a year with Helmut. A bold heroine, a daughter who desires her father, Myrrha must be first virginal and innocent, then, at odds with Aphrodite, she must become surly adolescent. In dishonouring the goddess, Myrrha is fated to begin a treacherous descent. Overcome with forbidden passion for her father, she will transform to cunning temptress and seductress. Once her desire is sated, Myrrha will be eventually recognized by Cinyras, her irate father, who will draw his sword to slay his contrite daughter, now pregnant with Adonis and reduced to shame and devastation. In terror, she will think to flee and appeal to the goddess for mercy. Myrrha's pitch will turn to feverous madness until her final transformation to a Myrrh tree, when the goddess finally pities her. The final strains of Myrrha's aria mark the birth of Adonis—soon to be, in a fitting turn of ironic fate, Aphrodite's ill-fated lover—and the traces of her tears of bittersweet perfumed sorrow. Then the erring woman is at last silenced.

When she allows herself, Mirjam wonders at a daughter who might possibly desire a father. This part of the story is a huge leap of imagination, where she must use her utmost acting prowess, and if she considers the theme too deeply, it makes her gorge rise. Ovid and the ancient writers who recorded the story were frankly ridiculous, and Mirjam considers the tale likely to be an inversion of a father's incestuous desire for his daughter, a tale told by a male patriarchy to vilify and muzzle women. That she would ever desire her father in such a way, even unconsciously, seems too impossibly perverse. When she is in the role, rather than think of Danilo, she thinks instead of Helmut, who is fifteen years her senior and achingly handsome. Only in such a way can she muster the corresponding desire so necessary to this crucial aspect of the character.

In jeans and T-shirt, Mirjam steps into the cab she has ordered, her gown and a cocktail dress for the after-concert party in a garment bag.

"Where you going?" The cabbie looks at her in the rearview mirror. A rosary dangles over his ID card: Josef Bogdonović.

"Jackson Singer Hall, please."

"You are going to show?"

"I'm performing."

"Oh, you are singing? You are singer?" He grows excited. "That is why you are looking so beautiful."

"Thank you. Yes, I am one of the performers."

"What? What are you singing?"

"A concert opera. It's a debut."

"Very nice." He turns and they drive past the Saddledome. "I am singer, too."

"You are?"

"Back in old country. I sing songs in my language."

"Where are you from?" Although Mirjam already recognizes his accent.

"Dubrovnik."

"Ah yes."

"You know my city?"

"Jewel of the Adriatic."

"Ah, so you've been?"

"No."

"You should visit sometime. Croatia."

"Not really a good time, right now, wouldn't you agree?"

"Bah. Crazy people. Neighbours for forty years now shooting at each other. That's why I come to Canada. To get away from the crazy."

"You don't want to go back then?"

"Maybe someday. I miss my beautiful city. But now it is rubble—is still not safe, I'm believing. Here, I have a son and a little daughter. Anyway, I want to become Canadian. And I will apply for my citizenship in three years."

He pulls up in front of the Calgary Centre for the Performing Arts and she directs him around to the backstage door. "Good luck with getting your citizenship."

"Good luck with your concert, nice lady. What is your name, so that I can tell my kids I met a famous singer tonight?"

"Mirjam Pope."

"You are Catholic?"

"No."

"Well, I will pray to Saint Cecilia for you anyway, nice lady, Miss Pope."

Mirjam tips him well.

In the dressing room, she meets Judith, who will sing the role of Aphrodite, and gives her a quick hug. Mirjam pokes her head into the other dressing room to give another to William, who will soon become Cinyras, her father. She offers a greeting to members of Spiritus Chamber Choir who are gathering in the rehearsal room. The stage manager comes to check on all the singers and to give the one-hour call. Right behind him is Helmut, who kisses the leading women on both cheeks, wishing them well, before ducking into the change room with William.

Under the bright dressing table lights, Mirjam applies a little more makeup to her eyes, her lips and cheeks. She takes a few moments to do a little yoga and some breathing exercises. The two women help each other into their gowns, laughing about how one day soon, after the roaring success of tonight's concert opera, someone else will be hired as their official dressers and makeup artists. Over the crackle of their dressing room speakers, they can hear a few players of the philharmonic orchestra in the adjacent room, tuning and warming up.

The stage manager gives the fifteen-minute call and Mirjam and Judith warm up together, sotto voce. Miriam lifts her shoulders to her ears and drops them, breathing deeply. She and Judith practise a few of the passages, a cappella, until they are summoned to their places backstage right. Members of the choir shuffle quietly to offstage left. Mirjam can feel her nerves trying to swim to the surface, but she continues to breathe and drinks a little water with lemon. She and Judith and William grasp hands and squeeze. They whisper to each other wishes for a good show alongside murmurs from the audience and final arpeggios from the musicians. Mirjam breathes herself to stillness. The choir enters the stage and ascends the risers behind the horns. In the near darkness, she feels Helmut breeze past her onto the stage.

Backstage, the applause from the front of house sounds appreciative and expectant to Mirjam's ears. She hopes her mother and father—for whom Luba bought a last-minute ticket, despite the daughter's protests—have good seats, but then, every seat in this theatre is excellent. From her vantage point, she can see Helmut take a deep bow, then shake the hand of the principal violinist, the concertmaster. As Herr Weinstein assumes his place on the podium, a hush descends upon the auditorium. The stage manager cues the three singers to take their places on stage, and applause rises again to greet them warmly as they enter. Mirjam feels a flush of excitement across her face once she reaches her place stage right of the maestro. The lights are very bright and warm, and she remembers to smile, even though it is difficult to see anything much beyond the downstage edge of the platform. Herr Weinstein, too, smiles at his soloists, takes his brilliant baton in hands and briefly raises the tip to his nose then places it in his dominant hand, raises both, and with his downbeat, the first notes of the concert opera commence.

Cellos begin a soft theme in E flat minor with the first violin in a sad descant above the main melody, attended by delicate plucked notes of the harp. Violins enter and several bars later, the violas. As the music takes on depth and texture, the double basses begin a foreboding undercurrent. The tension waxes to the crescendo of the overture and then a gradual rallentando. Vibrations from the music move up and down Mirjam's spine. She feels enveloped in the notes. Beside her Aphrodite sings:

> *Daughter of Cenchreis*
> *Your mother claims your beauty*
> *Exceeds even that of Aphrodite*
> *Mortal pride shall*
> *Ever meet with retribution*

One may not insult a goddess
Without some grievous cost

Judith, as the goddess, begins her full aria and Mirjam, listening to her swell, breathes and centres her own focus. The chorus rises as Aphrodite finishes, to comment on the erring ways of humans and the jealousy of the gods. In this piece, placed in Mirjam's higher register, she feels vocally eased into what will be her increasing role in the narrative.

Myrrha is adolescent and wayward. She prefers to shrug off restrictions and does not heed the goddess.

I do give the offerings
Recite the words
Attend to the rites
What more would you ask
Of a girl who is fifteen and free?

Aphrodite retorts that a girl her age should choose a husband from her suitors, but Myrrha is not yet interested in marriage and rebukes the goddess for trying to make her too early a wife and a mother. Aphrodite and the chorus invoke the Fates and cast warnings that continue to go unheeded by the capricious Myrrha.

Throughout this portion of the concert opera, Mirjam feels confident that she is matching the energy of the soprano, executing the rapid-fire notes and absorbed by the role. Collectively, their music blooms and reverberates through the fine acoustics of the auditorium. As the chorus repeats a cautionary refrain, she lifts a defiant chin and catches sight of the maestro's strong profile, a bead of sweat at his left temple. He turns to cue her entry and their eyes meet. She pours her desire into the text.

So begins the first of her arias. Mirjam has disappeared; she is but a vessel through which music and feeling pour. Time has shifted to the musical measures and the mercurial time of the narrative. Her voice resonates in her head with the poetry of the text and the beauty of the notes. Her body is consumed and there is no self. There is only a lifting of the diaphragm, a releasing of sound, a confluence of breath and belief and music.

Part Two draws to its climax. Aphrodite connives and storms while the chorus, functioning as Myrrha's nursemaid, admonishes the girl for considering suicide, surely a worse option than sinful consummation. Instead, the chorus invites her to sate her desire for Cinyras for three nights of Demeter's festival. And so begins the seduction.

Convinced by the chorus, caught up in the web Aphrodite spins, Myrrha plies her father with wine and visits him in the darkness of his bedchamber. And in what will likely be the most controversial moments of the concert opera, the rising chorus and the intense bowing of violins above the thrumming double basses mimic the first forbidden coupling of father and daughter.

Sombre notes from the cellos and violas mark the final movement of the concert opera. Mirjam, back into herself for the moments of these measures, realigns her posture and lifts her ribcage as she breathes. The demanding passage is upon her.

Tonight, do I go again to my father's bed
Or do I, sinner, run from this place
And throw myself to the sea?
Still my clay feet lead me to his door
What kind of woman makes this choice?
A girl no more, I have already crossed this threshold
Knowing that to know in this way
Condemns me to Tartarus.
Shall I turn away?
No. I choose and freely.
Once transgressed, I will wear the mantle:
Willingly, eagerly.

As Myrrha sings, Mirjam senses that her aria is flawless. Those oft-rehearsed difficult runs and the tricky timing feel beautifully and masterfully controlled. The timbre of her mezzo voice feels vibrant, the emotion within the song marks this moment as the showpiece Helmut intended. Myrrha's pain and honesty make Mirjam quiver.

Breaking convention, the audience applauds spontaneously and loudly. When they quiet, Herr Weinstein raises again his baton and brings the philharmonic orchestra and the chorus to the moment of discovery, when Cinyras lights a lantern to discover his daughter in his bed. The tremolo of violins and a cacophony of full strings mark the violent chase and Myrrha's escape up to the final moving measures of her transformation to myrrh tree when she utters her parting words to the goddess.

Take the child within this trunk
Beneath this bark
Near my heartbeat as it ceases
Raise him up and love him
May he not break your heart
As you have mine, cruel Aphrodite ...

Silence follows the maestro's articulated cut-off. Several seconds tick by. Then an explosion of clapping and cheering confronts the performers. Mirjam is dazzled by the sound and at first glances down demurely at the sequined beading of her gown. Then she recollects herself and raises her head. Audience members are on their feet throughout the glittering auditorium, as far as she can see. She and the other principal singers take their bows, Helmut with them, to shouts of "Brava! Bravi!" while the orchestra players tap their bows on music stands. Herr Weinstein gestures to the orchestra to rise, and they do, and he urges the chamber chorus members to also take their bows. Four young women bring bouquets of flowers out to the singers and the conductor, and the applause continues, still hearty and appreciative. Mirjam feels the warmth of exultation in her breast as she, Helmut and the others take a third bow. The adulation continues for a full seven minutes, until finally easing off, and the principals, musicians, and choristers exit the platform.

Backstage, Helmut warmly embraces his three singers, then overcome at her triumph, clutches Mirjam in a passionate kiss. It is the first and only time he will acknowledge their relationship in public.

21

I know now that she called the police and had me arrested. I know it was Mirjam.

How can you be sure, Dan?

Who else could it be?

The neighbours?

Pah! They had nothing to do with us.

The walls are not always soundproof in a condominium.

Besides, I know Luba phoned her, our daughter. Long distance to Calgary. Told her I—

Go on.

I was hitting her. I had hit her.

Then what?

I pulled the phone cord from the wall, so it couldn't have been Luba. Soon afterwards the RCMP came to the door. Put me in cuffs and then into the cruiser and took me away. I was in lock-up for a week. Alone. And then she—Lu got a restraining order.

That must have been hard.

Dan shrugs. He won't give this shrink the satisfaction of thinking he can know such a complicated man as himself.

There are some things—many things—that should remain secreted in the heart. Private. Kept hidden to the grave.
Then tell me how you feel about Mirjam.
She's the daughter. She was protecting her mother.
So you can sympathize with her actions?
She betrayed me.
Wouldn't you have done the same for your mother had you received such an upsetting phone call?
It's not the same.
Why? Because it was you?
Children should respect their fathers.
What about husbands their wives?
Yes, that, too. And I do respect Lu. I just—She just makes me so angry.
Why? What does she do to make you angry?
Sh—she turns away when I'm speaking to her. She made this decision to move here to Calgary and did not take my feelings into consideration. She just made up her own mind.
Why did Luba want to move from Mission to Calgary?
Because of her ... because of Mirjam. She'd just received a fancy scholarship to attend a fancy music program. And Luba wanted, no decided to go back.
Your wife thinks of Calgary as home. Why?
We've lived there several times.
But I thought your family hailed from Drumheller.
That dry old broken place, a dead boomtown. We needed better horizons, and we found them. It took many moves, but by god, we made it.
Luba wanted something different for her retirement.

I'll say.

She wanted the nearness of her daughter and her family.

I guess.

You find that unreasonable?

I find it unnecessary. We were fine together, the two of us.

You were happy?

Yes.

Luba was happy?

She didn't say she wasn't.

So you assumed.

I didn't think about it. It's only after all these talk shows on television that she started getting ideas. Before these so-called experts on everything to do with a man and a woman. Were my parents happy? No. But they got by. They raised a family.

Until your mother slammed the door on your father who died alone, forsaken and cursed by his wife.

Th—that was later.

And you think that your wife should have stayed beside you, even after you hit her?

Yes—no. I don't know. You're tricking me with words!

I'm not trying to trick you, Dan. I'm trying to understand and to encourage you to understand.

Dan took a sip of the water the psychologist had poured him. It was cool and welcome. He tried the silent counting technique he'd learned in group therapy. Tried to extinguish the heat with the water and with numbers.

She should not have sung that song.

The concert last week?

It was not a song for a daughter to sing.

I read the reviews. They were glowing. Your daughter is a rising star. Some part of you must be very proud.

What a song to sing about your own father.

It wasn't about you, Dan.

I believe she sang it to spite me. Just like she meant to torment me by locking me up in jail.

Have you ever considered that you might be tormenting yourself, Dan? That you might be your own jailer, not to mention that of your wife and daughter?

Look. Lu moved back in with me of her own accord. She made her own choice. I don't control her.

No.

I don't control my daughter, either. There is no controlling that one.

So whom do you have control over, Dan?

Dan thought this over. Was it another goddamn trick question? He did not like this man, this therapist. If only Luba would get over her notions about his need for therapy. But it was her condition of their living together. And by god, this time she was firm.

I don't know.

Yourself, Dan. Would you like to have control of yourself?

Dan swallowed, then reached again for the glass on the table before him. He felt his eyes watering. Jesus Christ. What was this about now? Was he crazy? Or just tired. Come to think of it, he hadn't had a very good sleep last night. The ulcer was bothering him. He'd risen to get a glass of milk and some Maalox and had been startled at an image in the darkened kitchen window: that of an old man with a broken face looking in at him, a vagrant, or so Dan thought at first. Until he realized it was himself, his own reflection.

Dan?

Yes. Yes, I suppose I would.

His voice, like his arthritic hand replacing the glass, shook.

22

Their companions worsened. Two more dreary days passed much in the same manner as the one before. Four slept while two slaved. Building the fire. Tending the horses. Setting the snares. Stirring the stew. Mopping the brows. Watching the camp.

The young woman and the harpist took turns trying to rouse and spoon-feed the ailing travellers, but their efforts were nearly futile. As if enchanted, the guards and Elenya slept on. Glumly, the musician and Sudbina sat by the fire to muse.

"We might turn back; we might go forward, my lady. I am at your service."

"Forward, I think. But we must leave these to do so. And ..."—she glanced at Elenya's supine form, still as death in the tent— "we may lose them before we can return."

"True. But to stay here may be our own death. And I will not let a despot's daughter perish in the wood. What kind of song would that be to sing?" He smiled ruefully at her as he tuned his harp.

Sudbina laughed. "Only you, harpist, can bring me to smile or to sing when I am otherwise sad and have most need."

"I suppose it is my way, my lady."

Sudbina thought about his words. She thought about this kindred spirit, this fetching young man who had been a musical companion and accompanist so many years in her father's court. Now he accompanied her through this dark passage, caring for her friends at her side, easing her anxieties with his words and his music and his presence. She felt something alight again near her heart and lay her hand upon his arm. "I like your way, harpist. Very much. I confess I have always done so."

He felt the heat from her palm and looked down at her fingers. "You and I are from different places, Despoina. It would be well I remember mine."

Sudbina moved her hand to his shadowed cheek and brought her face closer. "And where else is that place but beside me?"

So in the dense forest, while their fellows slept unknowing, the harpist put his singing lips to Sudbina's. And their melody lasted the night.

She awoke at dawn in the musician's arms. He smiled at her and she at him, and they rose to a sad discovery.

Another guard's heart had stopped while they slept.

And so six were now five.

Their own hearts heavy and despite their misgivings, Sudbina and her lover filled their packs with food, their skins with water, tied the team of horses together, and rode off along the path on their own mounts, eastward towards hope.

But the trail grew faint and clouded in mist, so that they lost their way and wandered as if in circles until night shadows came upon the two, damp and downcast. With the chill darkening appeared the first of the glittering, travelling lights, as before. Then another and another. This time the weary travellers nodded one to the other and followed carefully through the growing shadows in pursuit of the dancing beacons. They wended through the trees until these thinned to a clearing. In its centre stood a humble peasant's cottage on chicken legs, encircled by a crude fence. The lights danced a mad parade about the thatched roof and finally settled in the eyes of the skulls upon the fence posts. At its gate stood a wizened old crone holding up a lantern that underlit her haggard face with its sharp horn in the centre of her forehead.

Sudbina and the minstrel knew her, had known her all of their lives, had harped and sung dark songs about her.

A gnarled hand reached out to unlatch the gate and offer a greeting.

"Come children, you must be chilled to the bone on this night. Come to my home, to my hearth, and I will pour you a glass of *rakija* to ease your travellers' shivers and aches."

"Why Mother," Sudbina spoke as she and the harpist dismounted, "how do we know you are not an evil fairy or the witch Baba Roga?"

"Why indeed, I am she! But the stories you've heard about me are but old wives' tales meant to frighten the innocents. You can see for yourself. I am merely a humble old peasant herbalist offering a haven for you lost ones and your beasts."

Sudbina took a step towards the open gate. The harpist put his hand on her shoulder. "What choice have we?" she whispered. "And more to the point, perhaps we can convince her to help our comrades." The despoina took another step towards the ancient mistress with her lantern.

"What are you called, child?"

"Sudbina."

"I bid you welcome, Sudbina." And the young woman strode boldly over the threshold. Adjusting his fez, the harpist followed, leading the horses.

"Those fine creatures will find oats and hay and water in that shed." Baba Roga pointed a crooked finger to the northern part of her yard. "Shelter them, then come you quickly to my fire, lest you catch the spring fever that runs amok through this cold forest."

The despoina and the minstrel tended to the seven horses that were grateful for the attention and the oats after their meagre fare of a week in the woods.

Then hand in hand, the two stepped towards Baba Roga's cottage, where she stood framed in the light spilling through the doorway, gesturing to them to hurry and enter.

"But Mother," Sudbina peered into the aged eyes, "what if you mean to trick us into some trap within?"

"You are a clever one to mistrust, but look to see for yourself." Baba Roga swept her arm back to reveal the amber glow from the stone fireplace and three steaming bowls on a rough-hewn table. "There is no trap, only hot soup and a crackling fire."

So once again the two young travellers stepped across a threshold, this time into the warmth of a witch's cottage. They were quickly ushered to the table. The old woman scuttled back and forth from table to cupboard, bringing a black loaf of bread, a flask of brandy and three pewter cups. She poured generously and raised her cup to her guests.

"*U zdravlje*, dear children!"

The harpist raised his cup uncertainly, and Sudbina peered into the contents of her own.

"Mother, if what I hear is true, these contents may well be poison or potion to enchant us."

"*Da*. Sometimes poison is medicine and medicine poison. So see me drink first, and let your own wits be your true guide, rather than the prattling housewives' warnings."

Baba Roga drained her cup, touched it to her horn, and, chuckling, poured another. The despoina and her companion drank also and swallowed the familiar heat of plum brandy.

"Trust you then to eat some supper?" Baba Roga lifted her spoon to her mouth, then dropped it, noisily and suddenly to the wooden table. "You are not being honest if you burn your tongue and don't tell everyone else that the soup is hot," she cackled, taking another sip of *rakija*. Her aged hands next cut the bread into generous pieces that she passed around. She stuffed a piece into her own toothless mouth, nodding in amusement, as her supper guests nibbled theirs.

Finally, the soup cooled and the three ate. No one died or turned to stone. Sudbina and the harpist began to feel at ease as the plum brandy warmed their blood.

Baba Roga rose to clear the plates. "And now, you might give us a song." She eyed the fine harp that was set by their packs in the corner, away from the heat of the fire.

What could they do but comply? The harpist played a tune and the despoina sang, a tale of travellers lost in the wood and of highwaymen and of fortunes lost or turned. When the last note sounded, the old one clasped her hands and crowed in delight.

"It's been many moons since music last graced these walls! What dexterous fingers you have, lad! What beautiful notes you sing, Daughter! I have a mind to keep you both!" She chortled at their shock and indignation. "Fear not. I'm not that sort of witch woman. I'm much fonder of eating children in search of sweets than two wayward lovers lost in the woods."

"We are not wayward lovers!"

"Well then."

"I am the despot's daughter."

"Did you think I didn't know that, Sudbina dearie? These old ears hear everything. I knew you were in a pinch some days ago. Did you not see my lights? I sent for you. I sought to help you. Certainly you tarried long enough, the pair of you."

"Can you help us then, Mother? Our companions lie ill back at our camp. They lie still as death from some fever—is it the one you described?"

"Very likely. Did you pay homage to the trees when you entered?"

Despoina and harpist shook their heads.

"Well then, you reap what you sow. This ancient forest demands and deserves some offering. You erred."

"Others have travelled this way—surely not everyone knows this lore."

"Some are simply lucky."

"What reparation might we make?"

"Ask me no questions; I'll tell you no lies."

"Now you turn to riddles, Mother?"

"I can give you herbs. I can give you tinctures. The rest is up to you, children. But I suspect the true answers lie ahead rather than behind."

"So you suggest we carry on this journey, to reach the castle of my sister, but first pay homage to these deep woods."

"Perhaps."

"You are maddening, Mother. I can't think what else to do, except to go forward to my sister's keep."

"Your sister's keep may keep the answers ... or more questions."

"But beyond her husband's lands?"

"Are the infidels," the harpist chimed.

Baba Roga shrugged. "'Tis not the destination that counts, child Sudbina. A journey may be both path and answer."

"Your tongue ties my thoughts in knots." The harpist's slightly slurred rhyme hung in the air for a breath.

"Some say minstrels are dunderheads; others say cutpurses and foreign-born robbers," chuckled the aged crone.

"And what say you, old woman?" He eyed her sharply.

"I say ... well, I say we should be off to our beds!" she chortled. And with a flurry belying her age, the crone whisked their drained cups from their hands and set the flask back in its cupboard.

She bade the harpist check the embers of the fire, then ushered the young travellers to their beds: Sudbina to the featherbed in the loft, the harpist to a pallet by the hearth. The old witch locked them all soundly in the cottage with an iron skeleton key, then curled herself up in her huge mortar near the door and her broomstick and soon set to snoring.

But some hours later, in the deep blackness of the cottage, Sudbina started awake to find Baba's face near her own in the loft. A soft light danced behind the wrinkled woman's left ear, throwing her horn into silhouette.

"Sudbina ..." her whisper was laced with onion and garlic and rakija.

The despoina sat upright in her feather bed. "What, Mother?" Her heart pounded as if to escape its ribcage pen.

"Your father—"

"What of my father? Go on."

"—is not the man you think he is."

Ire threatened to replace the fear in her belly. "He is lord and master over these lands and over you—"

"No child! No one is lord or master over Baba Roga. But he is a cruel master unto others, and this you should know."

"He is my father. He is a good lord."

"So you say, but so you do not know. Tell me, what is the difference between an infidel and a tyrant?"

"An old woman riddles again!"

"Nothing." And at that moment the small light quitted and Sudbina was thrown back into darkness.

"Baba Roga!" she spoke aloud in the sudden quiet.

A soft snore rose from below. Disquieted, the despoina settled back under the coverlet and tried to convince herself the visitation was but a dream. In the morning, she would tell the harpist and confront the crone.

But by daybreak the matter had entirely slipped her mind.

23

Luba likes the new house well enough.

It is a modest home that they now own clear title in pretty Inglewood, near the bird sanctuary that Luba sometimes visits. She finds that walking in the park is a great pleasure and a respite from Dan. This afternoon is another reprieve; she is alone in the house and the day is fine and yellow-gold with the falling leaves outside the kitchen window overlooking the back garden. In the solitude, she bids welcome the memories.

When the giant furniture franchise, Leon's, offered to buy them out and to set up an outlet store at their Mission location, Luba leapt at the prospect, convincing Dan that this was at last paydirt. They need never fear bankruptcy again and would live their retirement years in affluence and in Calgary.

It has not been ideal, this new co-habitation. But it has been sufferable. They have separate bedrooms, separate TV rooms. Dan plays golf on fair-weather days or goes off to *parbuk* with other Serbs at Tim Hortons. Luba watches talk shows and frequents the library. They eat meals and sometimes have coffee together before one or both of them head out for the day. Luba has kept her own car, and, with it, an independence previously denied her. A suitcase packed with essentials is tucked into the trunk, should she hastily need to leave. A spare key to the car is secured behind the driver's side wheel. She has a new flip phone with important and emergency numbers in auto dial, although she often forgets to turn the device on and can't operate it without the reading glasses she frequently misplaces. There have yet been no harsh words between husband and wife, nothing violent or threatening from Dan, particularly as they avoid loaded topics like those concerning their daughter. Their companionship has been amenable. Dan has been faithful to his promise to attend group and individual therapy. A hotwire current still runs through the house, but Luba dares to hope that it may at last be insulated and grounded.

As he agreed, Dan has surrendered the accounting and banking to her, with good reason beyond Luba's ultimatum. He's never been good with their money, and he made stupid purchases during their separation, like yet another overly expensive luxury car and, worse yet, all that heavy bland furniture they had to sell for a song, redundant once they moved back together. Luba has quietly re-consulted her expensive young lawyer about exactly how to proceed should she need to freeze the accounts in the future. She has purchased GICs in her and Mirjam's names and maintains her own banking and savings account and credit cards. In a security deposit box are all her important documents. Dan, for his part, has signed the papers and mainly kept his nose out of financial affairs, content rather to discuss the old country and Serbian woes with his pals, to show off and brag to these acquaintances about his business acumen, his many career accomplishments, the war and his heroism, and to live once again in Luba's care. His loneliness is abated. Hers is not, but she is content enough and her daughter is near. Luba feels more like her old self than she has in decades.

She does not miss Mission; she does not miss Edmonton. She does not even miss her family, though they are relatively near and she has the means and time to visit them. Luba does not feel any particular compunction to do so, now beyond intimate connection after so many hard years. There is one female friend, Ruby, from her days at the post office, still in Edmonton, and every now and then Luba calls her. But when Dan last uprooted their lives as the recession hit the province in the 80s, Luba kissed that city goodbye, like all the others in her past. Edmonton in the rearview mirror, Mission became just another stopping place along the way, especially as Mirjam never joined her parents there. In their decade in Mission, Luba helped Dan to achieve financial security for the first time, assisting with the books and staying on top of consumer trends. She kept the house and another job to help pay for Mirjam's education and bi-annual visits to Montreal.

On one such trip in Mirjam's final year of her undergrad, Luba heard the girl sing in concert, and she recognized that her daughter had moved from competent to world class. Luba ached from the pride of it all. How could she deny Mirjam when she sought to continue her music education with a graduate degree in performance? Despite Dan's grumbling that such degrees were worthless in the real world—and what did the man know of degrees and the real world, having lied about completing even high school—Luba supported Mirjam financially, although the girl still worked during the summers, won scholarships, and, against her mother's advice, took out a student loan.

Mirjam stayed on in Montreal after her graduation. Faithfully, Luba followed her daughter's concerts in the east, and occasional performances in Vancouver or Victoria, attending whenever she could.

And Luba tried to ignore Dan's nonsense, dancing around his distaste for the organist Miriam had followed to New York. That folly had lasted maybe four months, until Mirjam came home broken-hearted and penniless. She'd failed to temper her husband's aversion to bassoonist Nigel Smith, in Dan's words, a pompous bastard Englishman. Luba also fretted about this woodwind musician who seemed untethered in life and tethered only to his instrument, while, oblivious, Mirjam flitted along into further heartache. And there had been others; she and Dan had lost track of them all, and likely ones they knew nothing about. Mirjam had a tendency for attraction to the wrong kind of man.

Lu had spent hours on the phone consoling their girl, even arguing about her unfortunate romantic choices. After one such telephone confrontation, Lu and Dan spent a stark Christmas alone when Mirjam refused to come to Mission for the holidays. That particular rift wasn't healed until Luba bought a plane ticket to Montreal and spent two weeks reconciling with her daughter. After that, Lu tried to keep mum on all of Mirjam's liaisons. Hers was already a house perpetually divided. She wouldn't also lose a daughter in a futile battle of words or wills.

And now here they are together in Calgary, after all these

years, even if it has cost her. Even so, they are a family still. And hasn't Dan seen what talent their amazing daughter possesses, at last? Luba leafs through the program pamphlet again at her kitchen nook table, pouring over Mirjam's biography hungrily, studying her lovely headshot, remembering the triumph that was her concert opera performance. She tucks this into a scrapbook of Mirjam's various and numerous performances. Luba has several of these books commemorating the girl's earliest days as a child soloist, through her university years, and her professional life. But this last concert, Luba understands, is Mirjam's singular best. She knows it will launch the singer forward and her heart catches at the possible thoughts of where and how far away.

Life intrudes into her thoughts. There is a pile of Dan's laundry in the laundry basket. She should run the vacuum over the floors and the area rugs. And the windows are streaked from the fall rain. Lu does not feel that she merits a housecleaner even at this point in her life. Dan certainly never offers—either the help or to help. She picks up his soiled socks and where she left off. Mirjam comes for supper on Sunday, and there are still a casserole and a dessert that need her mother's careful, caring hands.

Luba does not know, nor does Dan, that this will be a last supper of final parting, of ultimate division. Mirjam will leave. A tsunami and floodwaters will come between child and parents. Resentment and anger, like a virulent cancer, will invade the cell of the nuclear family and take pernicious hold. All because of a watch and the time it takes to finally break three hearts.

Their daughter arrives late for Sunday dinner, pours herself a large glass of orange juice, the last of the carton, and this irks Dan. She is full of chatter about the concert, its aftermath, the critical reception. Luba hangs on her every word, but Dan feels he is outside of a fishbowl looking in.

Dinner is delicious and features the daughter's favourites: Luba's moist roast chicken, spicy *sarma* or *holubsti, burek sa sirom* or *šuplja pita* in all its delicate layers of filo pastry, buttery and thick with melted cheese curds. Mirjam is appreciative, at least, of her mother's efforts on her behalf. Dan loosens his belt buckle a notch when they move to sit in the living room.

"I'm going to miss this." Mirjam eats a forkful of Lu's pie.

"I can always make you another."

"No Ma, that's not what I mean." She faces her father. "I'm going ... I've been invited to Germany for the debut of Helmut's piece in Berlin. I am going to Berlin with him."

The mantle clock ticks audibly.

"You love him."

Mirjam allows a beat to pass as she pours the tea that has been steeping in the brown betty at the centre of the coffee table. "No. I thought I did. But I don't."

"Well, of course, you have to go." Luba's hands flutter with her napkin.

"It's an enormous opportunity to sing at Konzerthaus Berlin."

"Your European debut. How exciting, right Dan?" Luba spies his darkening expression.

Mirjam, sensing the changing temperature, searches for an

escape. "Thanks, Ma, for ..."

"For what?"

"For everything. The gown. Your support. Your belief in me."

"We're your parents."

"Maybe you can fly to Berlin for the opening."

"Maybe. We'll see."

"She's not getting any money for this grand pie-in-the-sky scheme."

"She hasn't asked for any money, Dan."

"Well, what does she want?"

"Nothing. Except maybe our blessing."

"I'm right here!"

"I think this is crazy. Who do you know in Berlin?"

"My conductor, my teacher."

"Who will she turn to when it all goes sour?"

"It won't sour, Dan. Don't you want this for her, this fantastic advancement for her singing career?"

Dan is now up and pacing the room. It is done up in the roses and greys of their furniture moved from Mission, an expensive set that Luba picked out, but that Dan got wholesale from their furniture and appliances business. She sits in one of the wing-backed chairs as though she wishes to take flight.

"Of course, I do. But Mirjam gets herself into so many crappy situations. And then it all hits the fan. When her love affairs don't work out, she runs back home."

"What's wrong with that?"

"She's wasting her life!"

"How am I wasting my life?"

"It's like she's trying on shoes. Then deciding not to buy."

"So?"

"So someday you have to settle on a pair of shoes, goddamn it!"

"Can't she try on as many as she chooses? Buy a few pair? Buy a hundred? It's her life, Dan. We have to let her live it. And this could well be the break she needs and has been working so hard for all these years."

"And this Herr Wein *scheiße* …"

"Weinstein."

"Wein scheiße. He could ruin her."

"How could he ruin her?"

"He could knock her up."

"Jesus, Dan."

"For fuck's sake." Mirjam covers her face with her hand.

"I wouldn't put it past him. Or her."

"Mirjam is smarter than that. She's ambitious. She's careful. He is her teacher."

"I don't trust teachers."

"You don't trust me." Her voice is pianissimo.

"What about your schooling? Your fancy scholarship? You'd leave it all for some new waste-of-time German assh—"

"Helmut," Mirjam swallows and resists looking at her father, "has spoken to the department. They agree this is a splendid prospect for my career. I can resume my studies when I—if I return."

"What are you going to do with that Kraut?"

Mirjam recognizes the flames leaping to Dan's eyes, the same ones licking at her self-control. "Helmut is my teacher …

and my lover." She steels her eyes to her father's. "So I expect I'll be singing and screwing."

"Mirjam ..." Luba recognizes her daughter's defiance welling, as though striking match to tinderbox.

"Just what I thought!" The flame catches Dan.

"Dan, calm down. Your daughter has every right to see whom she pleases."

"She's throwing herself at some German."

"He's an artist, Dan."

"That's what I mean. Another flake!"

"This is my career, Dad. I'm doing this for my career. And Helmut Weinstein is an influential conductor who will help me to make a European debut on a world stage. Surely you can see—"

"What I see is a wayward girl who is running away."

"Running away? From what?"

"Responsibility. Her mother. In her old age."

"Dan. I'm not in my dotage! And Mirjam is no longer a girl!"

"Running away from making a reasonable life."

"Right. Settling down. Settling."

"Yes!"

"When will you get it into your head that I'm not some kind of puppet you can manipulate? Some kind of mirror to tilt in the right direction to reflect you back in the best light to yourself, Dad?"

"What are you going to do for money, eh?"

"I've got money."

"You've got nothing but debt!"

"That's not true. I have most of my scholarship—"

Dan rises from the table. "Where is it?"

Both women look at him in bewilderment.

"Where is what?" Mirjam feels the flames reach her ears.

"Where is it? My mother's watch?"

"What the hell? Dad, what are you talking about?"

"You pawned it, didn't you? You and your Heinie lover. To get money for this latest stupid scheme of yours. You sold it!"

"Jesus Christ, Dad. Gramma's watch? I never touched it. It's where it's always been." Mirjam tries to follow the logic. Pawning her grandmother's broken watch. Would it even get her ten dollars? What is this man thinking? Why is his colour changing to that telltale ruddy of rage?

"That's what you do, Mirjam. You take and you take. You're a selfish little bitch! I know you sold that watch. I know you did. For the goddamn money. You have no sense of what your grandmother did. What that watch meant. You have no sense of decency, whoring around with—"

"Dan, Dan." Luba's voice is a moan at Mirjam's elbow as the young woman turns her full gaze on her shaking father.

"For Christ's sake, Dad ..."

"If you didn't want it, you should have returned it to me so that I could have given it to somebody who really wanted and deserved it like—like Stefan—who appreciates tradition and family."

Mirjam wills herself not to spit out Stefan's name. Instead, "You're fucking crazy, Dad. The watch is downstairs in the spare room in a box with some of my other stuff from when I was a kid." Mirjam pulls up and away from the table.

"Don't you walk away from me!"

Mirjam gives no answer. She turns her back to the incendiary maniac who is her father. And then the camera slows to fifteen seconds per frame. A chair falls to the floor as Dan reaches for his daughter, attempting to turn her around. Luba lurches for his arm. But Mirjam eludes his grasp and heads towards the hall leading to the stairs that descend to the spare bedroom. Spitting venom, the father pursues his child, threatening to strike. Luba sees clearly his menace and stumbles after him, clutching his shoulder. In the narrow hallway, Dan snarls at her, whips around and throws Luba into the wall. Mirjam whirls then to see her mother shrieking, sinking, shrinking to the floor. She pushes her face close to Dan.

"Don't you hurt her!"

"Shut up, you little witch!" Dan raises his fist.

Mirjam looks at it poised above her head. "Don't you dare hit me! Don't. You. Dare."

And then Dan slams the cudgel into her face. Her head. Once. Twice. An ocean fills Mirjam's left ear. Luba, still on the floor, tries feebly to ward off further blows upon her daughter. Dan's fist is raised again. Mirjam roars—grief, hurt, fury rolled into one paroxysm of pain—and pushes back with her full body weight, both arms level with Dan's shoulders, her hands at his neck. So surprised, he has no time to react. She thrusts him to the wall and into the family photos now hanging by thin wires at reckless angles. One falls, its glass face smashing to pieces.

"Stop! Stop now, Daddy, or I'll call the police!"

Luba is sobbing. Dan's eyes, too, are welling. The entire scene flames Mirjam's pent-up years of swallowed resentment and fear and rage. Instinct prods her to squeeze Dan's throat. To slice open his jugular. She need only pick up a shard of glass…

And yet the man before her is spent and pitiful. Her body weight full upon him, hands rigid about his neck, her father is red and now openly weeping.

Her grip releases from Dan. The net of wrath loosens, permitting Mirjam to regain some sense of her sane self. Still dazed, she leaves both parents in the hallway, staggers to the steps and manages the descent to the basement.

In the downstairs closet, after a mere minute of searching, her shaking hands locate the cigar box and her grandmother's watch. When she returns to the main level, her father sits steaming in his La-Z-Boy near the dangling photographs. Mirjam can hear her mother weeping as she sweeps up the broken pieces.

Dumping the contents of the box into her father's lap, she speaks in staccato triplets, "It was here. In your house. All along." The watch in its shroud of tissue is tarnished and dull in Dan's shaking hand. Tucking the empty cigar box into her handbag, Mirjam moves to the entrance closet and pulls on her fall coat.

But Dan's voice assails her with the quiet and keen edge of an assassin's knife. "Nobody is ever going to notice you over there. You'll sing your little songs. Have your little concert. And disappear. No one will remember. No one will listen. You'll see. You'll learn. When you do, *picka,* don't come crawling back to us."

Something is hurting in her shoulder. Her cheek and mouth feel as though they are swelling up. Something else slams in her heart. Nothing stops her words.

"Goodbye Daddy."

In satisfaction, she watches her baby picture crash from the wall to the ground, glass shattering, fragments flying towards her father's stricken face.

Mirjam closes that door, leaving the scene of her near crime. She would have killed him, wanted to. And he her. How familiar, father and daughter.

A crow caws as Mirjam fumbles with the keys to her car. She fights off a wave of nausea, wonders for a moment if she should even attempt to drive. Sensing a descending cloud of self-pity and loneliness, she switches on the car radio that is set, as always, to CBC Radio Two. Beethoven's Piano Sonata No. 23 "Appassionata." Perfectly synchronistic and perfect company.

The engine catches and the daughter tears tempestuously away.

Part 2

1

He plays her like his beautiful cello, a Guadagnini, the one standing upright on its stand in the corner. His name is Alban, and he is breathtaking, full of feckless swagger.

They met at her resplendent performance of Helmut's concert opera, three months after Mirjam's arrival in Berlin in January. Their friendship was easy, grounded in a mutual passion for music and admiration for each other's considerable talents. Throughout the summer, Alban introduced her to many musicians, took her to free outdoor concerts and helped her to negotiate the city. They have been lovers since Christmas, when they first tumbled into bed and the dream of each other.

Still in his twenties, Alban is perfecting Tchaikovsky's *Rococo Variations*, practising and rehearsing with great fervour. And he is equally and deeply passionate about Mirjam, who is teaching him how to fall in love with abandon. He is an apt pupil, indeed, a virtuoso. His fingers find the notes along her nape, her breasts, her stomach. Cellist and singer have not left his tiny flat in six days, and the room smells of sex and red wine.

She has been wet between her legs for most of the duration, and when she thinks she is finally spent, he takes up his bow for the sixth variation and she is lost again.

When Mirjam rouses after the coda of post-coital slumber, she leaves the bed, Alban asleep and tangled in the sheets, to boil water for tea. Berlin is covered in snow, and the city's lights have come on in late afternoon. Mirjam pulls a scratchy, red woolen wrap about her shoulders. The apartment is old and the windows draughty. She sips her rooibos tea. In a few hours, she and her lover will venture out into the snowy streets to one of their favourite pubs, the rustic Alt-Berliner Wirtshaus in Mitte, for a meal and to meet friends from the university. Afterwards, Alban will pull her by the hand. Half-mad, half-drunk, they will weave back along the walks to Weinbergsweg and return to their flat to fall back into lovemaking. This has been the theme of the past nine weeks.

Tomorrow she must return to work at Hochschule für Musik Hanns Eisler. She has papers to grade. An appointment with Helmut. And she must resume rehearsals for the International Leyla Gencer Voice Competition. Her preliminary audition is set for June 7th at the Schiller Theatre right here in Berlin. But the meeting with Helmut is more immediately pressing.

There is a fermata over their relationship; the prolonged note of it ringing shrill. Since taking up with Alban, she has determinedly avoided Helmut. She has weaned herself of his influence and his baton.

The maestro begins before she even has time to take a seat. "You told Hannelore. My children."

"Yes." Mirjam glances at the clock, wonders how many minutes this unpleasantness will take, decides she will give it fifteen at most. "I also told your mistress."

"After all I did for you. *Du Fotze!*"

"Sit down, Helmut. You'll give yourself apoplexy." She knows he fears a stroke, his own father and grandfather having suffered and died from the same.

"I'm ruined." Helmut sinks to the seat behind his cluttered wooden desk.

"You're triumphant. You've returned to nothing but applause and professional accolades."

"She's thrown me out, you know."

"She'll take you back."

"I have no home. She's changed the locks."

"I suspect this isn't the first time."

"Why would you be so cruel, Mirjam?" He blinks bleary eyes at her. "You're a rising star. I introduced you to the right people. Put you in their sights. All I've done this past year …"

"All *I've* done!" Mirjam rises from her chair and moves to the glass case of concert batons on display. There are fifteen batons, glittering in their boxes. Ivory, ebony, olive wood, horn, with decorative mounts in silver or gold, some elaborate, some engraved, some not, most from the early twentieth century, the oldest from the nineteenth, and of course, the Mahler, closed up in its case to protect it from the building's uncertain winter climate. "I sang the soul into that role, Helmut. I believed in you. That night at the Konzerthaus—the ovations, the flowers, the public praise, the sex: how was all—any of that cruel? And since then, with each concert, with each of our performances of the concert opera, your reputation has grown exponentially."

"As has yours!"

"True."

"But my wife, my sons—why tell them? We could have gone on as we were." Helmut rises suddenly from his chair and draws near Mirjam. "*Liebchen.* Darling Mirjam. I love you, I—"

Mirjam pulls away from his kisses, his fumbled fondling, and buttons her cardigan to the neck. "Helmut, stop." She faces him. "This is over. We are over. I'm glad for all you've done for me. Grateful. Truly, I am and always will be. But I gave back to you. Your career is soaring. You'll take another mistress or two. Or your wife will give you a new key. Your sons will get over it. You'll go on as you've always done." She loops her satchel over her neck and arm. "And you'll have the satisfaction of saying you discovered me. Fucked me. That's all yours."

He turns his back on her. Touches the glass cabinet and winces at her reflection. "Get out."

"This is how you want it to end?"

"*Verpiss dich!*"

"As you wish." Mirjam looks at him, a small man poised before his prize collection. He trembles and she thinks to touch him one last time. "I—" Helmut's back stiffens. "*Auf wiedersehen,* Herr Weinstein."

The door clicks shut behind her. The maestro unlocks the door of the old oak cabinet, unlatches the case of the Mahler baton, and finds the ivory wand within has cracked in half.

Mirjam rehearses with Hans Schlick, the pianist, who has offered ingenious interpretations and coaching. She has been preparing two initial arias: "Una voce poco fa" from Rossini's *Barber of Seville* and Bizet's "Habanera" from *Carmen*.

Though these are iconic works in the opera canon, she and Helmut felt they would best represent her voice and her talent for acting and performance in the competition. If she makes the finals—and her new voice teacher, Frau Littgenstein, has every confidence she will—Mirjam has two other arias she is preparing with Hans—Richard Strauss's "Wie Du warst" from *Der Rosenkavelier* and "Smanie Implacabili" from Mozart's *Cosi fan tutte*—plus Myrrha from Helmut's concert opera. Frau Littgenstein has agreed to mentor her in preparation for the audition, now that Mirjam has severed ties with Helmut. Demanding and exacting, Frau L. has given excellent instruction. She is all work and no nonsense. The singer appreciates the woman's fine ears, despite their pendulous lobes. Today and throughout this week, the Frau works Mirjam's singing in Italian, German, and French with strict precision. The spartan little rehearsal room is chill and Soviet in its minimalist design. At least the piano, an upright Steinway and a fine instrument pre-dating the war, is in good repair and well tuned. Every half hour or so, Frau L. turns on an ancient space heater for a few minutes so that the pianist's fingers can warm up for play. Mirjam wonders vaguely if the thing will ignite, setting fire to the piano, sheet music, teacher, musician, and vocalist. For a ridiculous moment, she imagines Alban weeping and bereft over her dead but curiously uncharred corpse, envisions her mother and especially her father, contrite at last, weeping over her casket. She eyes the door nervously, marking an escape route.

Hans, her fine accompanist, is sensitive to Mirjam's phrasing and her breath. He is most supportive and intuitive, perhaps the best pianist she has worked with to date, with beautiful fingers. After rehearsals they go to a nearby café, for despite her longing to return to Alban's arms, she knows she must resist so that they can both get some work and rehearsing accomplished, return to some semblance of living beyond the bed. Over beer and cigarettes, Hans tells her that he is desperately in love with an older man, one who reciprocates affection only at his leisure or convenience. His expressive hands gesticulate his frustration. Mirjam listens attentively and is not without empathy as snow continues to powder the streets of Berlin. She looks away from the window and up to the Van Gogh reproduction on the café wall, *Wheatfield with Crows,* and allows herself to wonder where the path may lead.

On the way home, she purchases a fresh loaf of bread, some onions, green peppers, tomatoes, and a package of stewing beef. Tonight she will cook a stew for supper. As an afterthought she picks up a bottle of reasonably priced Rioja to share with her lover. Snowflakes are huge and wet, the walks not well cleared as they would be in Canada, and her packages feel all the heavier as she trudges toward Weinbergsweg. The lift, as usual, is not working and the seven-flight climb leaves her quite breathless. She fits the spare key Alban has given her into the lock of emptiness. He is still at the academy, no doubt puzzling over some phrase of Tchaikovsky that eludes absolute perfection or consulting with fellow cellist Kürt Koch over some finer points of cello technique.

Singing the Bizet refrain softly, Mirjam first cleans the kitchen, then chops vegetables and sets the stew to bubbling. She sits before the window as the day darkens to evening and she must turn on the overhead reading lamp. Pulling out the papers still ungraded and a pile of letters retrieved earlier in the day from her mailbox at the academy, she begins to sort them. There is one from her mother. Her breath stops as she opens the envelope.

Crossing an ocean to leave her father, Mirjam had not anticipated how much she would miss her mother. After the father-daughter schism, she and Lu had spent a sober Christmas day together and then, with Helmut, Mirjam left Calgary and the country without a backward glance. In February of the new year, Luba had been ill, hospitalized with pneumonia, just before her daughter's March debut at the Konzerthaus. Though she'd recovered, Lu was yet too weak to make the journey. Mirjam was disappointed and wracked with worry, but when her mother assured her that she was absolutely fine, turned her full attention back to the concert opera. And then her new life in Berlin. And then her new lover.

Weekly, they spoke on the phone, made plans for Luba's impending visit, but something always seemed to intervene: family visitors, Lu's new job, or was it Dan forbidding her to travel? Had he hit her? Luba insisted not and promised she would book a trip soon.

But another Christmas had passed; a whole year had spun by. Mirjam felt a rueful mixture of guilt and longing.

Dear Mirjam,

How are you my darling daughter? We had a Chinook followed by a blizzard these past two weeks. With the thaw and freeze the sidewalks were a mess and I had a fall. Don't worry—nothing seriously injured except my dignity. Mr. Probst, the nice neighbour to the south, was walking Sylvie, his border collie, and they helped me to my feet with kind care and some sympathetic licks. I've had to wrap my wrist, which I must have strained to break my fall. Since then we've put some salt down, but the kind that is doggie friendly, in respect for my canine saviour.

Thank you for the clippings from your last concert. They are lovely and you look glamorous and glowing in the photos. I'm so glad of your success, dear Mirjam. I wish I could have been there. I just didn't feel I could take time off work, new as I am to this job. Work at the Inglewood Bird Sanctuary is really a treat. I can think of no better employment than to hang out with the birds—so much better than Woolco or handing out cracker samples to Safeway's customers! The Nature Centre is a great place—sometimes peaceful, sometimes mayhem when the school groups arrive. I like to have something to do that is different from retail but still involves the public.

I missed you so much at Christmas. I just didn't feel festive with my daughter on the other side of the world. We had your father's friends over for drinks after New Year's. It was all very dreary. They spoke in Serbian most of the evening, nattering on about their homeland and the grand Serbian struggle. I was glad to close the door on them when they left.

Your father is fine, if you're wondering. He's missed a few appointments with the psychologist, but I've reminded him of our agreement. He went to the doctor for shortness of breath but it's nothing but old age, I guess. Lately, he's been parbuk-ing more than usual with his Serb friends at the mall food court, rehashing the war. I asked him if they ever talked about the atrocities. He asked me if he could bring the priest to bless the house. The Orthodox priest! As if Dan's ever had a religious day in his life. Suddenly now he finds the path to righteousness? I told him no. He told me to call him Danilo. Usually, I don't call him anything at all except for supper. Ha ha.

Well, I thought I might have a chance to report that an early spring has hit the Prairies, but not yet after this latest wallop of snow, I'm afraid. I'll let you know when I hear or see the first robin. Or maybe a returning crow. My vantage point at the bird sanctuary should give me a first glimpse. Hope you are finding your second winter in Berlin bearable. Best of luck as you prepare for your audition. Maybe you can make me a recording?

And just for your information, at work one of the girls is showing me how to work the PC so one day very soon I will try my hand at this e-mail thing. Looking forward to your Sunday call. You can reverse the charges. Do you need any money?

Oh, and say hello to Alban. I really hope to meet him soon.
    Love,
    Your mother (whom you like to call Ma)

P.S. I finally had your baby picture reframed. Back on the wall and good as new!

Mirjam studies the snapshot of the Inglewood Bird Sanctuary Luba has sent along in the envelope. In the foreground, Lu stands in her blue parka, smiling at the camera and pointing to the entrance of the Nature Centre. Her image makes Mirjam smile, too. The thought of her mother happy eases the ache behind her ribs just a little. She will send a quick note of reply and a box of marzipan that Luba loves. Any thought of her father she pushes aside at the sound of footsteps on the stairs.

And then Alban bursts through the door, cello case in one hand, bouquet of winter flowers in the other.

"I have closed the door on Helmut."

"That must be a relief."

Mirjam pours the last of the Rioja into the glass, raises it and shrugs, "*Živeli.*"

"*Prost!*" Alban tucks a loose strand of her hair behind her left ear. "What were you doing with that old man, Liebchen?"

"Building a career." Her smile is wry, "some would ask what I am doing with this young man?"

"Building a life."

Mirjam drains her glass and wonders.

Afterward, after the lovemaking and the pillow talk, when Alban is deep in sleep, she rises and paces the chill apartment in only her woolen wrap.

The night is uncharacteristically clear and bright. A half moon lights up the flat like a grainy black and white film. Mirjam pauses before the full-length mirror, an old thing that had come with the flat. By daylight one can see that the silver is wearing away from the edges. It clearly dates from the war, and though it might once have been fine, the wood frame is pockmarked and somehow has seen water damage.

Mirjam utters the familiar fairy tale refrain of Snow White's stepmother.

The mirror speaks and does not speak.

It does not say this is the best and worst of times. Or that when life hands you lemons, make lemonade. Or that everything that happens, does so for a reason. With a slight warp to the glass, the image exposes that 289,080 hours have passed, that fleshy bits are hanging looser now, that scars never fade completely, and that death is certain and closer than yesterday's glance in the mirror.

Mercifully, a shadow passes the moon, and the room darkens so that the dimpled thighs seem in softer focus, the beginnings of crow's feet fade, and the earnest gaze appears, at least for a heartbeat, younger and still hopeful.

Outside, early morning Berlin traffic begins to bark but does not call attention away from the mercurial, quicksilver image of a woman, half done, half undone, bare and breathless.

2

Dan is up to his knees in mud. His hand reaches for his cigarettes, but then he thinks better of it. A match struck in near-darkness, a butt glowing at dusk—sure beacons for the enemy. He doubts that in this wretched rain the bloody fag would even stay lit. Instead, he sits craving the nicotine, scratching the lice miserably, and uneasy on watch. It is quiet now, in this dawn pissing light. A single crow swoops by, cawing for his mate or for sorrow, Dan doesn't know which but wonders. Anything to break the monotony, free his thoughts from what happened to Boyd, Aksaniak, Cecchetti. To so many buddies from back home. He doesn't know what gets to him most about this aspect of warfare: the tedium or the anxiety or the sheer terror.

Beside him are two of his best remaining buddies from home, Chester Smith and Gordon Landon. The other is Scotty Sutherland, back behind them with the rear guard. Somehow all three have made it to Ortona, Italy, same division and brigade, though Gordie is in the Hasty Ps and Dan, Chester and Scotty are 48th Highlanders. That was the easy part for three green boys from Drumheller. The Toronto recruiting sergeant asked what they wanted to get into, and Chester, Dan and Scott answered in unison, "the army." Without an upward glance from his papers, the man said, "welcome to the infantry." None of the three knew then what he knew now: each might have served in the Medical or Service or other noncombatant corps. Instead, here they were along with Gordon, "D-Day Dodgers" in Italy facing the Germans at the Moro River. It will be forty years after the war when Dan finally learns that seventy-eight percent of all casualties were infantrymen.

For now, Dan is a decorated sergeant. Early on he showed leadership and level-headedness in making decisions in the thick of a skirmish and for that he was awarded some ribbons and a third stripe. Gordon is a new private with only three weeks training, but Dan doesn't lord his authority over his friend. All four are in this nightmare together, comrades in arms as they were comrades in the Badlands, now fighting for their lives and those of the other boys. The daily reports of Canadian casualties bring the bile to Dan's throat. He and the rest are bitter that resources seem bound for other parts of Europe instead of here where they are much needed. Barely trained kids from home are being sent into this slaughterhouse. Anyone with a brain can see this advance on Ortona for the trap it is.

Gordon took in the news about the deaths of so many Drumheller boys soberly. He'd read friends' names on the casualty lists before coming overseas. Now these four kids from Drum were reunited in some grotesque twist of fate. They'd been best school chums, Dan, Chester and Scotty, a few years ahead of Gord. Together they'd been an inseparable shit-disturbing team—overturning outhouses, egging windows, swimming in the Red Deer River, playing shinny on the frozen water through the long Drumheller winters. Three Anglo boys and a Serb. They'd accepted Dan. Joined in on the punches when the other town pricks called Dan a bohunk or a stinking foreigner.

They'd had his back. Now they were four again. Dan had spared Gordie most of the grisly details about their other pals. But his own restless nights were haunted by dreams of baseball games that never seemed to have enough players to make a winning team.

For his part, Gordon told him about his meagre three weeks of training. Dan shook his head in wonder. Five years into this asshole of the universe called the infantry, he knew that twenty-one days of training prepared no one. Shit. No amount of training prepared you for the fucking horror of it all. But three lousy weeks? He didn't share this with Gord, who seemed, in his uncharacteristically sober mood, to know it anyway. Dan knew that in the midst of this mud and shite, even for his inexperience, the younger man still had his back.

A sniper's bullet pings dangerously close to the pair on watch. Dan looks behind him and sees his lieutenant give the signal. He taps Gord's shoulder and the two soldiers crawl awkwardly through the mud, retreating to their lines on the shores of the Moro. Back amongst their regiments that have joined together, they receive their orders as the first shells start to fall. A group of infantrymen drops to shimmy on their stomachs across the mud and through the puddles toward the onslaught. Earth tremors rumble beneath his belly, and Dan fights to keep calm amidst the furor that seems to his ears as if mythical giants are hurling battle cries and berserkers are running rampant over the world. The company wriggles forward like filthy worms for perhaps fifty yards. As he was bid, Dan and several others rise to a crouch. He, like his fellows, fishes out a grenade, pulls out the pin and lobs the pineapple towards the area from which the machine gun fire emanates about a hundred yards away. Nearby, comrades duck for cover.

Dan's aim is sure—those halcyon days as a hardball pitcher in the Drumheller semi-pro minor league pay off—and the weapon detonates, raising a sea of mud and debris, as the other grenades similarly find their deadly marks. Dan sees parts of the machine gun apparatus fly up and land some twenty feet away from its original site.

Retaliation is swift and lethal. Artillery fire and shelling intensify, forcing the advancing Canadians to seek immediate shelter. They abandon their fallen comrades on the field and scramble to some safety behind a farmer's rock wall. With relief, Dan greets the guys, Chester, Gord, and Scotty among them, with a grimace.

"Bullseye, Dan!" Chester claps him on the back.

This is no time to celebrate. They've lost two men. Jerry is on the offensive and they must focus and take aim, keep their heads down, their wits about them, despite their sleep deprivation. Dan's stomach is a knot of live wires. When they try to abandon their refuge, he doubles over in pain. Scotty looks back in concern. He and Gord each grab a shoulder. Taking advantage of a momentary break in the battering, they stumble—a six-legged beast—to where the others are now headed behind the rubble of a collapsed stone farmhouse. Gordie mouths something at Dan, whose ears are ringing so he can't make out the words. Not for the last time he wishes he could exchange this hell for the hell of working in the coal mines back at home. One grave for another.

By evening, the regiment has been removed to an allied encampment near San Vito Chietino. The bloody rain has stopped, at least temporarily. Dan has seen the combat medic, who feels certain the soldier is suffering from "soldier's stomach." He's given him packets of bromide powder for any future attacks. Feeling foolish and as though he will be perceived as a whiner, or worse, a fake, Dan sits outside the medic tent smoking his cigarette in the darkness. He can hear Fenzie inside, first talking with the medic, then blubbering.

Gord comes from the canteen with two cups of the swill they call coffee and offers one to Dan.

"What'd the doc say?"

"Just a bit of upset. Maybe constipation. Probably the food."

Gord snorts, "Hell, yeah."

From inside the tent, Fenzie half-sobs, "But we just left him there."

"How many of Jerries do you think we offed today?"

"Wish it were the bloody lot."

"Bastards."

Dan nods and they drink. The small camp is low lying and at best dimly lit. A few stars creep through the clouds. Off in the distance are the occasional boom and reply from the forces still fighting.

"Jesus, he's my twin. What'll my folks say if they know I just left him there? Left him behind with the Krauts and for the fucking crows?"

Gord coughs and spits. "Nice night if you aren't in a war."

"Here we are. Vacationing in Italy." Dan reaches for another cigarette.

Murmurs from the tent and the sounds of Fenzie's weeping are drowned out as someone in the darkness nearby begins to sing to the tune of "Lili Marlene":

We're the D-Day Dodgers out in Italy
Always on the vino, always on the spree.
Eighth Army scroungers and their tanks
We live in Rome—among the Yanks.
We are the D-Day Dodgers, over here in Italy.

Putting on his best voice, despite the cigarettes and fucking fatigue, Dan joins in:

We landed at Salerno, a holiday with pay,
Jerry brought the band down to cheer us on our way
Showed us the sights and gave us tea

From the shadows step Chester and Scotty, and other guys further along begin to join in, including Gordie, as usual off key:

We all sang songs, the beer was free.
We are the D-Day Dodgers, way out in Italy

No one's quite sure where the song began or who wrote the words, but no one misses the irony. No one is dodging anything but bullets and shells in Italy, as far as Dan can see. That cuntish Lady Astor made some comment somewhere back behind the safe walls of the British Parliament, about the Italian holiday the troops are enjoying, or so the story in the field goes.

He'd like to see her here for five minutes. Damn bitch. She'd piss and shit her pants before the time was up. He'd bang her back to London. Or this war would.

There's a girl he thinks softly of—Sophia. A buxom young thing he'd met in Santo Stefano in Aspromonte, the little village they'd liberated where the Italian soldiers marched towards them and just surrendered their weapons while the citizens cheered as the 48th piped through. That night Italian and Canadian infantrymen drank vino rosso locale with the Italian soldiers and lay down with Italian girls. He'd clipped a lock of her black hair and tucked it into a pocket of his kit with his cigarettes. Somehow in the madness of ensuing days, he must have pulled it out with his cigs and lost the damn thing. Now all he had to physically remember Sophia was the infestation of crabs that were celebrating with the lice on his body. Christ, he yearned for a shower and a de-lousing. Not to mention de-crabbing. But that was weeks away. Maybe more.

But he would have liked to have Sophia's breasts in his rough hands again tonight. That kind of wisdom would be some kind of relief from this shit storm.

Dan glances over at Gordie's dark form beside him, curled over his cold coffee can, out for the night. He removes the cup and still-glowing butt from his friend's hands, takes a final drag and punches it out on the ground.

Accompanied by the distant artillery lullaby pounding the crap out of Italy, Dan, mired in filth—the Moro's and his own—drops to exhausted sleep.

3

Despoina and harpist woke in the morning to find the old woman, mortar and pestle gone from her hut on its skinny chicken legs. On the crude table were set a bottle of tincture and a bundle of herbs, as promised, the skeleton key, a skein of silk yarn, and a cloth bag of food, presumably for their journey forward or backward or there and back again, wherever their paths might lead.

At that moment, a mouse ran by and startled the despoina so that she squealed. It stopped to turn small beady eyes on her, then rising to its haunches, spoke in a human voice not unlike the old crone's, "Some medicines are poisons; some poisons medicines. Silk is stronger than hatred. One key, many doors; the right key, the right door." Then the riddling creature scampered away.

The harpist, as astonished as Sudbina, shivered beside her. "There is bewitchment about this place. I've always thought such tales the stuff of fancy, but now," he swallowed, "having seen with my own eyes, heard with my own ears ..."

"Best to quit the witch while we're ahead!" Sudbina snatched up the offerings left by Baba Roga, her bow and quiver, and together the companions stuffed their travel packs.

The horses were rested, and they mounted two, leaving the others of the team in the rough-hewn shed.

"I sense that our hostess intends these beasts no harm," Sudbina spoke loudly to the gated yard, as though believing the old baba was somehow within earshot. "I imagine that if we return, we can repay her hospitality with some treasure—whatever that might be."

The harpist nodded and clicked his horse towards the gate, which he opened, then closed behind them as horses and riders left the yard. In the strong sunlit morning, they found their way easily back to the encampment where their comrades still slept deeply and unaware. Together, they gently wound silken threads thrice about the remainder of the company—Elenya, Dragan, and Budimir—hoping that Baba Roga had meant the gift as a talisman of protection. Indeed, the skein seemed no smaller than it had been, as if magical proof of the old witch's intention. After forcing a few spoonfuls of boiled herbal tea into each slumbering mouth, the pair considered the direction of their leave-taking.

Before departing, they strode over to the tallest tree at the periphery of the clearing, an oak and clearly ancient.

"If we have offended you or your kin in these woods, we offer apology," the despoina spoke softly. She placed a sprig of wild hyssop at the foot. Then she and the harpist sang an old lay about a beautiful enchanted forest, hoping their humble offering would appease the woods and its silent creatures. When the harp stilled, a susurration through the leaves almost convinced them they'd been heard. So with lighter hearts, they took again to their horses.

Once more in the direction of Baba Roga's hut, the pair guided their mounts along the path. When they came to the spot of the witch's abode, true to lore, it had somehow vanished.

Sudbina and her lover travelled westward for three days and rested for three nights. No brigands or marauders accosted them in shadow or sunlight. Indeed, the journey was eerily quiet, and the despoina often wondered if they were under some protective enchantment. For whatever reason, either the forest or Baba Roga or both felt the travellers deserved warding.

On the afternoon of the fourth day, they sighted the battlements of her sister's castle. A company rode out to greet them, and Sudbina and harpist trotted into the castle walls with great good cheer. Milosti was beside her pregnant self with excitement, as were her children, now wild as weeds. Her husband proved an accommodating host, and together with the family and their attendants, the two guests drank deeply and supped rich fare at the grand table in the grander hall.

For her part, Milosti, having expected her sister some days prior, was relieved to have Sudbina within arms' reach. She sent an immediate dispatch to their father, lest he likewise be worried. While Sudbina was very glad to see her sister, she remained haunted by the sickened company who still lay comatose in the woods. In response, Milosti's husband sent out a small guard with carts to retrieve the sleepers. By week's end, only one of the group returned, clearly out of his head and babbling that the others were lost to some bewitchment that the lord immediately attributed to the horned hag, Baba Roga, despite Sudbina's protests to the contrary. He prepared to send out a larger company, armed to battle the witch, the following day.

Distraught, the despoina sought the harpist, some hours before cockcrow.

"Sudbina, you are dressed." The sleepy musician raised himself to blink at her from his pallet in the servants' quarters. "I can only surmise you are leaving—either to return to our friends or to ..."

"To go onwards to the unknown realms. I think I am meant to journey thence, for I think there lie the answers. And somehow, I hope to warn Baba Roga."

The harpist rose to don his garments. "But you know what will happen when you are discovered gone."

"I do. First my brother-in-law and then my father will send out their parties to seek and apprehend me. And likely to punish you for participating in my foolishness."

"Wheresoever you go, so will I."

"Even to our deaths?"

He kissed her. "Even so."

And hence, like two skulking bandits, the young woman and the man stole from the castle, past snoring guards, into the royal stables to retrieve their horses.

Behind her, Sudbina had left an empty bed, a burgled larder, and a hastily written note to her sister.

Before her, she well knew, lay the threat of the hated Turk. Though she had never met one, she hoped that she might outwit any who intended her harm. Failing that, she had her trusty bow and arrows, though but three remained in her quiver.

Thereafter, she hoped to charm from any Ottoman encountered the answer to the mystery of sleeping fellows in the woods. Tales of the Turks bespoke their clever ways with numbers and medicines.

She had heard her life long the ugly stories of the conquerors. The bloody battle of Kosovo was the theme of many songs and poems. Indeed, her harpist had performed these oftentimes in her father's court. Then there was the curse that rang in her father's and forefather's ears, told to her by her wet nurse, and oft repeated through her childhood:

> *Whoever is a Serb and of Serb birth,*
> *And of Serb blood and heritage,*
> *And comes not to fight at Kosovo,*
> *May he never have progeny born from love*
> *Neither son nor daughter!*
> *May nothing grow that his hand sows*
> *Neither red wine nor white wheat!*
> *And may he be dying in filth as long as his children are alive.*

Sudbina had always wondered at the cruelty of the verse. Why so much antipathy directed towards those who did not participate in the battle? Why, after so many years, did her people harbour such grudges against the Ottomans? Was it simply because they had lost at Kosovo? Weren't her father and the other lords relatively free to live as they pleased under Ottoman rule? She shuddered to recall the stories of women's breasts and men's heads hacked from their bodies. The infidels, she'd always been told, were monsters.

But she had also heard marvels of the Ottomans. Indeed, the minstrel, several nights back, had harped and sung a tune of great wonder about the city of Carigrad, or Constantinople, and its erudite people. Thoughts of its domes and spires, its fabled library, beautiful towers, minarets and churches intrigued her. She herself had never seen the sea. Might she one day see the Marmara?

Such thoughts kept Sudbina occupied as she and her harpist wended their way through the woods that day, travelling at a brisk pace, keeping an eye out for her brother-in-law's men. That night they fashioned a lean-to and huddled together under its shelter before a small fire. And together they improvised a song of warning, hoping the words would somehow reach Baba Roga's old ears.

4

Lu stops on the trail where the chickadees like to gather, as she's done before. She reaches into her satchel and pulls out two handfuls of wild bird sunflower seeds. Elbows to her sides, she stands with her hands outstretched. It is not long before the yellow breasts flutter closer. Perching on the bare branches, they eye her warily. Finally, one dares closer. Another alights. And then several take turns landing and darting away for a number of heart-stopping moments. Lu barely allows herself to breathe, so entranced by this afternoon's magical ave.

When most of the seed is gone, she gently lowers her arms, sprinkles the remainder in the light snow around the bushes, and dons her gloves.

Turning to resume her walk, she is startled by a stranger on the path who has trained his Nikon camera lens upon her and what she thought had been a private moment. She stiffens, feeling flustered and slightly violated.

He apologizes instantly. "I ... just came across this beautiful sight. The light was perfect. I hope you don't mind. I didn't mean to intrude."

His smile is warm and bright and there are deep laugh lines

at his eyes. Lu thaws and smiles a little back at him.

"How do you do that with the birds?"

"Patience. They'll come to you, too, if you're still enough. You must know about stillness, being a photographer."

"I suppose I do. But I'm only a novice nature photographer, you see. My specialty has been—still life. Or more often the case, still and dead."

"Beg your pardon?"

"Sorry. I am—I was a medical photographer. I took pictures of patients, diseases, apparatus, autopsies. I often worked in the hospital morgue."

"How ... morbid sounding."

"Well, yes. But it was all very technical and clinical. And for me ... I came to see a kind of peace in death, a kind of honouring through the photos, if you can imagine."

"I guess so."

"Or perhaps I just told myself that," he looked down to snap his lens cap on the Nikon, "and how I was helping to document medical science. So after all those years in a hospital, I'm at best an amateur bird photographer, really. My name's Hodi, by the way."

"That's a nice name."

"It's a nickname. It means 'hello,' a greeting, instead of a North American doorbell, when you approach someone's door in my village back in Kenya. As a small child, I used to visit my grandmother and relatives often, crying out at the top of my lungs, 'hodi!' So my grandmother began calling me *Hodiii Hodiii,* and it stuck. My family still calls me Hodihodi, but I shortened the name when I began work in Canada. What is yours, may I ask?"

"Lu. It's short for Luba."

Imperceptibly, they begin to walk slowly along the path together past a trio of frost-rimed mountain ashes. The earth is frozen, and their footsteps make a pleasant crunching rhythm. Hodi is her height and his strides match hers.

"What does it mean, your name?"

"I—I don't know. My mother never told me. And now it's too late. She's been dead for many years."

"You must find out on the Internet then."

"I've never thought of doing that."

"So that is why I've met you today, Lu, whose name is short for Luba. To prompt you to find the meaning of your name." Hodi's big laugh startles the nearby sparrows.

The sun is trying to warm the February chill, but their breath fogs the air.

"Have you lived in Calgary for very long?" Luba immediately regrets and blushes at her own typically white question.

"I have lived in Canada for many years, Luba. My wife and I came over in the fifties. We raised a family—two boys and a girl. Now they are off working or studying at universities in Ontario, and I am here. Alone, since my wife died of cancer three years ago."

"I'm sorry."

"Yes, it was a bad time. I came out West last year because I visited the Rockies once and always hoped to return to live nearer. They are something aren't they?" He sweeps his hand westward to the violet shadows peaking along the horizon.

"Do you ski, then?"

"Oh no," he chuckles.

"Climb?"

"No, Luba. I am more of a walker. I always choose the easy and flat trails."

"Me too." Their eyes meet, and she feels herself flush. "You must have been lonely, adjusting to your new life here."

"Well, the adjustment was much more difficult coming from Kenya to Canada. Though I was educated in the British system—my father worked for a British school headmaster and I was granted opportunity to attend—I found there are a great many differences between what I thought I knew about Britain and its colony, Canada, and, of course, between my country and yours."

"I'm sure."

"And Calgarians are such friendly people. Of course, my children have been a blessing—they visit often. Or as often as I send money for a plane ticket." There is that easy laugh again. "My girl—she studies human rights law. My two boys—one is a chef at a fancy Toronto restaurant; the other is working on his Master's in computer engineering."

"You must be very proud of them."

"Oh yes. And you? Do you have children?"

"A daughter. She's an opera singer."

Hodi smiles broadly. "Really? I love opera. Do you attend?"

Luba shakes her head. "Not often. Usually only when Mirjam is performing. We weren't exactly ... raised on classical music."

"Nor I, but we listened to it at the British school and I developed a special fondness for it. My teacher, Master Simms, who was very fond of me, gave me an old victrola and a collection of opera 78s as a gift when he retired. From that point on, our house was always filled with this music. Though my mother hated it, preferring the songs she grew up with, I learned to love the voices of Caruso and Callas. I appreciate the spectacle, the intrigues and scandals and the scale of human drama, you know? When I came to North America, I discovered Jessye Norman. Have you ever seen her in concert?"

Luba shakes her head.

"Breathtaking! But then, I love all kinds of music," he shrugs, "except perhaps rap. I come from a musical family back in Kenya."

"Did your father sing?" Luba thinks of Dan's earliest influence on Mirjam, his ease with a melody, their early, shared affection for singing together.

"My father was the photographer." Hodi raises the camera, as if in salute. "He received a camera from his employer, the headmaster I mentioned, who supplied him with film and permitted him to use the dark room in the school. And then my father taught me. I still have that camera. It was something we shared until his death.

"No, my mother and grandmother were the singers. Oh, my mother had a glorious voice—rich and resonant! It rang out through the house, through the village as she worked, and at the church. I wish you could have heard her and my grandmother, both. Unfortunately, they did not pass their gift to me. I would love to sing, but—we don't always get what we want, do we? I have to be content with taking pictures. And you, Luba, what is your gift?"

"I—"

They have looped around one of the shorter trails and are now in front of the sanctuary office building. "This is where I work."

"Ah, so that is how you know the birds so well."

"I suppose. I've always liked birds, but I find I like them more than ever as I grow ... older."

"I, too, like the birds. They are much different here—quieter, just like Canadians—than back in Kenya."

Luba removes her glove, reaches out her hand. "It's been lovely to meet you, Hodi." He takes hers in his and it is warm and reassuring.

"May I take your picture, Luba?" Hodi removes the lens cap and lifts the camera to his face. "This time with your permission?"

Suddenly shy and awkwardly aware of her dishevelled hair and her overall drab appearance, Lu nods, hesitantly.

"Say 'hodihodi!'" He laughs and aims the camera, snapping a shot of her caught in a genuine, if surprised, smile.

Packing the shortbread cookies in folds of wax paper and then in the cardboard box that she will parcel and send to Mirjam, Lu recalls that afternoon's chance encounter. A man from Kenya. She looked it up on the world map: a country in East Africa. Capital Nairobi. A place of lions and wildebeests, elephants, and rhinos. Creatures she's only seen in pictures or at the Calgary Zoo.

What does she know of Kenya or any other part of the world? Nothing but what she has gleaned from books and the

CBC, occasional *National Geographic* articles and TV programs. Her life has been so small, she thinks ruefully. Except for a family trip to California and Disneyland, and one to Yugoslavia with Dan, Luba has been nowhere else but Western Canada and to visit Mirjam at McGill. She has lived in a series of houses, unpacking, cleaning, packing and cleaning, leaving, to survive in a loveless marriage in order to raise a daughter. If thoughts of seeing the world ever rose to the surface, she choked them down again.

This evening she considers, wonders beyond her front door, her marriage, her daughter, the bird sanctuary. Dan sits in his easy chair watching the boxing match on television and she brings him his coffee, willing her hand not to spill its scalding contents over his thick head.

The crossword she is puzzling over at the kitchen table doesn't much hold her interest. One of the words is "Millay" for Edna St. Vincent, and Lu is instantly transported back to the final year of her inadequate Rosedale education, when she was asked by Miss Minster, who saw in her an apt and talented pupil, to memorize and recite several of the poet's sonnets. This same teacher was the only person disappointed at Luba's departure from school by her father's decree. She recalls that teacher, her one-room classroom, fondly. And now on this Friday evening some fifty-four years later, Luba can remember but a fragment from one of the sonnets: "I was not one for keeping/ Rubbed in a cage a wing that would be free."

Perhaps she should take night classes for her high school equivalency. Wouldn't that be something after all these silly years? Would she be able to retain anything in her old noggin?

She laughs at her own folly and wishes she could call Mirjam to share this bit of nonsense. But it is 3 a.m. Berlin time. No time for crazy talk from a mother to a daughter.

Her book and a cup of herbal tea are all she needs. A shake of the head to dislodge the cobwebs of solipsism, another word from her crossword. A good night's sleep. She calls out goodnight to Dan and locks the bedroom door.

Framed pictures of Mirjam adorn her walls—as a beautiful baby, a toddler, a kindergartner, a gangly teen, and then her concert photos and her professional headshot. As Luba spins around the room, it seems the time turns just like in that old Malvina Reynolds' song. With her daughter now living so far away, what is Lu's purpose? Has she become the old woman in *Mary Poppins* who feeds the birds? This makes her laugh at herself. She makes a mental note to share the joke with Mirjam in her next letter as she moves to shut the blinds.

Above the alley, the moon is haloed by the frost that persists through this cold February. Everything looks silvery in the frozen garden below. The birdbath is a sheet of ice. The weathervane is hoary and perfectly motionless on top of the garden shed. This is a scene fit for a chorus of dancing frost fairies, if one believed in such things. Mirjam used to, and Luba had indulged her fantasies until the girl reached adolescence and its accompanying smart-ass omniscience. That was a hard time of crossed wills and of keeping daughter and father from murdering one another. Bruises then were purple or deep, some still lingering these many years later.

Luba's slippered feet cross the carpet into the ensuite. The lights above the mirror are bright and her reflection tells no lies. She washes her face, touching the scar above her eyebrow where it met with the sharp edge of a counter during one awful fight with Dan twelve years ago. There are new lines and age spots, it seems, since yesterday. Encroaching age mocks her. She is already much older than her mother was when she died. How many more years will be granted her? Trying to see the positive, she mugs a smile for the mirror. Luba's teeth are good, and only one has needed a veneer when it broke in another altercation with Dan, she can't remember how long ago. Wiping away traces of the day, she arrests the washcloth in mid-air. Her eyes have caught her off guard, those same that have seen nothing and too much. Wise and foolish. Why doesn't she walk out of this house and away? Past the bird sanctuary and into a new life? Why can't she be like the woman in the book she is reading—resilient and self-possessed? Why is she a woman possessed?

Lu considers taking a little blue pill but thinks better of it. The doctor has warned of a dependency. She doesn't want to be further locked in some *Valley of the Dolls* stereotype. Not for the first time, Lu wishes she had a friend, a close confidante.

She creeps under the bedcovers.

Her bedside light is good, and she reads until 10 p.m. when she clicks on the TV for Peter Mansbridge to tell her what kind of day it's been. In Bosnia the rumours of ethnic cleansing continue. UN reports reveal a mass starvation strategy by the Serbian Special Operations Unit against Bosniaks in Srebrenica, despite its being declared a UN Safe area. Milošević is an ugly, ugly man. Why does the world not stop his hand?

Sometimes, she thinks, she should forego watching the

news. At 11 p.m., she snaps the light off and settles into shadows. It takes a long time to surrender to sleep.

When she does, Luba dreams fitfully the night through—of babies in cauls and birds flying into windows.

5

If I was a young man, I'd go.

Back to former Yugoslavia?

Serbia. Yes. I'd go and join the forces there. Fight for the mother country. To protect Serb culture, the Serbian people.

O—kay.

You believe all the crap that's in the media?

Well, I've heard some pretty damning things about Milošević. And I've been doing some reading ...

You've heard exactly what the spin doctors want you to hear. It was worse under Tito.

Seen some terrible images out of Srebrenica. Burning villages—women and children—

Have you seen what the Ustaše did to the Serbs?

I've read about the Ustashas, their fascism, their killing campaigns. But I'm sure I don't know everything. It seems hard to know which reports and whose statistics to believe. But this is now, fifty years later. Are the photos I'm seeing on the nightly news—is that just tit for tat, a retaliation against the Ustasha by today's Chetniks?

They can do anything with photographs these days.

Yes, they can, but Dan ...

Danilo.

Sorry, Danilo. Tell me more about the—the cause you would like to defend.

Look. It's not that there aren't atrocities probably going on. On all sides. But the Croats started all that in the Second World War. Hell, the Ustaše in league with Hitler perfected ethnic cleansing. You should look up Jasenovac concentration camp, do a little historical searching into that dungeon of horrors, take a look at the *Srbosjek*, the 'Serb cutters,' knives used to kill our people quickly and efficiently by the hundreds and thousands, in that camp and others. They used to organize killing competitions to see who could slaughter the most. And then read how Tito made Serbia into the nightmare that was the former Yugoslavia. All the Serbs have ever wanted is their own land back.

Borders get redrawn all the time, especially after a war.

Exactly. It will take a war to restore what is rightfully ours.

Ours.

The Serbs.

Aren't you a Canadian, Danilo?

Yes. And a Serb.

Weren't you born here?

No. I was born in Bunić. I came over as an infant.

Dan feels his fingers curling into a fist as the man before him checks the file to re-read notes from some previous session. The point of the matter, he can see this Anglo pseudo-doctor will never understand, is that when one has Serb blood, one is always a Serb. His mother made that clear to him, whether he was born on this or the old country's soil: *wherever Serbs live and bury their dead should be part of Serbia.* Her village Orthodox priest had pounded that into her brain, and she in turn had pounded it—sometimes literally—into his. So now when Bora and Stanko meet him in the mall to tell stories of injustices that still persist back home, he is filled with an impotent rage. All he would like, besides finding his daughter and cutting her out of his life once and for all as he plans to do with his will, is to be of some service in Republika Srpska and in the regaining of former Serbian lands. To be at the side of other brave lads trying to do the same. He points a finger at the doctor.

You don't understand ... when you fight together—there's a kind of kinship. You would die for each other.

Yes. Many do.

And in the heat of the battle, you take all kinds of risks. Because you are brothers. Because you are kin.

Do you miss your brother, Danilo?

What? What kind of stupid-ass question is that? I—I—of course, I miss him, but he died years ago.

From blood poisoning, wasn't it?

Yes.

Is your blood poisoned, Danilo?

What are you getting at?

Okay, let's take a step back. I don't mean to be confrontational. Maybe I can come back to the question a little later. Tell me a little of the difference between Yugoslavia and the current Balkan states.

Nation. Serbia is a nation and has been for centuries.

Sorry. Nation. Tell me the difference between Serbia and

SFR Yugoslavia.

Tito ruled with an iron fist under a guise of 'brotherhood and unity.' He lived like a czar and screwed his way through dozens of women from Belgrade to Moscow. He didn't give the Serbs what we deserved: our own king, the return of Kosovo. Instead, he split the country into six and made for more bad blood—poison you called it—between us all. It was a recipe for disaster. And that's what's happened. Anyone could see it coming. Even my mother: she spat whenever anyone spoke his name.

When I got back from the war, she was ill, so she would look at *Life* magazine—my sister Bosilka got her a subscription to help Majka pass the time. There was Tito's arrogant Croat face, on the cover in 1949, staring right at her. Because she was illiterate, she couldn't read the article or write to the editor, but she took her pen, the one she used to sign her X on the rent cheques, and she drew horns on the bastard. Later, I took the cover out to an open field for BB rifle practice with my young cousin Arsa, and we shot out both of Tito's eyes. After that my mother made Bosilka cancel the subscription to *Life*.

So your mother hated Tito. What did your father think of him?

He was dead by the time Tito came to power.

Yes, of course. Sorry. Do you think your father would have hated him as your mother did?

My father was a Serb. Serbs had good reason to hate that dictator.

Your father was an educated man who spoke four languages, yes?

Five, counting English.

Was he a vengeful man?

Danilo thrummed his fingers impatiently. Why was everything in these sessions about his father and mother? How was any of this helping his own marriage? Fifteen minutes to go. He fought to keep his cool.

No. All of my sisters agree Tata was a patient man. Not an aggressive bone in his body.

And that bothered you.

It sure as hell bothered my mother. She thought he was spineless.

What did you think, Dan?

I thought—I used to think he was weak. But now, I don't know ...

Go on.

I—I think it was just his nature. He was a kind man. Someone the neighbours called on for a favour. Kids loved him. My mother was the angry one, the one who held a grudge. My dad—he liked being Serbian and kept the holidays and the saint days, but he—he also liked being Canadian. Hell, they came here to get away from ...

From what?

I don't know exactly. My father wasn't a religious man, despite observing the saints' days. He was tolerant. They left Bunić and Lika for a better life, one that wasn't hardscrabble and subsistence farming in some god-forsaken mountain village. A life far away from the Orthodox church.

Dan watched the therapist scribble.

Did I tell you that my father was supposed to be a priest? But he didn't pursue it. He turned away from the church, though I don't know why. I can only guess that he didn't go in for all the hocus pocus and swinging of the incense censer and ...

And?

Hate-mongering that seemed to bubble up through the orthodoxy.

But you'd go back, Dan? Even knowing this about your father and the Orthodox church's complicity in the whole affair in Serbia?

Yes. I would. Because I am Serbian. And for me, it's about that. Not the church. Like Prince Lazar said, 'It is better to die in battle than to live in shame.'

The famous Prince Lazar who died on the Field of the Blackbirds in Kosovo, when was it?

Dan waited as the man checked his notes.

Right. 1389.

You *have* been reading.

I'm a history buff, actually. And I've been boning up on Balkan history in light of your interest in Yugo—in Serbia.

So you know how important Kosovo is to the Serbs and our national identity and why we want it back.

I have some inkling. But 1389 was a long time ago.

We Serbs have long memories.

Apparently. And you would join the bloodletting?

If I was able.

The hate-mongering your father seemed anxious to escape so that he came to Canada to give his family—you, his son—another life, a better chance? To keep you safely away from all of that? Still, you'd return?

Tata would understand.

Would he want you to take up arms for this cause? Again? After all you lived through in six years of WWII? Risk your life once more? Kill others once more—maybe some of them even Serbs? Women? Children? Old people?

War is ... never fair to the innocent, common people.

No. It certainly isn't.

There was a long silence. Dan considered telling the shrink about his recurring flashbacks. But then he swallowed.

Or is vengeance the wish of your mother, Danilo?

Call me Dan.

Okay. Dan. What do *you* really want?

I want this fucking session to be over.

It is. You're free to leave. To be a Chetnik or a Canadian. To be a good husband. A loving father. Or a tyrant. The choice is yours, Dan. See you next week.

6

They sit holding hands over *Turk kahvesi* amidst the lively conversation, the piped-in old music on the sidewalk tables of Fazil Bey *kahvehan* in Kadiköy. Alban is smoking a noxious Turkish cigarette, as are most of the other patrons; Mirjam is the exception. Instead, she is licking the delicate powdered sugar of the *lokum* from the fingers of her left hand, delighting in the sweetness and the lovely pistachio nugget at the centre of the jellied candy.

Alban returns to his paper, and she to her surroundings. She loves this city and all of its colourful difficulties: Istanbul with its chaotic, beautiful mess of cultures, people, ideologies, of East meets West, modern and ancient, of Muslim, Christian and Jew, Byzantine and Ottoman. She feels enlivened by the music and the pulsing of the place even with the recent undercurrent threat of violence from rebel Kurds.

"Perhaps the Kurds—and the Serbs—learned their lessons from the Turks. All those centuries of brutal Ottoman occupation," Alban muses over his empty coffee cup. He holds up the article by *Agence France-Presse* with its harrowing account of the recent August PKK bombings near Taksim Square. So near their apartment, and yet, mercifully, they'd been absent for the blast, the shock and the bloodshed. Yet the cause made sense—over decades Kurds had been displaced and disappeared by the Turkish government. Why was the solution of the mighty always and finally to abuse, to extinguish?

Mirjam shrugged. "I guess it wasn't always brutal. The Ottomans were by many accounts tolerant of those they conquered."

"Yes, but wearing a yoke? When does that lead to peace?"

She and Alban have taken a small furnished flat in Beyoğlu, several streets off lively İstiklal. He has been invited to play in two paying concerts, and she will sing in the September finals of the Leyla Gencer vocal competition. So far, summer on the Bosphorus has been glorious, and they have spent wonderful weekends with friends at a summer home on Büyükada. The weather continues to be as hot as a Turkish temper.

They are running out of money.

But there is enough this week for coffee and cigarettes, some food and to pay for the flat.

Next week? Alban waves it away with his newspaper, like so much smoke from his bad habit.

She has been singing well. Ever since Berlin, Mirjam has been in excellent voice. Frau Littgenstein was as pleased as she ever had appeared and pronounced the young woman's final rehearsal prior to the preliminary audition, *"Gut, sehr gut!"* which Hans assured her was the best praise Mirjam was likely to hear from the tough old bird. The pianist had been permitted to accompany the singer for the preliminary, and he'd played brilliantly. She'd felt that tingle down her spine when she knew command of her voice, her technique, the language and the piece with the accompaniment—when all the components came together after hours, weeks, and years of rigour, determination, and practice. Her interpretation of Rossini's Rosina was determined and wily, her runs cascading and dexterous. The Strauss was pure ardour, as Mirjam-cum-Octavian insisted that he loved and would always love his older mistress. As Carmen, she turned dazzling and sensual, her mezzo so suited to the tantalizing Bizet character, this role she was meant to play ever since finding her grandmother's watch in the cigar box, the one with the beautiful femme fatale she'd longed to emulate on its cover. With the final "prends garde à toi!", she looked out into the darkness of the auditorium where the jury sat whispering together in a small pool of light. Boris Anifantakis, whom she knew from Berlin, and Umberto Finazzi, whom she did not, from Milan, thanked both her and Hans warmly, as the two performers bowed and left the stage. When the letter arrived on June 30th, Mirjam opened it with a gut-level prescience that she'd made the semi-finals.

Alban was ecstatic with excitement. Within days of the news, he'd sublet the Berlin apartment and together they'd packed up their few personal effects. He'd made contact with a university conservatory in Istanbul where he was to teach cello to Efe Baltacıgil, a teenaged wunderkind. Alban's support of her opportunity was so ardent, Mirjam thought she might burst from gratitude and love. He'd helped with visas and purchased the plane tickets from his meagre savings. Through a Turkish friend at the Hochschule, Alban located a potential English teaching position at Ata Koleji for Mirjam, one that she was eager to begin in early September, if all went well. Being with this man brought her a mixture of terror and elation. She was aware of the difference in age between them and worried that he would leave her. He laughed away her fears. Why would he leave when they had so much in common as a couple, so much music to make, so much love?

This filled her with momentary joy—no man had ever said such things to her, vowed such devotion. But in too many dark sleepless hours, while Alban slept twitching in dream beside her, Mirjam would be frozen in certainty and dread that he would tire of her. Maybe not this year, nor the next, but in ten? Fifteen? What then? Who would she be? How would she mark the time without Alban and his beautiful cello?

"Would you like another, my darling mezzo?" Alban's grin is open and reassuring. He gives her shoulder a squeeze and goes in search of the *tuvalet* and the waiter.

While he is away, Mirjam watches a crow crack a nut on the sidewalk and allows her ears to tune to the scale of the music playing over the *kahvehan's* speakers. She can recognize the *bağlama*, noticing how similar it sounds to a Serbian *tamburica* or a Greek *bouzouki*. She hears similar nuances between the nasal woodwind *ney* and the Croatian *sopila* or the Serb *zurna*, and the Turkish *kemençe* players reminds her of the Serbian *guslars* who are masters of the *gusle*, the strange-sounding violin-like instrument. Though foreign to her Western-tuned sense of scales, these musical pieces all seem so familiar and so interconnected. But then, of course, hundreds of years of Ottoman influence spread virally over the Balkans and brought with it foods, songs, dances, and so many cultural precepts to her forebears. Did the Ottomans bring a bloodthirst, too, she wonders, thinking of her father, then of the current ugliness a mere ten hours away by car. Above the music, she can hear the strains of the call to prayer from the nearby mosque. The crow, having captured the prize at the heart of the walnut, flies off. It is Friday, the holy day, and *öğle*. She feels her stomach rumbling for something more than coffee and sweets.

Alban returns and Mirjam convinces him to cancel their second cups and leave for the nearest *kafeterya*, an inexpensive little place in the neighbourhood where one can buy *çorba* with good fresh bread, *köfte* and a green pepper and tomato salad—all so similar to the comfort foods of her own family. Her mouth waters as they enter and find a seat in the crowded room full of noisy, smoking men, those who are not among the faithful at the mosque.

They are shortly joined by musician friends, two men and a woman, from Mimar Sinan University. The woman is a Turkish Jew, and the men are from Serbia and Bosnia. Assembled, they make a multi-cultural breaking of bread rather than skulls, thinks Mirjam.

She has been reading the English newspapers, especially the *Guardian* and *The Independent*, which report in alarming detail the atrocities going on in her—no, her father's—no her grandmother's—old country. Many fingers point to the Serbs as the aggressors. A few to the Croats and the Bosniaks.

Alban and she and these and other friends have often discussed the complexities deep into many nights of wine and *rakı*.

So many disparate threads in the unravelling tapestry of the Former Republic of Yugoslavia. A perplexing number of players:

Tudjman, Milošević, Karadžić, Ratko and so many acronyms for different guerrilla factions and invading or defensive armies. Victims, however, are mainly Bosnian Muslims or Bosniaks, so the awful reports go. She's learned that the hideous euphemism *ethnic cleansing* was first mentioned in Western media in 1992, but that its precursors were used by various fascist regimes including the Ustaše, Nazis, and Soviets. The razing of villages and cleansing of undesirables, she's read, have been part of the warring Balkan strategies—and apparently all of the area's various ethnic tribes—since the inaugural wielding of a club against another.

First-person accounts of systematic rape of girls and women, but also boys and men, especially sicken Mirjam. Images of mass graves and bodies frozen ghastly in death she cannot erase from her mind. How to grasp that she is happily sitting with these multinational friends while atrocities and men playing gods are but a few horrifically disputed borders away?

Particularly, the idea that so much of what is happening *over there* radiated from this very city where she sings and plays and makes love, makes her shudder.

A confluence of so many religions and ethnicities is Istanbul. She has learned of its many names, but Constantinople is the one that links the city to Serbia. In fact, the symbolic head of the Orthodox Church, Bartholomew I, the Ecumenical Patriarch of Constantinople, still resides in this city, providing direction to his Orthodox flock throughout the world, including Serbia. Somehow religion—Catholic, Orthodox and Islam—and power-mongering empires—Ottoman Turks and Austrian-Habsburgs—are all wrapped up in the virulent nationalism that has a stranglehold on the former states of Yugoslavia. It's the stuff of great plays and great tragic operas. But in the final act before the new millennium, it's not the fat lady who dies.

Mirjam has covered her auburn hair to visit the beautiful Blue Mosque with its glorious tiles in geometric perfection, its stunning dome and cupolas, sunlight from the glass windows lighting up the ceramics, deepening the blue hues. The winking of the lanterns, the beautiful calligraphy with verses from the Quran, the intricate patterned prayer rugs spread across the floor—all of it inspired within her a kind of peace.

Similarly, she's admired the Aya Sofya, Byzantine jewel and once seat of the Orthodox church, Christendom's first great cathedral and a feat of architectural genius, now neither church nor mosque but a museum. Though the reddish outer walls seemed to her representative of how much blood had been spilled because of this basilica and what Sophia symbolized to both Christian and Turk, once within those frescoed walls, Mirjam, an avowed atheist, almost dared to believe that God was present. A hush of wonder filled her. She trod the worn stones, imagining whose famous feet had preceded her own. Mirjam wished she could sing aloud under the beautiful sunlit dome, but the stern-faced, moustachioed security guard made her think better of the idea. Especially charmed by the cathedral cats that slinked between her and Alban's legs, she unofficially appointed the felines "the Aya Sofya *kediler*."

Despite the peace floating like motes within Sultan Ahmet and Aya Sofya, Mirjam knew the Ottoman Turks could be paradoxically cruel conquerors and hard-fisted masters, even as they tolerated the presence of other faiths and permitted some autonomy within communities. Miniatures and fabled folktales told of the cutthroat and capricious nature of the sultans and their minions who wielded scimitar and knife and bowstring and specialized in the gruesome tactics of torture and execution, with a special penchant for beheadings. Did such examples spread plague-like across the Balkans?

The Turks who wrested this city from the Christians in 1453 and renamed it Istanbul were the successors of those who'd marched in 1389 to the fields of Kosovo and soundly trounced the Serbs and Prince Lazar featured in the folksongs her father so loved. This history, she now knew, had fanned the ire of her father her life long. It seemed a stupid grudge to hold for so many centuries. But then seemingly with a single speech on that hallowed ground, now home to so many Bosnian Muslims and a rabid Serb minority, Milošević fanned the embers that had smoldered under Tito for forty years into the wildfire raging across the Balkans today. Did something reside in Serbian DNA that brought on a voracious appetite for long-lived vengeance and violence?

"I'm a pacifist," Andrej insists, his gold tooth glinting, "so it's not in *my* Serbian DNA, although my cousin Borys looks and acts like a Chetnik—so who knows?" When he's not studying the violin, or busking on the Istanbul streets to make a few liras, Andrej is a member of an underground grassroots organization that, among its many efforts, supports the work of the local woman's shelter, recognizes the Armenian genocide, and from afar, denounces the atrocities happening in his home country.

"My mother is Muslim and Croatian and my father a Serb, and so far neither has killed the other, though back at our house in Sarajevo they've had some ear-splitting arguments," Mustafa, a classical guitarist, chuckles. His entire family fled and found refuge from the siege of his city with a distant relative in Üsküdar. Then he sobers, "It's an awful business—neighbour turning against neighbour, intermarried families sometimes having to choose which side they belong to: Serb or Muslim or Croat. I—I am Bosnian." And he draws his hand through his blond hair as if to emphasize the point.

Ester touches his arm. Her tenderness is not surprising. She is smitten with handsome and clean-shaven Mustafa, who looks more German than Slavic. "Of course, what a union ours would be, Mustafa," she says in perfect TOEFL English. "Think what the Chetniks would make of a mixture of Jew, Croat, Serb, and Muslim. It beggars belief."

And the five friends chuckle drily.

Later that evening they perform together for tourists on lively İstiklal near the belit Galata Tower. Well-heeled foreigners gather at the Galata Güney Restaurant to drink pints of Guinness, and the more they imbibe, the freer they are with their liras and American dollars. The group—with Mirjam as singer, Alban on cello, Andrej on violin, Mustafa on guitar, and Ester on darbuka—performs familiar pop songs and makes nearly three hundred American dollars, which they share five ways. Over glasses of Efes at the much cheaper bar in an alley off İstiklal, they celebrate their earnings and their time in this ancient city, while leagues away, 8,000 men and boys are gunned down and buried in mass graves.

7

Sudbina and the harpist travelled the second morning without mishap along the well-worn cart tracks of the forest. By midday, the intrepid travellers stopped to water their horses at the nearby stream. Her back to the minstrel, Sudbina bent to fill their water flasks. Smiling, she turned to make some quip to her companion, and the colour drained from her face. Her harpist had been seized by a handful of men dressed in colourful garb and peaked helmets. One had his knife to the musician's throat.

Spahija! The mounted cavalry corps, loyal to the sultan, fief holders her father so hated and skirmished with almost constantly over all the years of her life. Their horses must be nearby, but clearly these men had crept up by stealth and on foot to seize the hapless two.

Another stepped from behind a thick mass of bushes along the shoreline. He was clearly the leader. Though not a tall man, he was impressive in gleaming chain mail. Within several strides, he was before the despoina, who rose steadily to her feet and met his hard gaze.

"Fine beasts," hissed one of the other *spahija* as he seized the reins of the two horses, both nervous and sensing something amiss with these newcomers.

"Here is another," smirked his superior, spittle forming at the corners of his mouth. "I am Mahmud Pasha Anđelović, and I think you"—he dared to touch the despoina's hair with a thick finger— "are one of my loyal serfs."

"She is no serf, *kučkin sin*!" the minstrel cursed and was met with a harsh cuff to his face.

"I am the daughter of the despot."

"Interesting. And now you will be my concubine."

"He will pay a large ransom if you return his favourite," the harpist blurted.

"Will he? Then I shall be doubly rewarded: the pleasure of this sweet flesh and the pleasure of sweet silver."

He spoke sharply in Turkish to the others, who tied the hands of the harpist and those of the despoina and forced them to remount their horses. Reins in firm fists, the *spahija* and their pasha travelled on foot several hundred metres to where their own horses and additional members of the corps waited, dismounted and lazing in the sunshine. Greedily, a few rifled through the packs of the captives like hungry curs, fighting over and devouring the food they found. For jest, they tossed the harp between them and plucked its strings tunelessly, until bored, they stuffed it carelessly back into the minstrel's pack. One unstopped the cork of Baba Roga's tincture, grimaced at the smell and dropped it back into the satchel on the despoina's horse. At the raucous command of their leader, the party mounted and, in a matter of moments, was cantering northward towards Vojvodina. Hands secured to the horn of her saddle, Sudbina looked back at the harpist, tethered similarly to his horse. His eyes seemed shadowed with worry.

Sudbina counted five days and nights. She and the harpist were not ill-treated, but they were travel weary and saddle sore. Food and water were offered freely. The despoina slept alone in a small tent each evening, the harpist in another, some distance from her. No one spoke to them and the pasha paid them little heed, except to leer occasionally at his female prisoner, and the pair were permitted no contact with each other. Most of what passed between them were glances, Sudbina hoped, of reassurance. She wanted her love to know that she fared well enough.

The dusk sky was a bruise on the sixth day when they approached a great half crescent of tents silhouetted against the dwindling light. A semi-circle of fires burned before these tents, tended by men roasting spitted beasts. Harpist and Sudbina were heaved from their horses, then separated, she to a large tent of lurid colours and he to a smaller. Serving women were given orders to attend the beautiful captive. After providing her a supper of lamb and lentils, they cleaned the grime from Sudbina's face and hands and helped her into fresh garments and bedclothes. Exhausted, she slept solidly until she awoke to a sunlit morn on the seventh day of her captivity.

Summoned to an afternoon audience before the pasha in the grand tent that dwarfed all the others of the encampment, Sudbina weighed her options. For now, compliance seemed the necessary and only option. She acquiesced and the two waiting guards accompanied her through the grounds.

"Where is the harpist?" Sudbina tried to disguise the quaver in her voice, but neither man knew her tongue or, if they did, deigned not to answer.

The flaps to the pasha's tent were thrown open and she entered.

Walls and ceiling richly lined with intricate patterned blue-gold silks, thick cinnabar carpets covering the ground, at the rear of the tent were a desk and lectern on which sat an open Quran. In the fore, Mahmud Pasha squatted on an embroidered sofa, sipping chai from a small glass cup, his deputies and subordinates nearby. One held a calligraphy pen and paper in hand, ready to record the pasha's every word.

"I trust that you are refreshed, Despoina."

A servant bade her sit atop a tooled-leather ottoman and poured her a cup of the tea, dropping a cube of sugar into it. Mahmud selected a date from a copper plate beside him.

"I am."

"We know whose daughter you are, and"— he admired the curve of her new garments for an uncomfortable pause—"what a prize we have captured."

"My father is a mighty—"

"Your father has been at war with the Ottoman Empire. He has not been a loyal vassal of the sultan."

"My father will never bow to the sultan's yoke!"

"Indeed, he has proven a menace to our rule and has put to sword many an Ottoman Turk."

"No more than have fallen at your hands, I'm sure."

The servant moved to refill their cups, but the pasha waved him away. "I'm told your name is Sudbina."

"I am she."

"Despoina Sudbina. Know you this: I have sent a dispatch to your father, the despot. Your ransom has been set at a thousand pieces of silver. He will pay, insha'Allah, or your life will be the forfeit."

"He will answer you with fury."

"If so, we will meet that fury with the mighty sword of Allah."

Sudbina lifted her chin defiantly. "Where is my companion, the harpist?"

"Who? Kemal?" The pasha cracked a crooked smile, then continued mildly.

"Don't look so puzzled. Why, he has been right here all along, listening to us."

From behind a silk hanging, the harpist appeared, sumptuously dressed as an imperial Turk. He stepped forward. He did not or could not meet the despoina's eyes.

"Allow me to present to you, Despoina, daughter of the Despot, the long-lost son of our wondrous Sultan Qayser-I-Rûm, Şehzade Sultan Mustafa whom we affectionately call Kemal. Stolen by your father in a raid of an Ottoman company. We thought him dead to us near twenty years. We raised a fine tombstone in his honour. Songs were sung. His poor mother nearly died of grief. But he lives, praise be to Allah. The sultan ... let us say, he will be overjoyed to have his son returned to him."

"I—I—"

"You are surprised, yes? As were we. But he bears the birthmark in the shape of a harp on his forearm. You have perhaps seen it?"

Sudbina searched the harpist's immobile face. How could this man be the son of her enemy, her father's enemy? How had she not known? Why had he not told her? A rush of questions tortured her mind. She had given herself to this man, this imposter, and thought she'd known him, but here he was, a complete stranger before her.

"I think, Pasha, that the despoina grows faint," the harpist who was Kemal, the sultan's son, spoke carefully. "Let us not lose the treasure before the ransom is delivered. Let us speak again when she has recovered from her shock."

"As you say, Şehzade Sultan Mustafa. Your wish is my command. Guards! Help the woman back to her tent. Make sure the attendants see to her needs."

Hoisting her from the ottoman, the two wiry men seized Sudbina by the arms and escorted her from the pasha's tent.

Indeed, she did feel queasy: truly from shock, but more from anger. Her love had betrayed her. A rage turned molten in her veins. How had she allowed this? She, the daughter of the despot? Had the harpist led her into this trap all along? Was he the tunesmith of this ugly song?

She spat in the dust. The guards handed her over to the servant women and eunuchs. Confined to the tent for the remainder of the afternoon, Sudbina refused food and drink, fuming about her own part in exchanging one prison for another. At dusk, the tent flap opened and the harpist entered. In less than fluent Turkish, he bade the women and eunuchs, slaves themselves, to leave. Used to the ways of the sultan's court, though his son was new to them, they demurred to his wishes. The despoina turned her back to him, wishing she had a knife secreted on her person so that she could slit his treacherous throat. Or perhaps her bow and a trusty arrow ...

"Sudbina, I thought to tell you a thousand and one times. I could not while I was in your father's court. I dared not."

"You are a Turk."

"I am."

"You lied to me—all these years."

"I kept the truth close. I am not proud of this."

"You could have told me. You had many a chance. We have been ... together. I trusted you."

"And I hope to win again your trust. The words I spoke, the songs I sang—these are all true, my lady. About this and how I feel for you, I told no lies."

"I cannot think ..."

"Despoina. Please sit and listen." He motioned to the sofa where he sat. Hesitantly, she joined him but kept a distance. The harpist sighed. "What I say will be hard to hear but say it I must. I—I— was abducted by your father because my father abducted your father's only son and heir."

"Liar!"

"Search your heart, Sudbina. You know your father longed for a son. In truth he had a son and lost a son through the blood tax of *devşirme*—the taking of Christian boys for service in the Ottoman Empire—a young boy who is now a man and very likely a Janissary in my father, the sultan's, court. No doubt he has risen in the ranks and has considerable power and prestige.

"As revenge, your father had me stolen away from my mother's apartments in Carigrad. A slave was tempted and convinced. Much silver was exchanged. I was brought to and reared in your father's court."

"You told me you were a minstrel who travelled far and wide to perform. A minstrel my father invited as paid musician into his court!"

"Could I tell you the truth? That he ripped me from my home and secreted me away until he could find a use for me? Why would I tell you this? Turn you against your father and possibly against me?"

"So you presumed a bagatelle of lies would serve you better?"

"I—"

"And the charming tale about your grandmother? Your uncle who taught you how to craft a harp? More fancies to beguile me?"

"No, no! My earliest memories are of my grandmother harping, singing. Despoina, I only sought to..."

"Deceive."

"I learned to craft instruments in your father's court, from Miroslav, the old minstrel in his employ—he taught me. He took a shine to me. Who knows why? I was a young boy, and he'd also lost his son and wife to plague. The attention and the kindness he offered this stolen child made me an apt student. And he recommended me to your father: I was no threat to the court. Because of Miroslav, I was accepted, taught to ride and hunt, and eventually, when my teacher grew too frail and old, I replaced him as court minstrel."

"I have no recollection of this Miroslav."

"Why would you? He died when you were still with your wet nurse."

She studied his finery. He looked every bit the infidel. "How can I ever again trust you, Harpist? Kemal? Son of a sultan? Whatsoever imposter you are?"

A silence fell between them. Sudbina could feel her pulse in her ringing ears. The harpist looked at his hands.

"I swear by these hands and my music, I intended you no harm, Despoina. I feel … Well, in time I hope to show and convince you again of what I feel. In the meantime, I hope to bring you, at least, to the brother you never knew."

"A Janissary is a slave."

"As am I. As *was* I …"—the harpist bowed his head— "until you chose me to accompany you on this journey. You freed me, dear lady."

"I have freed my father's enemy."

"When have I been enemy?"

"Now! Now that you are free, you will return to your father and cut the throats of my people as we sleep. It is the way of the Turk."

"It is not my way, and you know this well."

"How can you not? Even if you choose, your father will never grant leniency. He will put to sword my father, my family …"

"I will never allow it, Despoina." He reached for her hand, but she pulled sharply away. "Upon my return to Yeni Saray, I will confer with my father. Yours will be granted clemency in this matter, or …"

"Or what?"

"Or I shall leave Carigrad, never to return to my father's court, this time of my own volition."

"And what will become of me? The ransom? My father's ire? How will you avert a war?"

"Therein you play a necessary part, my lady. If you will accompany me, we will to the Sublime Porte ... to Constantinople, and our music will convince my father the Sultan of the wisdom of my plan."

8

Luba opens Mirjam's letter and the clippings about her triumph at the Leyla Gencer singing competition in Istanbul. Istanbul is hard for her mother tongue to pronounce. Her family called it Carigrad. Miss Minster in the one-room school in Rosedale called it Constantinople. It is harder still to believe that her Western-raised daughter could be in such a foreign, exotic place.

Mirjam's phone call had jarred her awake. Luba dreads late-night calls that always seem to bear bad news—her sister's illness, the passing of her father. But this is often the hour Mirjam chooses, because of the time difference. And so, when an elated daughter called very late in the Canadian night, bubbling over with excitement and too much champagne, Luba tried to match her exuberance.

"Ma! I won!"

"Oh, my darling! I'm so proud of—so excited for you!"

But that was a month ago now. It has since taken this long for Mirjam to write.

Carefully, Luba spreads open the newsprint and sees a dazzling Mirjam engulfed in a bouquet of roses, beaming confidently at the viewer.

> *Canadian Mirjam Pope is a singer with vast potential and a resumé that needs only a welcome boost from the opera establishment. The Leyla Gencer First Prize honour will bring her deserved recognition within the opera world. With a kaleidoscopic voice of voluptuous richness and a seamless wide range, a convergence of dramatic sincerity and vocal brilliance, the ability to interpret complex characters through deft control, tonal lustre and musical sophistication, Ms. Pope is clearly a star on the rise. Accordingly, she was awarded three months of study at the Accademia Teatro alla Scala, in addition to her prize money.*

The audacity of her daughter's life takes Luba's breath away. Once again, Mirjam has invited her to Istanbul and now in the new year to Milan, but Luba is unsure if she can take the time off from her work at the bird sanctuary for travel to either city. Is she afraid of something? No, she resolves, making a promise to herself to ask for a leave without pay. Surely, her supervisor will grant her this request. But the thought will slip her mind when she returns to work on Monday.

Luba tucks all of the papers into a shoebox that she locks away safely from Dan in her overnight bag. He has not uttered Mirjam's name aloud in the house since she left, claims he has no daughter to relatives who telephone, probably says worse about his child to his *parbuk*-ing friends at the mall.

Mirjam never asks about her father in either letter or phone conversation.

Luba bites her tongue around the both of them.

Last week a mail order do-it-yourself Last Will and Testament package arrived in the post. Luba believes that Dan is hard at work on this document, behind her back, in a move to disown their daughter. It is a waste of effort. She suspects she will outlive him and because everything is jointly in their names, there's nothing he can withhold from Mirjam as long as Luba lives. As long as she lives.

They've both been coughing, but that's likely the asthma doctors say is an epidemic in Alberta. Both are reformed smokers, but Dan surrendered a pack-and-a-half-a-day habit, while Luba was much more casually addicted. She's noticed that their steps have slowed these past years and that Dan's packing on more weight, largely as his appetite has replaced his nicotine cravings. Yes, health-wise, there's every likelihood he'll beat her to death. If he doesn't beat her to death.

When she'd thrown out the package with the will, thinking it junk mail, Dan leapt to fury. She'd confronted him about his idiotic plan, and he'd taken a swing at her. This she dodged neatly, evading him and any contact. The man was getting old, losing his grip and certainly his aim.

In sudden realization, Dan dropped his hands and his guard, beginning to weep and apologize profusely, claiming he'd never intended to hit her.

"But you swore you had your temper under control, Dan!"

"I do, Luba. I do. I— I'll be sure to discuss this with the headshrink. This week. I promise. I—"

"You do that."

"I'm sorry."

"Those words are a bit hollow after all these years, Dan."
"I swear I'll ..."
"I'm not Mirjam."
"Of course not ..."
"Nor all the people who've let you down."
"I know that."
"We made a deal. Are you in or out?"
"I'm in, Lu. All the way in."
"Then keep your fists in your pockets. Or go for a damn walk."
"You're right. I will."

Later when she took out the recycling bin to the alley, she discovered that the will package and its contents had been retrieved, no doubt secreted away. Luba didn't care to investigate or to see Dan's venom, spilled ink across the pages.

She pads through the hall and finds that Dan has fallen asleep in his recliner in front of the television. Managing to find the off button on the annoyingly complicated channel changer, she dismisses the shouting late-night trash-TV to silence and oblivion. Dan snores on. She leaves him there and turns off the remaining lights.

Her bedsheets are cool and lonely. Whom or what does she miss exactly? Mirjam, of course. But missing one's child is a natural progression of life, Lu reasons. And Mirjam hasn't shared her bed since her little girl dove into her mother's covers seeking comfort from night terrors. And Lu had never slept well those nights; Mirjam was such a squirmer.

With a start that sends a tremor along her back, Luba knows absolutely that she misses being touched. The feather lightness of fingers against skin, the whisper of breath at the nape. An arm draped across her waist. A gentle hand to her cheek or her hair. Did Dan ever give these things, these small but important gestures? She thinks not, yet she misses them as profoundly as she misses her youth when she sometimes catches her sixty-nine-year-old self reflected in a shop window.

Her heart climbs into her throat. There is so much she has missed. Marrying this man, then staying with him, when she could have had touch and warmth at the centre of her life. There could have been more lovemaking, more passion. She might have looked into the eyes of a lover and found lasting connection and real meaning in their coupling. Someone might now be here with her, treasuring her heartbeats. Instead, she has no one. No one but herself and her own hand gently caressing her own soft shoulder. The wonder of this and the sense of touch and loss make her skin burn. In the ten years, maybe twenty, maybe fewer, remaining of her life, is this how it's meant to be? A chorus of sighs from missing? Lu draws the covers of self-pity to her chin and moves her hand tentatively to her inner thigh. It is not enough, not nearly enough, but it will have to do.

"I finally looked it up, after all these weeks. Your name—Luba. It means *someone who has love or is beloved*."

"Ha!" Luba takes a handful of popcorn from the bag Hodi has brought for the birds but mainly has shared with her.

"I think it's a lovely name."

"I've hated it all my life. I wanted an exotic name like Vanda or Raquel."

"Neither of those would suit you."

"I suppose not."

"Your husband must like your name."

"I don't know. He mainly calls me Lu."

She is very conscious of their hands touching in the bag: his, dark and slender, hers, pale with liver spots. Lu feels a redness rising to her cheeks, a warmth that has nothing to do with the unseasonably mild weather. She reaches for the thermos of sweet tea she has brought and pours them each a steaming cup. They sit together overlooking the small marsh and the water birds as they land and take off on this sunny late-autumn day. There is a whispering of secrets in the reeds at the water's edge.

Luba feels as if she has a secret, too. His name is Hodi. He comes every Thursday afternoon on the pretext of photographing birds. Though he does take pictures, often his lens is focused on her. This is both unnerving and flattering. He has shown her some of his shots. She loves his images of the birds, less so of herself. But he insists she is very photogenic. They have become friends. Maybe something more, if Luba allows herself to consider, but Hodi interrupts her thoughts.

"I would like to invite you to the opera, Luba. If you think you wouldn't mind seeing a tragedy ... *And* if your husband wouldn't mind."

Of course, Dan would mind, but Luba pushes him from her racing thoughts. Is Hodi asking her on a date?

"For next Thursday—*Otello.* Verdi. At the university concert hall."

"I— I— don't know much about opera, Hodi. Only a little from my daughter, and only the songs she sings."
"Then you will be pleasantly surprised, I hope."
"Wait until I tell Mirjam I'm going to the opera!"
"Then, yes?"
"Al— alright. Yes. Thank you."
"At 7 p.m. Where shall we meet?"
"In the lobby?"
"In the lobby, it shall be!"

Hodi's eager smile sets her pulse apace. Luba feels giddy as the child she once was, standing above the precipice overlooking Horseshoe Canyon in the Badlands. Dan has never been interested in the opera, even when their daughter began performing arias as part of her training, then later as she assumed professional lead roles. He always went to her shows begrudgingly, claiming he did not like the music or the melodrama, even though he was proud of Mirjam and her dexterous, polished voice. So he does not take much note when Luba informs him she'll be attending *Otello* with a friend. As long as there's a meal in the fridge that he can heat up and eat in front of the TV, Dan is satisfied. She does not tell him her friend is a man and an African. Dan, who himself suffered the arrows of xenophobia, sees no irony in his own intolerance.

That weekend she buys three new outfits and returns two, finally deciding on a black jacket and pants with a white silk blouse. She wanders into Birks to find a pair of silver hoop earrings, which she considers bold and pricey, but succumbs to the purchasing urge. Alejandro at Scissorhands sneaks her in after a cancellation, trims her bob and touches up her roots. At

Arnold Churgin's, she decides on a pair of comfortable Italian pumps that don't make her feel like a doddering granny. When she looks in the mirror, Luba is satisfied and without a hint of buyer's remorse about the $1,200 she has put on her Master-Card. She doesn't feel or look a day over sixty, she thinks, as she steps out into the first snowflakes of the thirtieth of October. Just in time for all the poor little clowns and hobgoblins, she muses.

The opera is thrilling, even though she finds it rather hard to concentrate on Verdi's plot and her barely remembered study of the play with Miss Minster, ironically the last she ever read before she went out to work at fifteen. Lu is embarrassed by the heat she feels sitting next to Hodi, watching an opera about a black warrior— played by a white man made up as a Moor— who marries then murders his Venetian, very pale wife. Hodi smiles over at Luba every once in a while, which brings more colour to her face. At intermission he buys her a glass of wine, and he is eager for her reactions to the first acts. Lu confesses that she is impressed with the three leads and wonders if her daughter will ever sing the part of Desdemona. She corrects herself, thinking aloud that the role might be a vocal mismatch for Mirjam.

"Ah, so she is a mezzo soprano."

"Yes! That's what she's called." Luba is much more at ease talking about her child than about herself, her own impressions.

"I would like to hear her sing someday." Hodi drains his glass and waits for Lu to drain hers. He returns them both to the bar and takes her arm to guide her back into the theatre.

"If she returns to sing here, I'll invite you. But she is away in

Turkey and then Milan."

"Such an accomplished daughter!"

"No more than your children."

"Yes, we are equally blessed, aren't we?" As the theatre house lights dim, Luba can still see Hodi's teeth gleam in the near darkness.

One of Lu's few Calgary acquaintances stops them in the lobby after the opera: Cerise, a woman who chairs the Neighbourhood Watch for the Inglewood neighbourhood. After introductions, the woman can obviously not contain herself.

"Where's Dan tonight?" She glances at Hodi.

"Watching the tube, I'm guessing." Luba works hard at keeping her tone mild. "Did you enjoy *Otello*?"

"Why, yes! And you, Luba? I never knew you enjoyed opera."

"We all have our surprises, don't we?" And she pulls Hodi away, knowing that this encounter will no doubt be the topic of conversation—after soccer, dance, and the passels of children that need discussing—at the next Neighbourhood Watch meet and greet. Luba silently makes a pledge not to attend.

# 9

Ata Koleji is the Turkish version of bedlam.

The school itself is a disaster, a filthy, wretched little building with neither working flush toilets nor toilet seats, hand towels nor toilet paper, hot tap water nor soap for students or haggard and overwrought staff. An unscrupulous *palas lisesi* for the rich and lazy, the private school purportedly serves the nouveau riche, but in reality, caters to the pampered sons and daughters of the Turkish mafia. The owners charge a hefty school tuition fee, and for this the students receive a substandard education in a draughty, ill-equipped building, with the promise of a diploma no matter how poorly they perform. Mirjam tries to teach the rude and ungrateful *çocuklar* English, augmenting her lessons with music appreciation. But the teenagers are willful and disobedient, calling her disgusting expletives in Turkish behind her back, plotting means to upset her, breaking into soccer rally songs when she tries to share music, whether Turkish or Western.

As Mirjam balances over one of the toilets missing a seat, or worse, a squat toilet with a cold-water bidet for clean-up, she considers the similarities between these descendants of the Ottomans and those of their Serbian vassals. She'd visited the sultan's toilets in an exhibition in Bodrum on a weekend jaunt: Ata's, though less ornate, are not dissimilar. She's been assured that such toilets are the norm throughout the Balkans, especially in rural areas. So is the Janus-faced character of this city likewise mirrored in cities in the former Yugoslavia? Turks, like her own relatives, are such impeccable hosts, quick to graciously offer food and drink, eager to sing, eager to dance. But she's also witnessed sick violence in the streets of Istanbul, has learned about ugliness harbored and directed against Armenians, Kurds, and gypsies that reminds her of the ethnic violence that fogs the thoughts and hearts of Serbs and Croats. Had the Ottomans taught their lessons well to the peoples they'd conquered and subjected to five hundred years of rule? Where did violence begin but with the father, whether sultan or family patriarch? Who could lead better than by example?

And women? Whether covered by traditional Serbian or Croatian *marama za glavu* or Bosnian Muslim *hidžab* or Turkish *başörtüsü*, what influence in this part of the world do women really have? It seems that everywhere women raise sons to fight and die in ethnic skirmishes. Though she'd read of women who fought alongside husbands and sons with nationalistic fervour, more often reports come out of small towns and districts like Grabavica that women weep for their disappeared children, fathers, and spouses or for the systematic rape that is a deliberate military tactic of Milošević and his war cronies. And what history books tell her about ordinary women in ordinary Ottoman households is scant and abbreviated. Surely, they too grieved the loss of their menfolk who were in the sultan's thrall or who laboured and fought in servitude.

So the school with its daily hallway scuffles, its haughty young men who question female authority and choose violence over diplomacy, seems a microcosm of the worst of Balkan sensibilities.

For their part, the Turkish staff are hostile and understandably aggrieved because the foreign teachers make triple their meagre salaries and are paid in American dollars rather than the rapidly inflating Turkish lira. Her demoralized colleagues offer Mirjam little to no assistance with her unruly pupils, saying nothing when she enters the barren staffroom, drinking their tepid chai while casting her suspicious and sullen glances. Resentment swirls thick as the noxious Turkish cigarette smoke that hazes the room.

The spineless American headmaster—whose name, Mr. Jucker, summons an unfortunate yet appropriate rhyme—is utterly useless in a role considerably beyond his abilities. With no discipline or management policy to deter them, the students run roughshod over him. His favourite job seems to be the rearrangement of office and hallway furniture, followed by a retreat into his office.

Back in her second-world classroom that floods every time it rains, Istanbul deep into its rainy season, she learns that heat does not come on in the building until the fifth period of the day. Centipedes crawl across her desk and mushrooms sprout from the walls. Five times the handle has been ripped from her classroom door, forcing her to summon the foul-smelling and lecherous caretaker who tries to peer down her blouse as he works his master key suggestively in the keyhole. Once classes finally commence, Mirjam is the victim of chalk missiles hurled at her back, frequent verbal abuse, constant inattention, and eruptions of Turkish expletives. Most of her students cheat on exams and exercises. Only a minority of sincere and apt pupils are deeply embarrassed by their peers and apologize for their behaviour. It makes a little difference, but not enough.

Daily, she feels her temper rise and tries to project her voice above the din, fearful of the vocal damage she might be incurring. One afternoon, Mirjam is treated to a synchronized, post-lunch vomit-fest by the entire class of students, and she dashes madly about the room with the garbage can, trying to collect the spew and control her own gag reflex. On another, she chides herself for being drawn into a shouting match with three belligerent boys who offer no respect to any female Westerner, especially one in a position of power, with the end result being that one of the trio aims his arse to fart directly toward her face.

At night she weeps in Alban's arms. He assures her that she does not have to go back to Ata Koleji—study in Milan is mere months away—but she knows his tiny income will never suffice. Jobs are scarce for English-speakers in Istanbul. Without her wages, how else to pay for the water, the gas, the rent, the food they eat?

After leaving Alban in tousled bedclothes each morning, she descends the seven flights, sets her jaw and walks into the sodden day. On her way to and from the school, Mirjam keeps her eyes always downcast to avoid misconstrued invitations, her handbag tucked tightly under her armpit, while anger and bitterness seethe beneath the surface of her foreign skin.

The bus route to *Bešiktaš* bottlenecks, so the tumid bus, sardine-packed with dark men who look like her father and male relatives, creeps snail-wise towards the school. Twice she has been groped and pressed upon by men who seize opportunity in the crowding. More than once in solidarity, a kind woman—sometimes in *başörtüsü,* sometimes not—made room for her on a seat. At such kindness, Mirjam finds herself close to tears in gratitude.

With the Leyla Gencer competition over and ending so well in her favour, she wonders why she is still in this country. Her time as a TOEFL *öğretmeni* at the Ata asylum makes her feel the honeymoon in Istanbul is decidedly over. True, her job at the *lisesi* supplements the few concerts and Alban's small income. But why stay in this country at all? Why not move on to Milan in preparation for the coming year and her studies? Or why not back to Berlin in the meantime? What does a nation full of men like her father have to offer her but the humiliation of always looking down?

It has been almost two years since she's been in Canada. Why not accept Luba's open offer of a return flight to Calgary?

Her father.

Though she has not seen him in the nearly two years since their confrontation, his voice is ever an earworm, ringing with admonishments about her shortcomings and failings. For Dan has made it his objective to point out to Mirjam throughout her life how completely inept and irresponsible she is with money. How stupid about men. Returning home with nothing but another lover will give him opportunity—perhaps not immediately, but eventually and inevitably—to point out her numerous inadequacies. To humiliate her and her chosen career. No doubt to unleash his temper upon her or her mother or Alban.

She shudders at the thought fueled by memory.

No, Mirjam promises herself. She will not be returning home any time soon or ever.

Unsure whether the solid ground under her person exists anymore, Mirjam imagines her feet dangling midair as she hangs on, barely, to a tightrope.

Because it isn't just the students who deflate her spirits: the city in winter seems sinister with shadows, the streets a dripping mess of the homeless, the mad or disabled, with miserable street cats and dogs fighting cacophonously amongst themselves to survive another day or night. Pewter-coloured clouds embrace the pollution coughed out from the many cars and coal-burning heaters in homes. At times the sulphur dioxide count in the atmosphere is dangerously high, but no warnings are ever issued for citizens to remain indoors. Turks believe themselves immune. Turkish government agencies know otherwise, but keep mum, so that the business of progress continues uninterrupted. In a city of fourteen million, casualties of commerce are but collateral damage. Daily, Mirjam wonders if she is breathing in the carcinogenic pathogen that might end her career or her life.

And there are so many other disincentives to remaining in this city. At the bank, as she waits her turn for a teller, Mirjam sits beside quite possibly the filthiest human she has ever seen. She is sure he has shit himself as evidenced by what emanates from his dozing form, leaning towards her. Filth seems to follow filth. On the polluted shore of the Bosphorus, she and Alban have been swindled by gypsy shoeshine boys and flower sellers. Sneaky fingers have twice picked their pockets in the Grand Bazaar. When the couple discover a family of scorpions in their rooftop apartment, Yaşar, the obliging landlord, sends over an exterminator who is set to fumigate with DDT until, in horror and just in time, Alban stops his hand. They agree thereafter to live with the ugly creatures, shaking out shoes every morning, treading carefully in the darkened hallway at night. When Yaşar next sends workers to fix the leaking rooftiles, the men prove inept at the repairs. One, who does not understand the physics of flush toilets, leaves a massive fecal gift in the toilet while the couple is absent from their flat. Alban takes to bleaching the entire washroom, while Mirjam strategically places all of their pots to collect dirty rainwater from the leaks in the ceiling.

They laugh, make music, make love. But still Mirjam's spirits plummet.

She does not like who she is becoming. Her anger makes her cruel—a fact she tries carefully to deny and to control. She'd called a lippy young female student a bitch, something she'd never fathomed she would do. Always, she is steeling herself for a battle, sensing the worst in everyone—whether student, colleague or shopkeep—too quick with a nasty tongue in retort. For each Istanbul denizen is suspect, potentially unscrupulous, eager to rip off the Westerner or assume she is American and, therefore, licentious. On a busy streetcorner, she'd slapped an older man whose umbrella had lightly tapped her thigh. He apologized, holding up his hands to show her the offending article, and she had been ashamed of her reaction. But this encounter did little to reassure her, even as she reminds herself that she knows so many accommodating and hospitable Turks. The turmoil in Mirjam's stomach makes her feel very much her father's daughter.

Repeatedly, their Turkish friends reassure Alban and her that these incidents are but blips on a screen, insisting that Istanbul is a cosmopolitan and enlightened, if crazy, city, but when Mirjam ventures back into the streets after a recuperative weekend, she is nonplussed by the tantrums of the bus drivers, the road rage of motorists who come to fisticuffs over a minor traffic infraction, the cars that bump her in the crosswalk and pay little heed to pedestrian safety. Two weeks into Ramadan, she is pushed by a black Mercedes impatiently trying to exit the alley by the school. Mirjam raises two be-ringed fists and pounds them onto the gleaming surface of the Mercedes' hood. She grinds the rings against the black polish for good measure, then runs to the safety of the guards at the school entrance, evading the swearing Turkish driver too fat from privilege to roust himself quickly enough from his car.

Receding in memory are the halcyon days by the Galata Bridge in late summer and the happy dream of coming to Istanbul. It seems eons since she's sung confidently or with joy, and Alban begins to worry.

Several days before Eid, the school photocopier breaks down. Mirjam dashes across the street to the copy shop to pay out of pocket for copying that day's exercises. When she returns, one of her students, Kerim, a hulking, brutish son of a reputedly prominent Turkish mafia family, has pinned a much smaller boy to the lockers, no doubt to extort something from him. Without a thought, she wrenches Kerim away from the boy and shoves him by the throat into the locker. Though much taller, he is caught off guard and seems at first unable to respond. Mirjam can feel a rumble of fury about to erupt from him but keeps her hand at his throat. The younger student flees down the stairs, leaving Kerim and Mirjam to scream at each other.

"Teacher, Teacher!" Mirjam feels several strong hands pull her abruptly off the teen, whose rage has brought spittle to his mouth. "You mustn't! Kerim ... His family!"

She resists their warnings, instead hissing at Kerim, also now being held back from her by his peers, "You bully! If you ever attack a smaller boy again ..."

"What? What will you do?" Kerim's eyes are a Balkan blaze. The boys tried to drag her away from Kerim, but she resists. "Don't touch me again, Teacher, or you'll regret it!"

"Don't you dare pick on a younger boy ..."

"*Sürtük*, my father will kill you!!!"

At last, the boys push Mirjam into the staffroom where one of the other foreign teachers of the elementary classes makes her sit and drink a cup of sweetened chai. Eventually, she returns to her classroom to find the door broken open and her room upended, files strewn about, some shredded, some muddied by boot prints, desks upturned with their contents strewn. Her ceramic pencil holder lies in shards, pens and pencils snapped in half or simply taken. *Sürtük! Sürtük! Sürtük!* is scrawled in chalk across the blackboard.

A few of the nicer female students peer in through the door.

"Oh, Teacher." And they help her to right the desks, clean the board and sweep up the detritus from her classroom. The

American headmaster ducks in and out without a word.

The next day, Mirjam attempts to resign and collect her pay, but Jucker will not listen. She stands her ground in his office demanding her month's wages. Their contest of wills grows in volume. She is contracted until the end of the term and has a duty to fulfill. Mirjam counters that she will not teach in a school where there is no assurance of her safety. In irritation and puffed up to all 5'4" of himself, Jucker moves from his desk and tries to physically push her out of his office.

"Don't manhandle me! You're an American, not a Turk!"

But he manages to thrust her over the threshold, slam and lock the door.

She storms down the stairs and past the cafeteria but hollering draws her inside where bloody pandemonium has erupted between two of her students and a host of cheering and jeering onlookers. Kerim is bleeding from a cut to his face; the other, Tibet, has a butcher knife and is also bleeding from slashes to his arms. Apparently, the knife has changed hands several times. Stupidly, Kerim, though now unarmed, keeps lunging at his attacker. As with the earlier ruckus in the hallway, friends of each are trying to shout reason and to physically separate the two. Gunam Hunar, the aloof Turkish principal whom everyone calls "the poisonous dwarf" peers into the cafeteria, apparently without concern. Then Tibet lurches at Kerim and a cloud of red spreads over the navel of the boy's shirt. Mirjam and Çiğdem, the young school psychologist, are the only two adults amidst the chaos. The two women try to assist in separating the boys but are shoved aside for their efforts. The cavernous cafeteria amplifies the shrieking Tibet who cannot endure Kerim's verbal slight of his mother, and Kerim's retaliatory shouts add further to the clamour.

Mirjam stands with rags in hand beside Çiğdem, who is trying vainly to call an ambulance on her cellphone. Blood seems everywhere. Out of the corner of her eye, Mirjam catches Jucker's momentary profile at the door.

Finally, the boys are torn apart. Finally, someone takes Mirjam's makeshift bandages and binds Tibet's slashed arms while another boy presses his Benetton school uniform shirt to Kerim's stomach wound. And finally, the boys, still hurling voluble insults at each other, are careened individually out of the cafeteria and presumably by car to a nearby hospital. Two surly caretakers bring their buckets and begin to mop up the mess of tempers.

It all reminds her of a postcard she'd purchased from a gift shop, a reproduction of an Islamic miniature of a *timarhane*, an asylum, depicting a scene of frenzied inmates attacking each other with knives.

A shaken Mirjam returns to her classroom. On her desk she discovers an envelope with $2,000 American inside—full pay for the month of December. Having briefly witnessed the bloody mayhem in the cafeteria, Jucker has apparently reconsidered.

That night she and Alban, together with an extended group of Turkish musicians and artists, get very drunk on a Bosphorus dinner cruise. They sing and dance along to Tarkan, the current darling of the Istanbul pop music scene. Too much Efes and too many stuffed mussels later find Mirjam barfing in the hole that is the toilet on board the vessel. She pukes so hard that a blood vessel bursts in her left eye.

Nursing hangovers the next morning, she and Alban manage to join their friends for coffee in the Pera Palas Oteli. Andrej, Mustafa, and Ester are already deep in conversation with other musician friends, Youssef, a tenor from Marrakesh; Tarik, a bass from Mostar; Özgür and Nora, the married Turkish couple, both singers, who have just written with Mustafa the music and libretto for a new opera, *Romeo and Juliet in Sarajevo*. Mirjam has helped them with the English text.

"Nora is singing the role of the mother; I'm the father. We have our Romeo in Youssef and his father in Tarik. But so far, no Juliet."

Mirjam and Alban sit across from their friends and beside each other. He opens a new package of Camels and offers them around the table.

Özgür plops two cubes of sugar into his cappuccino and stirs thoughtfully. "We don't know if we'll get to Sarajevo—we don't know if we can even get into the city, despite the ceasefire and this new Dayton Agreement. But we are going to as many places as we can, starting with Belgrade, moving across former Yugoslavia with visas we have managed to obtain, military escorts whenever possible, and fixers that Andrej has arranged through friends and relatives."

He shakes his head when Alban offers him a cigarette. "We have raised a little money to cover our living expenses. And we will perform this opera for free for the citizens of former Yugoslavia, as a show of solidarity and a symbolic gesture in support of peace."

"You'll all be killed for your efforts." Ester bites a hangnail.

"We won't do anything stupid, my darling," Mustafa tries to take her hand. "We'll perform only when and where it is safe."

"Really? And how exactly will you know that?" She rises abruptly and hurries out of the café. Mustafa rushes to follow her.

"She is upset because she doesn't want him to go back ... to Sarajevo or anywhere near the conflict." Nora's look is apologetic.

"I can understand why." Alban reaches for the ashtray.

"I'll go." Mirjam's voice is so soft that Alban asks her to repeat herself. "I can sing the role. I— I— would like to, if you'll have me."

"That would be great!" Özgür claps his hands and Nora beams. "We have found our Juliet!"

"Mirjam—" Alban's face is ashen and not from his hangover.

She turns to look at him and speaks quietly while the conversation about details and logistics circles around them. "I think it is something I should do; I would like to do."

"You'll be stepping into a minefield."

"They say it will be safe. Mustafa and Andrej—they know the country."

"Fuck this shit, Mirjam!"

"Music can be a healing, an elegy, a balm, Alban. You know that. Look at what Vedran Smajlovic did for his people."

"But Vedran Smajlovic escaped Sarajevo in 1993. Why would you want to go there to that madness? Those aren't your people—this isn't your conflict! You're Canadian."

"Yes, but I'm Serbo-Canadian."

"You're also Ukrainian-Canadian."

"But I've always felt that Serb blood runs thickest in these veins. Alban, I have never understood what my people are. I have always hated and loathed being Serbian, even more so with the atrocities we keep learning about. Maybe this is one way to learn, to bear witness, or at the very least, to resist becoming what they are. Since Ata Koleji I feel more and more like I am a too-near relative to the ugliness that is going on in my father's country."

"Mirjam, you beautiful fool." He runs his hands through his hair. "I'm coming with you, then."

"I'm not— I would never ask you to."

"I'm not leaving you to do this alone." Alban looks at Nora and Özgür as Mustafa returns to the table. "We're in. The both of us."

And when she returns to them, red-eyed Ester learns that she alone will remain in Istanbul for the remainder of winter.

10

Dan maneuvers his black boat of a car along Calgary Trail and into the city of Edmonton. He winds through the river valley and up to the Hotel MacDonald where he will spend two nights. Velvet curtains are parted to offer a view of the North Saskatchewan, greyly meandering between the verdant evergreens along its banks. Dan tips the bellboy, hangs his garment bag and searches for the phone number to the Edmonton Cemetery. He calls to make an appointment for the following afternoon.

At dinner, he wishes Luba were with him now on this solitary errand. He wishes Luba were with him. For though they live together, he knows they are not. Not really. She is interested in birds and more recently, the opera. Dan shakes his head. What has become of his vivacious wife, the one he fell in love with all those years ago, dancing in Drumheller? It has been many years since he held her in his arms. What has become of those years? He coughs. Maybe he shouldn't have had that wine with his steak. Sometimes wine congests him, not to mention gives him indigestion. Like so much he eats these days. That damn ulcer from the war plagues him into old age.

In Ortona he begins spitting up blood. They are mouse-holing through a series of old buildings in the ancient city. God knows what the structures had been before they became disfigured by mortar shells and grenades—certainly one was a *farmicia*, evident from smashed blue and brown bottles and the Rod of Asclepius which miraculously still hangs on a partial wall— but the others are indistinguishable, unidentifiable.

Last night a team of men had been surprised and bloodied by just such a building, booby trapped by the bastard Krauts. Three Canadians didn't come back.

Dan had spent a shaky night, lighting cigarette after cigarette, trying to calm his nerves and his aching gut. He'd thrown up a red mess at dawn, but there was no backing out of active duty that morning.

He spits again. Christ, what is wrong with his stomach?

Gordie and he stop to load the PIAT that Dan has been carrying. They crouch behind rubble in the *farmicia*, take aim, and Dan fires. The roar of the explosion ripples through Dan's arms, down his back, through his aching gut and along his sprawled legs. Dust and debris rain down, and they cannot see much beyond a hole in the brick and mortar. Gordie crawls over to the breach in the wall and lobs in a grenade. A second roar. The men take cover for a few choking minutes. The hole is sufficient to crawl through and so, when they can manage again, the two cautiously enter the powdery clouds of the adjacent building. Inside they can identify the remains of six members of the German 1st Parachute Division. Another is pinned under a slab of collapsed ceiling. Dan approaches him guardedly. The soldier's dusty face is smeared with red, and his jaw is clearly broken.

"*Mutter. Mutter!*" his lips somehow manage.

Dan removes his Colt pistol from his hip and takes aim at this man who is surely no older than he. The soldier's eyes flicker to Dan's as he pulls the trigger. He cannot look away from the bloodied pulp of the aftermath. He imagines a greying mother, maybe in Heidelberg, coming to the door wiping hands on her apron to receive the telegram, then collapsing to her knees. Dan leans in to ensure that the dog tags are still around what remains of the neck. Finally, Gordie drags his retching compatriot forward to the next wall.

That night, after several doses of stomach bromide powder, Dan collapses into exhausted dreams about a soldier crying for his mother. He fires and fires at the man who does not die but resumes his pitiable cry. When Dan looks into the half face of the soldier he is trying vainly to kill, he recognizes himself.

※

The lights of Edmonton twinkle across the river as Dan tosses and turns, sleepless. He reaches for the Maalox he has thought to bring along for his acid stomach and wishes again that Luba were with him. At 6 a.m., he tries calling their house in Calgary, but she does not answer. It is a dull Edmonton day, colourless and threatening rain and maybe snow. He dresses carefully in the new black suit and white shirt he has bought for this occasion, then chooses the navy tie with silver flecks instead of the red. His white hair is neatly Brylcreemed into place. He has always been a dapper man.

By the time Dan begins the drive to the cemetery, a weary drizzle has started. Turning the collar of his raincoat up, he curses the fact that he has left behind his umbrella. At least he remembered his felt trilby.

A helpful assistant at the cemetery office shows him on the map precisely where to walk. It does not take long. Perhaps a few minutes from the administrative office is all. The manicured grass is wet but mercifully not yet soggy. Still, the water seeps in through his new brogues. Dan finds quite easily the recently placed charcoal marble headstone: *Petar Maniljo Popović. Born 1882. Died 1933. RIP.*

What he does not know, he imagines. St. Joseph's Auxiliary Hospital has been lately repurposed into upscale yuppified condominiums. But nearly a lifetime ago, St. Joseph's Hospital for the Chronically Ill run by Sisters of Providence of St. Vincent de Paul, was the hospice where his dying father lay rotting from mouth cancer in 1933. His was likely a spartan hospital-green room shared by any number of dying men. A Catholic haven for an Orthodox man. But Dan guesses this little mattered to a father and husband who had otherwise been abandoned by his family and his church. Dan hopes that the nuns had been kind, that one or more had placed a cool hand on a fevered brow as Tata's breath turned to wisp and then silence. Dane's older sisters told him that half his father's face was gone, in the end. He'd seen worse in the war but envisioning the half-face of a father half-remembered makes him shudder. He hopes the morphine was sufficient. In the end we all die alone.

This before him is a pauper's grave. Several men are buried here together from the time of the Depression. One of them is Tata. Who knows or cares about the others?

It has taken some weeks of working himself up to make this trip and face this moment, but at last the son has found the father. Sixty years too late.

Marble is dear. Dan has purchased the monument with money from his veteran's pension. This great stone is no heavier than this moment and his heart. There was no stone here a week ago. And now there will always be a marker of his father living and dying in this city, this country. It is the very least a son can do. And far too little, the shiver along his spine reminds him.

The rain turns up the volume. By the time he returns to the cemetery office, Dan is drenched. The astute assistant does what he does best, and Dan is convinced into purchasing two plots, at a veteran's rate, an assurance for an assured future.

Danilo does not know that Luba will refuse to ever join him here—she will die, yes. But her place of rest will be ashes on the wind. As he walks back to his car, Dan cannot tell rain from tears. He drives carefully through the city and onto Highway #2 through the sleet for home. He will make this journey but once again. In sixteen months, he will also be beneath a black marble marker.

11

The sultan's silver-soled slippers whispered across the Golden Road of the Imperial Harem. After the lucky beauty was selected, his remaining *cariyeler* disappeared silently or absented themselves by stealth to one of the four hundred rooms of the sequestered dwelling. Evading the watchful eye of Hüma Valide Hatun, grandmother of Kemal and mother of the sultan, Sudbina slid into shadows. She had no wish to play concubine to the sultan, no matter what honour the Valide Hatun insisted this role would be. The despoina was well aware that the grandmother thought little enough of her and conspired to win her grandson's heart away by tempting him with other lovelies residing in the harem. Still, the old woman admired the musical voice of her captive and treated her well enough because of this, even though Sudbina hailed from the troublesome vassal state of Serbia.

Daily, Kemal the minstrel, the sultan's possible heir and her betrayer, sought an audience with the despoina. Though matters had warmed between them, frost still clung to her royal-born heart. Kemal returned to her the bow and arrow, Baba Roga's tincture and herbs, silk skein and skeleton key—all as a gesture of his good faith and enduring love. These she accepted and secreted away beneath the thick mattress in her chamber. He sang and harped to her. She joined him. But she would not join her body to his, nor reassure him with even the brush of her hand. At night, a great eunuch stood guard at her door. So Sudbina was neither concubine nor odalisque, but merely prisoner.

She knew that the sultan was overjoyed at the return of his son. The Valide Hatun had assured Sudbina of this and had also shared the news of the sumptuous feast that was given in Kemal's honour. The despoina had been deliberately excluded, she knew, though Kemal came quickly and apologetically to her after the fact. She knew also that a second, more threatening ransom note had been sent to her father by order of the sultan through the grand vizier, Mahmud Pasha. This revelation the minstrel hastily whispered to her with the repeated promise that Sudbina would be safe while with him. She had seen neither the sultan nor the pasha since her arrival at Constantinople, which the Ottomans called *Kostantiniyye*. She had, however, met Kemal's mother, the striking Gülşah Hatun. As the only son of her union with Mehmed II and, therefore, her darling, her maternal delight at his return was embarrassingly overwrought. She tried to keep him always in her sight, petting and cooing over Kemal as if he were some prized lap dog. Though Kemal's mother had little liking for the Valide Hatun, Gülşah respected and, moreover, feared her, so shared the older woman's distaste for the infidel who was apparently the son's consort.

They'd arrived at Carigrad in the midst of day. A resolute

sun sparked the waves of the Bosphorus. Their retinue had ridden along the Golden Horn and Sudbina's senses were quite overwhelmed with the reek of the harbour, the bold colours of the standards, the hucksters in the noisy bazaar, the salt in the air as she jolted along, tied to her mount. Her mouth gaped at the Aya Sofya bedazzling in the light and the towering minarets of the Fatih Mosque. Everywhere she looked was frenzied beauty and history coupled with the filth of too many people and animals.

She was exhausted when they reached the heights to pass through the Imperial Gate of *Yeni Saray* and was ushered away to the Imperial Harem. As days passed she glimpsed—she was never permitted to explore—the vast wealth of the sultan's palace and position of the Ottoman Empire.

In the gardens of the inner courtyard of the still unfinished *sarayı*, she could parade with the peacocks at leisure. And colourfully as a peacock, she was bedecked in the finest Ottoman silks. Never had such rich fabrics touched her flesh, though she was a despoina and accustomed to beautiful finery. On occasion she stole a look at the other parts of the palace—the porphyry columns of the treasury, the shining domes of the Privy Chamber—but was forbidden entrance. Only the kitchen workers bade her entry, as women have ever and always been permitted into sculleries and cookeries. The other women of the harem seemed to shun her, a Christian and, therefore, *kirli*. Only the squawking peacocks and the elegant gazelles were her companions. As they became accustomed to her traipsing through the gardens of tulips and jasmine, soon they ignored her, too. In loneliness and boredom, she awaited the hoofbeats of her father's men. All in vain, it seemed. Days turned to weeks.

Her father did not have such wealth as Mehmed II possessed. She had heard of an emerald in the royal treasury that was large as a man's fist. Neither did the despot have Mehmed II's might—the sultan was, after all, the *Conqueror*, he who had brought Constantinople to her knees and who had quelled every Serb uprising. What possible offense could her father muster against the Sublime Porte? How could her father rescue her, even though she was his favourite? Why would he? Such a risk would be his death. And perhaps hers, too.

Her hopes and her spirits faltered as the crows dipped and dived in the skies above, as though they were laughing at the peacocks trapped in the gardens.

"Despoina."

She turned to find the harpist come to seek her out. He wore the costume of his father's court—still handsome, still earnest and talented. But no longer hers. They sat together in the April sunlight.

"I have found your brother. He is, as I suspected, a well-regarded Janissary under the sultan's command. I have told him about you."

"What is his name?"

"Sokollu."

She recognized the twist on her family name.

"I will arrange for you to meet him."

The despoina swallowed. Perhaps her brother, this Sokollu, would help to free her? Together they might return to her father, she leading the prodigal son. It would be the happiest of days for her father, a triumph of the daughter over her own foolhardiness. She would be redeemed and not a drop of blood shed for her sake. She might bring the minstrel back with them for her father to deal with as he wished. Or she might leave him to his fate, here in his home. A caged heart is a curious thing.

Hers began to beat wildly, whether with anticipation, fear, dread or all of these, she did not know.

"Yes," she whispered.

And within the hour the minstrel brought to her a brother. A secret meeting behind the tallest cypress grove in the garden. Kemal kept watch nearby. If any should happen this way, he would engage the sultan's Janissary bodyguard as if in quiet conversation, and Sudbina would slink away amongst the trees.

Tall, with eyes of obsidian, dark hair meeting in a widow's peak so like her father's, her brother wore the dashing bright uniform of the Janissary. His beard and stashes were long in the style of the Ottoman, but all was trim and well-turned out.

"Sister." His voice betrayed nothing of the emotion she felt.

"I am Sudbina."

"You were born but eighteen years ago. Yes?"

"Fifteen. I have two older sisters."

He raised a thick eyebrow.

"We are but a year each apart. The eldest will be nineteen on St. Sava's Day. When were you taken, brother?"

"I was but eight summers."

"I did not know. Father never spoke—"

"Never mind him. What of my mother?"

Sudbina looked away from her brother. "She is gone. I was the child that broke her. She tried thrice more for a son and was disappointed each time. My birth ended her life."

Sokollu seemed to consider this. "It is never the babe's fault. Sometimes there is no help, no medicine."

She nodded. "But Father—"

"My father is dead to me. Sultan Mehmed bin Murad Han, Qayser-i Rûm is my father."

"But, but— Father would give anything—"

"He gave nothing. He did nothing. He watched me go."

"He took me in your stead," Kemal spoke mildly from the shadows.

"Ah yes. Revenge *devşirme*. It little mattered to me, weeping for my father, my mother, soiling my bed nightly. Until I recognized the honour that attended my new privilege. An excellent education. A good salary. The company of my brothers. And Islam: the one true religion. I left behind sheepherders and became a member of an honourable guard of fighting men. I have served on many campaigns, and I have won the sultan's favour." His voice swelled in volume, so that Kemal waved a cautionary gesture. Sokollu spoke next in undertones. "In time, so I am promised, I shall be Grand Vizier, insha'Allah."

"You are indeed grand, my brother."

"And now, sister, you will be with me. I will find you a suitable husband and you will have great honour within the expanse of Mehmed II's generosity. We will never again be parted."

"I— I— have no wish to be wife and play the slave in the sultan's court."

Kemal stepped towards them. "Sokullu, the despoina is mine."

"I am not!"

The Janissary eyed the son of his sultan. For a long sunlit moment, neither man said anything. Finally, Sokullu bowed his head slightly. "I meant no offense."

"I am not anyone's possession. No man's slave or wife!"

"Sudbina, hush. Come away. There are eyes in the grates." And indeed, several of the *cariyeler* peered out through the iron-crossed windows at the sounds in the garden. The sultan expressly commanded silence in the inner courts. Turning her back on the both of them, the despoina strode away. She entered her own apartment and slammed the door. What to do but while away the wearisome hours at her own grated window, silent like the mute servants, the harem women, the discreet eunuchs. Storm clouds battered her heart and mind. As if in commiseration, a crow landed outside her sill and cawed disagreeably throughout the tedious afternoon.

12

When she breathes, she aches. Luba has tried to shake herself of this nonsense, but it persists. She has tried her pills, more tea, less tea, herbal tea, coffee instead of tea, and lately has taken to gin and tonic in the afternoons. Sometimes more than one shot, sometimes more than one glass. Eventually, the gin works its way to her solar plexus and relaxes the knot of hurt that gathers there each waking morning, waxing through the day.

To take her mind away from the loss, she worries about her daughter. Mirjam has sent only the briefest of emails, presumably because communication from the war-torn cities is difficult, even impossible. So far, Luba knows that her daughter has performed in Belgrade, in battered Zagreb, and is bound for even more dangerous territories. She tries to check her mother's intuition, living in trepidation and in hope that the phone will ring.

Luba also agreed to take Dan for his medical appointments. Finally, at her urging he went to the clinic to see about his wretched persistent coughing. The family doctor ordered a series of tests.

"It's just a way to rack up extra dollars at the taxpayers' expense, Lu."

"Don't be so stubborn, Dan." She cleared their morning coffee cups from the kitchen table.

"I was hoping to go bet on the ponies with Bora and the gang."

"*Parbuk*-ing isn't a way out of this, Dan." Her back was to him as she washed up the breakfast things and placed them in the drainer to the left of the sink.

"You sound just like her."

"Like who?"

"Her. Mirjam."

"Will Bora and the gang come to visit you when you're dying in the hospital?"

"That's exactly something she would say."

"Go or don't. I'm not your mother, Dan." Luba dried her hands on the tattered dishtowel.

"I've heard the odds are in favour of Senga Breeze to win or place."

"That's nice."

"And Not-on-Your-Life stands the best chance for the tenth race."

"Okay."

"Plus, Bora got us free parking."

"Because you can't afford the $5.00 to park all day?"

"Can't you give me a break, Luba?"

"What are you so afraid of?" She snatched the racing guide from his hands.

"W—will you go with me?"

"To the races?"

"No, Lu. To the medical tests."

And so she had. Three separate tests on three different afternoons. Technicians took his blood, his urine, a fecal test, and finished with an X-ray of his lungs.

Now they wait in their little Inglewood bungalow for the doctor to ring. Or not.

Sitting alone in her little backyard garden, under the heat lamp on a mild but sunless afternoon, she remembers a day when she didn't have a phone, when she was a poor girl from Rosedale akin to nowhere. Raised in a one-room shack, she went to a one-room school and dreamed of a life with many rooms. When she started school, she spoke only Ukrainian. Outside in the schoolyard that was little more than a dirt field, she'd met the other coalminers' daughters, poor as she or poorer. They were a collection of immigrants' children with Slavic names—Bodnaruk, Eliak, Varga, Horvat, Stepanović, Svoboda, Kowalski, Kozdrowsky, Novak—all mispronounced by their marmish schoolteacher, herself a WWI widow originally from Cumberland and whose working-class accent worked its way into their own brand of Canadian English.

But when her family went to town, the young girl Luba always felt the heat of shame. Her clothes were hand-me-downs from her sisters, similarly her shoes of broken and worn leather, sometimes with the toes stuffed with newspaper to make sure they'd fit for two seasons or more. By contrast, the Drumheller town girls seemed freshly and prettily arrayed in store-bought clothes. Everything about them spoke of the huge divide between their trimmed green lawns and five mere miles and a non-Anglo background. When she encountered them at the popular swimming spots of the Red Deer River, she and her family or friends waded upstream to avoid their taunting giggles. At softball pitches, she heard what they called her and the other immigrant girls on the opposing team: the Bohunks. There were no dictionaries to define that slur, but she understood it viscerally. Then the fateful night behind the Napier Theatre, Luba, still reeling after the movie starring the dashing Errol Flynn in the role of Robin Hood, found her thirteen-year-old self alone, without cousin or sister, and encircled by five little town girls, emboldened by the twilight and their own pubescent sense of power. The tossing and pushing, hair-pulling, her falling to her knees and scraping them against the gravel she all vaguely remembers. But the shrewish cries haunt her with precise clarity to this day:

"Go back where you came from, you dirty bohunk."

"Your father's a filthy pig and your mother, too!"

"You stink of garlic."

"Learn to speak English!"

"We don't need you in this town."

"Get back to your own stupid kind!"

Somehow she'd fled, escaping their parting jeers to find her tear-stricken way to the rickety truck her uncle drove back to the Rosedale shack. In the bed she shared with three sisters, she wept herself to sleep that night, wondering why she was so reviled. She couldn't see the difference between herself and those others, except for wealth and accent, and the fact that her father led the miners' protests and strikes for better pay and conditions against the mine operators, their fathers. Luba awoke at dawn to see the sun creeping over the hills of home and felt herself trapped as a fossil in sandstone. It would take the rain of many more tears to loosen her Slavic bones and be freed, but in time she did escape ... or so she'd imagined.

Hodi had told her of his country's struggles for independence and of family casualties because of the fighting between his countrymen, the Mau Mau and the British. The conflict sounded brutish and ugly and senseless, like so many wars: colonizer against colonized, and African against African. She told him about the Holodomor under Stalin. So Luba and Hodi were both refugees of conflicts born of domination and intolerance, and immigrants to Canada. He had come here as a young man with his wife in the late 1950s and she as a child with her parents in the 1930s.

Many things had changed in this nation since then, but others had not. Three times while they were out together and riding in either her or Hodi's car, police had pulled them over, simply to inquire if Luba was alright. Her cheeks smarted with indignation and embarrassment for Hodi.

"It's fine, Luba." His voice sounded resigned.

"No. It's not, Hodi. It is not *fine*. We should be able to go for ice cream without someone thinking ..."

"You are a white woman. I am a Black man."

"That shouldn't even enter their minds!"

"Here, as I tried back in my own country, I must practise *ustahimilivu*. It translates as perseverance. Not all in this life is fair, dear Luba."

Hodi's manner of speaking to her quietly and frankly, of taking her seriously, was causing her to have lustful thoughts about him. She didn't dare suppose he felt the same until the surprising moment when he first kissed her. They were returning from an evening concert of the Calgary Philharmonic. It was unseasonably warm, and Hodi was walking her slowly back to her car. They paused as she unlocked the driver's door and when she turned to say good night, he cupped her face and kissed her with a tenderness she had not felt in years. Nothing but a kiss, a touch of his hand and he was away to his own vehicle. Luba felt as if she were fourteen.

Several meetings and several kisses later, his tongue found hers and she found herself awash with desire that had held its breath for nearly thirty years.

And kisses, furtive and deep, turned to much more.

"Luba, my dear Luba," he spoke to her from the other side of his futon. "*Nakupenda*." He brushed a stray wisp of hair from her cheek.

"*Ya tebe lyublyu*, Hodi."

She did not question what they were doing or why. She allowed her soft self to melt into his. Luba did not pause to think or care about being too old or too soft or too little or too much or too married for any of this. She allowed herself to accept the strong, dark coffee he brought to bed. She allowed herself to make love to him again and again in ways she'd never dared with Dan. She allowed herself to spend shady late winter afternoons naked under his snowy duvet, listening to recordings of his favourite operas or looking at his black and white photographs of people and his homeland and at his vision of this country that had become his home. She allowed herself to laugh at his jokes and to be late getting home to make supper for Dan. She allowed Hodi completely.

But when she met Hodi's daughter on her recent visit to Calgary, the seam of their illicit relationship ripped open. He'd been so proud of the opportunity to introduce the one to the other. For days he'd told her about his accomplished daughter, her commitment to legal justice for marginalized communities and the underdog. He was so certain she would like Luba and had chosen a lovely restaurant by the river for their first-ever meeting. But from the first handshake, Luba sensed a chill. Conversation stilted, Luba picked her way cautiously through her salad. She had trouble meeting Mwara's eyes.

"You're sleeping with my father."

"I— I—" Luba cast about desperately, hoping Hodi would return from the restaurant washroom.

"You have no idea about him or where he comes from or who he is."

"I am just learning."

"You're *not* my mother."

"I never intended to be—"

"My brothers and I and my aunt—we all want you to leave him alone. Get out of his life. You know nothing about what it means to be Kenyan-Canadian. He's not some exotic toy."

"Mwara!" Hodi had reappeared at the table, his face unhappy with shock.

"It's true, Baba." The daughter turned to him, "Someone has to say it to her before you go and make a fool of yourself again. The last woman almost took your entire savings, until I stepped in. It broke my heart. And she," Mwara glanced over at Luba, "broke yours. Or have you forgotten?"

"Luba. I'm so sorry. Mwara, apologize to Miss Luba."

"It's Mrs., isn't it? I'm fairly certain, Baba." She lifted a defiant chin in opposition to her father's. "I found her home number in your address book and telephoned her. Today before you arranged this stupid dinner. And a man answered."

"Th—that's none of your business." Hodi looked to Luba apologetically, then back to his daughter.

Luba busied herself looking for her car keys.

"You didn't know, did you?" Mwara's tone was drawing attention to their table.

"You had no right." Hodi lowered his voice. "And yes, I am aware."

"I do have a right! As a daughter protecting her father. It is my business when I'm the one who'll have to come back here to pick up the legal and emotional pieces. Like I did the last time, after the other white woman. Why Baba, when there are any number of beautiful African- or Caribbean-Canadian women, do you continue to undermine the struggle we face daily?"

"Daughter, be reasonable. I know you feel your struggle is mine, too. I am sorry that you've been so hurt and poorly treated. But I don't feel as you do. Especially not about Luba. She is different."

"She is white. How can she ever understand?"

"I'll leave, Hodi. I don't want—"

"Bye-bye, *mzungu*! Back to your own kind!"

"Mwara!"

Her mortification complete, Luba, still keyless, bolted without a backwards glance, like a stupid pup as Hodi tried vainly to recall her.

Days had dragged their feet across the calendar. Then a week hobbled by. Two. No call, no word from Hodi.

Halfheartedly, she put the Christmas decorations up and took them down a week later on New Year's Day. No Mirjam. All the effort it took to breathe through the day. Jesus, what was there to celebrate?

She guesses Hodi has seen the wisdom in his daughter's words. Would she not do the same if Mirjam had so intervened on her behalf against some ill-advised tryst? And Luba is ashamed that she'd not been more honest about her marriage to Dan. They had danced around it. Hodi did not ask. Luba did not tell. Adultery had always been a word that belonged to other people. In books and movies. To Dan's indiscretions. And of course, she had been afraid.

Of what?

Of losing this green tendril of love.

She dares again to admit that word. At this late stage of her unimportant life, she has dared again to love. And look what it has cost her.

There is nothing to do but put one foot in front of another. Try not to succumb to the vise that grips her, relaxing only when she finally surrenders to sleep each night. Concentrate on her life, Dan, her daughter, this slumbering garden, and hope to make it through to spring. Maybe with a little too much friendly gin.

The first flakes of a major January snowstorm drift downwards. A wind is up and Luba shivers. She looks upwards. The sky is such a zinc disappointment.

13

An RPG explodes, ear-splitting and incendiary, its target a tram paused at Museji stop in front of the National Museum at 6 p.m. on a January Sarajevan night. Silhouetted against the flames, the tram is a gutted tin can, its twenty occupants shredded into bloody cabbage. Amidst the screams and the choking ash and dust, Mirjam discerns a dire lament in A minor. She tries to shake herself loose of the terror to locate the source of the song. A child lies across what is left of his mother. He is clutching vainly at her hand that bears a gold ring, and he is moaning the root of the chord. Spattered with the blood of the mother, Mirjam recognizes her own wail on the minor third with ambulance sirens shrieking the final part of the triad. She feels she has intruded on a private scene of mourning; one she has no right to accompany. Though in shock, Mirjam recognizes she is part of this deadly Dies Irae, too.

A shaken Alban, who was in the trolley car behind hers with others of their touring company, has managed to find her amidst the carnage. He grabs the child and her arm and they scramble, crouching low, to what they hope is some semblance of safety behind a barrier of cinderblock wall and the rubble of what was formerly a school.

Nothing makes sense. They are musicians, visitors. There is a ceasefire, an accord. Why, but two days after Orthodox Christmas, have the Serbs on the hills sent this new reign of terror? Why this on this night, on the Feast of St. Stephen, mere hours after they have performed hymns asking forgiveness for aggressors as did Stephen for his executioners? What muddied notion of heaven and heavenly reward do these madmen harbour? Together, a sobbing child, a cellist, and a Canadian woman hold each other, bewildered, huddled in horrified solidarity.

Sometime later they are discovered by a member of their company and pulled away, crawling through shadows towards a waiting, if battle-weary jeep.

It is hours after they finally reach the Abdulah Nakas general hospital to surrender the child for treatment for shock, after threading a harrowing and labyrinthine course with their fixer escort and his grim, chain-smoking driver, that Mirjam realizes they did not ask the boy his name. How will he find his relatives in this city of chaos and bloodied roses? While this realization dawns, another comes: Alban finally speaks aloud to Mirjam, and she cannot clearly make out his words. His face is blood-smeared so she tries to focus on his lips. She can read nothing. Hear nothing. Her voice shrills a refrain of anguish.

Desperately, Alban tries to gain the attention of a member of the medical team on duty. They are all too busy and consumed with the casualties of this terrible January night. At last, he convinces an exhausted doctor to examine his distraught and dazed partner. The surgeon can only surmise she has experienced blast-explosive acoustic trauma and suggests that

Mirjam seek treatment immediately upon returning to Berlin. There is little that can be done given the current state of medicine here in war-torn Sarajevo. Besides, hearing loss is a minor issue at this time, in this place.

The doctor tries not to seem impatient, though he is dealing with imbeciles who have come to a war zone to make music when they were perfectly safe and far away with their liberal guilt mere weeks ago. Or so Mirjam imagines through the tinnitus that is raging battle in her ears.

She spends a restless night in the hotel, the scene of the blast replaying like the looped film of a macabre art exhibition. Mirjam does not hear Alban's groans from his nightmares. She stares at the pockmarked ceiling and wonders what she intended on this fool's errand.

But Belgrade had been a beautiful experience. She'd sung in museums and galleries with other foreign musicians who offered their gifts to the conflict-weary citizens. The stage of the National Theatre was another acoustic delight. Noon-hour crowds filled the seats. Mirjam had trilled her arias to enthusiastic applause. Handsome Alban was feted and adored, his cello technique much lauded. One evening, the opera touring company had been invited to join members of the rock group Rimtutituki as they played on the bed of a truck dashing about Belgrade, and together they'd belted out U2's anthemic "One." It was an exhilarating and defiant gesture met by the cheering of thousands of Belgrade citizens who lined Kolarčeva and Knez Mihailova streets and Republic Square.

Warm and welcoming, their Serbian hosts insisted on feeding their guests and filling their glasses with too much *šljivovica*. That week in the city by the confluence of the Danube and the Sava had been uneventful and hospitable, despite the shuddering chill. It was hard to believe that these same people were largely responsible for the atrocities committed just hours away.

But of course, they were not. They were neither rebels nor Chetniks. Just simple people who despised Milošević. Who were trying to get by. They shook their heads. Looked into their hands as if for answers. Many who hosted the couple and the touring entourage were musicians and artists themselves.

"Am I a murderer?" Zoran, a violinist in the Belgrade Philharmonic Orchestra, spoke softly, his voice breaking. "My friends, my colleagues are under siege. I know Croats and Bosniaks from music school and we have performed together. What can we do for them? We are powerless against this madman. And they blame all Serbs for him."

"All we can do is to offer shelter. Speak out against the tyrant. And play on." His wife, Nada, poured the Serbian coffee—elsewhere known as Croatian coffee or Bosnian coffee or Turkish coffee—into demitasses and set a tray before them. She played harp, and the instrument filled the better part of the living room corner in their tiny bohemian flat near Skadarlija.

In Zagreb, the company had workshopped a portion of the new opera to appreciative crowds at the Croatian National Theatre, its neo-classical yellow glory lately restored after the Serb rocket attacks. In this stately city, as in Belgrade, other musicians ate and drank with them. Teaching them phonetically some folk songs, they sang and played deep into the winter night. Zagreb was relatively calm after the assaults of 1995. But the people were still smarting from the senseless deaths and the defacement of their capital by cluster bombs. The Croats sang their sorrow into their *šljivovica* as the Serbs had in Belgrade. Resentment smouldered. No one could understand Serb aggression. Alban and Mirjam listened and tried to understand. Where had all this brutality come from?

"The Serbs have always been aggressors. They have been sore losers for centuries."

"But by your own admission"— Alban shared the last of his Turkish cigarettes with the Lazarević brothers, Borko and Nikola, horn players in the Zagreb Philharmonic Orchestra— "you have Serb and Bosniak friends, comrades you've made music with."

"Yes, and I would die for them. But! The rest of the Serbs are heartless killers. And have always been."

"Nationalism is the poison they drink," mused Vera Jurić, a Zágrepčānka and renowned dramatic soprano who'd shared the Lakmé "Flower Duet" with Mirjam earlier that evening. "It has been poured into their cups since the nineteenth century. They live and die to drink it. And so do we Croats, if we're honest, Borko."

"Religion," sighed Nikola, an avowed atheist named after a great Croatian saint. "It will kill us all in the end."

Under secrecy and darkness, they'd arrived via armoured vehicle in Sarajevo just days later. In the silver fog of dawn, the streets were a monochromatic maze of abandoned and burnt-out vehicles, pox-scarred half-structures, and piles of what had been the buildings of a once multicultural and reputedly tolerant cosmopolitan city—the glowing example of the Balkans. The Hum Tower was a blackened farce of its former self. The soccer field of the Koševo Olympic Complex was now a desolate cemetery. A profound sadness hung in the crisp winter air. Mirjam could not staunch her tears when they cautiously encountered the skeleton of Sarajevo's city hall and devastated National Library, then passed by the Vrbanja Bridge that was the actual site of the subject of their opera, the spot where Boško and Admira had been gunned down by snipers and lain for five days in May 1993.

And finally, they'd performed their opera in an underground theatre, ill-lit and poorly equipped, draughty and stale with the smell of cigarettes and drink. For three nights they'd filled the house and for each brought the weeping audiences—some Croat, some Serb, many Muslim—to their feet. She and Alban felt as though something important had happened in those performances. People had been moved to tell her so. They wished that the families of the dead boy and girl might attend, made the company promise to come back in better times so that they could.

Like the journalists who'd hazarded the worst of the siege, she and Alban stayed at the Holiday Inn, spending New Year's then Orthodox Christmas with artists, writers and musicians, some of whom had been living in shelters, others who'd had their homes seized by Serb militia and still others whose apartments had been destroyed by mortar shells. Everyone had lost someone. Some had remained friends across ethnic lines; others had seen neighbour turn against neighbour. What art could one make in such a nightmare, Mirjam had wondered. And yet artists painted, writers wrote, and musicians composed despite the onslaught and in reaction to and against it. Their courage was humbling.

Together with Özgür and the rest of the touring company, they'd given gifts of many cigarettes, sweets, woodwind reeds, strings for instruments, wax and horsehair for bows. All of them felt keenly how little they'd brought their new Sarajevan hosts and friends.

So she, Alban, and the others dared to stay another week, to sing at a number of free concerts, both impromptu and planned. That very evening had been one such.

But why else, she asks herself now in a stunned silence, why else had she come? In the bleak night, alone with her jumbled thoughts, she challenges herself: what exactly was she trying to accomplish? Was this something to do with defying everything her father stood for? Was he the Serbian culprit in the apartment in Grbavica who'd fired the shell at the tram car? Roiling in her body, her ire rises, the anger she has contained since leaving Canada and the final violent scene in her parents' home. It had burbled and threatened to surface, but she had managed to beat it down. Now she allows it to spread from her breast to her gorge to her mind.

She hates the Serbs who rain terror down on the hapless people of Sarajevo, not to mention Dubrovnik and Srebrenica and all the other places from tip to toe of these balkanized lands. Never mind that the Croats are also vile aggressors, that there are reportedly atrocities on all sides. She abhors the Serbs who prey on the old, the innocent, who lead thousands of boys and men to shallow graves, who rape old women and babies and girls and women, make them carry the fetuses in their wombs to full gestation, train crosshairs on people eking out a life in the rubble, fix rocket launching sights on the gorgeous architectural treasures of ancient cities and deliberately target hospitals, schools, libraries, markets. She loathes the Serbs who turn against former friends and even family members, taking over their apartments and possessions, turning them out with nothing but the clothes on their backs, burning down their own homes so that no Croat or Muslim can possibly use the abandoned dwellings as shelter afterwards. She is repulsed by generals and leaders who set these awful events in motion, but she also loathes those among them who propel it onwards or do nothing but turn a blind eye. Serbians and the republic and its nationalistic sickness sicken her. And Danilo, her father, is integral to her sickness. She longs to cut him to pieces, to take all the repugnant Serbs to draw and quarter to send them all into the ocean to wipe the smirks from their wicked faces. She tries to summon the potent magic she wishfully senses milling in her veins, to invoke some horrible gas to asphyxiate them all, wipe them from the earth, her father included—her father especially. What have the Serbs ever done but cement the term ethnic cleansing into twentieth-century consciousness, start world wars, slit throats, and add one apt and blood-curdling word—*vampire*—to the English language? She centres her hate and sends out her curse: that not one Serb will be living in the morning. Not a bloody fucking one.

And she half-knows at this moment, halfway through the night, that in cursing what she hates, she curses herself, daughter of Serbia. Violent thoughts, ugly dreams, atrocious wishes course through her veins, through the blood of her people. She is a Serb. This harsh truth is the tintinnabulation in her ears.

The dawn comes as it always does, even in a winter city suffering from collective post-traumatic shock. Snow is falling softly on Sarajevo, so softly that Mirjam cannot hear it. And Milošević and all the other murderous Serbs, including her father, are alive and well. As is she, but for her hearing. She has no magic. Or not enough magic—it little matters. For she cannot change a thing. She is just a woman approaching the halfway mark of her life. A mere singer. Or a woman who used to be a singer. Who can sing who cannot hear?

Nora knocks on their door and rouses Alban.

"We must go now," her hand, urging them to follow, is shaky. "Through Tunel Spasa, the tunnel ... of rescue ... of hope."

Hastily, they dress and throw their belongings back into suitcases. Mirjam tosses their blood-fouled clothing into the trash. Alban's touring cello takes up much of the decrepit taxi. The others of the entourage follow in similar makeshift vehicles through yet another thick fog towards what was once a residential neighbourhood now within Serb-controlled territory. Alban will not let go of her hand, but it isn't enough. Mirjam cannot get the image of the dead woman's gold ring from her mind. Her tears do nothing to quell the nightmare of the previous night or the blood or her recollected sounds of the wounded.

Maybe, she wonders, they will be all I ever hear.

The company reaches the garage of the Dobrinja apartment building, and the cars stop, everyone climbing out as though evacuating vessels mined with ticking bombs.

Mirjam is afraid of small spaces. Her courage left her days ago. "How will we manage your cello?"

Alban mouths something that she knows is meant to be comforting.

Someone within opens the door and hastens them inside, taking their permits, handing them each a gas mask. They must pay with German marks for each member of the company, extra for the instruments. She takes a deep breath. Alban kisses her. They don their masks. Mirjam steps over the threshold and descends the steps into the abyss.

Part 3

1

"Tympanic membrane or TM perforation, most certainly," the Berlin audiologist had pronounced carefully, writing it down for his patient, adding, "a perforation in your right eardrum."

They already knew this.

"But why can't I hear out of the other ear?"

"We don't know. There may also be mild TBI: traumatic brain injury or it may be psychosomatic or sympathetic hearing loss. We will also treat you for concussion. How is the vertigo?"

Alban wrote down the doctor's question and passed the notebook to Mirjam.

"I'm taking the Dimenhydrinate, but it only seems to put me to sleep."

Mirjam was bewildered by the charts and diagrams and statistics on hearing recovery after trauma. She had seen three specialists who had given her a diagnosis, but no prognosis. No one could seemingly predict the full impact of the injury to her ears. This latest doctor, Gutermuth, who reminded her of a balding Woody Allen, had scheduled her for endoscopic ear surgery, a progressive new technique. But a recent pre-operative audiometry had produced dismal results. She could hear a little sound as if from very far away, but the tinnitus and dizziness were sometimes debilitating.

"*Gut.* Now: sleep, eat, rest. Next week, we will perform this surgery. I am very hopeful."

"Herr Doktor, will I sing again?"

"*Wer weiß*, Fräulein? Try not to worry and we will take it one day by day."

In fact, the surgery in late March had gone well, so successfully that the doctor was excited to compose a medical paper focusing on Mirjam's treatment. The post-operative pain had been bearable, improving each day, though her thoughts had been muddied with the high doses of T3s for the better part of a week.

At their last consult, the doctor had been encouraging. She was to avoid stress. Rest, he assured her, was her best cure.

And that is all Mirjam has been able to do for weeks. She can manage short walks on good days but reading or videos with subtitles are more than her tired brain can process. Friends have dropped by with Kaffee und Kuchen. Even Frau Littgenstein and Hans came by with some spring lilies and to share some tea and sympathy.

The attention is welcome, but Mirjam feels inept at small talk, letting her visitors carry the thread of the conversations. They often forget that she cannot hear and neglect to write things down. She says nothing to remind them, worried that she is a disappointment to everyone.

Alban has been the most tender of caregivers. In the evenings, after he finishes at the Orchester-Akademie der Berliner Philharmoniker, he rushes into their apartment with a small bouquet of fragrant flowers, or a treat from the patisserie, or some joke that he writes upon the slate they use to communicate. He brings her the English newspapers and urges her to stay in the world, to write to their friends in Istanbul. She is learning to read his lips and finds solace in his nearness, his presence a multi-measure rest in a difficult musical score. He helps her cook their simple meals, cleaning up afterwards. She watches him rosin his bow and practise. Vibrations from his cello console and soothe her, as do his body and his mouth.

Still, Mirjam's days are long, and she alternates between fretting and despondency. She has tried to sing, but her pitch, always a signature of her excellence, is imperfect, she knows. Will she hear again? Will she sing again? What of Milan?

Frau L. has written on her behalf to request a second deferral from attending Accademia Teatro alla Scala, and anxiously they await the decision. It may well be that the request will be denied, with nothing to do but forfeit the marvellous opportunity granted her by the Leyla Gencer competition. Not for the first time Mirjam wonders why she did not immediately head for Italy when she had the chance. What a gift she has lost. Her regret is bitter and tuneless.

Mirjam has written home only once, enclosing a happy photograph from early days in Belgrade. Luba knows nothing about her daughter's auditory handicap, and Mirjam feels guilty for the evasion with her mother. But she can find no words to explain what she has lost and feels a profound shame for what at times seems a self-inflicted impairment. When Mirjam has a moment and the energy, she traipses down to an Internet café to research hearing loss. What she learns only troubles her further, and Alban has begged her not to waste her time on cyber-prognoses.

Since that January night in Sarajevo, she has read online and in the papers that there have been no further attacks. The shell-shocked city holds its breath in hope that the bloodshed has finally ended and that the Dayton Agreement will hold.

Mirjam has also learned that French troops searched the apartment in Grbavica from whence the deadly RPG was fired. No one was apprehended. No one party—Serb JNA or Bosnian-Herzegovinian ARBiH—could be officially deemed guilty. The Bosnian government has only recently declared the siege to be over and the citizens who remain have begun the terrible work of clean-up, restoration, and grief. She knows there is a mass exodus of former Sarajevan Serbs to Republika Srpska. Where can such segregation lead but to more hatred and division? Such thoughts make her head ring the louder.

Unexpectedly, a package arrived last week from Belgrade where her musical hosts had heard of her injury. Their card was written in broken, if heartfelt and empathetic English, and they'd wrapped carefully in tissue a small bottle of *šljivovica* beside a tin of homemade *salčići*, her favourite Serbian pastry. Only slightly drunk on the *rakija*, she'd penned a short note of thanks and wished them good health, glad that her foolish curse on all Serbs had been nothing but futile whimsy.

Attempting to clear her thoughts and wash away lingering hate and bile, Mirjam tried donning Alban's earphones, hoping to hear Bach's cello suites, but the music sounded as though under water and the ringing in her ears swelled to painful.

So, abandoning music, Mirjam often wanders through the Tiergarten to watch the rowboats on the Neuer See, or the dogs and children at play, or the artists at their canvases, or to meander the Flohmarkt. One day she pauses at a milliner's stall. A beautiful carousel plays calliope music nearby. She can barely make out its tinny tunes.

"Fräulein! You have such a pretty head. Please try." She hands him her notebook and pen, pointing to her ear and the carousel. The milliner's name is David, and his hair, trousers, shirt, jacket, even his nose ring and many earrings are vivid hues of purple. He gestures to a hat reminiscent of the 1920s. Mirjam takes the band from her hair and obliges. They spend a quarter of an hour trying his various creations, but there is one in a deep burgundy that cradles her head and reaches down her left cheek as if in cupped embrace. It is beyond fetching.

"You look just like Brigitte Horney, Fräulein!"

"Didn't she sing 'So oder so ist das Leben?'"

"Ah, so you know something about German cinema?"

"I know very little. But I know something of German music."

"Yes? You are a singer?"

Mirjam tries to keep her face still as she writes, "Yes."

"I must hear you sometime."

She pays her Deutsche Marks and accepts the package in which David has wrapped the felt hat, tucking his card into her handbag to discard discreetly later that afternoon.

Alban is happy that she has made such a purchase and opens his gift from the neighbourhood vintner, a bottle of very good Tempranillo. He urges her to model for him as he pours the wine. And then to remove her clothes but for the hat, and model again. They drink and he takes his forefinger, butters her nipples with the Tempranillo then tastes each one, pausing to repeat. He presses her against the tousled covers of their bed and makes love to her earnestly in adagio. Vivaldi's *Sleeping Drunkards* plays softly in the background, though only Alban can hear the strains, and the hat falls from her head to the floor.

In the aftermath, as Alban dozes peacefully, Mirjam wills herself to wonder if he will stay with her. What music can they make together now, beyond this reverie of lovemaking? Will some other cellist or perky coloratura catch his eye? Will his travels as a professional soloist take him to a composer's eager arms? Will life elsewhere captivate and seduce him? What can he share with someone who cannot even hear his bow caress the strings of his beloved cello? His arm is draped across her and, in unison, they breathe a rhythm she has come to cherish. She does not want to cling to him, and yet he is her harbour while she flounders on this sea of deafness. Mirjam dislikes needy women and has never thought of herself as one. But now, Alban she needs with a hunger. And that, she senses, is the surest way to lose him.

Tomorrow she will enlist Alban's help to call her mother. Tell Luba the truth of what happened to her in Sarajevo. Ask for advice about Alban, the future. And learn that her father has stage four terminal lung cancer.

2

"You will be returned to your father," Mahmud Pasha Anđelović was matter of fact. "We have received a missive that he will comply with our wishes. There will be an exchange on the Field of Crows. In Kosovo, he will pay tribute to the sultan and he will pay your ransom. You will be returned without a hair harmed on your Serbian head. Our sultan is just and merciful."

Sudbina had dared to request an audience with the Conqueror. The Kapi Agha had laughed at her folly, saying such was the stupidity of women. So she appealed to the harpist who appealed on her behalf.

Kemal himself met with the great sultan. He pleaded Sudbina's case and also clemency for her father. His Imperial Majesty would entertain none of it, thinking his son naïve and stupidly smitten with an infidel's daughter. Should he not be grateful that the Ottoman leader spared the heads of the despot and his daughter? What loyalty did Kemal owe either? Had he turned infidel these lost years? Though much contented that his son had returned to him, Mehmed II had no intention of seeking his council or granting him any further powers.

Instead, for the remainder of the meeting, the sultan merely tried to divert the harpist's attention with a particularly exquisite *çengi* dancer.

So there would be no audience. She was told she would never set eyes on Mehmed II. But the Grand Vizier spoke to her now in the ornate hall of the Imperial Council building, a grace she was meant to accept as a great privilege, considering she was a captive and a woman. Standing between the two most powerful eunuchs, Sudbina was allowed no word of reply or protest.

She was summarily dismissed and returned to her chambers where the women slaves of the harem had already begun packing her trunk. Doubt churning in her stomach, she wandered over to the harem kitchen and spoke with the confectionary cook who was pouring a clear liquid into a ceramic jar.

"Drink, sad Despoina." The elder woman offered a small glass cup to the young captive, who took and sniffed it.

"It will ensure your good health."

Sudbina took a tentative sip. It was tasteless. "What is it?"

"April rain. We gather it in those *nisan tası*," she indicated a shelf display of many silver, bronze, and brass bowls, some plain and others ornately scrolled. The woman placed the ceramic container onto a shelf with others. "This water has powerful properties for the sultan's health, insha'Allah. We collect these precious drops every April for his purification and cleansing."

"Would this liquid cure someone who seemed unable to wake?" The despoina thought of her somnolent companions long left behind in the deep woods.

"Who knows for certain? But I believe yes. Such are the

powers of April and rain."

Sudbina drained her drink and handed back the cup. The confectioner turned away to her mortar and began to crush herbs with a pestle. This gave Sudbina the opportunity to steal the jar and secrete it under her garments. Then she thought also to pilfer one of the lesser bowls. Unnoticed in the busy kitchen, she absconded with both, pulse throbbing at her temple as she imagined how she might best use the purloined liquid.

That night she poured a cup and gave it to Kemal. "This April rain is for your father. A means to thank him for sparing my life and in hope of my safe delivery."

The harpist eyed her. "I will deliver it to him. Shall I drink from it first to see if it is sound?"

"You may. If you wish."

Ten heartbeats passed in silence.

"Better I should save it all for the sultan."

"Perhaps, yes."

"I will go with you in the morning. I do not want you alone on this trek."

"My brother is to accompany me."

"So I hear."

"I will be safe with you or without."

"I know you are strong and capable."

"I am a despoina."

"I did not—I never meant to suggest, Despoina, that you were mine to possess. I—I did not want to see you married."

"Married off? Or to another?"

"Both, I suppose," he shrugged. "I know you have not forgiven me. But I swear to you now, Sudbina. Ask and I shall quit this place, this palace, this life. I am yours."

"How can I ask that you leave your people?"

"Who will I make music with?"

"There are many fine musicians in the sultan's court."

"Yes, but I have learned a different tune. Think Despoina: I could be a *guslar*; you a *pevač*. We could be itinerant musicians singing songs and stories throughout the empire of the sultan. It would be a different life, but an honest one."

"We would be beggars."

"It is likely."

"You are a dreamer, harpist."

"Yes. Moreso than a sultan's son."

"What need have I of a dreamer?"

"We all need our dreams, Despoina."

"So then, accompany me tomorrow with your harp and your dreams." The harpist's arpeggios that night took on a hopeful note.

Also that night, or so said the whispers in the harem, the sultan slept deep. He did not wake to bid the travelling party, or his son, farewell.

They met on a plain, the very same, former scene of Serbian infamy and defeat. A large group of soldiers accompanied the despot, but it paled in comparison to the mighty and disciplined regiment of the Mehmed II's Janissaries. Her father's men were as peasants on work ponies compared to the glory and might of their foes on fine and well-trained steeds.

As the horse hooves came to rest and the two camps faced each other, a tense quietude descended. Anxiety, like a long-legged spider, crept along Sudbina's flesh. She, the harpist, and her brother dismounted to face the despot.

Her father's head was high, as if in defiance of this symbolic meeting place, deliberately chosen by the sultan to pour salt on an ancient wound. To Sudbina, he seemed somehow older around the eyes, less grand and certain than the young man who stood across from him.

The despot greeted his long-lost son with great formality, his eyes betraying neither affection nor expectation.

"You have grown tall and sure."

"True. I have. I serve my sultan with my life. And you have grown old."

Sudbina saw her father's jaw change. "You have become a Musliman."

"Maşallah! I am a member of the Janissary."

"So it would seem."

Sokollu gestured to his sister. "Your treasure is returned."

The despot took a step forward. "A son should recognize his father."

The Janissary took another closer. "A father should recognize his son."

They stared one at the other, mirror obdurate images of pride.

"I could order my men to seize you." The despot's voice was hard. "Who knows? Perhaps even now one of my marksmen is fitting arrow to bow to take aim at your heart."

"Who knows?" Sokullu adjusted the gilt scimitar at his hip. "Perhaps, Despot, I will steal back in the night, slit your throat, and take your head back to the sultan, leaving, for all to see, your cowardly body impaled upon a stake in the centre of this field as feast for the crows."

Sudbina shivered at the frothing temper of these two men, blood of her blood. Finally, the despot turned away. The Janissary smiled thinly.

Her father next ordered two of his men to reveal a first chest, "Here is the tribute to your chosen lord," and he pointed to another, "and this is the ransom."

With a sharp command, Sokullu ordered that the two chests be loaded onto the back of the carriage drawn by a team of strong horses.

Sudbina stepped towards her father. "I am sorry for this trouble, dear father. I did not wish to bring you to this place or this time, but I am glad to be back with you ..."

He turned to her at last. "You, daughter, are hitherto not to speak to me unless spoken to from now until my death or yours. Your talking is what brought us to this awful place. Your insolence, your disobedience have cost me a great deal of gold and silver and more ..."

"But ..."

"Silence! We will return to the castle. You will wait out your days there and never leave until you are a bride. Know this: you will be wed to the first suitor who comes forth for you, no matter how old or poor or ugly. I am done. I wipe my hands of you!"

"Father!"

And with sudden motion, the dark-browed man took his fist to the left side of Sudbina's head, knocking her to the ground with his impact. She heard a ringing of bells. He kicked her hard as she lay trying to catch her breath. Blows continued to rain on her arms, her back, her stomach. She cried out but they did not slow. It was as if she were caught in a tumult of falling boulders. Sudbina wondered if she would die at her father's hands and feet.

"No! My Lord!" The harpist was at her side, and finally the blows ceased. He helped her to sit, then to gingerly rise to her feet and to balance.

"And you! Interloper! Inveigler! I gave you a roof, food, my protection—even my affection. And see how you betray me. You are ever the son of the sultan. The dog filth beneath my shoe. Out of my sight from this moment hence. Or you will not live through the day."

"Go, go," Sudbina managed.

Seeing there was no mercy in the despot's gaze, the harpist turned stiffly, then strode to his horse and mounted. "I will not forsake you, Despoina," he called in Turkish. He galloped towards the nearest bank of trees and disappeared into their midst.

Sudbina kept her eyes on the ground and so did not witness the final hateful look that passed between father and estranged son. Sokullu said nothing in parting to his sister and had done nothing to intervene in her assault. Issuing commands to his men, he turned his back on those who were his former family. The noise and dust of their leave-taking filled the air for many moments.

When she dared to look up, her father had quitted the field. She touched her bruised cheek, already visibly discolouring, and wiped her bloodied mouth. She could feel her left eye beginning to swell. The pain clutching her chest did likewise. Though she had difficulty walking, no one came to her aid.

Banished to a tent and under the charge of several terse waiting women, Sudbina, throbbing from the hurts of the afternoon, tried to assess her choices.

Her impulse was to seek again her father, beg his forgiveness. She could not fathom his treatment of her. Had she not been his last and favourite daughter? Where had his affection flown? Then another feeling flamed within her. Injustice was a sour taste in her swollen mouth.

What did she, a mere daughter of a despot possess? She had no horse to ride, and besides where might she go? Her sisters, fearing her father's ire, would offer no sanctuary, she was certain. She had once a bow and arrow, but these had been seized and forbidden her. She still had a key secreted in her bodice, but what door could she open? Likewise, there was an old woman's bag of herbs, a skein of silk, a skin of April water, a simple brass bowl, but of what use? Little else had she but her voice and her wits. Her brother was as if dead to her; her lover had taken to the woods and likely the hills. Sudbina tried to sleep, but her bruised body and mind permitted only fitful respite. She tried to summon Baba Roga, but all she heard were the light snores of the slumbering chambermaids and the cough of a guard outside the tent flaps.

The journey home was long and painful. As promised, her father did not deign to speak to her or inquire after her or see to her comfort. It was as if she were just another nameless member of his company. Her heart and body ached with the passing of leagues and days.

She had adored this man, even admired him. Defended any who suggested he was a cruel and exacting master, even as she came to know the rumours for fact. She had been his darling. Was this then the measure and depth of a father's love for a mere daughter? Only as deep as the reflection of himself she cast? And if that reflection proved unpleasant, there ended the love? There began the violence? Now shut out and shunned, she wondered if he had ever truly cared for her or her sisters at all, or simply favoured what they brought him in the way of allies and heirs, or in her case, entertainment and the passing of hours. The other girls had been meek. She had not. And her reward was a beating.

Where was the harpist? Where was the witch? Where in all this wide world was a friend?

Each day's dawn seemed another hard slap, a punch to her will. For even though summer neared, the chill did not seem willing to lift from the air.

3

Tired. He is so very tired.

Dan's shared room at the Tom Baker Cancer Centre is serene and his roommate is a decent sort, a Hungarian who immigrated to Canada in the 1960s. Luba comes every day, sometimes twice a day. She brings him sandwiches from the deli he likes and Tim Hortons coffee. Hospital coffee tastes like piss.

He learns that Mirjam is coming home to Canada in June, when the doctors say she'll be able to fly, and that she has had a horrible injury from a rocket blast. Dan is confused. What was she doing near a rocket? Where in Germany are the launching pads? And then it dawns on him what kind of rocket. Mirjam has been in former Yugoslavia, amidst all the hatred and violence. The ice wall he has been steadfastly building around his heart begins to melt and he allows himself to see her face. His daughter.

Luba patiently explains what she knows of the blast and the type of rocket and the injury, plus some of the missing parts of his daughter's life, puzzle pieces that gradually shape into a sense of what and who Mirjam has become. What was his crazy daughter doing in that awful place?

"She was singing for people affected by the conflict."

"But why?"

Luba sighs. "Because she is Mirjam. Because she is your daughter, after all."

His daughter.

"Will you ask her—ask her to come to the hospital?"

"Don't be surprised if she doesn't come." She helps him adjust his pillows and offers him a sip of water. "How were the radiation treatments today?"

"Same as two days ago. They wear me out."

"Then sleep, Dan. I'll be right here with my magazine."

Mirjam. Mirjam.

And he closes his eyes, but to remember, not dream.

He thinks of his daughter at her birth. So much love and pride mingle in his breast he fears he may explode from the might of it all. His beautiful child walking, then running, towards him. And then away from him, as children must do. As he did from Tata. And then, from Majka to the war.

Suddenly, he is back in Drumheller just returned from England in 1945. And he is running towards his home, his mother. His wide grin shows off a new set of gleaming false teeth courtesy of the Canadian Armed Forces. His hair has been dyed jet so that she will not collapse from the shock of seeing him turned completely white. She is there at the door of their house that looks depressingly old and weather-worn. He will get to painting it as soon as possible. He takes her in his arms. Majka diminished, has lost too much weight. They pass through the door and he is overwhelmed by his sisters and their young families. His eldest sister helps Majka to her chair, lifts her swollen feet onto a small ottoman. Moved by his mother's fragility, her pallor, Dan realizes she is unwell.

"Her diabetes and her heart are killing her," Maria speaks softly to his ear as she embraces her brother for the first time in almost six years.

They feast that afternoon. *Sarma* and lamb *ćevapčići* and *Karađorđeva šnicla* and his sister's flaky *pita zeljanica*, so buttery it melts on his tongue. It is a jubilant homecoming, and the house is filled with loud talk and laughter, even though Majka must leave the table and take to her bed by 6:30.

He joins her to say goodnight. She has knit him a beautiful blanket for whenever he gets married.

"Quickly, my Danilo, find a nice girl. Your Majka doesn't have much time left."

And though he tries to joke this away, he can see death's promise in her watery eyes.

"Mama, I brought you something." He produces a small, wrapped gift from his shaving kit, watches her gnarled hands tear it open carefully—she will save the wrapping—and a joy lift the shadows of her face. It is a fine Italian cameo encircled by delicate silver filigree. Dan stole it off a dead German soldier, but she need never know that. Like she need never know what he has seen and heard and done in the six years since she slapped him for joining the infantry.

Dust powders his mouth and sweat trickles a stream down his back.

Ortona had been colder than a witch's twat. Here he is months later on the Adriatic coast, heading for Rimini, and now it is hotter than Hades. What a country. Its climate extremes remind him of Drumheller.

A group of thirteen grimy men, most of them younger than him, stand glumly before Dan and the other Allied soldiers who've apprehended them. The 1st Brigade and the 48th have been ordered to take prisoners. Alright, by Christ, they'll take two. *The only good German is a dead German.*

Shovels and spades are thrust into hands. Someone barks: "*ausheben!*" And the men begin to dig, some stoic, some weeping openly. It doesn't take long—the ditches are shallow—until someone yells at the men to stand along the edge. Everyone, including Dan, takes aim. One young German turns to face the firing squad, whether in defiance or to plead for his life. It doesn't matter. None of the gunmen is deterred. Dan fires straight at his head and at other heads, then at fallen bodies bouncing in bullet dance. The two Germans selected randomly to be prisoners lie wailing and writhing but unharmed on the ground. Someone gets them up and walking, somehow.

Next, the Allied company members swarm the bodies, looking for trophies, trinkets to send home. Watches are ripped from wrists. Be-ringed fingers are cut from hands. Dan finds the Italian cameo in a soldier's breast pocket, no doubt looted by this bloody Kraut from some sweet, now dead Italian woman. He slips it into his kit without a second thought.

On the way back to camp, one guy the others call Lucky bends over to retrieve the dog tag of a fallen comrade. It has been booby-trapped by the Germans, and his arm is blasted away. He is screaming and two men try to staunch the blood that is pulsing madly out of what used to be his shoulder. Within moments his screams have stopped. Dan trudges by. Bad luck today, Lucky.

The Germans are ingenious at setting Schu-mines and Bouncing Bettys. An afternoon of body parts flying about and the shrieks of the dying and the tumult of explosions have loosened Dan's bowels, probably for the thousandth time in this goddam war. He has taken refuge behind an abandoned, burnt-out tank. Other guys are scurrying to join him, his buddies among them. Then the bastard Jerries, seemingly invisible in the hills, open fire. Instinctively, Chester dives for cover, straight into a mined gully. And he loses his head.

Dan shits himself and vomits up his rations mixed with blood. There over the head of his childhood friend, he makes a promise to himself: to get the hell out of this hell. Before it takes his head off, too.

In two days, Dan is toothless and recuperating in a field hospital waiting to be moved to England, shortly after his rifle backfires into his jaw. His bloody puking seals the deal for discharge. He will not witness the breach of the Gothic Line and could give a rat's ass. He has a bleeding ulcer that will remind him of the horrors of this war for the rest of his life. Lighting a cigarette, Dan closes his eyes and lies back in his bunk. He awakes with a start from a dream of Chester's severed head trying vainly to tell him something Dan desperately needs to know. His cigarette has dropped and the blanket begun to smolder. Dan tosses a cup of water to extinguish the flame and the remnants of the vision of Chester. He wishes he could wash away these last six years.

When he finally returns home, he is treated like a hero. Everywhere he goes folks clap him on the back, shake his hand, thank him for his service, buy him a beer. He easily gets a job at the Five and Dime store in Drumheller and manages to save a little money to help Majka out. Within six months, he buys her a Frigidaire. She, too, thinks him a hero.

Unable to relax, many nights he wanders the streets of his hometown wondering about his buddies. Where his youth went. Who he is. And remembering too much. Finally exhausted, he drops into bed around 4 a.m. and sleeps through his alarm. His manager understands when Dan, the decorated war hero, is late for work.

The Corner Café offers him, and all vets, a free cup of joe and a slice of pie for their service. This gift he accepts for the better part of a year, until he is too embarrassed to acquiesce any longer—he's a working man and can afford the two bits. After Victory in Europ, he is convinced to march with the other returned veterans in the celebratory parade down main street where the joy-filled citizens throng, weeping and laughing, to cheer them along, just as exultant others do elsewhere throughout the world. A couple of guys he knew from school but from different divisions take him for beer at the Elks later that night. They get stupid drunk and fall all over each other on the way home. Dan wakes in a pool of his own vomit, too sick to make it into work that day. His ulcer takes weeks to settle down.

Sometimes he is so terrified by the backfiring of a passing car that he dives for cover, once into the path of a very large, if understanding, woman. A stranger. She coos something sympathetic—her husband had been in the war, too. But he is red with shame and hastens into the nearest shop, Claire's Ladies Fashions, pretending to look for nylon stockings for his mother and sisters.

Dan is not really a heavy drinker, but he watches some of the vets turn to serious drink. He gets it. Liquor softens the edges on the madness. Instead, he starts to look for a wife, thinking this will be the best way to purge the war. Get married, start a family, move on and make a few bucks. Even as he invests in handsome new civvies and starts to date and dance again, insomnia and his troubled gut plague him. Always on edge, he is quick to temper, too quick, once actually hitting his sister, Jovanka, for failing to make coffee on a Sunday morning. In deep contrition, he finds her later that afternoon and apologizes weepily. Because he is her favourite, of course, she understands. His fury will erupt many times again within the confines of the family home. Dan does not understand its wellspring and prefers not to. He is a gas burner always on low flame.

Within two years, Dan buys a car on loan from the Canadian Imperial Bank of Commerce. It is a maroon-coloured 1947 Commander Custom Cruising Studebaker with beautiful white wall tires and a 2.8 litre engine and 80 horsepower. When he drives that baby, heads turn. He has a few dates with a gorgeous blonde from Calgary named Olivia, but she dumps him when her fiancé, Henry, returns from overseas. So he drives Majka, now very frail, all around Drum and East Coulee and across the eleven bridges to Wayne and through the hamlet of Cambria. She is bursting with pride.

And then quietly, on an unremarkable Thursday afternoon,

she dies. Dan thinks his heart will fall out of his body and into the earth. He has never before felt so alone.

She is buried in the Drumheller cemetery. For the first months after her death, he visits the grave weekly to clear it of weeds and place a handful of flowers in the jar. Who will do this for her when he and his sisters are gone? Who will place flowers on the hundreds of thousands of graves overseas?

Dan begins to cry. Luba looks up from her magazine and comes to his bedside.

"It's alright, Dan. I'm here."

"I know. I know."

4

When she picks her child up at the airport, Luba feels rent in two. Mirjam, pale from the journey, immediately collapses into tears the moment she sees her mother's face at the arrival gate. Luba enfolds her daughter in her arms as if to return her to the womb. Sniffling and blowing into tissues, they eventually break apart and join the mass of people waiting at the luggage carousel.

"How is your young man—Alban?" Luba enunciates clearly over the din.

"My flight was okay, but my ears didn't like the pressure changes much."

Luba, fighting tears, shakes her head and puts her hand to Mirjam's cheek.

"Here, Ma. This works best." She hands her mother a small black notebook with a pen and Luba scratches across the page.

"He's fine and in our flat in Berlin. I'll need your help to call him as soon as we're at your place. He made me promise. Alban really wanted to come, but we could only afford the single ticket. And he has the commitment to the Orchestra Academy of the Berliner Philharmonic. It wasn't possible for him ..."

"We'll meet him soon." Luba wonders how to make her written words reassuring.

Later over tea at the familiar table, in the house she left two years previous in dishonour and dismay, Mirjam fills Luba in on most of the missing chapters of the story. Her mother is quiet. There is little to say and nothing her daughter will hear.

Luba shares the names of several audiologists who come highly recommended. She has already booked three appointments for the coming week. Through her wilting hope and jet lag, Mirjam puts on her bravest face for her mother.

So Luba shows her the guest room she has eagerly prepared these past few days. A bouquet of irises, Mirjam's favourite, adorns the bureau and a lavender duvet and sheets, newly purchased, lie open and waiting. Gratefully, daughter takes to bed. Luba comes in to kiss her and stroke her brow. She checks back frequently as she sleeps, just as she first did when Mirjam was a baby.

As her daughter slumbers, Luba runs to the hospital to find her husband is also asleep. She returns home where Mirjam has risen and is making coffee in a copper pot on the stove.

"It's a gift I brought you, Ma. A *cezve* for Turkish coffee. I learned to make it in Istanbul."

She pours the dark brew into two small ceramic demitasse cups, covered with intricate scrolls and designs in red, blue, and green.

Luba thinks the coffee gritty and too sweet, and she gratefully sips the water Mirjam has also provided. Her daughter places a small plate of German chocolates on the table and pops one into her mother's mouth. "These are delicious—from our local *Schokoladenhaus*. Alban chose them for you."

Once again, mother and daughter sit together, as they have done so many times, discussing first teenaged, then later, adult concerns. Mirjam looks better rested, but there is something changed about her. Perhaps it is the set of her shoulders or the small lines near her mouth. Luba looks down at her own hands, then picks up the pen.

"He has asked to see you."

"I'll go. It's why I came home, Ma. And to see you."

"I'm sorry it all went so bad that you felt you had to leave, Mirjam."

"You've got nothing to be sorry about. And besides, you know I left for Helmut and the music."

"Yes, but you didn't come back. Not for two years." Luba wipes the tears from the notebook before passing it to her daughter to read.

"Ma." Mirjam looks at her mother's crepe-y hands lying on the table next to a mug of tea. Blue veins are visible under the thinning skin. Mirjam takes one of them in her own. "I didn't mean to. I—"

"It's okay, my sweet girl." Luba turns the page. "You'll find him changed."

"As in different? Or just sick."

"Older. Old."

"He's not that old, Ma. Seventy-five?"

"Yes, he is."

They decide Mirjam will visit him a day or two after his next round of radiation, after Dan has had a chance to rest from treatment. In the meantime, Luba invites her to the Inglewood

Bird Sanctuary for a daily walk. Lu is on compassionate leave from her job there, but they might drop in to meet her co-workers and her girl could use some sun even though, since the solstice, it's been very windy, a cruel and chilly June.

They wrap themselves in woolens and stroll past the signs and along the pathways and wooden boardwalks. Songbirds chirrup them along their way, but later along the path are usurped by the cacophonous crows that have taken up residence as they usually do in previous year's nesting areas.

Luba writes, "Have you heard of a crow court?"

Mirjam, glancing upwards at the black preening birds, shakes her head.

"Some say it is just old wives' tales but reports still circulate from time to time in the news about such things. A large, noisy group of crows gathers in a circle, falling quiet when one submissive bird steps into the centre and squawks as though defending itself. Followed by a kind of cawing judgement from the jurors in the circle. If found guilty, the crow at the centre is pecked to death."

"How awful. A real murder of crows."

"No one knows, or science can't seem to tell us, if the bird is truly guilty of some offense or is simply scapegoated."

"Crows sometimes seem to follow me."

"They're very smart. *Corvus brachyrhynchos*, members of the *Corvidae* family."

Mirjam thinks of crows surrounding the victim and Serbs on the hills surrounding Sarajevo. Was Mirsada Durić, the dead mother of the boy they rescued, like the scapegoat crow in the centre of an accusing court? Was she, Mirjam, also the accused?

She says nothing to her mother, having spared her the goriest details of the January 9th attack. They walk along peaceably through the budding willows as though terror and violence do not really exist in the world.

Then Luba stops still. A dark man ahead of them aims a camera at the crows' nests. He turns and freezes. Mirjam cannot read what passes between her mother and the photographer.

"Do you know him?"

Luba nods.

The man begins to walk towards them, as if hesitant.

"Should we be worried?"

"Don't be stupid, Mirjam!" Luba, annoyed, forgets she cannot hear and speaks aloud. "He is my ..." She remembers to write "friend."

"Hodi."

"Luba, my—my dear. Hello."

"This is my daughter, Mirjam."

"Hello Mirjam." Hodi extends his hand to shake hers. "I have heard so much about you and your lovely singing voice."

"Hodi, Mirjam cannot understand you clearly. She was in a terrible explosion and has lost her hearing."

"No!" Hodi shows genuine shock. "I'm so sorry."

"We are doing all we can. Mirjam will be seeing several specialists."

"I'm sorry—how awful. You are a singer. You must be ... I am sorry."

Mirjam understands he is apologizing for her impairment. She finds pity to be exhausting. Sensing her mother and this man would like to speak together, she escapes to the nearby park bench, dedicated to Marvin Fender, late of Calgary, beloved father and birdwatcher.

"How have you been, Hodi?"

"Luba, I—I am so sorry. For my daughter, her behaviour, her rudeness."

"I think I understand her. But I thought I might hear from you." She tries to keep her voice light.

"I know ... I did not call. I did not write."

"I can guess why." He says nothing but fiddles with his camera, so Luba presses him. "Did you know I'm on leave? Is that why you came today?"

"Luba, I did not. I came by, I've come by several times in hopes of running in to you as we used to."

"You have a phone."

"You're right. I could find no words."

"You're doing fine just now."

"I was so embarrassed ..."

"Me too."

"Mwara ... my daughter is not very fond of white people. She had some bad times in her school, perhaps because she was the youngest of our children and a girl. And she—"

"She wants to protect you. I suppose we're all guilty of wanting to stick with our own." She laughs. "I was really such an idiot. I had to Google your country to find out about Kenya. I was so stupid and ignorant. I still am. But ... Well. I have since taken *Petals of Blood* from the library, and I have another, *Mother, Sing for Me*, on reserve."

"Ngũgĩ wa Thiong'o, Kenya's greatest writer. His son is a

fine writer, also."

"Oh, that is how you pronounce his name. Thank you. Some say he will one day win the Nobel Prize."

"All of Kenya and the diaspora hope so."

"I know that word, too, now: *diaspora*."

"You are part of a diaspora, also."

"Yes, I guess I am. But I'm not much involved in my community or heritage. That desire was shamed out of me, I suppose." She looks over at Mirjam. "I think it is true for her, or it was. She longed to excise from her anything that was Serbian. Because of my husband. They do not ... see eye to eye."

Hodi's voice is apologetic. "That sometimes is the way of fathers and daughters."

There is a pause and a nearby meadowlark trills, a rarity in the city. Lu cranes her ear to the sound.

"May I—may we see each other again, Luba? I have so missed you."

"I've missed you, also." She struggles to keep her breath even, controlled. "But I don't think so, Hodi."

"I see." Disappointment etches his face.

"My husband is dying. Lung cancer."

Hodi turns to her. Takes her hands in his. They are both aware that Mirjam is watching from her perch on the park bench. "I am so sad for what you and your family are going through, Luba. I know what my wife ... I am here, if you need a—a friend. I will be here. You have my number. Please call me."

"Your daughter?"

"Is far away and back in Toronto where she lives her own life, usually quite unaware of anything to do with her father.

Her self-righteousness only rises to the surface when she comes to Calgary." He laughs gently. "Perhaps it has something to do with the proximity of the mountains so that she feels so eager to be high and mighty."

"I think for now"—Luba's voice is soft, but firm—"it's best we leave things as they are."

Regret tempers his half-smile. Hodi nods. "Goodbye then, for now." He waves to Mirjam and walks in the opposite direction. Luba tucks their conversation away for later.

Rising from the bench, Mirjam makes a mental note to find out more about this man from her mother.

5

"Wrong. I was ... wrong." It has taken several visits, many of them abbreviated because Dan seems unable to tolerate more than an hour of company, but now upright, he faces his daughter alone.

She cannot hear her father's voice, but she can sense it is weak. He is so painfully shrunken. "Please write it down."

Shakily, Dan takes the pen and pad.

Mirjam reads and nods. "Yes Daddy. It's okay now. It's past."

"Do you love Daddy? Daddy loves you. I shouldn't have hit you."

"No."

"But you goaded me into it."

Mirjam supposes she did. Wanting the finality. The deathblow. Wanting her father and her to be over. "I goaded you into hitting me. My fault. You're right. You always were." Though, of course, she means none of this.

Her remembering is visceral. Luba sobbing against the wall where he'd shoved her. The baby picture crashing to the floor, glass shattering along with the family. She recalls the verbal assault erupting from his mouth and her own well-wrought words of malice. Mirjam now knows too well that she has always been Dan's most astute student.

"Would you have killed me if you'd had a gun?"

Yes. As you would have killed me. But she does not write this. She will reserve it for later, perhaps.

For her mother has re-entered the hospital room with coffee and donuts.

Now they will sit together in the July sunlight streaking in between the bird-shite streaks on the window. They will break bread and drink to each other's health as if downing a shot of *šljivovica*. Come to think of it, Mirjam decides she will buy a bottle from the liquor store and share it with him next visit.

Except that he may be coming home, depending on how he responds to the radiation. Mirjam wills this not to happen, makes the excuse to herself that it would be best for her mother. But in reality, she does not feel she can stomach ever being in the same house as her father again. The thought of him near fills her with fear and revulsion.

She watches her parents through the afternoon. Luba is attentive and kind to Dan, who surely doesn't deserve it, thinks Mirjam. She has pretended forgiveness for her mother's sake. Luba seems happier because they are three again. But there hovers a pong of resignation about the room. Perhaps it is just hospital smell. Or is it the stench of disease? Does cancer have a smell? She supposes it may be the wafting acceptance of Dan's death, though after the radiation treatments, he claims to be fighting back. She can only see a man melting away before her. Maybe it is just the stink of recognizing they will all now play again their parts, dragging on the family drama, a long day's journey into night. Mirjam the prodigal daughter, Luba the doting mother and wife, Dan, a dying Lear-figure. Something about the way Luba's shoulders droop makes Mirjam anxious for her.

Tonight she will email Alban about all of this. He will be understanding and write to reassure her she is not mad to be back here watching her father die. She wishes he were here with her—he asks her repeatedly if he should come, but each time she declines. Mirjam fancies that her parents, her father too, would like the young cellist. At the very least, Alban could help her to sort out her feelings about all of this. But it is pretense. Dan will never like anyone she loves. And she will not bring Alban into the toxic mix of her family. So Mirjam vacillates between pity and resentment for the desiccated figure in the hospital bed. She worries for her mother. And of course, all tangled up in the matter is what is the matter with her hearing.

"You go to the specialist tomorrow?" Dan writes.

She nods.

"They'll fix you up. Great docs in Calgary. Thank Christ for our healthcare system."

She doesn't tell him or Luba that the system in Germany is very fine and that she has had the best of medical care and expert opinion. She imagines that if she can never hear or sing again Dan would be very glad of her need to finally settle down and get a real job.

When Luba excuses herself to the bathroom, Dan scribbles, "What was it like? Over there?"

"It was amazing and it was a nightmare—an amazing nightmare. Everywhere we went, we were welcomed by so many lovely and generous people ... who seem to want to kill each other. It is war."

Unexpectedly, her father tears up at this. "I understand war."

"I guess you do."

"I will write a little of what I saw and lived for next time."

As she promised herself, when Mirjam next returns with Luba, they each share a small glass of *rakija*. Her father coughs and she helps raise the hospital bed while Luba pats his back and gives him a sip of water. When he has calmed, he hands his daughter the notepad. He has written only a half-page of words in shaky penmanship.

"They stole our youth. Forced us to march and slog through Europe and into Africa until varicose veins mapped our legs. Forced us to stay awake for thirty-six, seventy-two hours and more. Forced us through the concentration camps. Forced us to look at what men can do. I saw terrible things, too terrible to share with you."

"They forced you to kill."

"Yes."

"You had no choice?"

"Court martial if you refused. Some did. Not me."

"You're proud of this?"

"No. Not proud. I was a soldier following orders. It was—it was war."

"Why are we talking about this now?" Luba's hands are restless as a bird's wings. She turns the radio she has brought to the

CBC to listen to Jurgen Gothe on *DiscDrive*.

Because Mirjam cannot hear, she decides to take a walk down to the visitors' lounge. The vinyl seats are coolly complaining as she sits. A television blares away in the corner. Mirjam is relieved that the smiling talk show host and his inane guests are muted.

Her father was a killer. Just like the Serbs in the hills around Sarajevo. He was forced to kill. And kill. She recalled him once in Safeway shouting at the German baker in annoyance at his poor customer service, "I killed better Germans than you in the war." She'd slunk away down the produce aisle in teenaged mortification.

Her father the killer. To protect the world. To keep us all safe. Kill and be a man. What lies we tell our sons.

She knows Dan hated war. But neither can he relinquish the tales of glory. "I'd go again," she remembers him saying, his eyes wet and Vera Lynn on the record player. He'd framed the medals. Collected the pension. Curled his hands into fists. And kept them that way throughout their lives together. Even taking the side of the maligned Serbs when Milošević came to power and people began uttering the word genocide. Dan the killer would not relent. Mirjam wonders what he would think of Serbs had he been in Sarajevo or Srebenica or Karaman's house in Foča.

But then she remembers her friends in Belgrade and is ashamed. She too harbours an intolerance.

So many stories of atrocities on all sides are leaking out of the sieve that is the former Yugoslavia. Who is the victim? Who is the torturer? Who is the executioner? Where will be the next theatre of ethnic cleansing with its horrors upon horrors? Violence and terror are the songs from this and that country, the songs of her father and of her ancestors. Does she, Mirjam, also sing the songs?

And yet Leno is interviewing Hugh Grant for some indiscretion half a world away from the real minotaurs lost in a labyrinth of hate.

She returns to Dan's bedside and they share a last bedtime shot of *šljivovica*.

"The chaplain came today."

"Did he?"

"I sent him away. The Orthodox priest, too."

"Maybe I should find a rabbi?"

But he doesn't seem to think her joke is funny. Or he has simply shrugged it off and gone to sleep.

Mirjam watches him while Luba dozes in the other chair. Unbidden, the opening strains of Holst's *Saturn: Bringer of Old Age* trickle across her memory's ear. Her father's hair is pure white. Though he is still swarthy, a jaundice settles now on his face and shadows deepen his sunken cheeks. A nurse had earlier removed Dan's teeth for the evening and now they sit grinning in a glass filled with cleaning solution. Her father seems a cadaver but for his shallow breathing, aided by the plastic nose tube fitted to the oxygen. How long before he succumbs?

In his narrow bed, Dan inhales raggedly and deeply. For a brief second, she wonders if this is his last breath. When he breathes noisily out and then in again, her disappointment spills like ink across a page.

6

Days turned to weeks turned to months.

A young woman alone, she sat in a tower like Zlatokosa of the famed folktale.

She recalled a song based on the story, but Sudbina no longer believed in happy endings. So she did not bother to sing it.

Gradually, her bruises turned from purple to blue to yellow, at last fading away entirely. While she nursed her soreness, she nursed her resentment. It was, in truth, her only enduring companion. Her favourite handmaidens had all been dismissed by the despot and replaced by strangers who paid her little attention or affection. They were empty-headed and completely loyal to their lord.

Her father remained a silent, hunkering presence in the castle. Even though she seldom saw him, she felt him always. When he travelled out on some tax errand or hunting party, Sudbina allowed herself to exhale. His absence helped alleviate her fear. But whenever she heard his heavy steps return through the corridors, her pulse began to race. Too often she awoke, shaken from night terrors wherein she'd been visited by a fiery dragon, very nearly succumbing to its flaming breath.

True to his word, the harpist had thrice visited her late at night, harping soft tunes from many metres below, having bribed the gatekeeper or addled his wits with drink. But Kemal was unable to climb the walls or otherwise trespass the despot's fortress. Sudbina remained too heavily guarded.

He sent her messages delivered to her windowsill by a clever blackbird he'd trained, but these brief and hasty notes bespoke of his love and little else. What had she hoped for? Deliverance and rescue? Doubt about the power of any man's love came to rest permanently in her mind.

Her quickly written replies were short and without hope. She was beyond penning words of love. Often, she found she had nothing to say at all. Still the blackbird came every day, faithfully, just in case she had a message for the harpist.

Listless, she spent her time at working, unwinding, rewinding and reworking the skein of silk, her gift from Baba Roga.

No other suitor had yet come to ask for her hand. Though she was much relieved by this, the despoina winced at the tales her chambermaids whispered behind their hands when they thought she dozed. As the summer passed, certain of them swore that the despot planned to lock his last remaining daughter away until she turned skeleton. Could it be true?

She was lonely and bored as a tethered young colt. After her many adventures, it galled her to think that this was to be her fate. This or marriage to some fat old *ujka*. Many nights she wept hotly into her pillow. Others she sang wistfully to herself and the maids; her father now never more asked for her songs. Her solitary heart grew sadder and harder. To be so ill-used and not even a chance to set matters aright. Sudbina felt as forsaken as a long-forgotten childhood toy. Broken.

Too, she wondered anxiously about the members of her first foraying party, still locked in deep sleep within the forest. She wanted to appeal to her father on their behalf so that he might send forth a cadre to bring them safely back to the castle. But her entreaties for an audience were met with sullen silence. To allay her worries, she turned to needlepoint and to the few books granted her. When the weather was fair, she was permitted to traipse along the garden paths, but always and ever in the company of some female chaperone. At least the sun on her face allowed her a short period of grace out and away from the greyness of her chambers. But always such relief was only too fleeting.

Letters to her sisters either went unanswered or the women were long in replying and could give her no assurances of a visit. Sudbina knew her father was behind this further indignity, and she felt the tendrils of hate begin to creep and then lodge firmly about her breast.

A young woman locked in a tower has a great deal of time to herself and a great deal to think about. Time permits one opportunity not only to dream, but to plot. Sudbina kept her thoughts to herself. But they began to provide a kind of hope, a kind of pleasure. And along with working her silk, she began to work a plan.

The first of the twelve great feasts was approaching and Sudbina's father enlisted the women of his castle to begin the preparations. At last, her sisters and their sprawling families were granted leave to travel to their paternal home. It would be a marvellous occasion, replete with feasting, dancing and music. Clouds of uncertainty began to lift from Sudbina's mind.

Rumbling carriages announced the arrival of Milosti and Vera, their children and husbands. Wet-eyed, the sisters greeted each other. Their first few days were filled with news and catching up with months spent apart, the doings of children, the vagaries of marriage. The castle seemed bursting with energy.

Finally, one afternoon, the sisters were alone together.

"But what, dear Sudbina," Milosti scolded softly, "were you possibly thinking, running from our midst and into the mouth of danger? You, a mere woman. And the daughter of our father. You have brought him such disgrace."

"I was not meant to be caged." Sudbina kept her eyes on the skein and the silk braid she worked in her lap.

"Caged? You are meant to be obedient and loving. To follow Father's guidance and direction. That is a daughter's duty."

"He beat me. Do you know this?"

"Sometimes a woman—well, sometimes we deserve it. It is the cost of disobeying father's love."

"You have cost him dearly," Vera echoed.

"His pride has cost him."

"Father paid a good fortune for your safe return."

"He paid a good fortune to ensure his kingdom remained safe from the Conqueror who could, with a mere flick of his wrist, smite Father from the earth."

"Nonsense, Father is powerful and—"

"Father would not last an afternoon if the sultan so commanded. Mehmed II is very mighty indeed."

"The Turk is a brutal tyrant!"

"Father is like a small mirror image of his foe."

The two sisters gasped at the third.

"Both are cruel masters and, at a whim, their cruelty extends to their subjects, to their families, if such is their displeasure, if the tax is not paid, or if the wind should change. They have learned well their barbarous lessons, each from the other."

"How can you compare our father to he who conquered our lands, subjugated our people?" Vera dabbed her kerchief to her eyes.

"You have grown willful and spiteful in the company of Turks," Milosti shook her head sadly.

"Wiser, rather."

"I know not what you have seen, sister," Milosti met Sudbina's eyes, "but you speak such lies."

"I speak what you both are unwilling to hear, what I myself denied for a very long time."

"But now! We mustn't fall to quarrelling amongst ourselves," said Vera, always the peacemaker of the three siblings. "We cannot waste the hours. Come, look what we have brought you, Sudbina! Milosti has sewn this fine gown, and I have trimmed it with lovely lace and ribbons. It is your very best colour: red. Within the hour we will suit you up for the feast! More time spent in our company—and Father's—will show you your error, bring you to your better senses. You shall see. And you shall find a way to apologize and soften his heart."

Not in this life, Sudbina thought but did not say. She excused herself, promising to return shortly, and descended to the kitchens, grateful for the freedom of movement that preparations for the family and feast had only lately afforded her.

That eve, in the grand hall and by the firelight, the family sat together at the many tables laden with roast game and harvest vegetables. Wine was plentiful as was the plum brandy. A merry mood echoed about the walls. Children played at games after the great meal while the adults gamboled to music finely wrought by the seven musicians hired for the occasion—two played *gadje* and *gusle*, another the *šupeljka*, a fourth the *tapan*, a fifth and sixth two *zurnas*, and the seventh, a bearded hunchback, played the *çeng*. Sudbina worked at her smile, pretending her pleasure at it all, never once looking at her father, nor he at her. But at last, the family begged her, their nightingale, for a song or two, and she graciously complied. Her voice practiced and polished, the despoina sang first an old favourite well known to the musicians, a country folksong with a lively chorus that invited everyone to join along. When the applause died, she moved to an unknown and unaccompanied ballad, beginning softly, her confidence rising in volume:

> *Once lost and wand'ring through a vale*
> *She came upon a wise old one*
> *Who bid her weave another tale*
> *And so upon the rising sun*
> *She took to horseback through the dale*
> *But oh, her luck was quite undone*
> *As sudden captive she became*
> *For so it seemed a prize was won*

Her heart was filled with fear and pain
And so another fate was spun

But not for love, when all was done
For once upon a field of shame
Much gold was passed from sire to son
She thought her captor was to blame
Yet kin was foe and hope outrun

Many are the songs we sing
For son and daughter key
To who they are and what they are
All wrought in melody

So split a heart or break a vow
And all your honour feign
Raise the cup of lies, my sire
The drink will be your bane

With the last note, Sudbina turned to look squarely at the despot, who rose, sputtering as if in a fit. He pointed at her, "Begone!" And the room fell very still. Her sisters dared not breathe. Everyone tried not to meet another's gaze. "Take the slattern away!"

But Sudbina had already started for her chamber. She did not lower her chin, even as two attendants each took an arm to propel her the faster away. Her feet felt light as she ascended the many steps. When the bolt of her tower room slid into place, locking her within, she leapt to action.

Tearing off her festive garments, she dug out of a chest her travel garb, still dusty but sufficient. Her satchel was already packed and hidden behind the arras. In it was food and her few treasures. Next, she fastened one end of the silken ladder, designed and knotted these many weeks, to the great oak door handle and dropped the other out through the window. Down it tumbled, metre by metre. Though she could only see a short way into the dark below, Sudbina had never been afraid of heights and descended surely, silken rung by rung. At the bottom awaited the harpist, beard and hunchback disguise thrown off, steadying two saddled horses.

They led the beasts quietly through the courtyard to the gate where the drunken keeper slept soundly. It was child's play to swing open and shut again the wooden doors. Within moments the despot's castle was at their backs. Then two dark silhouettes cantered away under the waxing moon.

Sudbina did not witness the foaming of her father's mouth, his agonized twitching as the poison worked its way through his writhing form while he lay abed. She did not see the terror that crossed his face in recognition of his end and who had hastened it. She did not see his fixed stare at the ceiling, his mouth locked in a death grimace or her sisters clutching his hands and sobbing when he was discovered in a pool of vomit and shit the next morning. Sudbina was leagues away by then. Leagues away and singing a joyous new tune.

7

I didn't think you'd come.

Of course, I would come, Dan. You've been my client for three years. And I've grown rather fond of you.

I—I was rude to you last time I visited your office.

Just the last time? The psychologist shifts his lanky form and chuckles.

Okay, a lot of times. I'm sorry for that. I'm sorry for not coming back. It's been quite a few months ...

It's fine. I've heard worse. And besides you called me this week and that's an excellent sign. As it happens, I'm pretty open in August—many people are off on vacation. And as for rudeness—well, I'm used to anger, being an anger management specialist and all.

I guess so.

You finished your course of radiation treatments?

Yeah, done. I thought I could get home, but I'm so damned weak ...

How is your pain?

Only hurts when I breathe.

Are you feeling able to talk? Should I go?

No, it's good that you came. Thank you for coming.

Something you'd like to get off your chest, Dan?

Not really. Just wanted to ... you know.

No problem. I can stay for about thirty minutes before I have to pick up my kid from his guitar lesson.

You got a kid?

Yup. Jadon, my teenaged son who is going on forty or thinks he is. Also thinks that I'm the anti-Christ of fathers. Too embarrassed by me to hang out with me much, but he lets me drive him places, so that's our quality time together. Lives with his mom. He plays lead guitar and has notions of being in a grunge band.

Dan doesn't know what that is but nods anyway.

Let's see. We were talking about your father the last time I saw you.

I found him. And I saw his grave. Drove up to Edmonton and paid for a monument marker.

How was that for you?

Sad. But a kind of closure.

You never got to say goodbye, did you, Dan?

No. And I missed him, I realize now. So much that I took off for the war, the first chance I got. Had to prove I was a man. To him. Or someone.

Is that what war does? Makes boys into men?

Yeah. Did me.

Hell of a way to grow up, isn't it?

I did some things. Awful things. In the war.

Do you want to tell me about them?

Not really. I just want to say out loud that I did them. They were wrong. I was wrong. I never really got over that stuff.

The psychologist shifts again, leaning forward.

How could you, Dan? How is any young man ready for what he sees when he goes to war? No one could prepare you.

I should have stopped myself. I could have said no.

But you didn't. You were a boy, and a fatherless one at that, sent over to do a killer's work. Can you see how that is a perversion of manhood? How it might cause a boy or a man to lose his grip? Make insane choices?

Dan sighs.

And when you came home, what support did Veteran's Affairs offer you?

A job. Schooling, if I wanted. My pension—

I'm not talking about that. I mean what did the VA know about PTSD or shellshock back then? What therapy or treatment was there for all those wounded boys returning after that terrible war?

Nothing.

Exactly. It's taken you fifty years to get here.

Is that why ... why I hit Luba?

Maybe. Probably. It's also a combination of how you were raised, your own temperament, a definition of masculinity that you adopted. But yes, when you have been the victim of terror, sometimes the victim becomes terrorist.

I'm not a terrorist.

No, not in a global sense.

Is there a connection, do you think?

We're pretty sure.

Jesus.

I think he was pretty much an anti-terrorist, Dan.

It is a lot to take in. Dan can feel his ulcer complaining, despite the bland hospital food he's barely been able to eat. He knows by now, of course, that his ulcer acts up when his anxiety or his temper are roused. So it shouldn't surprise him.

Is he surprised?

No. He'd sensed it all before. Killer. Terrorist. These are hard words to admit to himself. To know what and who he was. Is. The words aren't all he is, not all that make him Danilo, but they have long been a part of him. Suddenly, Dan is very glad that his father died before he became these things. His father only knew him as an eager boy, unspoiled and with all of life before him. Best he never knew the truth about his son.

Anything else you'd care to tell me? The psychologist's low voice brings him back to the room.

I don't—I don't think so.

I'd better be going then.

Thank you.

I'm glad I could come.

No, I mean, thank you.

You're welcome, Dan. Anytime.

But there will be no other time, Dan knows. He reaches out his hand and tries to control the tremor. The psychologist takes and shakes it warmly.

Hope you're able to get some rest, Dan. Some peace. He rises, heading for the door, then pauses.

You should know something, Dan. I'm glad, so many Canadians are glad of what you did over there. We do, I think, enjoy a better life because of you soldiers. Your sacrifices. I'm sorry that it cost you so much, Dan. But I am grateful for your service. I think your father would have been proud of you, too.

Dan nods, not trusting his voice, and the man leaves. It is quiet in the room. The Hungarian is asleep, his usual pre-supper nap. Exhausted, Dan craves sleep, too, but resists. Napping often troubles him. He'll often awake with a start, fearful that he will never wake again.

Did Tata feel like this? Dan wishes he could ask him. He longs for both his parents to be present, consoling him as they had at his childhood sickbed or after waking from some nightmare.

There is only the clock on the wall for cold comfort now. The second hand winds around and around, silent and accusing. He's wasted so much time being angry and afraid, those twin serpents in his mind. What can he do now with this knowledge of how he'd been broken by the war, come to him so late in his remaining hours? He wishes, above anything, that he could start all over again, just like the cheerful admonishment of that old 30s song from his childhood. But instead, he lies dying in a hospital bed, unable to do anything but breathe, and even that is a struggle. What good are wishes?

Luba. Mirjam. He can tell them what he's learned. Maybe they will understand. He will tell them tonight when they come to visit. And then find a way to truly apologize. He watches the clock. Only a few hours. And then he will finally say all that needs saying.

But instead, Dan slips into a coma.

8

Thank goodness, Luba thinks.

In early June they had revisited the will and Dan had left everything to her.

Gone was the clause excising Mirjam from any inheritance. The lawyer had been good enough to come to the hospital. Everything was signed and formalized.

She has the keys to his car, to the security deposit box, and all his paperwork and identification cards in hand. She has the personal directive with its order for no heroic measures, the abbreviation DNR stamped on the page and initialed clearly. She has the information from the Edmonton cemetery, the names and phone numbers of the relatives and Dan's *parbuk*-ing friends ready by the phone. She has to-do lists made and time to go over and over the lists. But she has no idea how to be a widow.

What is left of Dan lies, wracked with laboured breathing, in the white sheets of the hospital bed. Once he'd become unconscious two weeks ago, he'd been moved to a private room on the palliative ward. Doctors said it could be weeks; the nurses say probably only days, perhaps now hours. Luba has a cot at her husband's side. She's slept there fitfully for two nights. This evening Mirjam has offered to take a shift so that her mother can go home for a shower and a night in her own bed.

Luba looks at Dan who is no longer Dan. She's tried speaking to him, has tried to rouse him, but he is as if on another shore and far away from her. His head makes a deep indentation in the pillow and seems to arch slightly backwards. His toothless mouth gapes open in a cadaverous grimace. No one had told her dying was so ugly.

She'd lost her own mother at such a young age, and years ago her father succumbed to a sudden heart attack, so Lu knows nothing of her parents' final days or moments. Were they, too, reduced to empty shells as life flowed from them?

Listening to Dan breathe has become obsessive for her. Sometimes he seems not to inhale at all. This is followed by a sudden gasp of intake. His harsh exhalations often appear to be his last, and then Dan breathes again. Will this breath next be his final?

She applies some Vaseline to his dry lips and moistens the inside of his mouth with a wet oral sponge, as the nurses have instructed her. His nose tube seems fine, but she checks it anyway. Adjusting his blanket for the umpteenth time, Luba thinks to kiss him goodnight. But the sallowness of Dan's skin repulses her, and then she instantly feels guilty. As he lies dying, will he have no last embrace or touch? She wills herself to put her arms about him, as best she might, and lays her head upon his chest as she had often done after their lovemaking through the first good years of their marriage. Luba listens to Dan's lethargic heartbeat and presses closer.

"I loved you."

A gentle music from the radio creeps into her consciousness, an old Nat King Cole ballad from the 1940s and one of her favourites. She reaches to turn up the volume. Many times they had danced to this song in their young courtship.

"Maybe that's why we stayed together," Lu considers aloud, "for sentimental reasons." And of course, for Mirjam. The best thing she and Dan have ever done.

Once she is home, Luba becomes aware of how big, how empty is her home. Though she and Dan had often simply occupied the same space, still he was there. He had been a presence. Now the place is echoes and shadows.

Wandering out to the backyard, she takes her garden spade to the irises buried in the debris of nearly a year. This is a garden of neglect. It is wild and willful, she decides, a little like Mirjam. Lu stands and wipes the soil from her hands. From inside the house comes the whistle of the tea kettle. She'd put it on when she got home from the hospital—that was at least twenty minutes ago.

She wills herself to eat, to drink a cup of tea and try to rest. Instead, she tidies the unread newspapers strewn about the front porch. Maybe she should vacuum. Make a casserole for Mirjam. Luba catches herself in the mirror. Suddenly, she cannot bear to be alone, knowing that she will be.

The city's western night sky is showing off its dusky lavenders and pinks. It's only a few weeks until the autumn equinox. A lone robin calls out a final song for its mate or maybe to its fledglings, repeatedly and urgently, even as the sun fades from the day. Streetlamps glimmer softly and lights have only begun to flicker on inside people's houses. Lu walks through her neighbourhood, looking in the windows to catch a glimpse of the glowing lives within.

Luba watches as a family gathers together at a dining room table. She'd had this once, she thinks. All three of them had sat around the evening meal to share talk of school and business and the events of the day. So many meals prepared by her hands for her husband and daughter. So many meals over years and years of living and loving and love fading. So many meals and yet Dan and she didn't really know what they'd had. She'd like the chance to cook such a dinner again for the three of them.

Her feet are sore, and it is time to take her self-pity home, Luba decides. She stops at the corner liquor store to buy a bottle of red wine. Over the next few hours, she will drain the bottle as she looks at old photographs and remembers when she was a wife.

9

She cannot hear him and he can no longer speak. It will be another long, long night, thinks Mirjam. She has forgotten her book and there is no television to help her through the death-watch. The hospital halls and visiting areas are abandoned and only a skeleton nursing staff remains. In the overly warm room, Mirjam feels quite alone, quite lonely. Already bleary-eyed, she observes the slight rise and fall of her father's chest in the semi-darkness. Still. Alive.

In her mind's ear she hears the haunting strains of Mozart's *Requiem*:

What then shall I say, wretch that I am,
What advocate entreat to speak for me,
When even the righteous may hardly be secure?

This wretch, her father, so frail, so breakable. He doesn't even look like himself any longer, only the husk of the man who wrought terror in her life and Luba's. Dan's hand is curled stiffly, but it will never again make a fist. He is imprisoned in the coma, and she and her mother are safe at last.

She tries not to think beyond these thoughts, to what lies ahead after death. Curled into a C, Mirjam reclines on the cot, hoping to surrender to the sense deprivation of her hearing loss. But sleep is not her friend these days. Homesick for Berlin, she thinks about Alban, longing for his body, missing their life. But above all, Mirjam misses music. A simple melody. A bold concerto or a rousing symphony. And especially the sound of her own voice. Bella canta. Beautiful singing.

A headache has plagued her throughout the day, and the tinnitus is particularly jarring this evening. Mirjam gently presses the sides of her temples, the underside of her eyes and tops of her cheekbones. The high E reverberates, shrilly incessant, as if to drive her crazy.

Fearing this, she gathers herself to begin a longed-for conversation, long imagined.

"You have so many demons, Daddy."

"Yes."

"You were my favourite parent, at first. When I was little."

"Really? I thought Luba was."

"No, it was you. I was so worried when you went to the hospital. I was only four, remember? You were terribly ill with your ulcers. So ill that I spent one Christmas night all alone with Ma. Singing away her pain. And mine. Finding my voice, even then. When you came home, I thought I would break apart from joy."

"A happy new year."

"Back then you loved me, too."

"I've always loved you, Mirjam."

"You—you showed it better when I was a little girl. You were even playful. You're the one who taught me to sing, to love music by

your example, do you remember?"

"*I remember us singing together.*"

"*I had you wrapped around my baby finger. I was, after all, the baby: Daddy's little sweetheart. Your sweetheart.*"

"*You were a marvel. As a child.*"

"*Only as a child?*"

"*Then a woman.*"

"*But not the grown daughter you wished for.*"

"*I loved you still.*"

"*Your love is so capricious, Daddy. I will never understand how you can love someone and strike her down.*"

"*I come from a different time and place.*"

"*Long ago and far away ...*"

"*What did I know about daughters?*"

"*Well, raise a strong daughter in your own image and look what happens, Daddy. All she-hell breaks loose.*"

"*You certainly did.*"

"*I was so afraid of you. But I'm not now.*"

"*There's nothing to be afraid of. I'm an old, sick man.*"

"*You have a kind of madness, I think.*"

"*Maybe so.*"

"*I think I have it, too.*"

"*You can learn to control it. Better than I did.*"

"*Can I?*"

For a short while, Mirjam dozes, dreaming she is singing on a concert stage. All is going so well—her voice is mellifluous and faultless—until she forgets the words of the piece she is performing and a chorus of boos rises from the audience.

Waking with a start, Mirjam glances over at Dan, thinking

he has died, until once more his chest rises as if in defiance. She imagines the crackle of his breath in his throat. Quite unexpectedly, she is annoyed, angry. When will this be over?

With a sudden hot certainty, Mirjam is glad that Dan has cancer, eager for it to eat hungrily away at him, to consume him. To be rapacious and devouring as Dan's love. She wills it to kill him.

But his heart keeps pumping.

She considers putting a pillow over Dan's head to suffocate him, to put them all—she, Luba, Dan—out of their lingering misery. In a moment of dazzling clarity, it comes to her. Mirjam wants this power. To kill her father and so dominate the dominator, at last. And in so doing, in stopping his breath, she will finally stopper his voice.

All her life she has been listening. Even as she defied this man, her father, the head of the household, by finding her singing voice. For as long as she was in his house and even when she wasn't, she was told to listen. To shut up and listen: to his words, his opinions, his righteous anger. To his telling her that life was banal and without adventure, so who did she think she was to run off and have one or many.

Adventures or lovers.

"Listen to my words and don't dare think you have a right to any of your own. And watch that tone of voice young lady. Or else."

"I can't hear you, Daddy."

Perspiration beads Dan's forehead. Mirjam takes a washcloth and dampens it under the tap of the hospital room sink. Carefully, she wipes away the droplets. The *Requiem* plays on in her thoughts:

I groan like a guilty man.
Guilt reddens my face.
Spare a suppliant, O God.

Then she takes the cloth to her father's face and neck, his arms and hands.

My prayers are not worthy,
But Thou in Thy merciful goodness grant
That I burn not in everlasting fire.

When Mirjam finishes, she places the rag within arm's reach, near the radio on the bedside table. Will there be an everlasting fire for this man, her father? Mirjam does not believe. Her secular parents never once took her to the Orthodox church. She does not believe that tyrants burn for their crimes. There is no poetic justice for the killers of the world. And yet she sings as if there were.

"Goodbye Daddy."

She dims the room lights to dark and touches Dan's pillow.

Unbeknownst to Mirjam come plaintive strains of Peggy Lee's version of "Bye Bye Blackbird" from the radio speakers.

10

They paused at the threshold of the woods to pay tribute to the trees and the spirit of the forest. The soughing poplar leaves bid them entrance. Sudbina and Kemal clicked to their horses and ambled under the woodland canopy where the green had given way to gold and amber.

In the spot where they had left them were their lost companions, slack-jawed and snoring, with hair touching their shoulders, beards grown long and full, fingernails curved to claws. First, they cut the silken threads that bound the group with Baba Roga's magical protection. Next, Sudbina took her herbs and mixed these with the last remaining drops of the April rain. She and the harpist spoon-fed each of the three mouths, then, in relief, watched each dreamer finally rouse from slumber, dazed and uncertain of the surroundings, but otherwise quite well and cured of ague. Tongues were thick from disuse, so that strong, hot tea and small portions of food were offered and gratefully accepted. Gradually, the company cleared its cobwebs.

Sudbina and Kemal spent the next hours telling much of the astonishing tale of the past months. At last they paused, not daring to share the final moments of their escape from the despot.

Dragan was the first of their companions to speak. "Despoina, we must return you to your father's castle, posthaste."

"Why, Dragan, when my father is dead?"

Elenya and the two guards gaped in disbelief. "This cannot be!"

"It is true."

"How? When?"

"Poison, I believe. But these are details I leave you to discover for yourselves. I am sure that even now my uncles plot a usurping course, salivating at the thought of seizing his fortress and demesne. There is no place for me back there. But we will retrieve the horses and then you three, Dragan, Elenya, and Budimir, will be free to return or seek your fortunes elsewhere."

"We cannot leave you, Despoina," Elenya spoke, aggrieved.

"You can and must, Elenya. I am despoina no more. Nor have I any wish to be. I will go forward as my destiny wills me."

"Surely your uncles will find you a fine match," the waiting-woman protested.

"And that is precisely what I fear."

The harpist stirred the fire and added more wood. His voice was mild, "I have learned, Elenya, that Sudbina says what she means and means all she says."

"Nonsense!" Dragan stood unsteadily. "Tomorrow we will together gather the horses from the dread Baba Roga, curse her! Then will we return to the despot's castle and all will be well. We'll have no further talk of leave-taking or separation.

That is what got us into this plight in the first place. There will be no more misfortune for this company!" He strode off to relieve himself in the shrubs.

Kemal and Sudbina exchanged a glance and nodded. They moved into the trees on the pretense of searching for mushrooms. A huge moss-covered trunk made a good seat and so they sat. Kemal took her hand.

"What are you thinking, my love?"

"I think I will tonight visit Baba Roga."

"Then so will I."

"No, Kemal. I think it best that only I go."

"I fear that woman and her witch-trickery. Please, Sudbina—"

"My bones tell me that this must I do alone."

He sighed and took her hands to his lips. "You must promise to be careful, to watch out for her deceit and betrayal."

"I have learned to do this well."

Kemal bowed his head. "I did not do as I promised: to win my father's protection or save you from yours."

"I never looked for a saviour, harpist."

"I failed you."

"You are made of music and courage, Kemal."

"Moreso are you, beloved Sudbina."

She smiled at him and stood to return. He caught her hand.

"Will I see you again?"

"Have you finished that song you composed, the one about a certain despoina?"

"Ah, yes, I have."

"Why yes then, of course. I long to hear it."

That night was cloudy and the forest cool. As if they had taken a draught, the harpist, Elenya and the guards all slipped soundly to sleep. Sudbina lay awake, watching.

She did not wait long. The dancing lights arrived noiselessly, as before, circling around the camp and above her head. Stealthily, she moved from her pallet, snatched up her pack and followed their be-lighted path exactly to where she'd known they would take her. Once again the lights gyrated above the thatched roof then finally settled in the eyes of the skulls atop the fence posts.

Taking the skeleton key from her satchel, Sudbina fitted it to the lock of the humble cottage and turned. The oaken door swung inwards. There at the stone fireplace, her back to Sudbina, stood the old baba silhouetted against the flames.

"You have come, Daughter."

Sudbina closed the door and took the key. She stepped forward into the warm room. "You knew that I would, Mother."

"I did not know when. Though I cast the knucklebones, they do not always show the whole of the picture."

"Knucklebones?"

Baba Roga turned to face Sudbina. "You will learn, Daughter. You have so much to learn. But you will have time to study. So many years." She gestured for the young woman to sit once again at the rustic table, to raise a glass of *rakija* with her.

They drained their first, and Baba Roga poured a second.

"I promised a treasure, Mother, but I have no treasure. I could not seize a gem from the sultan, nor gold from my father. You spoke the truth about both—they are equally tyrants. They hoard their wealth; they subjugate the people. And under both their roofs was I prisoner."

"Ah ..."

"All I have is this *nisan tası*," she handed Baba Roga the small bowl for collecting rainwater, "and it is only made of brass. I stole April rain from the Conqueror, but alas, I have used it up."

"As well you should."

"As best I could. So, I come thus empty-handed—I bring only the gratitude in my heart for your herbs, your help and your hospitality."

"You are wrong, Daughter. Your gift is the greater, yet you know it not."

"Your riddles—"

"You, Daughter, are my treasure."

"What do you mean?"

"You. You will be the Baba Roga now."

"I? But there can be but one such witch!"

"Da. And now, you are she."

She rose to take her lantern to a darkened corner of the cottage. In sudden greenish illumination glowed the polished marble of her huge mortar and pestle. "I spent days polishing these just for you, Sudbina. Use them well. She and he are fit for herbs and fit for travel."

The young woman said nothing, so surprised was she. Baba Roga returned to the table. "I will be away within a fortnight, and of course, you will need them now. I think I will first journey to see my sister, Baba Yaga ..."

"How will you travel? By foot? By broomstick?"

The old crone cackled just like a witch. "Silly goose. You've been listening to too many twaddling tongues and fancy tales. Women of the craft don't fly on brooms. We do walk, but I have many leagues to fly."

"And I am to take your place? I am not a witch. Neither am I a baba."

Firelight and lantern flickered blindingly and there beside her sat a woman in her prime, bereft of hideous horn and warts. "Daughter, nor am I."

Sudbina rubbed her eyes. This woman was actually quite handsome and dressed not in rags but finery.

"I see your amazement. But we witches have our ways."

"Why do you—"

"Choose to be hideous? How else to keep the cutthroats and rapists from my door, but with illusion and trickery? How best to keep my own company, my own liberty? How better to survive in this world of men and swords and might? How to subvert and deceive and work my woman's magic? But to live in a house that moves from place to place, to take up mortar and pestle and to the sky, to scare the wits out of the folk, whether low or noble born. I choose to be hideous so that I can choose."

"Baba Roga—"

"I am no longer she."

"Then what am I to call you?"

"Vrana, I think, suits me well."

"But how ever can I take your place?"

"You already have, Daughter, from the first moment you supped and drank with me."

"You lied to me."

"A deliberate lie. But one that will save you."

"Trap me, the rather! How can I be a witch? I know nothing about the craft!"

"Ah! But so you shall, so you will!" Rising spryly from her chair, the woman who had been Baba Roga leapt with her lantern to the cupboards in the shadows and flung open the doors. There shone the gold-lettered spines of many books, and as the witch pulled one out another slipped forward into place.

"Incantations and Transformations." She withdrew another. *"Levitation."* And another. *"Herbs and Potions."* Another. *"Conjurations."* Another. *"Soothsaying and Shapeshifting.* You see, Daughter, a whole library to occupy your mind and your time as you learn the ways."

"So I am to be prisoner, once again. This time in a wretched little cottage."

"You are beginning to sound like an ingrate, Sudbina." Vrana closed the cupboard and returned with a book and the lantern to the table. "Consider your options, carefully. I am offering you a possibility. If you wish to go, you may. Simply surrender the key to my *koliba*."

Sudbina considered her empty cup. "Your life is so solitary, so lonely."

"Not so, Daughter," the witch grinned rather wickedly. "I have entertained in this rough abode princes and huntsmen, Janissaries and tinkers, wise women and healers, giant- and dragon-slayers. And every once in a red moon comes a despoina and a harpist."

"But why? If this life is as you say, why abandon it now?"

"I feel the urge to leave, to see the world. After visiting my sister, who knows what wonders will beckon? I have heard that people in other lands could use the good work of a witch in warding off conquerors and tyrants."

"So Baba Roga is a good witch, then?"

"That, my daughter, is all up to you."

"I have killed my own father."

"Then, you see, this is your safest course."

"Does that not shock you?"

Vrana poured more brandy from the flask that seemed never to empty. "How do you think I came to these woods?"

"Your father? You?"

"Kill or be killed." Neither spoke for several minutes. "We all kill, Sudbina, in some way, on some plane."

The young woman shivered and looked deep into the shadows. She took the skeleton key from her bodice and set it on the table. "I will stay then."

"A wise choice, Daughter."

Crisp and blue the morning dawned, and both women woke at the very same moment. Together they broke their fast. Together they set the horses free from the shed. Vrana whispered something into the beasts' ears and slapped each on the rump. Off they trotted, certain of their direction. Together the women moved to the centre of the fenced yard.

"A good day to travel, Sudbina." Vrana lifted her sharp nose to sniff the air. "The winds are favourable."

"Today? You intend to leave? But how?"

"I've a mind to take wing and set you to your destiny."

"Already? But I know nothing. I—"

"You have your wits, your clever mind and your able fingers." Vrana stepped away from her and began to turn counterclockwise slowly. "No long goodbyes for us!"

"But—"

"Fare you well, Daughter."

"*Zbogom*, Mother. Will I see you again?"

"Ask me no questions, I'll tell you no lies." She turned again. "Sudbina, move the *koliba*! Confound your captors. Consult the book I set upon the table."

"Da! My first task."

"May you live happily ever after, Daughter." A third turn.

"And you, Mother."

"Don't eat too many children, they caw caw cause indigestion! Ha ha caw caw caw!"

Wheeling thrice above her head, the blue-black sheen of a crow cast Sudbina a black eye and then swept away, sure-winged. The wizened old woman who had once been Sudbina turned and walked haltingly back into the cottage.

Within the hour, the chicken legs began to scratch and shuffle. Later that afternoon they settled deep in the heart of the forest where none but the very bravest of hearts dared ever travel.

11

One hundred sixty-four days from diagnosis, Dan is dead. The body is transported to the crematorium. Arrangements are made, an obituary written. Luba has learned that Dan wished to have his ashes placed in the plot beside the grave of his father in Edmonton with no ceremony and only immediate family. So on a particularly autumnal day in late September, she and Mirjam take the car and drive the three hundred kilometres under a blue Albertan sky. Thankfully, the roads are good, and though the route is flat, there is a kind of stark beauty to the many farms and rolled haystacks they pass along the way.

They check in at the Best Western near the Northern Alberta Institute of Technology and drop off suitcases in a modest, double-occupancy room. Luba drives to their former home in the west end, and she and Mirjam share her childhood memories as they cruise through the familiar neighbourhood haunts. They pass by the monster mall, opting not to enter and join the frenzy. Lu remarks in her notebook to her daughter how the city has grown and changed—she recognizes so little of it now. In the last of the daylight, the two walk along lively Whyte Avenue, stopping for coffee in the red and teal warmth of Grabba

Java. Later, Lu treats her to dinner and a little too much Chianti downtown at The Creperie where they work out a schedule for the following day and their return to Calgary.

A wine hangover coupled with the smoke detector on the ceiling blinking red and insistent through the night, disturbs Luba's rest so that she never quite slips into deep sleep. Finally, she gives up and stares through the curtains at Edmonton dawning grey to salmon pink to cerulean. This city was Lu and Dan's home all those years ago, but now it is alien and Luba feels a stranger here in this capital that seems to her the poorer sister of Calgary. Where at last is home, she wonders? Drumheller? Her valley family has scattered its bones across the continent, or they've grown old and demented or have simply returned to dust. Mission in British Columbia seems a green dream that ended badly; she has no fondness for that time and place, even though there were prosperous years spent there. Is it Calgary then? Her house in Inglewood and the bird sanctuary? Or does she have a home now at all with Dan gone and Mirjam going?

"Maybe you should travel, Ma," suggests Mirjam over breakfast.

Luba butters her toast, thoughtfully. She writes and shrugs, "Maybe."

"You could come to Berlin, visit me and meet Alban, at last."

"Actually, I think I'd like to go to Africa."

"Shit, Ma. As your first solo trip?"

"Why not?"

"I mean—well, sure, but ..." "But?"

"Are you chasing after something ... or someone, Ma?"

"Look who's talking."

Mirjam finds she is curiously moved by her grandfather's tombstone. Petar Maniljo Popović lying in a pauper's grave she discovered for her father years ago. Who was this man? She has the one stern family photograph, scratched and fading with age, and that is all. Why had her father not told her about his father? Now she will never know. Is it true, she muses to herself, that people are only alive for as long as their names are remembered?

Returning her gaze to her grandfather's tombstone, Mirjam wonders: was this a man who sang also? She recalls that music ran in her father's family. Did this Petar Maniljo's baritone reverberate through the mountains of his youth, across the valley of the Badlands where he immigrated? Did he sing in Serbian or English or both? Or was it rather her grandmother who was the singer? Now she will never know.

She wracks her brain for her grandmother's name. Anna, wasn't it? Or was it Angela? Anastasia? Yes, Anna. The next time she visits Drumheller, she will check the graveyard records and find the tombstone to be certain. But then she snorts ruefully to herself. When will she ever be back in Drumheller? Her life is elsewhere, and she is itching to get back to it.

Except that she cannot, not really. Without hearing, she will have no life of music. She cannot perform; she cannot teach. Of her almost thirty-five years, twenty-one of them have been spent on the pursuit of music. What will she pursue now? Alban?

How will she make a living? What life is there without song?

Yes, she diverts her thought, to avoid falling into the chasm of that sorrow.

Her name was Anna.

A cemetery attendant, formerly known as a gravedigger, has rolled up the sod and dug a hole for Dan's cremated remains. Luba places the small urn into the hole and throws in a spadeful of dirt. Mirjam does likewise, and then the attendant takes over, filling in the remainder and replacing the sod. The whole thing takes but five minutes.

Luba stands over the grave. She has been crying off and on since they drove through the gates of the cemetery this morning. Her tears are for the loss, she supposes—of her husband, her companion, their youth and dreams—all the usual reasons one mourns when a spouse dies. The finality of death, its shadow leaning close as she stands here, Dan's death and hers, and one day, her daughter's, too, though she prays that will be long after she herself is gone.

Will she miss Dan? She guesses she must. Returning to that empty house certainly doesn't much appeal to her, especially since Mirjam must soon return to Berlin.

But something else ripples into clarity: her tears are of relief. Though she cries, a weight lifts from within her ribs. She knows she has been carrying this for almost fifty years. Luba wonders if Dan knew how heavy he was.

Mirjam does not cry, has not cried since she arrived back

in Canada, nor when her father died. In fact, now that she has brushed away any troubling thoughts of her future, she is jubilant. This day is a release, she realizes, and her spirits soar suddenly as if caught up and rising on the brisk fall wind. She takes her mother's hand and tries not to register her joy. With her other hand, she plugs her right ear gently and sings Ethan McGrath's beautiful piece, knowing that Luba, who has no musical ability, will not recognize any pitch problems, hoping that perhaps the words will assuage her mother's tears:

When lilacs last in the dooryard bloom'd,
And the great star early droop'd in the western sky in the night,
I mourn'd, and yet shall mourn with ever-returning spring.

Ever-returning spring, trinity sure to me you bring,
Lilac blooming perennial and drooping star in the west,
And thought of him I love.

Luba smiles at her daughter's attempt to cheer her, then moves away to blow her nose and reapply powder and to compose her face. While Luba's back is to her, Mirjam plays in her own memory the later Whitman verses from Hindemith that she prefers:

Over the tree-tops I float thee a song,
Over the rising and sinking waves, over the myriad fields and the
*   prairies wide,*
Over the dense-pack'd cities all and the teeming wharves and ways,
I float this carol with joy, with joy to thee O death.

"Goodbye, Daddy. Goodbye Petar Maniljo Popović."

Together mother and daughter walk back across the cemetery to the parking lot, passing under the mature elms and glorious oaks that drape their fall curtains across the tombstones and monuments. A roost of crows caws animatedly across two of the largest oaks that are at least a hundred years old—certainly already planted when her grandfather died—perhaps the last of their flock that have yet to vacate the city for the south before winter's icy breath blows. Luba and Mirjam pause to look up at them.

"How long does a crow live?"

"If they survive the first year, most average seven to eight years." Luba scribbles quickly. "But they can live between fourteen to seventeen, I understand, and longer in captivity."

"That many years! I wonder how a crow measures time."

"By staying alive, maybe? Making it through another day, another winter. They certainly understand the changing seasons—all linked to time and its passing."

"And they're musicians, aren't they? So they understand music, so maybe they really do understand time as best as we do. Or better."

Luba hooks her arm through Mirjam's.

"But it's not a very pretty song, theirs, is it?"

"Can you hear it?"

"Faintly, in the distance."

"Not everyone has a pretty song to sing, Mirjam."

"I guess not, Ma."

They are quiet on the ride home. Luba is thinking about the daunting task of sorting through Dan's things. What will she do with all of the detritus of their life together? She doubts Mirjam will want any of it. Clothes are easy enough. They can go to the Salvation Army, as Dan would wish—he always thought fondly of the Sally Anners who gave out treats and cigarettes to the soldiers overseas. But all the tools and books, the Serbian histories in Cyrillic? The photographs of people Luba doesn't know and never did? A flea market perhaps.

Mirjam is thinking about the unexpected paradox that she is both free and trapped. She recalls the elation of the afternoon at the graveside, her soaring spirits, the song on her lips and in her heart. But then, too, the reality of her hearing loss reverberates like a slamming vault door. As she'd feared, the Canadian doctors had no more to tell her than did Gutermuth in Berlin. Though Luba had protested, Mirjam had insisted she cancel the third and final appointment. There was no point in rehashing what she'd already learned from other experts and specialists. There was no use. She has no use. These lines play a tuneless refrain in her brain.

Near Red Deer, Mirjam breaks the quiet and asks her mother if she would like her to take the wheel. Luba declines as she is fond of driving. But they stop for coffee and a donut at the faux windmill of the Donut Mill.

"Do you—did you love him?"

"Dan? Of course, l did." Luba's pen pauses. "But love changes, Mirjam. You have a child and …"

"No, I mean that man we met in the sanctuary."
"Hodi."
"Yes, him."
"We were lovers."
"Oh, Ma."
"So yes, I loved him. I love him. But it is ended."
"Why? Because of Dad?"
"Yes, and because sometimes it just—doesn't work, Mirjam."
"Could it?"
"I think I'm too old for all that."
They drink the last of their coffee.
"It's funny, Ma, you know? I think I'm too old sometimes. For all that."
"Don't be a goose! You're still such a young woman with your whole caree—life in front of you."

Back in the car, they continue onwards, looking westward for first ghosts of the Rockies, Luba driving in silence; Mirjam lost in hers.

Mirjam turns her face to the passenger window. The sun is setting earlier each day, she knows. It will be fully dark when they reach the city limits of Calgary.

※

That evening around midnight, Mirjam calls Berlin. She and Alban have been in constant email communication over the many weeks of her absence, and he has continued his offers to join her in Canada. This she has resisted, not willing to let him give up his opportunities just to watch her father, a stranger, die. Neither does she want to wrap him in the tentacles of her worry, fearing she will drag him under and drown them both. There is no consolation for the inconsolable. Trying vainly to cheer her, he has told Mirjam of an agent who wishes to connect with her—something about an opportunity to understudy the role of the Gingerbread Witch in Humperdinck's *Hansel and Gretel* this Christmas at Komische Oper Berlin. She laughed at this. But she tries not to let rue and despair seep into her messages to him, promising only that she will soon return to Berlin. It is difficult keeping up this pretending. She writes little of her wondering if she is any help to Luba or merely a hindrance. She intimates nothing of her worry that Alban and she are drifting apart. She reserves for herself the worst fears about her voice, telling him instead that daily she sings, to exercise and to fight resignation. Her courage withering, she turns the volume of her parents' phone up to the loudest setting, hoping to hear the barest trace of Alban's voice. But either he is too soundly asleep to hear the ringing or has already left the flat for his classes. The answering machine beeps at the edge of her hearing.

"I don't know if I'll ever sing again, Alban. I'm too old for you. I don't think I should come back." She hangs up then instantly picks up the receiver again. But the dial tone is a barely audible, imperfect cadence.

Luba finds her sobbing into her arms at the kitchen table, a scene out of some ending to a tragic opera.

"Mirjam!"

"I killed him, Ma! Dad is dead because of me."

Lu grabs the notebook, scratches feverishly, "What are you saying?"

"I did it."

"You think you have some kind of—magic?"

"You've always said I was touched."

Luba remembers the caul around the infant Mirjam. She remembers other things, too. "You have a gift, Mirjam, but ..."

"It's true."

"No, my darling," she writes, "no and no!"

"I willed it. I did. And I'm glad."

"It wasn't magic—yours or anyone's. It was cancer. And time. It's all about time, Mirjam. Time. It was his time." Luba takes her grown daughter into her embrace, thinking that if she had anything to do with Dan's death, she is not ungrateful. "And now it is ours to make of it what we will."

"I'm not crying about that. Not really."

"Then what?"

"I—I'll never sing again, Ma."

Luba hesitates, framing her thoughts carefully on the page. "Maybe not. But it's not for you to say. That doctor in Berlin—he wants to retest you. So go and be tested." She swallows, not quite believing her own words. "Go back to Berlin."

"I can't. I am so frightened."

"I know, Mirjam. So am I."

"I only have music. I don't know what else or who else to be."

"If you can't sing, you will find something else fulfilling."

"What, Ma?"

"I don't know the answers, Mirjam. But I think you need to return."

"To what?"

"To Alban."

"I have broken off with Alban ..." Her voice breaks into another sob.

"Oh, Mirjam."

❦

A troubled heart takes Luba back to the bird sanctuary. She checks in with her supervisor, shares a cup of watery, lukewarm coffee with her colleagues and agrees to resume a shift or two in the coming week. It will do her a world of good, she thinks, to occupy her mind, to pass the time, to be apart. Mirjam's sorrow has consumed her, and she is bewildered by her own helplessness. There is nothing she can do but shoo her away, push the nestling from the nest. Some sense tells her this is her daughter's only hope.

Walking briskly along the pathway, Luba keeps her sights out for blue jays and chickadees. The pungent smells of fallen poplar leaves and the jetsam of autumn decay fill her nostrils. Luba is glad to be walking along this leaf-strewn carpet, glad to have some moments she can call her very own. Though it is early October, the sun is still warm upon her shoulders and the light through the remaining leaves is golden. She pauses to drink in its gold, wishing she could freeze this moment in time. At the end of the loop, her legs are fatigued from the exertion and Luba is a little footsore, having spent too many recent hours in a hospital chair. Ahead, she spies a figure with a camera. Her pulse rises as she wills herself forward. But then she stops short. Hodi is with another woman, someone around his age or slightly younger. Luba cannot believe what is happening to her chest—it feels as if struck by a wrecking ball.

But his face lights when he sees her, and Lu is confused. "Luba! How lovely to chance upon you!" He brings the other woman around to greet her. "This is Njeri, my younger sister. She is visiting me from Toronto for Thanksgiving."

"Hello, Njeri."

"Hello, Luba. I have heard quite a bit about you." She extends a hand.

"Oh dear."

Njeri's face creases with laughter, revealing a gap between her teeth. It is a face that smiles often, and Lu feels almost instantly at ease. "My niece. She is a good girl, but she is strong-minded, overly protective of her father."

"That's not a bad thing," Luba takes Njeri's hand and, eyes meeting, they shake.

"You are right. Mwara had some hard times growing up in Toronto, especially with bigoted schoolmates in high school and again in her freshman year."

"I understand a little of that."

"So it is good to have a mind and a backbone."

"Especially for a young woman."

"Ah, we aunties and mothers, we know, don't we? We've seen more of life and its nuances, yes? In Mwara I see so much of my youthful, angry self."

"In my daughter I see her father."

Njeri raises an eyebrow.

"They never got along very well."

"A locking of horns?"

"Yes that."

"It was the same with me and my father. We don't necessarily get the parents we might choose." A little hardness creeps into Njeri's voice. "But"—she meets Luba's gaze—"maybe as she grows older, time will soften your daughter towards your husband."

"Maybe."

"And perhaps you will have the chance to meet Mwara again someday, to see her in a new light."

"I would like that."

Hodi is grinning wildly from one to the other woman. Luba finds herself blushing.

"My brother, it seems, is quite happy to see you."

"I should have called, perhaps, Hodi ... to let you know that Dan—my husband has passed away."

"I am so sorry to hear this news." Hodi sobers and steps closer.

"So sorry," Njeri echoes.

"It is alright. We, my daughter and I, are coping. His death was expected, merciful even. Lung cancer—"

"Such a sad ending."

"Yes, but in some ways, we've been saying goodbye to him for a long time."

"How is Mirjam? Her hearing loss?"

"It's hard to know. The specialists here all repeat what the doctor in Berlin says: that it may take more months to know with certainty. Of course, she's dragging her feet to return there, and I know it's because she's afraid."

Hodi nods. "For a singer, that makes perfect sense."

"She doesn't know how to be anything but a singer."

"This is such a difficult time for you both," Njeri says.

"We are getting by. I will be coming back to work, only a few shifts for the first while."

"That is good to know." Hodi swallows. "How are you, dear Luba?"

"I've been keeping busy. Despite almost no attention on my part, my garden is quite lovely." She looks around at the fall array. "Though it won't be long before the snow."

"No, it is like taxes in this country. A sure thing."

An idea occurs to Luba and she blurts, "Would you both care to join us for Thanksgiving on Sunday? I mean … I'm sure you have plans already. But if not, it would be very nice to have guests at our table. We are only two and—"

Njeri nods at Hodi. "We are also only two," he says. "So yes, Luba, four for Thanksgiving would be especially nice."

※

There is, of course, too much food.

"Ma, are you cooking for four or fourteen?" Mirjam chides as she chops more onion. "And they're bringing a dish, aren't they?"

"Yes, Njeri insisted they bring something," Lu writes.

"Ma, you look flustered!"

"Mirjam, I'm focusing on these pies." Luba turns to her oven, pulling two perfect pumpkin pies steaming from the oven, her sole nod to a traditional Canadian Thanksgiving dish. Every other is Ukrainian or Serbian or Kenyan or German.

"We'll have a real United Nations feast: *spätzle* and *pečena jagnjetina*, Daddy's *punjena paprika*, and what are they bringing?"

"Something called *sukuma wiki*."

Mirjam sounds it out from the written words. "What is that?"

"I don't know."

"Sukuma wiki and pumpkin pie with whipped cream. Maybe you should make mashed potatoes and gravy, too, Ma."

"Do you think so?" Luba casts her a worried look.

"Ma, I'm kidding."

"Stop teasing, Mirjam," Luba scribbles quickly. "I'm nervous enough as it is."

"Go get ready then, Ma. I can handle the rest."

At 6 p.m. sharp the doorbell rings and Hodi calls out, "Hodi Hodi!" Feeling a little like a flustered schoolgirl, Mirjam answers. Luba appears at her shoulder and they bid their guests welcome. Hodi has brought wine, and Njeri offers a hot casserole dish, redolent with cumin, and pops it into the oven to keep warm. Mirjam pours everyone a small glass of *šljivovica*.

"*Živeli!*"

"*U zdravlje!*"

"*Maisha marefu!*"

Lu takes the small glasses from Hodi and Njeri whose faces

reveal their distaste. "It's not for everyone."

"It is ..." Njeri wipes her mouth with her napkin, "very strong."

"An acquired taste," Mirjam offers her some water, which she accepts readily.

"But very potent and great for dancing."

Together they sit at the dining table, adorned with Lu's finest china and crystal. Mirjam watches her mother serve the dishes, then leap up frequently to make sure they are ever replenished.

"Sit, Ma. There's enough already."

Everyone laughs, overwhelmed yet delighted by the spread. Mirjam makes sure to keep filling the wine glasses. Hodi's bottle of Côtes du Rhône pairs beautifully with the succulent roast lamb. She opens two others from her mother's wine rack and the conversation flows easily, even as they pass the notebook. Mirjam learns that Hodi was a medical photographer at the Toronto General Hospital and that Njeri is a semi-retired child psychologist and an active member of the Congress of Black Women of Canada. Kindly, they keep the conversation away from any talk of her singing career. Everyone agrees that the meal is beyond compare; both Mirjam and Luba find the *sukuma wiki*, with its flavourful and spicy collard greens, a delicious addition.

Finally, the pumpkin pie is served with a flourish. Njeri accepts only a small piece, but Hodi asks for extra whipped cream. To finish their palates, Mirjam brings in the *cezve* and offers everyone Serbian coffee. They sit for a moment in contentment and satiety.

"I'm very happy to meet you, Hodi and Njeri."

"It has long been my wish to get to know you a little, Mirjam." Hodi writes, then drains the last of the wine into her empty glass.

"Your pumpkin pie would win a contest, Luba." Njeri finishes her final forkful, and Mirjam clears her plate. "The Kenyan judge gives it a ten out of ten."

They chuckle together. Then Njeri writes the joke down for Mirjam, and they laugh again.

"This is one of my happiest Thanksgivings," Luba sighs.

"Mine too," Hodi lifts his espresso cup to her.

Within the hour, they rise to leave, but Hodi insists that everyone gather for a photograph. He sets the timer and they grin dazedly at the lens. With a flash, the moment is captured, and the group breaks apart. At the door, both he and Njeri brush Lu and Mirjam's cheeks each with a kiss. Then Hodi hugs Luba, and Mirjam understands everything.

"That was a great meal and a great evening, Ma! All your hard preparation paid off." Together they are drying the good dishes and crystal and have already gone through a pile of tea towels. "They are both very nice. I approve of him. He is a good man for you, I believe."

Luba arches an eyebrow. She takes a stack of dishes to the dining room buffet, then returns to the kitchen. "Thank you for your help, Mirjam," she mouths. "Thank you for helping me through these hard weeks."

"Anytime."

Luba grabs the pen and notebook. "Well ... not really."

"Pardon?"

"It's time, Mirjam." She produces an envelope from a kitchen drawer, fighting against her maternal urge to grab her child and hold her near for the remainder of her life. "This is for you."

Mirjam unfolds a sheet of paper and within it, a plane ticket from Calgary to Toronto to Berlin.

"You kicking me out, Ma?"

Luba writes, "Alban will be there to pick you up."

"You phoned him?"

Her mother nods and writes again. "I believe you have more songs to sing, Mirjam. Many more songs. I am not giving up on you and neither is he. Go home, Mirjam."

⚜

At 35,000 feet she has a bird's eye view of the world. Patches and squares of quilted green and gold, trickling rivulets that are raging rivers, mountains that look like crusts of bread rising from the earth. People are invisible and that perhaps is a good thing. There is no sense that they are busily destroying the planet and each other when one is headed into cotton ball clouds.

Mirjam is no closer to any understanding of the violent appetites of her father and her father's people. She does not understand such impulses of her own. What she most wishes is to make music in contravention of those impulses, to make music and keep anger and grudge ever after at bay. And yet, now that she has found this particular key, she cannot keep the tune.

It is naïve and simplistic, she knows, to think that something like music could solve the world's problems, could heal people of their desire to eradicate the other, whoever the other is this particular week. She thinks of what she and the company tried to do in the land of her grandparents. Was it folly or hope or both? Perhaps this is all there is, the only possible response when madness drives one to pick up a rock or a knife or a rifle and end a life. She understands that she, too, could wield stone or sabre, but she hopes she will always now choose not to, that she will choose music—even if only dimly heard—instead.

The Tegel Airport is crowded and Mirjam maneuvers her way along with the other arrivals, salmon swimming upstream. She spills out with the rest through the doors, and there is Alban, gorgeous with a bouquet of amber-tipped yellow roses. Immediately, she is in his arms.

"You beautiful fool," he says over and over, crushing her in his embrace, heedless of the blooms. *"Leibling, liebling ..."*

Later in the Audi he has borrowed for the day, he drives her to Erholungspark Marzahn as Mirjam is yet too wired from her flight to consider sleep, even as she senses the oncoming jet lag. The park is flush with autumn colours, and on this particular day under a few stray cumulous clouds, the trees are absolutely still, as if willing her to notice their vivid red and orange displays. Hand in hand, she and Alban traipse along one of the many paths and Mirjam wonders aloud if her happiness is a dream.

"I should have come to see you, regardless of the cost," Alban writes when they sit together near the fountain.

"No Alban. I had to work something out."

"Have you?"

"No. I don't know. Maybe. My father is dead. I may have killed him."

"Oh Mirjam. You didn't." Alban scribbles fiercely. "Just like you had no effect on the maniac who sent that rocket blast in Sarajevo, just like your curse on all things Serbian did not destroy Milošević or Karadžić or Ratko or any of those bastards or the Serbian people as a whole. You're not a witch, Mirjam. Just a half-mad woman I am quite mad about."

She leans back against the bench. "You're right, of course. It's even arrogant to think such thoughts about myself."

"Well, you *are* half-Serbian," he squeezes her knee.

"Serbo-Canadian and Ukrainian-Canadian. Whatever that means."

"And I'm the grandson of an SS Officer. We can all open locked closets and find family monsters, Mirjam."

"Probably."

They watch a mother with a pram trundle by and a father shouldering a sleeping toddler.

"I was beside myself when I heard your voice message, Mirjam."

"I'm so sorry."

"*Danke gott,* your mother called me."

Mirjam allows her tears to fall and shares her fears—all of them—at last with Alban, under the listening trees.

"I'm not that man, you know. Someone who would leave

you."

"Not even for a younger woman."

"No."

"Not even if I never sing again?"

"You will sing again."

"I feel hopeless, Alban."

"We will go to the doctor."

"And what if the news is bad?"

"Then we will work through it. Together, Mirjam."

She kisses him. "No more running away."

They rise and wander towards the exit. Mirjam is beginning to wane from the long hours of the journey. She leans her head on his shoulder and tries not to think of anything, to simply enjoy the cool fresh air and this singular day.

And then Mirjam halts on the path. "Alban, do you hear that trilling?"

He angles his beautiful head to the sound, smiling, nodding. "'Ein Lied im Schlüssel des Lebens,' a song in the key of life. *Es ist wunderschön!*"

She holds herself very still, closing her eyes, concentrating intently. It's a songbird. A skylark.

"Yes."

Acknowledgements

Over the years of writing *Songs*, I met with many people and consulted numerous sources. This book would not exist without their expertise. Any poetic license or errors in historical time and fact are mine alone in this work of fiction.

A note on the sources:

Poem and libretto: Sonnet 47 from *Fatal Interview* (1931) by Edna St. Vincent Millay and "When Lilacs Last in the Dooryard Bloom'd" (1865) by Walt Whitman.

For the fairy tale, I found many collections of Baba Yaga (or Baba Roga) tales helpful, but especially illuminating were *Baba Yaga Laid an Egg* by Dubravka Ugrešić, *Egg and Spoon* by Gregory Maguire, *Serbian Fairy Tales* compiled by Vuk Stefanović Karadžić, selected, translated and introduced by Jelena Ćurčić.

I also found "Serbia Under Ottoman Rule" by Tatjana Katić to be informative history for the fairy tale narrative. For the roots of Sudbina's father, I drew from historical information on Despot Djorde Branković and other titular despots under Ottoman rule, and for her brother, from Sokollu Mehmed Pasha (Mehmed-paša Sokolović). Their familial relationship is entirely my own invention. In the tradition of the fairy tale, I also took a number of artistic liberties with time, but the story is set roughly during the reign of Mehmed II, in his city and harem.

A dizzying amount of literature since the 1990s has been published about the conflicts in former Yugoslavia, including about

the Siege of Sarajevo, but I found these sources instrumental in my understanding, flawed though it may be: *New York Times* (June 20, 1994): "Sarajevo Journal; In the Very Ashes of War, a Requiem for 10,000" by Chuck Sudetic; *Fall of Yugoslavia* by Misha Glenny; the graphic novels of Joe Sacco - *Stories from Bosnia No. 1* and *Christmas with Karadzić* and *Fixer;* Brian Hall's *The Impossible Country: A Journey Through the Last Days of Yugoslavia;* Åsne Seierstad's *With Their Backs to the World: Portraits from Serbia;* Simon Winchester's *The Fracture Zone*; Mark Mazower's *The Balkans: A Short History;* Branimir Anzulović's *Heavenly Serbia: From Myth to Genocide*; John R. Lampe's *Yugoslavia as History: Twice There was a Country* (2nd edition); and Ivo Andrić's *The Bridge on the Drina.*

There are many online sources as well, but I found especially helpful for my understanding: of music, turkishmusicportal.org and leylagencer.org; of Canadian campaigns, 48th highlanders.ca (and its online museum), and for the effects of injuries sustained during war "The Mind and Stomach at War: Stress and Abdominal Illness in Britain 1939-1945," *Cambridge Journals Medical History;* Comparison of Endoscopic Tympanoplasty to Microscopic Tympanoplasty," by Choi, et. al. in *Clinical and Experimental Otorhinolaryngology*; and "Auditory Effects of Blast Exposure" by Jeanne Dodd-Murphy.

Also pertaining to my understanding of Canada's role in WWII Italy were the invaluable *The D-Day Dodgers: The Canadians in Italy, 1943-1945* by Daniel G. Dancocks and my father's own journal.

And with gratitude:

I am deeply indebted to Barbara Tolevska and Miki Andrević for guiding me to the inimitable Jadranka Jovanović, Prima Donna, National Theatre Belgrade, whom I humbly thank for her advice and for sharing her knowledge of artists performing during the 1990s Yugoslav Wars.

For their insights shared about musical accuracy, choice of repertoire, knowledge of professional world singing and competitions, I thank Judith Richardson and Robin Slade Phillips for reading an early draft of the novel and offering such important advice about the life of a singer.

To Tololwa Mollel for his sensitive reading of my book and characters, his guidance, and his knowledge of Kenyan author Ngũgĩ wa Thiong'o, thank you, my friend.

To my dear friends—Sylvia Strojek, Doris Car, and Yunus Kaya—who helped me with German, Croatian (Serbo-Croatian), and Turkish, respectively, much gratitude and respect.

To Catharina de Bakker, my careful, astute editor, and the team at Great Plains, thank you for the time and energy you put into making this book. I'm so happy you welcomed it (and me) to your publishing house.

To my beautiful Šobat family in Belgrade—Velimir, Tanja, Milan, and Marija–thank you for your love and hospitality. One of the best things about writing *Songs* has been getting to know you.

My profound love and thanks to my first readers and cheerleaders Carolyn Pogue, Geoff McMaster, Thomas Trofimuk, and dear Duane Stewart—my life and words are the richer for your presence. And of course, thank you to my mother, Jeannie, ever in my heart.

A final thanks to my musical, complicated father, Dušan (Douglas) Šobat: ours was a troubled sometimes tortured relationship, but this fiction, published twenty-seven years after your death, has helped me to arrive at some understanding of you and your own wounding as a boy too soon forced to be a man.